D0965552

Flight of the
Golden Harpy

BOOKS BY SUSAN KLAUS

Flight of the Golden Harpy

Christian Roberts Novels
Secretariat Reborn
Shark Fin Soup

Flight of the Golden Harpy

S U S A N K L A U S

A TOM DOHERTY ASSOCIATES BOOK
NEW YORK

FLIGHT OF THE GOLDEN HARPY

Copyright © 2014 by Susan Klaus

A Tor Book
Published by Tom Doherty Associates, LLC
175 Fifth Avenue
New York, NY 10010

www.tor-forge.com

Tor® is a registered trademark of Tom Doherty Associates, LLC.

The Library of Congress Cataloging-in-Publication Data is available upon request.

ISBN 978-0-7653-3755-9 (hardcover)
ISBN 978-1-4668-3506-1 (e-book)

Tor books may be purchased for educational, business, or promotional use. For information on bulk purchases, please contact Macmillan Corporate and Premium Sales Department at 1-800-221-7945, extension 5442, or write specialmarkets@macmillan.com.

First Edition: June 2014

Printed in the United States of America

0 9 8 7 6 5 4 3 2 1

To our vanishing wildlife.
To Brad Pitt, who inspired my beautiful and hunted protagonist, Shail,
when we were on the movie set of *Ocean's Eleven*.

ACKNOWLEDGMENTS

My children, Christopher and Kari. My sister, Sharon Burns, for her support. Susan Gleason, my literary agent. Bobbie Christmas, my Atlanta editor. Piers Anthony for his pep talk e-mails. And to my harpy-dinner critique girls, Jana Hoefling, Julie Ross, Lynn Ernst, Iris Meyer, Maryann Burchell, Pam Hennessy, and Sue Talkovic, for loving my harpies and insisting I publish the manuscript.

Flight of the Golden Harpy

1

Kari crouched as motionless as a doll beneath the ferns and stared across the lake carpeted with purple lilies to the trisom trees on the opposite shore. The towering trees swayed in the breeze; their branches overloaded with sweet fruit at this time of the year. After an hour of patient waiting, the eleven-year-old brushed her sweaty locks from her forehead and fretted. Her two-mile hike through Dora's hot jungle had been in vain. Nothing but birds and small-winged mammals had come and feasted on the fruit.

She heard a pair of squabbling kilts, squirrel-type creatures, and lowered her gaze to watch them as they tussled, rolled, and chased each other up and down the vines. So entranced with the kilts, she failed to notice the male harpy who had flown in and landed in the trisom trees. She rose to leave and saw the flutter of his pale yellow wings before he folded them against his back.

She ducked back down and swallowed. "He's a golden. A real, true golden harpy," she muttered, watching him. He picked a ball of fruit, leaned his slender, humanoid frame against the white bark, and nibbled.

Her chest pounded with excitement, realizing she gazed at the rarest creature on the planet. Numerous times, she had seen brown-winged harpies, but the blond, yellow-winged species were nearly extinct. Prized by hunters, the goldens were considered the ultimate game animal and slaughtered for their trophy wings. The golden flung the shoulder-length hair from his boyish face and sniffed the air before hopping to another limb, out of view.

Kari dismissed her father's warnings about dangerous harpies and crawled from her hiding place for a better look. Approaching the lake's edge, she was so captivated she never noticed the ripples of water created by a stalking mogel. It shot out from the murky depths and latched its mouth around her leg. The giant eel-like beast knocked her down on the muddy bank and dragged her toward its watery domain. She screamed for help, but was too far from home and her father to be heard.

With her free foot, she frantically kicked the beast's leathery black head and silvery eyes, but the mogel remained undeterred, holding on to its meal. Its sharp fangs clamped down and released their venom. While thrashing in the shallow water she felt a burning pain enter her bite wound. She grabbed a large rock and clung to it, but with the mogel's strength and steady pull, her hands quickly slipped over the algae-covered stone. Total paralysis from the poison and drowning would soon end her struggle.

Through a haze of tears, she glimpsed a flash of yellow. Like a seabird after bait, the harpy dove toward the lake surface and dropped on the mogel. The startled creature let go of her leg, and she scrambled backward to the shore. From there, she watched the battle: sky creature versus water. Half bird, half mortal, the light weight harpy was pitted against a six-hundred-pound mogel. The harpy wrapped his arms around the wide girth of the mogel's neck, and throttled the alarmed water monster. The fifteen-foot-long indigo body broke the surface and swirled in a circle, its huge jaws wildly snapping at the elusive harpy that rode its back. The tranquil lake erupted with splashing, and the fight flattened the lilies. The mogel, like a boa that constricts its prey, coiled and heaped layer upon layer of its thick body over the golden, engulfing him within a massive ebony ball. The two adversaries vanished below the surface.

Kari brushed her tears away and stared at the calm lake. Had the harpy drowned? After a minute, the mogel's head broke the surface. Its mouth gaped and its silver eyes closed. Its whole limp body soon floated on the water with the harpy still maintaining his stranglehold.

The golden unclasped his arms, made a reprimanding hiss into the mogel's tiny ear, and slipped off its back. Wading waist-deep toward the shallows, he glanced over his wing at the dazed monster and made a sniffling sound. The mogel swished its fanned tail and plunged to the lake's depths.

The harpy stepped from the water and ruffled his wet feathers before walking to Kari.

For the first time, she saw a harpy up close. His sleek frame was tall, nearly six feet, and his bronze muscles shimmered with dripping water. The creamy birdish wings lay tightly folded against his back, and he moved with a graceful tiptoe stride. He bent down alongside her and tossed the wet, glittering locks from his flawless features. Softly panting from the battle, he stared at her with intense royal-blue eyes. Only one word could describe him: beautiful.

The harpy wrinkled his small nose and sniffed her. Animal-like, he lacked the ability to smile or frown, but his large eyes displayed emotion—curiosity at first, but when she cringed with pain from her injury, his eyes narrowed with concern. He picked her up and carried her from the shore. Under the giant blue ferns, he placed her on some velvety moss and examined her wound.

The searing pain shot through her leg, causing her eyes to water. "I must get home," she cried, and pointed to the wound. "The mogel poison—it will kill me."

Not understanding her human language, he tilted his head like an inquisitive dog. He stood and spread his wings. With a leap, he became airborne.

"No, come back!" she called, but he disappeared into the trees. Harpies were terrified of people, and she had obviously scared him. She struggled to rise but was too weak as the venom took hold. A feverish sweat now covered her body, her heart raced, and she felt nauseated. The wound stung, and she detected the numbing pain moving up her leg. Her face in her arms, she wept in anguish.

A few minutes later, the golden sailed down and landed beside her. Holding a fine green moss, he smashed and rolled it in his hands, turning it into a gummy paste. He crammed the paste into her punctures, and her pain immediately subsided. He tore off a strip of the sash that hung on his hips and hid his genitals. She recognized the webbed linen that the groff insect wove within caves. He wrapped the material around her leg to hold the paste against her wound.

Kari watched him treat her wound. "Dad is wrong. Harpies aren't evil monsters."

He tilted his head again. Her sound apparently puzzled him since harpies were silent creatures, known to be mute.

"You must understand. I have to get home or I'll die," she said, attempting to rise.

He clenched his teeth and created a low hiss that conveyed discouragement. He swept her up into his arms. She gasped, unsure of his intentions. With his nose, he nuzzled her cheek like a gentle pony, reassuring her before he bounded toward the sky.

Just above the multicolored tree canopy, he flew west over the logging road, the same road she had traveled to reach the lake. In a short time the harpy landed in the sprawling meadow that surrounded her large home. Still cradling her in his arms, he nuzzled her again and laid her down on the soft grass, but then the dogs barked and men yelled. They had seen the harpy.

The golden released her and stood, facing his enemies. He arched his wings, angrily tossed his long locks, and seethed at the approaching men. The goldens were known for their bold nature and only these blonds had the nerve to stand their ground, but Kari had also noticed his shorter wings and pale yellow color, proving he was not full grown. Now he foolishly challenged armed men—further evidence that he lacked maturity. A laser blast came dangerously close.

"Go," she pleaded. "Leave before they kill you."

He glared at the men, his ruffled feathers displaying irritation. A second blast zipped passed his head. He longingly glanced down at her before fleeing into the sky.

Kari struggled to her feet and screamed at one of the men. "Charlie, he saved me. Don't hurt him." She collapsed on the ground unconscious.

Kari woke in her bedroom as Maria, the plump Hispanic housekeeper, bent over her and wiped her forehead with a cool towel. "Miss Kari, you gave us quite a scare," she said, and called to the open doorway, "Mr. Turner, she's awake."

Her father came in and sat down on the edge of her bed. "Thank God, you're okay."

Kari gazed up at her strapping father and his concerned eyes. Day-old beard stubble told her that he had not taken the time to shave. "The golden harpy," she said, and tried to sit up. "Charlie didn't kill him, did he?"

Her father grinned and stroked her head. "No, sweetie. That cocky young male got away, but you need to lie still. Doc just left and said you were very lucky. He recognized the mogel bite and caught the venom in time."

"A mogel grabbed me at a lake, and the harpy fought it and brought me home. He saved my life, Dad. And he was so handsome and gentle. Promise you'll protect him. You can do that . . . just keep the hunters off your estate and he'll be safe. Please, Dad."

He forced a weak smile and petted her head, but didn't answer.

Over the coming days, Kari had numerous arguments with her father over the harpy.

"The harpies aren't dangerous," she said. "People kill the poor harpies, and they're the ones that are evil and dangerous."

"Look, young lady," said her father, "you don't know anything about those flying devils, and furthermore, your days of wandering in the woods and searching for harpies are over. I want you in this house or at school. That's it. End of discussion."

She glared at him. "You can't keep me from him."

Ten long years had passed since those events in the jungle and Kari's encounter with the golden harpy. Now a young woman, she sat aboard a spaceship bound for Dora and recalled those childhood memories. Unfortunately, she had learned that her father could keep her from the harpy. Once her mogel injury had healed, she was placed on a spaceship bound for Earth and its schools.

Arriving on Earth, she found that the trees, animals, and all of nature had long ago disappeared. Nothing remained but vast concrete cities that lay under see-through domes revealing a sunless sky. Her classmates, as inhospitable as the chilly climate and the hard, gray buildings, chastised a girl born of the jungle. They claimed her home was barbaric, that only an idiot would want to dwell on the uncivilized and obscure planet of Dora.

Over the years, Kari became quiet and aloof to avoid criticism. She prayed for the day when she could return to her jungle home and walk beneath the towering fan trees, hear the songbirds, and breathe the fragrant, humid air.

Her only relief from despair and homesickness had been a weekly visit to a small solarium. Sitting under the modest trees, she told an elderly gardener about Dora, a small planet similar to Earth during the Jurassic period, when giant reptiles and colossal ferns and trees ruled the landscape. And, of course, she talked about the harpies, and the stunning teenage golden who had rescued her.

The gardener would always end their visit by saying, "If I was young and had the credits, I'd move to your home, Kari."

The old guy was her only friend and reminded her of Charlie, her grandfatherly Indian companion on Dora. During her last week on Earth, she went to the solarium to say good-bye but learned the gardener had passed away in his sleep. Perhaps he had needed her as much as she needed him.

Kari now gazed out the window at the twinkling stars as the mammoth starship made a path through the deep void in space. She pressed her forehead against the cool window, feeling the vibration of the vessel's engines. "Five more days," she sighed. "Just five more, and I'll finally be home."

Still thinking about the golden, she reached in her handbag for a small box. Opening the plastic lid, she took out a strip of tattered material and carefully twisted it through her fingers before bringing it to her nose and lips. His sweet, kittenish scent still lingered. The web linen from the golden's sash had sustained her on many a lonely and desperate night. Gazing at the insect material, she still saw the faint bloodstains from the mogel wound. "I'm coming back to you."

Her thoughts drifted to her father. After all these years, she remained bitter toward him and his decision to banish her to an Earthly prison. She had refused his trans-planet com calls and tossed away his gifts, but she'd soon have to face him. During the five-month space voyage, the meeting with her father lay heavy on her mind. Could she control her anger to even say hello to him?

She glanced out the window at the approach of Duran, Dora's sun, and smiled. Sitting at a stainless-steel table, she took a few raisins out of a bowl, popped them in her mouth, and gazed at the empty dining room. She heard the muffled laugh of a kitchen cook through the closed door. Shortly, this large room would fill with hungry passengers, and Kari would slip out, seeking solitude in her cramped cabin. She twisted her long blond hair, dreading her confined quarters, but she dreaded people more. Her lonely existence on Earth had turned her into a recluse.

The dimly lit dining room flooded with bright lights, Kari's cue to leave before the other passengers arrived and filled the vacant seats. She stood as several people entered the room, laughing and plainly happy that the voyage was ending.

"More colonists," she grumbled to herself, "to destroy the jungle, hunt the animals and kill my harpies."

"Harpies?" said a man's booming voice. Kari turned and saw a tubby, balding man and a woman as they seated themselves at a table. "If you want to see one, there's a few at Hampton Zoo, but the wild ones have been exterminated. And good riddance to those thieving, raping pests."

"Rape?" the woman exclaimed.

The man grinned. "Yeah, male harpies use to raid towns and steal women. Even if a poor girl was found, she was suicidal or her mind was gone. But like I said, most of the flocks have been wiped out."

Kari sank back into her seat and listened to the man ramble as others joined his table. Was he telling the truth? She closed her eyes and felt ill. Over the last decade could the harpies have been so hunted that they were on the brink of extinction? Was he dead—her majestic golden whose image had kept her from going crazy all this time?

She wondered about the man's accusation that harpies were thieves and rapists. Her father apparently believed these allegations. The mere mention of a harpy had sent him into a rage, cursing them as his worst nemesis and often calling them monsters or thieving winged devils. She glanced at the linen strip still in her hand. The golden would never harm me. She straightened. And he just can't be dead.

She stood to leave as the man talked about the gruesome harpy hunts. "Hunters hang the wounded ones from trees," he said, "so the wings bleed out before they're cut off. Amazingly, those ugly beasts don't make a peep while they're being dressed out."

Kari could handle no more. On her way to the exit, she stopped at his table. "I heard you talking about the harpies," she said politely.

The man gazed up with a looming grin. "Aren't you a pretty thing? What would you like to know about them, honey?"

"I am not your 'honey,'" Kari said. "And, sir, you're lying to these people about the harpies." She turned to the woman. "I've seen them. Harpies are harmless and resemble a gorgeous angel. It's criminal they are hunted and killed." She turned and glared at the crude man. "The only beast I see is one you'll find in a mirror."

Kari bit her lip and hurriedly left, hearing chuckles in the dining room. Back in her cabin, she drifted to sleep still clutching the woven strip.

The following day Kari again sat in the deserted dining room. A young man with wavy brown hair entered and walked to her table. "Hi," he said. "I had to meet you. One of the stewards said you come here when the place is empty. May I sit down?"

Reluctantly, Kari nodded.

He took the seat across from her. "I heard you last night." He grinned. "You were terrific. You really put a gag in that windbag's mouth. It was hilarious."

She lowered her gaze. "It was impulsive and wrong. I shouldn't have embarrassed that man and made him the brunt of a joke."

"I see." He raised his eyebrows. "Well, look. My name is Ted. I'm hoping you can tell me about Dora and its wildlife. Have you really seen them—the harpies?"

"Yes, I was born on Dora."

"Wow, a real native," Ted said, and leaned closer. "I didn't know Dorians were so attractive."

Kari blushed with the compliment, but it wasn't her first. As a teenager, she had many boys ask her out, but the dates always ended uncomfortably. Years of seclusion had made her reserved, and she hid her true passions. Having no interest in their modern machine-run world, she ended the dating drudgery, declining their offers. She sensed that Ted was more interested in her than in Dora's wildlife, but she tried to be courteous. "What do you want to know?"

"Well, everything," said Ted. "Tell me about the harpies."

"The harpies are very intelligent, but shy creatures. They have striking human bodies and large wings that—"

"I've heard their mounted wings are worth twenty-thousand credits," Ted broke in. "That's a year's salary for me. Is that true?"

"I wouldn't know," she said, standing. "I have to go."

"Wait a minute. Since you know Hampton, maybe you could show me around. I'd love to buy you dinner."

"I don't think so, but you'll find plenty of Hampton girls who will give you a tour and tell you the price of a dead harpy's wings."

Kari left the dining room and walked down the long corridors that led to her cabin. Halfway down the empty hall, she stopped and leaned against a railing. A tear rolled down her face. "What is wrong with me?" she stammered. The friendly young man couldn't have known that the subject of trophy wings repulsed her. She heard footsteps and glanced up. It was Ted.

"I'm sorry. I apparently upset you." He kicked at the floor and shook his head. "I get so darned nervous around a pretty woman and always end up putting my foot in my mouth. You really care about harpies."

"Now I feel ridiculous," she said, wiping away the tears. "I should be apologizing to you. I don't deal well with people, and become overly offensive when it comes to harpy hunting. I should've explained that I owe my life to a male harpy."

"Really?" Ted leaned against the railing. "I can see why mounted wings would rub you wrong. Do you think you could give me another chance? I left everyone I knew back on Earth, and I'm rather lonely here. I'm hoping to make Dora my home, so I'd like to learn more about your planet."

"Okay," she said, and they walked back to the dining room. Sitting down at the table, Kari told Ted about her home. "Dora is half the size of Earth, but similar to Earth; it's mostly a freshwater ocean with one large continent and hundreds of islands to the west. Except for the cold mountains, the tropical temperature doesn't vary much, warm during the day and cool at night. There are two seasons, the wet and dry. The multicolor jungle trees are enormous. Timber is Dora's main export. Like the harpies, half the animals have wings to navigate through the thick foliage. But Dora's most notorious creatures are the large, warm-blooded reptiles."

"Dora sounds like one great adventure," said Ted.

Kari smiled. "It's a dangerous adventure if you don't know your way around. There're man-eating plants, and the red dragons resemble a giant T. Rex. During the wet season, the torrential rains and storms are hurricane strength. That's why you won't find any high-rises on Dora. Even technology is limited due to the wet climate and since Dora is off the beaten path."

She then talked about the harpies, and the young golden male who had risked his life to save hers.

"I always thought harpies were nasty female monsters."

"That's Earth's old fabled definition, but it doesn't apply to Dora's harpies. In fact, I've never seen one of the females."

Ted leaned back in the chair. "Fighting that eel creature, harpies must be pretty gutsy."

"Actually, they're terrified of people and very elusive, so little is known about them except they're voiceless, tree-dwelling vegetarians. The brown-winged, dark-haired harpies are the most prevalent. The goldens were a rare subspecies, more aggressive, and known to dominate the flocks. Sadly, hunters want them the most. When I left, they were nearly wiped out." She bit her lip, and said softly, "I hope the golden I met is still alive."

Ted reached across the table and took her hand. "I hope so, too. I can tell you care about him."

"Very much." She smiled and changed the subject. "So, why are you going to Dora? You don't look like a lumberjack or hunter."

"Hardly." Ted chuckled. "I'm afraid I'm your average city boy. I have a degree in computers and spacecraft repair, but jobs are scarce on Earth, so I answered a Dora ad for a job in Hampton Port. I hope it works out."

Kari heard his uncertainty. "It will. And once you see Dora, you won't have any regrets."

"I don't regret this trip. After all, I met you. I sure hope we can be friends, Kari."

Kari stared into Ted's brown eyes and had noticed his good looks. They were both the same age of twenty-one and recent college graduates. More important, she detected his sincerity and kindness. "Ted, I believe we are friends."

"Then as a friend, Miss Kari Turner, I'll make you a promise. I'll do all I can to help your harpies."

Ted was delighted to spend the next few days aboard the ship with the stunning blonde. His heart fluttered every time he gazed into Kari's big blue eyes. The ship maneuvered into orbit around Dora, and they wandered to the crowded observatory to see the planet. "I need to start work as soon as we land," he said, "since I'm low on credits."

"You asked me to dinner when we met. How were you going to swing that?" Kari joked.

"If you had said yes to our date, I would have gladly spent my last credit and slept in the streets."

Kari's eyes brightened. "That's sweet of you."

A woman standing nearby talked to her small daughter about their new home on the planet.

Kari leaned toward Ted. "I wish I had known my mother."

Ted had heard about Kari's father and their rocky relationship. After all this time, she still resented him. But she had never mentioned her mother. Turning from the window, he asked, "Where is she?"

"She's dead. She died when I was a baby—some kind of accident. My father refused to discuss it. I just wonder how my life might have been if she had lived. Would she have saved me . . . stopped him from sending me to Earth? Would she have understood my love for the harpies? Just questions I have."

"Some questions are never answered." Ted put his arm around her slender waist. "I don't know your dad, but I think I know you. With your passion for nature, Earth must have been a living hell. Whatever his reasons, your father was wrong to send you to those schools."

She put her arm around him, and they gazed at Dora in silence.

The following day, large shuttles pulled up alongside the spaceship to unload the passengers and cargo. Kari and Ted were among the first to board for the trip to the planet. An hour later, the shuttle descended and landed inside Hampton's spacious domed port. They gathered their belongings, departed the shuttle, and walked past the huge off-loaded crates containing small hovercrafts, terrain vehicles, and even cattle fetuses. On the other side of the port stood towering stacks of Dora's exotic timber that would make the return flight. The blue, red, yellow, and white colors displayed the variety of trees on the planet.

They walked to an information counter and got in line behind a few people. "Ted, you don't have to wait with me," said Kari.

"I'm not scheduled for work until tomorrow. I'll wait and make sure you catch the next hover to Terrance."

Kari smiled, happy for the first time not to be alone. Eventually, she approached the counter and a middle-aged woman. "I need a ticket for Terrance."

"There are no more flights today," said the woman. "The earliest one leaves at noon tomorrow."

"I'll take a one-way ticket on it," Kari said, doling out her credits.

"We have one more night together. I'll buy dinner if you show me around Hampton."

"Don't be absurd," Kari said as they walked toward the exit. "I have more credits than you, and besides, I don't know this city. I was here only once when I was a kid."

"How about Dutch on dinner, and we'll explore Hampton together, unless you're tired of me."

"Not yet." She smiled.

"Great. Let me ask those cargo guys about a decent hotel. I've heard some places in Hampton are rough." He jogged over to three men unloading crates and returned in minutes. "They say there's one down the street that's decent and reasonable. Prices are cheap here compared to Earth. I might also stay there."

They stepped outside, and Kari paused to gaze at the two- and three-story wooden buildings that lined the street. A warm breeze pulled her long hair off her shoulders as she breathed deeply. After a decade of stale, filtered air, she inhaled the wonderful aroma of trees and flowers even in the heart of the large capital city of Hampton.

Ted stood back and watched her before glancing up at majestic blue trees that shaded the buildings and street. Ten-inch purple flowers adorned the spaceport and surrounding buildings. He reached down to pick one.

"Don't touch," she said, pointing to a warning sign. "They bite. They're insect eaters but might mistake your finger for dinner. Like all of Dora, they're beautiful, but hazardous." Leaving Ted, she bounced down the port steps like a child at a theme park.

He caught up with her on the sidewalk. "Do you want to get a ride to the hotel?"

"I'd rather walk," she mumbled, and stepped to the first tree. Dropping her bags, she put her arms around its trunk as if the tree were a long-lost friend. She stroked the bark and sniffed its sweet resin.

Ted put his hand over his mouth, concealing a grin. "You're one unusual girl, Kari—definitely different from Earth girls. I've never seen anyone hug a tree."

Kari withdrew from the tree. "I just missed them."

They walked down the street, and periodically, she stopped to admire another Dora treasure. They arrived at the hotel and entered the quaint lobby adorned with massive yellow beams.

"Let's drop our bags in our rooms and meet back here," she said. "I can't be indoors now." Ted agreed, and they soon were back on the streets of Hampton.

Kari felt a renewed sense of well-being as though the humid air contained a magic potion that healed her tortured soul. They walked for miles, discovering the city of wood. Beyond the buildings, kaleidoscopic forests covered the distant hills. They reached the coast and stood on a cliff, overlooking the emerald ocean that blended with a pale purple and green horizon. The waves lapped against the black rocky shore, leaving white foam as they receded.

"Jesus, Kari," Ted mumbled. "I've never dreamed a place could be so beautiful."

She nodded and stared up the beach at the seaport. Several large hydro-plane barges laden with lumber maneuvered into the docks. "I wonder if the timber came from my home."

"Your home in Terrance?" Ted asked as they walked a winding, sandy path to the beach.

"My father's estate isn't in Terrance," she said, "but Terrance is the only town in the western outback with a large airport for commercial hover-crafts. My home is on the west coast near a little village called Westend. When I reach Terrance, I'll rent a terrain vehicle and drive the five hundred miles on the dirt highway through the true jungle. It'll take two days, but it's worth it."

"Alone? That sounds awfully risky. Maybe you should . . ."

She stopped walking to glare at him. "Ted, this is my home. I'm safer in that jungle than I was on the streets of Earth."

"Okay, okay," he said. "It's none of my business."

"Thank you," she said, and resumed walking.

"Why did your father move so far from civilization?"

"It was my grandfather who settled the outback. He'd traveled to Russia and witnessed the fall of the last great forest. It disgusted him. When he, my grandmother, and a young Indian named Charlie came to Dora, they hacked out a living in the remote jungle. My grandfather was a great man and a nature advocate. For every cut tree, he planted a seedling, and he taught me everything about the jungle. I still remember our long trips with Charlie into the wild. When grandpa died, Charlie became my mentor and guide. I really have missed that old Indian. He's the only person who never gave me grief for my fascination with harpies."

Walking the coast, they came upon a run-down seafood shack, built half over the water. "I don't know about you, but I'm getting hungry," Ted said. "You want to try this place?"

"It's perfect," she answered. Sitting on the outside deck, Ted inhaled a large bowl of seafood chowder, and Kari relished a dish of Dora's exotic fruit. They finished the meal with white cakes covered in a wine-drenched berry sauce.

Ted stretched back in the rickety wooden chair as a gentle ocean breeze whipped at his hair. "I've eaten in some fancy, expensive places," he said, "but who would have guessed this shack offered the best food and scenery."

"Dora's fresh food is superior, and the ocean view is lovely."

He leaned over the table and gazed into her eyes. "I wasn't talking about the ocean."

Kari grinned shyly. Ted was obviously smitten with her and was cute in his sometimes awkward hints to let her know.

Darkness crept into the sky, and the first of Dora's twin moons appeared on the horizon. Kari and Ted made their way down the quiet streets until they reached the hotel. In the lobby, Ted took her hand. "I guess this is good-bye. I hope I'll see you again."

"You will. When you get settled, call me." She got up the nerve and kissed his cheek before leaving for her hotel room.

Her room was small but comfortable. Kari took a quick shower and collapsed on the soft bed. She felt exhilarated. This had been one of the best days she could remember, and she liked Ted. He was easygoing and fun, but more important, he didn't criticize her convictions. "Maybe there's hope for me yet," she thought, and snuggled under the sheets. She soon drifted to sleep.

In the middle of the night, Kari felt his lean-muscled frame over her and his soft panting breath against her neck. She opened her eyes into layers of tumbling blond locks that shimmered in the moonlight. Pushing his hair aside, she met his gaze—the same royal-blue eyes from the past. His yellow wings nervously fluttered, and she stroked his head. Calmed by her touch, he relaxed and the feathered limbs collapsed, encasing them. She was engulfed in his sweet animal scent as he nuzzled and tenderly nipped her neck.

"God, I've missed you," she breathed.

The golden harpy lifted his head and stared at her, his eyes sparkling between the thick lashes. He made a subtle sniffle conveying that he, too, had longed for her. Kari's heart pounded and she shivered, inflamed by the seductive creature. He pulled away and rose. His emotionless face gazed down at her, but then he swallowed down a sigh. In a puff, he was gone.

Kari jolted forward on the bed and looked around her empty room. Drenched in sweat and trembling, she made her way to the window and door. She found them securely locked. "It was a dream," her shaky voice said, "but so real." Never had a dream been so vivid. She sat down, collecting herself, and thought about the breathtaking harpy. Many times she had dreamed about him, but none of those dreams were this intense. Eventually, she drifted back to sleep.

2

The morning light filtered through the drawn blinds and woke Kari. As she showered and dressed, her mind was focused on the dream. She closed her eyes and could still see him, feel him, smell him. She then remembered the terrible man on the ship had said there were harpies at the Hampton Zoo. She hastily packed and rushed to the lobby.

"How far away is the Hampton Zoo?" she asked the hotel clerk.

"Not far, but it doesn't open until nine," he said.

Kari thanked him and wandered into the hotel restaurant for a light breakfast. Her hover flight left at noon, so she had the time. Glancing around the dining area, she hoped to see Ted, but he wasn't there. After eating some biscuits and juice, she caught a shuttle to the zoo.

Kari waited as the zoo cashier opened the gates. "Three credits," the woman said.

"Do you have harpies?"

"We have two brown fledglings," the cashier responded, taking Kari's money.

Kari entered the sprawling grounds and hurried past the exhibits, glancing briefly. Each animal brought back a cherished memory of encounters in the wild. She could have spent days in this place.

A sign read WINGED, and she hurried down the path, passing aviaries of flying reptiles and birds. The last were the mammals. Many were batlike creatures, the size of a large dog and smaller. They fell into the six-limb category.

Finally, she came to a large cage. HARPY was posted on the bars. Peering up into the tree branches, she saw them. All her excitement diminished to sorrow. They weren't the majestic creatures she remembered from her childhood. Instead, she saw two pathetic male fledglings with tattered wings. They slept curled up on the wide branch with their frail arms wrapped around each other for warmth and security. With their thin nude frames, matted locks, and broken quill feathers, they resembled five-year-old children who were refugees of war.

"You poor little guys," she said softly.

One fledgling opened his green eyes and gazed at her. Spreading his tiny wings, he glided down to the cage bars, curiously slanted his head, and studied her. After a moment, he put his arm through the bars and made a grabbing motion, but a rope strung between the cage and the path kept them apart. More zoo visitors approached, but the fledgling ignored them. Soon the second fledging joined him and his antics.

"I don't have any food," Kari said, hoping to appease them.

An older man wearing a zoo uniform approached Kari. "You're not allowed to feed the animals, miss," he said sternly.

One of the onlookers broke in. "She hasn't fed them. We've been watching."

The zookeeper rubbed his chin and watched the small harpies. "They usually keep their distance and only come close at feeding time," he said. "For some reason, miss, they like you."

"And I like them," Kari said.

"You must've recently arrived on Dora." The zookeeper chuckled. "The local Dorians consider them pests, like rats."

"I did arrive yesterday from Earth, but I was born on Dora and have always liked the harpies. They're so elegant, and resemble humans. I don't understand the Dorians' animosity toward them."

"I admit harpies are pretty things, but they have an ugly reputation. Harpy is a Greek word meaning 'to steal,' and in Greek mythology, they were loathsome, winged beasts. When Dora was first settled and there were many harpy flocks, men had to guard their wives and daughters since harpies would take them. That's why these creatures were named harpies."

"I don't believe those old stories," Kari said flatly. "A harpy saved me from a mogel and flew me home. He had plenty of opportunity to kidnap me."

The stout keeper frowned at Kari. "And when did this happen?"

"Ten years ago in the outback." She reached down and pulled up her khaki pants. "Here's the scar from the mogel bite."

"Would you mind talking to our new vet? He's doing research on the harpies but hasn't had much luck with information. He'd love to hear your story."

Kari glanced at her timepiece. "I have to catch a noon flight, but could spare a few minutes."

The zookeeper escorted Kari to a building marked for employees. She waited in an office and heard men's voices behind a door.

"She's in the office, Doctor." The door opened and a middle-aged man appeared, followed by the zookeeper.

The doctor raised one eyebrow, scrutinizing Kari. "I'm Dr. Watkins," he said, extending his hand. "Mike says you like harpies and had physical contact with one. Would you mind telling me about it?"

The vet's skepticism matched her own. "Why are you studying the harpies?"

"Dora's government hired me," said Watkins. "I'm a genetic expert and conduct studies on threatened species, their habits, and environment. If I can find hard evidence that harpies are endangered, new laws may be imposed to limit or ban hunting until they recover."

"I see," Kari said. "Since your study might help the harpies, I'll tell you about my incident, but it happened when I was a child. I don't see how it'll benefit your research now."

"Any information on these mysterious creatures is valuable," said Watkins.

Both men listened intently as she told them about the lake and the golden harpy.

"That's remarkable," Watkins commented when she finished. "Plenty of men have documented their hunts, but you're the first woman to discuss an encounter with a feral and uninjured harpy." Dr. Watkins seemed no longer dubious of her story. "You asked this golden male to take you home, and he flew you there, knowing where you lived?"

"Yes," Kari said. "Is that so amazing?"

"Yes," he answered. "Either the harpy understood the English language or it sensed your desires and where you lived. It's unlikely a wild harpy knows our language, so it relied on its instincts. The sixth sense or instincts allow animals to communicate with one another. I'm betting you also have strong instincts." Watkins smiled. "The creature probably sensed you liked him. That's why he helped you."

"But, Dr. Watkins," the old keeper said, "those fledglings understand and come when I call, especially if food is involved."

"Most animals can be trained to respond to certain words, but Kari spoke to a wild harpy, and not only did it take her home, but he also treated her wound and tied a strip of cloth on her leg. It proves these creatures are intelligent, even gentle."

"Have you ever tried talking to an adult harpy?"

"Talking?" He sighed. "There's never been time for talk. I was told that the adults die in captivity, but a month ago, I had the zoo purchase two stunned males from hunters. The harpies immediately curled up in a ball and suffered from shock. I managed to treat the shock, but one still died the following night from a heart attack. The remaining harpy wouldn't eat or drink and had to be tube fed. I was finally making real progress with the little fellow and released him into a larger cage. Before he could be restrained, he flew against the bars and broke his neck. I've never dealt with such difficult and fragile creatures. Learning how they communicate or if they're intelligent are on the bottom of my list."

Watkins wearily rubbed the back of his neck. "It's impossible to get an accurate count on the flocks, and the few harpies that are sighted, caught, or killed are always males. Their females and breeding grounds have yet to be discovered. It's rumored they nest on the western islands. Our zoo's fledglings came from there."

Pausing to take a deep breath and control his frustration, he continued. "And now I'm dealing with a pair of loca eagles that the zoo recently acquired. I learned that harpies have fifty percent of the same DNA as locas, proving they're related. The other fifty percent of a harpy's DNA is human. This gives credibility to the stories of harpies stealing and molesting women. Since no female harpy has ever been found, it's conceivable that male harpies used female locas, women, or both to create their offspring. These harpies are so baffling it's hard to know what is truth or fiction when studying them."

"I've never seen a loca eagle," Kari said.

"You won't, unless you visit the western islands. One hundred years ago they covered the continent, but overhunting reduced their numbers to a few remaining flocks. That's always the trouble with endangered animals. By the time a study is done, it's almost too late."

Kari lowered her head. "Is it too late for the harpies?"

"I hope not."

Kari glanced at the time. "I must go or I'll miss my flight. If I can help you in any way, please let me know. I do owe the golden my life."

"My research is stalled here, and I can't learn much from these captive fledglings," said Watkins. "I may come to the outback for my answers. Perhaps you could show me this lake."

"I'll do anything if it ends the hunting," she said, leaving the office. The old zookeeper accompanied her up the path toward the harpy cage. The fledglings were curled up on the branch, sound asleep.

The old man motioned to another aviary. "The loca eagles are over there." Kari rushed down the path to the huge cage. The two large winged creatures were perched on a tree limb, but they looked nothing like an eagle. Their six-foot bodies were covered with small brown feathers, and they resembled a furry ape with wings. Only their large, green eyes and elfish facial features were similar to a harpy's. She hurried toward the exit to catch the shuttle.

Reaching the street, Kari hopped aboard the shuttle. A short ride later, she arrived at the port. She gathered her things and walked toward the large circular ship. Before stepping inside, she heard a familiar voice calling her name. "Kari," Ted yelled from beneath a small spaceship. "I'll miss you." She blew him a kiss and stepped inside the hovercraft.

A stewardess confirmed her ticket and said, "You can sit where you wish. This flight does not have assigned seating."

Kari took a window seat across from an older businessman. She looked out the window in anticipation. The hovercraft rose through the port doors and moved rapidly west. Within minutes, the city of Hampton and surrounding small farms disappeared from sight. Beneath the ship lay the vast jungle. Like a giant painting, the landscape exploded with the multi-colored trees. She had been starving for this feast of beauty. The breathtaking view became overwhelming. She swallowed the lump growing in her throat and fought her moistening eyes. She truly was home.

As the jungle drifted past, she settled down, her gaze glued to the scenery. Glimpses of the highway appeared beneath the thick underbrush. The road ran from coast to coast across the continent. "That's my road," she thought, considering her journey. After Terrance, the highway would become a narrow, ill-kept path through the true jungle. Periodically, she saw a store with nearby homes and farms—remnants of civilization encased in the wilderness. Several small towns briefly appeared but were quickly replaced by the countless trees. Once she passed the river city of Terrance, very few settlements existed, much to Kari's delight. In three hours, the flight would end and her adventure would begin. She twirled her long hair in anticipation.

She glanced at the businessman consumed in his reading. Without looking up, he said, "This must be your first trip across the continent. It's very impressive, isn't it?"

Kari sat back in her seat, realizing her enthusiasm must have been obvious. "I was born in the outback, but I haven't seen it in a long time."

"So you're going home to Terrance?" He kept his eyes fixed on his reading machine.

"My home is north of Westend, near the coast."

"I'm familiar with Westend. It's a quaint little town. My name is Dan Roberts. I'm an appraiser for the Hampton Bank, so I travel a great deal."

"Kari Turner."

For the first time, the man took true interest in her and put aside his reading machine. "Any relation to John Turner?"

"He's my father."

"Well, it's a great pleasue to meet you, Miss Turner," he said, smiling. "Your father is one of our best customers and has the largest timber estate in the outback. About now, he must be a worried man."

"Worried?"

"The beetle swarms—they're consuming the western continent," he said. "Surely you've heard about them."

"No, but I only arrived yesterday from Earth, and I haven't spoken to my father in some time."

"The farther west we travel, you'll begin to see the damage from these wood-eating insects," said Roberts. "They destroy everything—houses, farms, and timber. Nothing kills them. Every insecticide known to man has been sprayed to no avail. Even surrounding them with fire has failed. The beetles simply spread their wings and fly away. I'm appraising a few farms north of Terrance that were hit by a swarm. Only the equipment may be salvageable. At the rate the beetles are multiplying and destroying timber, the whole economy of this planet will be in the toilet in a few years."

"Have they struck my father's estate?"

"Let's take a look." Roberts pulled a narrow computer out from under his seat. Tapping the keys, he scanned the Turner Estate—one hundred miles wide that ran six hundred miles north along the west coast into Dora's highest mountain range. The residence and wood mill were located at the southern tip, ten miles north of Westend. "Your father's been lucky so far, but the beetles struck some homes south of Westend a few months ago. How are you traveling from Terrance to Westend?"

"I'm renting a terrain vehicle and taking the old road."

"By yourself?"

Kari nodded.

"That's a two-day journey on a dilapidated road through the heart of the jungle," he said. "If you have trouble, you'll find few places to stop. Besides the dangerous wildlife, there are the swarms that can clog an engine and leave you stranded."

"I'm not worried."

"Well, you may have trouble renting a vehicle to such a remote area, but even a small hovercraft is dangerous. Several hunters recently died in a hover crash when the engines became clogged with beetles. This large hover flies too high for the swarms to be a threat." He closed the computer and shoved it under the seat. "In an hour, you'll see some of the areas that have been destroyed."

Kari turned her attention back to the window. When they approached the middle of the continent, she saw the blackened dirt of the forest floor—evidence of a swarm strike. Nothing remained. Like locusts, the beetles had consumed everything. The giant hovercraft swiftly moved over the vacant land, and jungle appeared again. She looked at Roberts. "I saw one. The swarm damage is unbelievable. How long has this been going on?"

"It started two years ago," he said. "The first swarm struck the southwestern territory, but now the swarms are everywhere in the west, and there's no consistency to their movement. It's only a matter of time before they head east. So far, no town has suffered a direct hit, but people are plenty concerned."

Kari shook her head and stared out the window. Her father would be one of those concerned about something so devastating that it could destroy everything he and her grandfather had sought to protect. Her thoughts turned to her grandfather. She remembered trailing him through the forest with his bag of seedlings. For every tree cut, he'd replace it with a seedling. When they entered an area scheduled for harvesting, he'd mark the massive thousand-year-old trees with red ribbon so they'd be spared.

Tying a ribbon around the wide trunks, he'd say, "These old ones have stood the test of time through hurricanes and drought. They've earned our respect, Kari. And mankind doesn't deserve their wood." Saving nature was a religion to him.

After her grandfather's death, her father had continued the practice, so the Turner Estate was different from other timberlands. The trees were harvested, but the jungle remained. Other timber companies practiced clearcutting. Every tree, young and old, was taken, leaving the land as marred as if a forest fire had struck. Like her father and grandfather, her passion for trees was bred into her.

Her father faced a battle to save what she also cherished. Feeling sympathetic for him, she decided to put her bitterness aside and give him the opportunity to rectify their damaged relationship. He didn't need additional trouble from her.

Out the window, the northern mountain range appeared and sloped southward. The sleek black peaks jetted out of a kaleidoscope jungle, piercing a grayish-green sky. The large hovercraft was nearing the outback. Mr. Roberts had gone back to his reading, and Kari kept her vigilant watch of the ground. As they approached Terrance, she saw more barren places created by the swarms. Some areas were vast and miles wide and others encompassed only the equivalent of a few city blocks. With man's advanced technology, why hadn't anyone found a solution to the destructive beetles? Man had beaten nature on Earth, but sadly, at a terrible cost.

Mr. Roberts closed his reading machine. "We'll be setting down soon, Miss Turner. It was nice meeting you."

"Same here and thanks for the information."

"You be careful in that jungle when you head home. You're far too lovely to be lost."

She nodded and looked out the window as Duran, Dora's sun, was setting in the west. The sky filled with pinks, oranges, and gold. The warm-toned rays shot through the wispy purple clouds on the horizon. In the distance, Kari saw the mighty river that snaked its way through jungle camouflage. The hover slowed, passed the river, and descended toward Terrance. Large barges loaded with precious lumber floated on the wide body of water and journeyed southward toward the ocean, then on to Hampton. From Hampton, the exotic wood would travel the galaxy to other planets.

Terrance rose from the riverbanks with a display of colorful Victorian buildings. Kari saw the meadows and farmlands merging into distant hills. A large black void of barren land rested to the north, and she recognized the swarm's deadly mark. The town had barely escaped a strike.

The hover set down on a large paved lot. A building stood nearby and off to its side were assorted small hovercrafts parked in no particular order. Farther out, were two large timber freighters. Hearing the hover doors open, Kari and Mr. Roberts picked up their belongings and moved up the aisle. "It's not as fancy as the indoor port at Hampton," he commented.

She reached the exit. "I think I like it better. This town has a lot of charm."

He smirked. "Well, this open port is not so charming during the rainy season."

Kari walked toward the building with the other passengers. Once inside, she went to the information desk to inquire about a vehicle rental.

"Westend?" said the man behind the counter. "There's no connecting office in Westend, and we don't rent vehicles to go that far. I can get you on a hover shuttle tomorrow. That's the best I can do."

Kari sighed, "Okay, book me on it."

"Sounds like you need a ride," said an older man's voice over her shoulder.

Kari whirled around and saw Charlie. She dropped her belongings and threw her arms around the old Indian. She choked up with emotion. "Oh, Charlie, I'm so happy to see you."

"And I, you. You are a sight for my old eyes." He hugged her tightly. After a long heartfelt moment, they pulled apart.

"Why are you in Terrance?"

He scowled. "To take you home. I figured you might try to drive that deserted road alone. Did you think your father or I would allow this? The jungle is still very dangerous, or have you forgotten?"

Kari beamed. "I haven't forgotten, and there's no other person on the planet I'd rather be with on my trip home."

Charlie picked up her bags. "My vehicle is this way." He strolled to the doorway.

Kari smiled. Charlie was never one for much talk. She followed the old man with long gray braids toward the parking lot, and he stopped at a green vehicle. He stored her bags in the back and opened Kari's passenger door. "The light will be gone soon," he said. "Do you want to stay in Terrance and start fresh in the morning or travel the road tonight? There is a small inn a few hours away. It is not fancy, but the food is good."

Kari glanced at the vibrant buildings decorated with carved wooden posts and white lattice. "I'm sure the hotels here are superior to the inn on the road, but I'd prefer to be in the jungle. I've had my fill of civilization."

They climbed into the vehicle and Charlie pushed the start button. The terrain vehicle rose a foot off the ground. He glanced at her. "You have grown into a beautiful woman, but your soul remains the same. This pleases me."

Kari was also pleased. Charlie's hair was grayer and his face more wrinkled, but her Indian guide was the same great companion.

Charlie navigated through the Terrance streets, and they soon left the quaint river city. After passing rolling hills of pastures and farms, they started their journey on the dilapidated, westbound road. The light faded and they entered the deep jungle. The magnificent trees lined their path, and their branches connected overhead, creating a canopy. Darkness came and vehicle headlights lit the way through the cavern of trees.

"If you're tired, I can drive," Kari said.

"It is not far, but I will tell you if I grow weary." The terrain vehicle moved slowly on the dirt road that was full of dips, fallen trees, and boulders. Had the road been smooth, the vehicle was capable of rapid speeds, but they were in no hurry.

"I heard about the swarms," Kari said.

"Yes, your father and I are very worried. He is doing everything to find a toxin to kill them. At the mill, the storage room off his office has been turned into a lab. Every night he experiments with chemicals on beetles we captured. He does not trust the government to solve his problems."

The pride in the old man's voice was obvious, as though John were his own son. She listened quietly as Charlie continued.

"When a swarm struck two homes in the south, your father stopped work at the mill. He supplied the lumber and sent his men to rebuild those families' homes. He is a good man with a good heart."

"Maybe to others," Kari said, unable to control her smoldering resentment.

"Such anger, still." Charlie breathed deeply. "Earth was hard for you."

She tried to respond, but couldn't. His few words brought back all the misery. Like a dam breaking, tears flooded down her cheeks, and she lowered her head and sobbed. He stopped the vehicle and held her as she trembled and wept in his arms, unable to control all the pent-up emotion. She gasped, "I'd rather die than go back to Earth."

"It's all right, it's all right now," he said softly.

The forest grew dark and echoed the sounds of the nocturnal. After some time, she pulled away and attempted to apologize.

"Shhh," he said, shaking his head. "I worried for you all these years. Our hearts are similar. I am old, but I still remember my life on Earth. It is not for the free of spirit. I tried to tell this to your father, but he would not listen. But it is over now, my Kari. You are home and the jungle will heal you."

"Yes, I'm home, finally," she sniffled. "The only thing that kept me sane was knowing I'd come back."

Charlie started the engines, and they traveled in silence.

"The inn is near," he said. "We shall eat and sleep. Tomorrow will be a good day."

"Just being here with you makes everything all right."

Charlie parked in front of the inn office. The building was made of rough timbers, and to the side were individual small cabins. He went inside to check in while Kari waited in the vehicle. In a few minutes, he returned. "The second cabin is yours," he said. "I am in the third. They stop serving dinner soon. Do you want to freshen up before we eat?"

Kari nodded and took her small bag into the cabin. She went to the bathroom sink and splashed water on her face, a ritual she had practiced on Earth. She soon joined Charlie outside.

"Better?" he asked.

"Much better."

They walked to the office and small restaurant. They found the place was virtually empty of customers. Charlie ordered a reptilian steak with a spicy herb sauce, and Kari had grilled vegetables, all native to the jungle.

Charlie talked about the beetles and how over the years he had seen small nests, but the insects had never multiplied to vast numbers until now. Kari listened and ate in silence. He told her of events she had missed—his last great hunt, killing a large zel stag with ten-point antlers.

"Charlie, I don't remember you talking this much."

"Nor I," he answered. "I guess I missed you."

"I really missed you, too."

They ordered a cobbler dessert with wild berries, and Kari ate every bite. "You were hungry," he said.

She smiled, a little embarrassed. "For ten years, I've been ravenous for Dora's food."

"It is good you eat now, for tomorrow we camp, and you must endure my cooking. The inn before Westend is closed."

"I'd rather camp and never went hungry with your cooking."

The dimming lights in the restaurant signaled it was about to close. Charlie paid the bill, and they walked to their individual cabins.

"Tomorrow we start early," he said, standing in front of Kari's cabin.

"I'll be ready. Good night, Charlie, and thank you for letting me cry on your shoulders."

"My shoulders are always yours." He grinned and left for his cabin.

Kari went in and took a shower. She lay down on the bed but couldn't sleep. The clicking, screeches, and bellows of the night jungle seemed to call to her. Dressing, she stepped outside, thinking a short walk might help her relax. A moist breeze whipped at her hair and made a musical sound through the branches. Dora's twin moons were full and lit up the deserted dirt road. Mesmerized by this magical night world, she ignored the hazards and sought the comfort of the wild. She walked among the breathing shadows, drawn farther and farther from the inn. Her senses intensified. For the first time in years, she felt alive. It was like a dream— a dream she had longed for.

In the distance, Kari heard the low growl of a grogin. Glancing back, she saw the far-off inn lights. Another growl came and it was closer. She knew about the sleek brown predators. Resembling a cat and weasel mix, grogins weighed in at one hundred pounds and were deadly. Hunting in packs, they could bring down Dora's largest reptiles. If one existed, there were others. Running was not an option. She might stimulate an attack, appearing like fleeing prey. She started walking back to the inn and safety. Only several feet away, she heard a snarl in the thick brush and froze. Any movement now would invite a grogin to pounce. Her heart beat fast as she listened. The snap of twigs and the underbrush giving way told her that several grogins were behind and alongside of her. She was surrounded.

Kari moved her foot from side to side in the dirt until she felt a baseball-size rock. Slowly she picked it up. The crackling leaves and growls came closer as the pack converged on her. Sweat ran down her body, but she dared not move. The outline of a large grogin, the female pack leader, appeared on the road. Her escape route to the inn was now cut off. She carefully raised her hand and threw the rock. It struck the female's ribs. The grogin released a surprised snarl and jumped into the bushes. Kari hastily searched for another rock, but only grasped a handful of pebbles. She sent them flying toward the animals behind her. The growls and crash of bushes conveyed that the animals had been startled, but pebbles would not scare off a pack for long.

More leery, the large female returned to the road and stalked Kari. With each step, the grogin paced closer and snarled, the moonlight exposing her long, white fangs. The grogin postured, hoping to intimidate and make Kari run.

Too late, Kari recalled as a child that she should always carry a large stick. Charlie had told her, "A good whack on the nose will make most wild animals think twice." She searched for a broken branch or makeshift weapon, but could find none in the dark. Calling for help was out of the question. She was too far away to be heard, and the noise would incite a charge.

When the female pounces, I must go for her eyes, Kari thought—the only option left to surviving a mauling. The animal moved in and crouched. Kari trembled, preparing for the ill-fated fight.

A dark shadow abruptly fluttered down, landing between her and the grogin. The brown wings were fully extended to appear more menacing. The frustrated grogin fiercely growled at the intruder, but when the male harpy hissed and stepped toward the animal, it backed off. Not satisfied by the grogin's retreat, the harpy tossed his dark locks, flapped his wings, and leaped at the large female. The female grogin cried out and sprang for the underbrush, the pack following her lead. Their anxious cries and yips echoed through the distant trees.

Shocked, Kari couldn't move or speak. The brown harpy folded his wings and approached her. The beaming inn lights caught his large green eyes. She gazed up at the tall, lean frame, and fascination replaced terror. He was so handsome and majestic. His chocolate wings and sweeping brown hair glistened with silver created by the moonlight. Except for the golden harpy, she'd never seen a more attractive male. He sniffled, and his asking eyes held concern.

"I'm not hurt," she said.

The harpy deliberately closed his eyes as though he understood. He raised his head and stared toward the inn. Backing away from her, his self-assured features turned to fear.

"What's wrong?" She glanced down the road. "There's nothing there." She looked back, but the harpy was gone. She whirled around, searching the starry sky and shadowy trees, but like a ghost, he had vanished. She now heard Charlie calling her name.

"I'm here," she answered and hurried down the road to meet him.

"Are you all right?" Charlie asked. "I heard grogins on the hunt, so I got up. Then I found your cabin door open and you gone. It scared me."

"I'm okay, Charlie. The grogins ran away when they heard you."

"I should scold you for wandering in the night jungle," he said sternly. "But I think you have learned that lesson tonight."

"Yes," she said. "I won't go in the jungle again unless I have a laser gun. I'm sorry I worried you."

"The worry I can live with. I am only grateful you are unharmed."

They reached her cabin, and after saying good night, Kari went inside and collapsed on the bed. She shuddered, reliving the near-death experience, but then she thought about the brown harpy. For the second time, a harpy had saved her life. It couldn't be coincidence. Perhaps she did have a strong sixth sense, and the creatures detected she liked them. She tried to envision all the details of the encounter, recalling she had told the harpy that she was unharmed.

"He asked me," she said, stunned. "He asked if I was hurt." The harpy hadn't uttered a sound, but she heard his question enter her subconscious. Kari rose and paced the room. "Is it possible that I can understand them, and they can understand me?"

She dropped on the bed and felt guilty about lying to Charlie as to who really had saved her from the grogins, but she had experienced such grief as a child when exposing a harpy encounter. To confess the truth would raise concerns from Charlie and her father—concern that for some reason, the winged creatures were drawn to her. She crawled into bed and shut her eyes.

3

Feeling his presence, Kari reached up and wrapped her arms around his neck, pulling him close. He snuggled against her and tenderly kissed her lips. Exploring his sleek muscled frame through touch, she ran her hand across his shoulder and down his ribs. His body quivered, and he panted softly. He nuzzled his face deep in her hair and licked and kissed her neck.

Kari shuddered with excitement, caressed by his gentle hands. The golden moved to her breasts and suckled. She breathed hard and firmly grasped his long blond hair to control him. Unfazed, he rubbed and wiggled his lightweight frame again hers. His yellow feathers fluttered with sexual stimulation. She felt the pit of her stomach rise and fall, aroused by the gorgeous creature.

Pushing his locks aside, she stared into his longing eyes and detected his reluctance to leave. "Don't go."

"Soon," was his answer, though he made no sound. Suddenly, he was gone as quickly as he had come.

Kari jolted from the bed and stared around the vacant room. Perspiration ran down her face, and she heaved for breath. Flinging her damp hair from her face, she jumped up and checked the windows and door. Again they were bolted. "Another dream," she said, sitting on the bed. It was the same dream, but more powerful than the last.

On Earth, she had often dreamed of the golden harpy—the rescue from the mogel, him treating her wound, the flying, but these Dora dreams were very different. They were filled with passion. And he was different. The golden was no longer a stranger or a curious creature protecting a young girl, but he was now her lover. She then remembered something else. He wasn't a slight teenager with short, creamy wings, but had matured into an adult, his shoulders broader and his long wings were now a rich buttercup-yellow.

Why the golden? she thought. A gorgeous, brown-winged harpy had just saved her. Why hadn't she dreamed of him? She crawled into the sheets, preoccupied with the dream.

Kari woke to the sharp rap on the door, and morning light flooded the cabin. Stumbling out of bed, she murmured, "Charlie." She opened the door and found the Indian waiting outside. "I'm sorry I overslept," she stammered. "I won't be long."

"There is no hurry. I will be in the restaurant," Charlie said, and headed toward the main building. Kari showered, dressed, and packed her small bag. She met Charlie in the empty dining room. He was eating fried lizard eggs with a zel steak and coffee. Kari ordered a bowl of fruit and told Charlie about the grogins, but again excluded the brown harpy and his intervention from her story.

She and Charlie soon were back on the narrow highway. Charlie slowed the terrain vehicle when a large herd of deerlike creatures called zels crossed the road. Their dark green bodies with yellow stripes glistened as they darted into the safety of the trees. Once among the foliage, they raised their rust-colored heads up to see the vehicle.

An hour later, Charlie was forced to stop the vehicle. A twelve-foot red dragon lay across the road, sunning itself. Charlie got out of the vehicle and yelled, "Go on, you big bum." He grabbed a downed fan branch and prodded the giant carnivore. The reptile seethed and snapped at the branch before standing and sluggishly moving off into the brush, its long tail swishing with annoyance. Charlie chuckled and climbed back into the vehicle.

"Most men would have killed that dragon," Kari said.

"Perhaps, but it would be a senseless kill. A lazy dragon is a fed dragon and no threat."

"Would you call harpy hunting also a senseless kill?"

"Yes, but I am an Indian and think differently than other men. I kill only for food or to protect myself and would never harm a harpy."

"Why do men kill them, Charlie?"

"You have asked me this question many times as a child."

She glanced at him. "I'm not a child anymore, and I still don't understand why men kill such beautiful creatures."

"On Earth, you learned about that planet's past wildlife. The tiger, the white seal pup, the elk, the shark, and countless others—all beautiful and all gone from hunting or loss of habitat. The harpies will share their fate. Dora is a remote outpost with no protective laws for its wildlife. Knowing this, many men travel here, seeking the thrill and glory of the hunt. With a harpy's instincts and intelligence, they are the most challenging game animals in the galaxy, causing their wings to soar in value. Some men come, hoping to get rich off these feather trophies. And the Dorians believe that harpies are dangerous, so they are content that the hunters wipe out this threat."

"Like Dad?" she said. "I've heard the rumors of harpies stealing and raping women."

"They are not rumors, Kari," said Charlie, "so do not judge your father so harshly. Now that you are older, he might tell you why he hates the harpies."

"I doubt it," she snapped. "He's always kept things to himself, and besides, I don't give a damn about his reasons. A harpy helped me, and Dad's phobia cost me ten miserable years on Earth."

Charlie massaged his chin. "Your father's dislike of these creatures has lessened. After you left for Earth, he was grateful to the young golden for saving your life and placed a ban on harpy hunting that covered the entire estate. The harpies found a sanctuary there, and all these years, they have flourished in peace."

"Dad kept his promise to protect him," Kari murmured, more to herself. She looked at Charlie "Maybe my golden male is still alive."

"He is. I saw him a few years ago. If he had been caught and killed, I would know. Such news would spread quickly through Westend."

"Where did you see him?"

"On one of my hunts near the coast. He stepped out on the path and stood before me. I had a laser gun and could have easily shot him. He stared at me for a long moment and then flew away. How he has survived all these years is a mystery. I've never seen a more brazen creature. That fearless nature has led to the goldens' downfall."

Kari leaned back, barely able to contain herself. "I knew he was alive. I just knew it."

"I never told John about the golden," said Charlie. "And I hope to keep it that way. Though grateful, your father still does not care for harpies. He protects them only for his love of you."

"I won't say anything."

Charlie grinned slyly, looking at her. "It might also be unwise to mention the brown harpy that chased the grogins away last night."

"You saw him?"

"I am old, but my eyesight is still good." He chuckled. "I had my laser sights fixed on the grogin and nearly fired when the harpy landed and scared the animal away. I watched and made sure no harm came to you."

"I'm sorry I didn't tell you about the brown harpy," she said. "I was afraid it would cause more trouble."

"I understand," he said. "You were unfairly punished when the golden saved you. A second meeting with these creatures would alarm your father."

"A vet at the Hampton Zoo thought I might have strong instincts, and harpies can sense that I like them. That's why they come to me."

"This vet is right," he said. "You've always had a way with wild creatures, and most animals can detect danger, fear, and acceptance. The golden knew that I, too, would not hurt him. The harpies may look human, but they are animals. For one hundred and fifty years, their instincts, fast flight, and wit have allowed them to survive despite man's technology and weapons. Humans couldn't prevail under those hunting pressures. But, Kari, why the harpies come and want you alive is unknown. Be very careful and don't trust them."

Kari reflected on Charlie's last statement. The old Indian obviously admired the harpies, but something was amiss. Perhaps it pertained to her father's hatred of the winged creatures. She changed the subject not wanting to ruin the day. She was traveling through the enchanting jungle with the knowledge that her golden male still lived.

She and Charlie laughed over past adventures when she was a girl. "I remember you brought a poisonous lizard home and wanted it for a pet," he said. "You nearly gave me and your father a heart attack. Why the lizard didn't bite you, I'll never know. You were as wild as the creatures in the forest and very stubborn. I pitied John at times."

"I suppose I was a tomboy." Kari grinned. "Never did care for dolls." The mood was merry on their westward journey.

Evening approached, and Charlie pulled into a small clearing with a stream. Like when she was a child, Kari gathered wood for a fire while Charlie set up camp, erecting a small tent. At dark, the meager fire snapped and crackled, and the cries of the night animals came alive under a star-filled sky. Rather than use the vehicle's heating element, Charlie prepared the food over the open fire, claiming it would taste better. The smell of the grilled meats, vegetables, and Charlie's biscuits enhanced their appetites.

Kari sat on a log, enjoying dinner, and stared at the fire. "Tell me, Charlie. What made you leave Earth and come to Dora with my grandfather?"

"You wish to hear more?" he asked. "Never have I talked this much."

Kari smiled, knowing this to be true about the quiet Indian. "I enjoy listening to you."

"I came here for the same reasons as your grandfather," he said, "to live among the trees and nature. My reservation was a dead desert—even the snake and scorpion were gone. The tribe sold it to developers, and I received a few credits. I did not wish to live under the city domes, so I left for the cold north. I met your grandfather in the last great forest. He was there to save it from the ax. We had much in common, your grandfather and me. When he failed to protect the trees, he told me of Dora, a small planet covered in jungle. He offered to pay for my trip if I helped him build a new home. The reservation was gone, but it was a hard decision for a young man. There was an Indian girl I loved and had to leave. I promised when I made enough money, I would send for her. The time came, but by then, she had married another." Charlie shrugged. "I knew she did not want to live on a wild planet, but it is hard to find love again."

"Charlie, that's so sad," Kari said.

"I have no regrets," he said. "When your father was born, I loved him like a son, and you, like a granddaughter. If I had stayed on Earth, I would have loved her, but been miserable in those cities. And she would have grown tired of an unhappy husband."

"I lived under those domes, and it is no life for people like you and me."

Charlie rose and left the fire. "It grows late. I will take the tent, and you, the vehicle."

"Good night, Charlie," she said, climbing into the comfortable vehicle bed. Exhausted from the lack of sleep on the previous night, she quickly fell asleep.

The golden harpy nuzzled her until she lifted her head. She stroked the silky hair hanging against his face. He turned his head and kissed the palm of her hand. "Do you have a name?" she asked, using her subconscious instead of her voice.

"I am Shail," he answered with his animal telepathy.

"Why do you come to me, Shail?" she asked.

He pulled back and stared at her in confusion. "As I am yours, you are mine. This was always meant to be," he related. He leaned over and tenderly kissed her lips before rising to a kneeling position.

"Don't go," she conveyed. "There is so much I want to know about you."

He tilted his head, perplexed. "You know. The light comes. It is time." He stood up and extended his long, yellow wings. With one flap, he was airborne. He fluttered for a second, gazing down at her, then vanished.

"Come back, Shail," she cried. "Please come back." She opened her eyes and saw the faint rays of dawn. "A dream," she said, looking at the locked vehicle doors. She shut her eyes and smiled, thinking of Shail.

Kari heard the songbirds and smelled the campfire. She sat up and looked out the window at the neatly rolled tent and stacked camping gear. Charlie gazed at the fire, sipping a cup of coffee.

"Guess I overslept again," she said, leaving the vehicle.

"The biscuits are warm, and the coffee still hot," he said.

She nodded and walked to the stream. After splashing water on her face, she returned and sat on a log, enjoying a biscuit.

"You did not sleep well?" he asked.

"What makes you think that?"

"I heard your calls for someone named Shail. You seemed very upset. I nearly woke you to end the nightmare."

Kari bit her lip. "I'm sorry I woke you, Charlie, but it wasn't a nightmare. Since I came back to Dora, I've had this crazy, passionate dream. It's so real I wake up and check the locks to make sure I'm alone."

"So Shail was a lover." He grinned.

"I've loved him for ten years," she said, without thinking.

"Ten years? He's from Dora?"

Kari's eyes widened, and she remained silent, realizing her mistake. She had unintentionally revealed the identity of her dream partner.

"You meet the golden harpy then," he said, solemnly. "Is Shail the harpy? Does he come to you in your dreams?"

"Yes, Charlie, yes."

He tossed his remaining coffee on the ground and straightened. Flinging his long gray braids back, he stared upward through the branches at the sky and murmured, "God help us." Coming out of this trance, he turned to Kari. "We must go now. Your father must learn of these dreams."

Kari saw that Charlie was very upset. Instead of neatly packing the gear, he threw the equipment into the vehicle. "What is wrong?" she asked, walking to him. He didn't answer. "What do these dreams mean? Why must Dad know?" When he ignored her questions, she grabbed his arm, forcing him to face her.

"The dreams are not yours." He sighed. "They are the harpy's. They mean that after all this time, he still wants you. He enters your mind when it is weak and receptive with sleep. There, he weaves his spell of seduction.

Your father sent you to Earth to protect you." He shook his head. "John must be told, and the golden must be hunted down and killed. Had I known this two years ago, I would have shot him when I had the chance."

Kari was in shock and stumbled backward, away from Charlie. "They're just silly dreams—my dreams, Charlie. Please, don't tell Dad."

"They are not your dreams or silly," he said sternly. "This golden has marked you, and the reason the harpies rescue you is now clear. When you met the golden, you were both very young. John hoped that distance and time would break any spell. He thought you would return, forgetting the harpy, and the young male would find another mate. But none of this happened. You wonder why your father hates the harpies. They are a threat to you. To be taken by this Shail will bring you great grief and even cause your death."

"If you tell Dad . . . if he kills Shail . . . ," she whimpered. "Don't you understand? He saved me not only from the mogel, he's the reason I didn't commit suicide on Earth." She fell to the ground and wept.

Charlie watched her for some time. He finally went over and placed his hand on her shoulder. "All right, Kari," he said quietly. "I will not tell your father. Just promise me. When the golden comes, you will be strong and reject him."

She stared up at him through a blur of tears. "I promise. If he comes, I'll reject him, but not for my sake. I'll reject him for his."

They climbed in the vehicle and moved slowly down the road. After an hour, Kari asked, "You really believe that harpies can bring grief and death?"

"Yes," Charlie said.

Kari remained quiet the rest of the morning, confused and saddened by Charlie's words. She knew the Indian would never lie to her. Were the handsome harpies really seductive monsters that preyed on women?

At noon, they came to a barren patch of land. "The swarms have been here," Charlie said, pulling the vehicle to a stop.

Kari got out and surveyed the damaged land. "It is terrible." For several miles the black ground was exposed, and all life was gone. A few sheared-off stumps remained where the beetles had stopped eating. An eerie feeling crept over her. The only sound was the whistling wind sweeping through the vacant land, blowing the smell of sour soil. She climbed into the vehicle. "It's like a great storm came through and blew everything away."

"Yes, these beetles are like a storm, but worse, for they know no season and give no warning. And, unlike a storm, they destroy everything in their path." He started the engine to the terrain vehicle.

They soon were back in the jungle. The sounds of birds and aroma of flowers filled the air with music and perfume. She glanced up at the towering trees that hung over the road, making it cool with their shade. It was similar to traveling in a beautiful colorful cave of light and splendor.

Charlie stopped for lunch along the road. Kari spotted wild berries and picked some for the journey. The land became hilly as the northern mountain range dipped southward. They crossed two more barren areas devoured by the beetles. "That is the last," Charlie said, "unless they struck while I traveled to meet you."

Between the vivid hills, the sun was setting in the west. The black mountains gleamed in the distant north. Charlie pressed the communication button, and a small screen appeared between the two front seats. "Hello, Maria," he said to the image.

"Charlie, where have you been?" Maria growled. "Did you pick up Kari?"

"She's here," he answered.

"Mr. Turner is having a fit! He's tried to call you several times."

"I turned off the com," said Charlie. "Tell him we will be home before dark and in time for dinner."

"Mr. Turner will be upset, making him worry," she scolded.

"It won't be the first time. See you at dinner." He disconnected before Maria could respond. "That woman would call me every hour if she could," he grumbled.

"Some things haven't changed," said Kari, remembering the contention between Maria and Charlie, but she knew deep down they were fond of each other.

Darkness covered the landscape, but Kari recognized some old buildings as she and Charlie neared the turnoff to Westend. They passed a road and an old painted sign saying, WELCOME TO WESTEND. They continued on the highway for another ten miles until she saw the wrought-iron gates of the Turner Estate. Turning into the drive, Charlie said, "You are almost home." The jungle was replaced with large rolling meadows and herds of cattle. After a mile, the drive forked. The road to the left went to the house, to the right was the wood mill and the smaller homes of the employees.

Kari felt a tinge of nervousness when Charlie veered left at the fork. What would she say to her father after ten years? She saw the imposing grand house that sat on the largest hill with the jungle beyond. Outside lights lit the white columns and front yard. The vehicle traveled through the hills and came to a stop at the front doors. Two Irish wolfhounds leaped to their feet and greeted the familiar vehicle and the Indian who drove it. Kari stepped from the vehicle and petted the large dogs that her father always kept.

The front doors flew open, and the old housekeeper rushed out. Maria ran as fast as her short, plump legs would carry her. "Miss Kari, Miss Kari," she cried, throwing her thick arms around her. "I'm so happy you're home." Tears of joy ran down her round cheeks.

Kari hugged Maria, who was the closest person to a mother she had known. "And I'm happy to be home."

Maria let go and stood back. "My word, you have blossomed like a beautiful flower."

Kari looked up, and standing in the doorway was her father. Amazingly, he hadn't changed that much. His thick blond curls hid any strains of gray and his chiseled face was slightly more weathered. His tall, well-built frame strolled toward her. She stared into his pale blue eyes as he lightly embraced her.

"It's good to have you home, Kari," he said quietly.

"I'm glad to be back." Kari put her arms around his waist, but felt the tension between them.

He released her. "I hope you're hungry. Maria's been cooking all day."

"I am," she said politely, "but I'd like to wash up first. We camped last night."

"Of course. Take your time," he said, grabbing her bags as Charlie unloaded them.

Kari and her father walked into the foyer and Charlie followed. She took the smaller bag. "I won't be long," she said, and ascended the stairs to her old bedroom.

As she reached her room, she heard Charlie and her father's low voices. She froze and listened.

"How is she?" John asked.

"Bitter, but you can't blame her, John," Charlie answered. "If you want her to stay, you had better open your heart and tell her all."

"I will." John hesitated. "Charlie, I know that look. What else is troubling you?"

Kari held her breath and prayed that Charlie would keep the secret of her dreams.

"She is like her mother. That is all I will say," said Charlie. "I must unpack the vehicle now."

"I understand. Thank you, Charlie."

Kari heard the front doors close, and she crept into her bedroom. Time had stood still in the room. All her old things remained in place except for a large vase of fresh flowers sitting on a dresser, obviously the labors of Maria. Kari picked up a stuffed toy animal that rested against a bed pillow and held it, remembering how it had comforted her in the night. She walked to a dresser and picked up a picture of her mother. The woman was dressed in a long white gown, the jungle behind her. She was radiant, Kari thought. Long blond hair flowed down her shoulders and partially covered her petite body. Kari saw the similarity between herself and her dead mother. Is this what Charlie had meant? In all these years, she had never heard Charlie refer to her mother.

Kari returned the picture to the dresser. "No more unanswered questions," she said firmly. "He's going to tell me how she died." She gathered a clean change of clothing and went into the bathroom. After a quick shower, she dressed, came downstairs, and entered the dining room. Her father poured a glass of wine, and Charlie sat at the table. Maria placed a steaming bowl of vegetables in front of them.

"It smells wonderful, Maria," Kari said, breaking the uncomfortable silence.

"I hope you didn't get spoiled on Earth and still like my cooking." Maria smiled.

"Spoiled?" Kari said sarcastically. "That was hardly the case." She seated herself in her old seat next to her father and across from Charlie.

"Did you enjoy Earth?" Maria asked.

Kari glanced at Charlie, who lowered his head. Her father nervously sipped his wine. "It was all right, but I prefer Dora." She took a drink of water. The half-truth stuck in her throat and was hard to swallow. She quickly changed the subject. "So tell me about the swarms, Dad."

John breathed deeply with relief. He obviously knew that an Earth discussion could create an outburst of anger or tears from his estranged daughter. "The swarms are very bad and will get worse if we don't find a remedy soon. I'm expecting a new insecticide from Hampton that the government assures me will work."

Through dinner, her father talked about the beetles, obsessed with the problem. She couldn't blame him. When Kari, John, and Charlie finished, they went into the spacious living room, and Maria cleared the table.

"I am tired," said Charlie, "and you two need to talk. I will help Maria clean up and see her home."

"Okay, Charlie," said John "Have the men start on the shipment of red in the morning."

"Good night, Charlie," Kari added, settling into a large stuffed chair.

John bent down and lit a small fire in the fireplace. "Was Earth really all right?" he asked, watching the growing flames.

Kari felt her animosity rise, the betrayal churning in her gut. "No, it wasn't," she bit out. "In fact it was so bad I don't care to discuss it."

"I'm sorry," he said, rising from the fireplace. "I know you're still angry and probably hate me for sending you away. I just hope you'll give me a chance to explain. I did it to protect you. There are things about Dora—"

"Dad, I'm tired," she interrupted. "Can we talk later?" She was ill prepared and too agitated for this conversation, feeling the urge to scream, curse, or cry.

"Of course," he said. "We'll talk in the morning if you're up to it."

Kari saw her father was trying to mend their relationship. "In the morning, then." She rose to leave the room. At the threshold, she stopped and glanced back at him. The once strong, determined man appeared frail, his gaze dejected. "I don't hate you, Dad. I just hate what you did to me."

4

Kari entered her bedroom and opened the balcony doors. A cool breeze blew the curtains into the air. She stepped out on the terrace and stared toward the jungle. Squawks and screeches of creatures rang out from the dark. Beyond the trees was the small hidden lake, the lake where she had met him, the golden harpy, years before. A longing crept over her to go to it and find him. She then remembered Charlie's warnings. Stepping back inside, she closed the doors, and locked them. She surrounded herself with the numerous pillows and drifted to sleep.

The dream overtook her, and she was wandering through the jungle. Pushing the colossal ferns aside, she searched for the golden. A dense fog covered the fantasy jungle, and she couldn't see far ahead. "Shail, where are you?" she called, drifting through the trees. In a small clearing, she saw him. He was curled up beneath a tree, and his wings were slightly extended, covering his body. She walked up and knelt beside him, pushing his hair from his sleeping face. He sadly gazed at her. His large eyes had lost all their fire and passion.

"You found me," he related.

"We must talk. I was told you hold a spell over me."

He reached up and gently caressed the side of her face. "Do not fear," he said with his soft male voice. "The spell shall soon be broken. Only know, my love has always been yours." He shivered and breathed hard. Kari saw panic and pain fill his eyes. She tried to embrace him, but the mist covered him, and he was gone.

She screamed his name, but the forest was empty. She raced through the trees, frantically searching for Shail. Detecting his pain, she was petrified, and her dream had become a nightmare. She trembled and continued calling; a terrible feeling crept into her mind that she would never see him again.

"Kari, Kari!" she heard a voice in the dream, but it wasn't Shail's low silky voice. It was the deep voice of her father. She opened her eyes to the bright bedroom lights, her father's hand shaking her to awareness. "Kari, are you all right?" he asked.

She tried to catch her breath and compose herself. "It was a dream," she said with relief, wiping the perspiration from her forehead.

"Sounded like a bad dream," John said.

Kari rubbed her eyes, tried to focus and think. "It was bad. I'm sorry I woke you, Dad. I'm fine now."

"Do you want to talk about it?"

"No!" She bit her lip. "No, I'm all right."

"Okay. I'll go back to bed." He left her bedside.

"Dad, is old Doc still in Westend?"

"He's still there, but somewhat retired. Why?"

"I'll go see him tomorrow. Maybe he has something so I can sleep through the night."

"I'm sure he can take care of that. See you in the morning," he said, turning off the lights and shutting the door.

Kari curled up in the pillows and stared into the shadowy room. Shail had admitted there was a spell, but it soon would be broken. What did that mean? Was he releasing her or was he coming for her? He had said that his love was always hers. She smiled. The moment she saw him, she also loved him. Now she agonized over his pain and fear. Why was he so scared? It was uncharacteristic of the bold golden. In previous dreams, she had detected his devotion and passion. Why was this dream so different and horrible? "My imagination is getting the better of me," she said. "They're only dreams."

The morning light spilled from the balcony and illuminated the floor. Kari slowly opened her eyes and smelled baking bread. The household was up and already at work. Throwing on a robe, she ambled down to the kitchen. Maria was slicing the bread.

"Hello, Maria," Kari said, walking into the expansive kitchen.

"Good morning, Miss Kari. What would you like for breakfast?"

"Some juice."

"That's not much of a breakfast," Maria grumbled while she poured juice into a glass. "Your father is in his den. He wants to see you when you're finished eating."

Kari took a sip. "I'll see him now." Leaving her drink, she walked to the den door and knocked.

"Come," was the answer behind the door. Kari went in and her father looked up from behind his desk com. "Just fix it," he ranted to the person on the com screen. He pushed the disconnect key, and the screen dissolved into the desk. "Sorry—business," he said to Kari "Have a seat. I'm glad you're here." He stood up and paced the room. "Did you sleep all right?"

"Yes, I don't remember any more dreams."

"Old Doc can help, but be warned, he's still cantankerous as ever," he said with a nervous laugh. He walked to a window and stared out. "What I must tell you is very hard. It has to do with your mother. Because of her, I sent you to Earth. Do you know anything about her?"

"Not really. Grandpa said she was killed in some freak accident," Kari said.

John pushed the hair from his forehead and sighed. "She's been gone twenty years, and I still miss her," he said. "You're very much like her. When I saw you yesterday, I thought I was seeing a ghost. She was strong and beautiful and loved the jungle like you." He put his hand to his mouth and cleared his throat. "We were very happy together. I want you to know that. And when you were born, I thought my life was complete. I had the two most beautiful girls on the planet under my roof." He smiled. He turned away from the window and stared at Kari. "A lousy golden harpy took all that away from me."

He returned to his office chair and slumped into it. "The harpy swooped down and grabbed your mother. I pulled out my laser gun and fired at it," he said, breathing deeply. "I missed and the blast hit your mother. She died instantly, but my second blast killed that damn beast. It was the first time

I killed a harpy. I was foolish back then, believing harpies deserved to live in peace on my land. After your mother died, I invited every hunter to come to the estate and exterminate them. When I heard the dogs barking and saw you in the arms of another golden, it was like reliving the past. I wanted to protect you, Kari, but you were so crazy about these winged devils, and too young to understand the danger. Before long that blond male would return, and you'd go to him, no matter what I said or did."

Kari knew he was right. "Dad, I wish you had told me this earlier."

"How could I possibly tell my young daughter that I had killed her mother?" he asked. "I planned on telling you when you were a teenager, but that mogel incident escalated things. I couldn't protect you on Dora. I'm sorry I sent you to Earth and for the pain it caused you, but I couldn't risk losing my daughter to another harpy. The harpies' numbers have declined, but they're still a danger to women."

"I was very miserable on Earth, but it was compounded by the fact that I thought you didn't care about me."

"Kari, I love you very much." He got up and wrapped his arms around her. "I don't know if I was right or wrong, but I was only concerned about your welfare. I hope we can start fresh and you'll give me the chance to make things up."

She embraced him. "Dad, I'm so tired of being unhappy. I just want some peace now. Telling me about Mom has helped me understand your motives. I do want us to at least be friends." She pulled away and looked up at him. "I know you hate the harpies, but Charlie told me you banned hunting on the estate."

"Yes, I stopped the killing. You asked me to protect that young golden—wanted me to promise. For a year, that gnawed at me, and every time I thought about the mogel pulling you under, it scared the hell out of me. Despite what he is, I owed the golden for saving my little girl. Some of the men spotted him last year, so he's still alive."

"Thank you, Dad, for protecting him but I know you also did it for my sake."

"Yes." He nodded. "It was the least I could do after what I put you through. Well, the golden has been a mature male for some time and probably has paired with a female, so I no longer consider him the threat he once was. But enough talk of harpies. I have something for you, a coming-home present."

Kari followed him through the house and outside. A new terrain vehicle was parked in the drive. "It's beautiful."

"It has everything. In the compartment is a new laser gun," he said. "Please keep it with you when you leave the house. I need to get to the mill, but I'll see you at dinner. Kari, this is a lot to take in. If you wish, we could discuss it further tonight."

"That would be fine."

He kissed her on the cheek and strolled to his small hovercraft. "I'll be home around five," he called, hopping in the hover. In minutes the hover was airborne and disappearing beyond the first hill.

Kari slowly walked back to the house, reflecting on her mother's death and the golden harpy that had tried to take her. Charlie had said that she was like her mother, and Kari now knew it had nothing to do with looks. It was the correlation that goldens sought her and her mother and understood Charlie's and her father's fears. But could Shail be evil? He loved her in her dreams. Maybe Charlie is right, she thought. Shail obviously hasn't found a mate and is seducing me to leave. In real life, maybe he is dangerous. She thought about the brown harpy on the road. If Charlie hadn't come, would the brown have taken her?

Doubts cluttered her mind as she thought about her mother's kidnapping and death. Have I been wrong all these years? Have I lived with a false childhood illusion about harpies, and everything I believed is a lie?" she questioned. "Can all Dorians be wrong about these creatures?

Her stomach was in knots, feeling like a loved one had died. Her fondness for the harpies had been replaced with suspicion. In the foyer, she sat down on one of the stair steps.

"Are you okay, Miss Kari?" Maria asked, polishing the dining room table.

Kari looked up. "Maria, did you know my mother?"

"No. I wish I could help you, but your father hired me after her death. I never met her, but I've seen pictures. She was very lovely," Maria said with melancholy.

"Yes, she was." Wanting to take her mind off the agonizing doubts, she changed the subject. "Did you see my new vehicle?"

"The whole town saw it." Maria smiled. "It was unloaded from a harbor barge a month ago. It's very lavish and such a rich red color. Are you going to take it for a drive?"

"Yes. When I get dressed, I'm going to Westend. See if the place has changed."

Maria laughed. "It's the same, a few more stores and houses, but it still a quiet little town that will bore you to tears."

"I'm ready for some boredom." Kari walked upstairs and dressed. She came back down to the awaiting terrain vehicle. With the push of the starter button, the shiny vehicle rose a foot off the ground and began to hover. Her schooling on Earth had taught her to operate all types of transportation equipment as well as learn intricate technology. She was taught about everything from weapons to communicators and was capable of using or fixing any of them. It had seemed like a waste of time and education because she intended to spend her life on Dora, a planet with limited technology.

She maneuvered the vehicle down the drive and stared at the vast green meadows dotted with a bright array of flowers. The grass seeds of the meadows had been imported from Earth because Dora had no grasses before man inhabited it. Along with the grass came the cattle and other domestic animals from Earth. Even the Irish wolfhounds resting on the large front porch were originally imported. She reflected on that first dog. She was very young, but still remembered the long trip to Terrance to get her new puppy. She smiled now, recalling the disappointment of a frozen fetus in a bag. "In a few months, you'll have your puppy," her father had explained. "If they sent a puppy on the spaceship, it would arrive as a big dog."

Glancing at the meadow, she thought about the devoted dog, and a tear coursed down her cheek. He had died the same year she was sent to Earth. In the night a male red dragon had jumped the high electric fence and was attacking the cattle. The wolfhound sounded the alarm and fearlessly charged the elephant-size reptile. Her beloved pet was killed defending the herd. Her father broke down and wept as he carried the dog's large body from the pasture. It was the only time she saw her father cry.

While she traveled through the estate, her mind was flooded with childhood memories. The meadows ended, as did the last view of the house. She turned onto the dirt highway surrounded by the jungle trees and drove east. After ten miles, she came to the weathered sign and road to Westend. Small wooden homes appeared before she arrived on Main Street. A modest grocery store and other meager shops stood in the heart of town. Maria was right. The little town hadn't changed much over the years. She came to a yellow cottage and stopped. Moss-filled trees lined the front yard, and at their base were beds of flowers. A decrepit sign reading DR. WHITE hung between the peeled-paint posts. She got out of the vehicle and went to the front door on a well-shaded porch, and rang the old-fashioned bell. A grizzly silver-headed man appeared. "Hello, Doc," she said when he opened the door.

"Who are you?" he asked gruffly.

"Kari Turner."

He rubbed his beard. "Any relation to John?"

"I'm his daughter."

"Thought you looked familiar," he said. "I delivered you. That was a hell of a night. Well, what do you want? If you're selling, I ain't buying."

"I'm not selling anything. I need your help."

"Well, come in." He scowled. "I got better things to do than stand in a doorway all day." He walked in the modest living room, and Kari followed. "I'm fixing fresh lemonade. Want some? Can't stand that crap that comes out of those confounded machines." He ambled toward the kitchen in the back of the cottage.

"No, thank you."

"Kari Turner," he mumbled. "Now I remember. Never were sick much, but didn't a mogel get hold of you?"

"Yes," she said. "A golden harpy saved me and brought me home."

He raised an eyebrow. "That harpy did more than save you from the eel. That little winged guy put licing moss on your wound. Drew the poison out. Without the moss, you'd be as good as dead by the time I got to your dad's. That was quite a discovery in the field of medicine. I did a medical research paper on the properties of licing moss. I imagine that harpy has saved scores of lives over the years."

"My father never told me about the moss," she said.

"I'm not surprised." Doc chuckled. "John don't care for those critters, and he ain't about to give one credit for anything."

"He blames a harpy for my mother's death."

"Yes, that was a real tragedy. Losing his wife made John plenty bitter," he said, pouring a glass of lemonade. "And your mom was a real looker, prettiest thing I'd ever seen. Say, you look a lot like her. So what's your deal? Don't look sick or hurt."

"I'm having trouble sleeping."

"Walking the floors, huh? You're too young to have problems."

"No, I fall asleep fine," she said. "I just have vivid dreams, and they wake me up."

Doc stared at her. "Can't help you."

"You must have something to help me sleep through the night."

"I do, but I'm not giving a heavy sedative to a young, healthy woman. That's what it'd take to stop a dream. You don't need or want that kind of drug. Everyone has bad dreams occasionally. They'll pass. Wish I could dream more often," he said, walking toward the back door. "Let yourself out. I gotta get back to my garden. The rainy season will be here before you know it."

Kari watched him stroll to the backyard. She walked through the small cottage, noticing a small bedroom converted into a hospital room. Old medical equipment surrounded a single bed. On the porch, she glanced up and down the street, her mind on the unsolved problem. What if Dad discovers the nature of my dreams? He would kill Shail. When she approached her vehicle, she saw a skinny young woman hurrying toward her.

"Kari!" the woman called. "I saw your vehicle at Doc's and was waiting for you to come out. How are you, and how was Earth?"

Kari recognized her old schoolmate. "Hello, Carol. It's nice to see you," she fibbed. She remembered how Carol chattered endlessly about nothing and bored Kari to tears.

"Now, you must tell me everything about Earth," Carol began, fluffing her bobbed hair. "I'm so jealous. I wish my parents had the credits to send me. They could have at least sent me to school in Hampton, but they want me to help them with a new store—clothing, of course. I was sick of the grocery store. You have to come in, and I'll show you what we have in stock. What am I talking about? You just came from Earth. I bet your closets are full of the latest fashions. Oh, you must let me come over, so I can see them. It will help me with my orders, and . . ."

Kari listened politely, fighting the desire to flee, and Carol rambled on and on, asking questions, but not waiting for the answers. Kari realized the people of Westend had also remained the same. Carol paused slightly to catch her breath, allowing Kari to break in. "We must discuss all this sometime," Kari said, "but I have to go."

"You're not sick, are you?" Carol asked. "I hope you're not using Doc. He's not altogether there, if you know what I mean, and so rude. I wouldn't go to him if I were dying. You should go to Terrance. That's where we all go. They have a great hospital. Paul went—"

Kari cut in. "I really have to go, Carol."

"Let's get together tomorrow night," Carol said excitedly. "We're having a cookout on the beach. Some of the other girls from school will be there. You could tell us all about Earth. I want you to meet my boyfriend, Jake. He and his buddies went hunting and fishing on the islands. They usually cook what they bring back. It's so much fun. And I have just the guy for you. He's single and real cute. Please say you'll come."

Kari sighed with the thought of an evening with Carol, but maybe the others would be fun. "It sounds great. What time?"

"Around six," Carol said. "It's the last dock after the harbor, right by the old shack. You remember the shack?"

"Yes, I know where it is," Kari said, slinking into her vehicle. "I'll see you tomorrow."

She waved to Carol and drove down the main street. What in the world was I thinking? The quiet of the vehicle consoled her. She wondered if any of her old schoolmates also had harpy encounters. They were her age. Perhaps she could learn from those girls. If not, she would enjoy seeing the west coast again.

Kari left the town and drove west toward the estate. She brought the vehicle to a stop in front of an overgrown trail. It was the old logging road that ran parallel to the back of her home and passed the small lake. The hover vehicle idled as she stared with indecision. Of all the places on Dora, the lake held her most cherished memory and now her worst fears. She closed her eyes and envisioned the golden male's deep blue eyes and cascading blond locks. "I have to go and confront this spell he has over me."

Despite the warnings, she turned the vehicle onto the ancient road. Not used for years, the road had huge ferns growing in the center. Kari adjusted the height of the terrain vehicle to the full capacity of four feet, clearing the foliage. The vehicle glided over fallen tree trunks, victims of great storms that came in the wet season. Large bushes and young trees encroached upon the narrow path. The jungle was reclaiming the man-made corridor. After several miles, she came to a massive uprooted tree. Resting on its side, the tree created an impassable obstacle, the tall limbs stretched upward.

Kari killed the vehicle engines. She got out and surveyed the tree. There was no way around it. She knew the lake had to be near. Traveling on foot, she would reach the lake but be on the opposite side from her childhood visits, and she'd be under the trisom trees. She closed the vehicle door and took a few steps into the dense forest, but stopped. Returning to the vehicle, she took the laser gun from the compartment. "For the wild animals," she said, tucking the gun into her belt. She shuddered with a rush of anxiety, realizing the gun was needed against an abducting harpy.

Kari crept deep into the forest, stepping quietly as she moved between the shadows on the jungle floor. Small flying lizards leaped from branch to branch in front of her as she roused hidden insects. Pushing some blue ferns aside, she jumped back. Massive purple vines grew on the trees and encroached on the path. The vines looked harmless, but the carnivorous foliage could take down large prey. Detecting a victim, several tentacle branches rose from the ground and reached toward her. She sidestepped the vines and proceeded more cautiously. She passed some white-barked trees and stopped to observe a flock of brightly colored mockingbirds.

"Aren't you guys cute?" she said.

"Aren't you guys cute?" several mocked, holding trisom fruit.

Kari grinned and moved on, hearing the growing choirs of, "Aren't you guys cute?" The birds would repeat this all day until they heard something else of interest. Seeing the fruit in the birds' arms told her the grove and lake must be near. She passed several trisom saplings growing in low, wet soil, further evidence she was on the right trail.

Finally she saw the towering trees that bordered the edge of the lake. Although late in the season, a few branches still held the sweet yellow fruit. She walked beneath trisom trees and stared across the lake at the beach. Beyond the beach and under the blue ferns, the harpy had held her and treated her injury. "Oh, Shail, I don't know if you're dangerous," she murmured, "but God, I miss you." She glanced upward toward the empty branches, no animals. She sat down on a boulder in the shade of the sway-ing trees, and relished a strong breeze blowing across the water.

Time passed, and the late morning drifted into the afternoon. Kari found it hard to leave the place. Her spirit was renewed, and as Charlie had said, the jungle was healing. Glancing at the time, she rose, considering the long, hot hike ahead. Scattered fruit lay on the ground, and she picked up the undamaged ones, deciding Maria could make a tasty pie. Placing them in the front of her shirt, she reached for the last one.

Although she heard nothing, Kari suddenly sensed a presence behind her. She whirled around and saw a brown harpy several feet away. Started, she jumped, releasing the collected fruit. One of the yellow balls rolled to his feet. Kari now recognized the harpy as the same one who scared the grogins away on the road outside of Terrance. He had traveled several hun-dred miles, and this wasn't a coincidental meeting. She jerked the laser gun from her belt and pointed it at him. "What do you want?"

Her weapon didn't frighten him away, and the harpy stood quietly. Though scared, she couldn't help admiring the tall, handsome creature. He flung his lengthy hair and made a sniffling sound with his nose, then stared across the lake toward the beach, the same beach where she met Shail.

"Are you going to take me?" Kari asked.

He slightly shook his head. His silent voice entered her mind, "You are his. Go to him."

"I am not his," Kari said out loud.

The harpy reached down, picking up the trisom fruit at his feet, and walked toward her. She saw the anguish in his green eyes and knew he wouldn't harm her. She lowered the weapon and took the fruit from his extended hand.

"Shail needs you," he relayed mentally.

Kari was mystified and totally perplexed by the harpy. She watched him raise his wings, and with one leap, he was airborne. He flew across the lake and vanished into the trees. She dropped the trisom fruit and staggered to the boulder, slowly sitting down. Her hands were shaking and her heart raced, as though she had stepped off a fast thrill ride, experiencing a mix of fear and joy. She dwelled on the harpy's words, though they were few. If Shail needs me, why didn't he come? She put her hand over her mouth, realizing her weapon was useless against a harpy. Like with Charlie, they instinctively knew she wouldn't harm them. If Shail had come, would he have taken her?

The scarlet horizon signaled the approach of night. Kari jumped up, knowing she'd be late for dinner. She gathered the fruit and darted into the woods. By the time she reached the logging road and her vehicle, she was dirty, sweaty, and tired. She tossed the fruit and her laser weapon on the empty passenger seat and hopped into the vehicle. Flipping on the headlights, she drove down the dark, overgrown trail. "Dad is going to be unhappy and concerned," she agonized. Reaching the highway, she raced toward the estate.

Kari parked the vehicle in front of the house and stepped out. The dogs bounded out of the shadows to greet her. She petted them, not realizing that Charlie was with them. "We've been worried," he said.

She jumped. "Charlie, you startled me," she said. "I'm sorry I'm late, but I was delayed in town."

"You should have called."

"Perhaps I dislike coms as much as you." She smirked.

He glanced into her vehicle. "Your laser gun was needed. It is out of the compartment, and you brought back trisom. They only grow in water, and none is sold in town this late in the season."

Kari knew she was busted. The wise old Indian should've been a detective. "After town, I went to the lake. I had to go. Shail wasn't there." She hurried toward the front door to avoid a lecture.

She found her father in his den. "I'm sorry I'm late, Dad. I ran into

Carol Baker and was held up. She's invited me to a cookout tomorrow night."

"That sounds like fun," John said, "but I'd appreciate a call next time you're late."

"I will. I'll just need a minute to clean up," she said. Walking to the foyer, she met Charlie. His arms held the trisoms.

"Should I take these to the kitchen?" he asked.

She lowered her gaze. "I don't like deception," she said quietly, "but I'm upset and confused. I need answers, but I don't want Shail killed because of my dreams or because I went looking for him. Dad told me about my mother's death, but I still can't believe that the harpy would harm me."

"Already, the harm has begun," Charlie said, and left for the kitchen.

Kari went to her bedroom and climbed into the warm shower. Nothing made sense anymore. The golden harpy was like an addictive drug. Despite the warnings and danger, she longed for him. He had definitely woven a spell she couldn't break. To protect him, she had become dishonest, like an addict.

Kari dressed and stared at her bed. "When Shail comes tonight, I will tell him that this must end, these dreams must end." Before long, her father would learn she was still drawn to harpies and that might seal Shail's fate.

She went down the stairs, and Charlie and her father were waiting in the dining room. Her father's grin told her that Charlie had not revealed her lake visit.

"It's great you're getting reacquainted with your old classmates," John said, "but I'm surprised you were talking to Carol. As a child, you always avoided her."

"I've grown up," Kari said, sitting at the table that held assorted fruits, jungle yams, and roast beef. Her father sliced the meat and offered some to her.

"No thanks, Dad," Kari said. "I still don't care for meat, but I'd like a few yams."

"Still a vegetarian," he said. "So tell me about your visit to town. Did you see Doc, or was he off fishing?"

"I saw him, but he wouldn't give me anything for sleep," she said. "He did tell me about the licing moss that the golden harpy put on my mogel bite. Said the moss drew out the poison and saved my life."

"If they'd sent more scientists to this planet, we'd have known about the moss years ago. Just like these goddamn swarms," John grumbled. "If they'd put some money into research, I'd have an insecticide that worked now."

Kari and Charlie remained quiet.

"I'm sorry. I'm a little edgy," John said. "A swarm hit in the northeast, barely missed the estate. They're getting closer." He patted Kari's hand. "And the mention of a golden harpy is still upsetting. I still worry about you."

"We won't talk about harpies anymore," Kari said.

"That's not what I want," John said. "I want us to be open with each other. Keeping quiet has brought too much misery. After dinner, we'll sit down and talk."

After supper, Charlie excused himself. He walked outside and the dogs greeted him. He wanted no part of the coming conversation between father and daughter. Would they be honest? He loved John and Kari, but knew their hearts and differences. Though Kari hadn't admitted it, she still carried a torch for the golden. Ten long years on Earth hadn't extinguished the flame, and the harpy sought her in dreams, proving he still longed for her. Such a bonding would be disastrous.

Before long, John would figure out his daughter was still devoted to the harpy, and then he'd kill it, ending the threat to Kari. The fragile father and daughter relationship would forever be destroyed. They were too headstrong in their convictions with no middle ground.

Charlie foresaw the coming conflict, and all his advice to John and Kari would fall on deaf ears. He was an old man caught in the middle. He walked through the meadow under a star-filled night. The two wolfhounds walked alongside, wagging their tails.

John and Kari settled in the living room. John poured a glass of wine and offered it to Kari, but she declined. "You don't like wine?" he asked. "Didn't they teach you the finer things in life on Earth?"

"Is it a finer thing? You seem to drink more than I remember."

John seated himself across from her and took a sip. "I suppose I do, but it helps me relax." He leaned back in the chair. "I'd like to clear the air tonight."

"I've been thinking all day about our morning conversation. It's understandable why you hate the harpies."

"I'm as much to blame as the harpy that went after your mother. When I saw him put his hands on her, I was filled with rage. I wasn't thinking. Normally, I'd have set the gun to stun, and your mother would still be with us. I'll take this guilt to my grave."

"Dad, it was just a terrible accident."

He gulped the last of the wine and stood up. "It was no accident that harpy tried to take your mother."

"Why do you think he wanted her?"

"To force her to bare his offspring," he grumbled, and poured another glass. "Those goddamn harpies."

"Is that what other women have said when they were taken by a harpy?" she asked quietly.

"Other women?" he said, puzzled. "Most women are never seen again. The few that have been rescued can't speak—their minds are gone. They usually commit suicide."

"Maybe they're like men, and there are good and bad harpies."

"Kari, they're not like men. They're wild animals. It's like saying there are good poisonous snakes and bad ones. They're all poisonous, all bad, all dangerous."

"But the golden who saved me," she argued. "You were even grateful to him."

"I knew he'd come up. You were a child, Kari, and he was too immature for breeding. His wing length proved he was a teenager and pretty naïve. I still can't believe that nervy young rooster ruffled his feathers and confronted my men even after a round was fired at him." He massaged his chin. "He probably saved you and risked his neck since he planned to take you later. It might have been a big mistake, protecting him from hunters all these years."

Kari grew nervous and changed the subject from the golden. "I heard in Hampton that no women have been kidnapped in a long time."

"That's Hampton. The harpies have been exterminated in the east. But this is the outback, and there are plenty of flocks." He gazed at her with a sudden realization. "You're trying to come up with excuses to defend these creatures."

"I'm trying to understand," she said. "The golden kept me alive. It doesn't make sense he'd hurt me."

"He'd hurt you, Kari. That son-of-a-bitch would put you in his nest in a tall tree where you couldn't escape and then rape you over and over until you lost your mind and were pregnant. You'd be a vegetable, producing his male fledglings year after year." John drank down his second glass of wine. "That's what those devils do to women."

Kari stared at the floor. "He was so gentle. It's hard to believe he could do such a thing."

His eyes narrowed, studying her. "You still have feelings for that cocky bastard?" he growled and rose from the chair.

Sick of lying, she didn't answer.

He paced the room, shaking his head. "Thought you'd meet a nice guy on Earth, thought all this harpy craziness would be gone. Guess everything backfired on me." His angry tone kept elevating. "Then I stupidly chased the hunters off my property and let the damn golden live, goddamn it."

"Please, Dad, understand. I can't change overnight. I was miserable on Earth, and the only thing I had were the fond memories of the harpies. I'm very confused now. I need some time. That's why I'm going to the beach party tomorrow night. I want to talk to people my own age and ask them about the harpies."

"Perhaps I should end your confusion and kill that blond buck."

Kari stood. "I'd leave and never forgive you," she said with conviction, "and the harpy would be another innocent victim of your rage. If I caused his death, I'd live with the same guilt you carry for Mother."

John collapsed in the chair and shook his head. "All right, Kari. I'll give you time. I don't want to lose you again, but know I'd sacrifice our relationship and your peace of mind if it came to your safety. If that golden comes sniffing around, I'll kill him."

"I'm going to bed now," she said, leaving the room.

Kari crawled into the soft bed, feeling ill. Her honesty might cost Shail his life, but she had difficulty concealing her feeling and beliefs. Despite the consequences, she felt truth was always better. I am bewildered by the harpies and my mother's death, she thought. Better that Dad knows, but if he discovers my dreams, and the brown harpy encounters . . . maybe I should leave. She closed her eyes, firmly committed to ending the dreams with Shail.

Kari woke to the sound of singing birds and morning light. She realized that she had no memory of a dream. The golden hadn't come. "Shail said the spell would be broken," she mumbled, disappointed and relieved at the same time. She climbed out of bed, dressed, and went downstairs. Maria and her father were in the kitchen. "I hope I didn't wake you with my dreams," she said to her father.

"You didn't wake me," John said. "I went in and checked the locks on your balcony doors, and you were sound asleep. I have to get to the mill." He leaned over and kissed her forehead. "The barges are arriving at the harbor today, and we're running at full capacity to get the timber out. I'll see you tonight."

"I'll be at Carol Baker's cookout," Kari said. "I probably won't be home until late."

"Call if it's real late." He headed for the kitchen side door.

Kari hung out in the kitchen talking to Maria. She saw Charlie working in the small vegetable garden alongside the house. As he weeded a row of tomatoes, she wandered out to him. "The golden harpy didn't come in my dreams," she said. "Perhaps this so-called spell is broken. I'm rather relieved."

Charlie glanced at her. "Your relief tells me the spell is not broken. You worry John might discover your dreams and kill the harpy. Your worry proves the golden still holds your heart."

"Maybe I'm relieved that I'm rid of him," Kari voiced. Charlie didn't respond. His assumption was right. She picked up a rake and began working alongside him. "Besides, Dad learned that I'm still fond of the harpies, but is uncertain what to do."

"I'm sure you saw John's anger," Charlie said, "but it comes from frustration. He wants to protect you, as do I. You travel a foggy path of choices. You are blinded by the fog, blinded about your feelings for the golden. Follow the wrong trail that leads to the harpy and your life will end in tragedy. When the fog clears, when the truth is revealed, it will be too late to turn back. Do not choose the harpy, Kari. He is a handsome creature, but his arms only hold unhappiness."

Kari nodded. The serenity of the plants and soil consumed them. By late afternoon, the garden was free of weeds, and the new seeds had been sown. She went inside to prepare for the cookout.

By four o'clock she was in her vehicle, heading west toward the coast. She was forced to slow when she came upon a truck loaded with vegetables. It was apparently traveling to meet the barges, destined for Hampton. Westend's main export was the rare timber from her father's estate, but the area's small farms also brought their surplus produce and livestock to meet the barges. The ocean barges that traveled the southern ocean were the cheapest and fastest form of transportation, rather than crossing the continent by trucks or hovercrafts.

The dirt highway ended at the harbor, and Kari was surprised at the growth of additional docks. She passed the box-shaped barges and the men working the loading equipment. Several piers away, the flat barges held brightly colored sheets of lumber. She steered her vehicle toward them. Noisy machines lifted large wood bundles off vehicle transports and placed them on waiting barges. She noticed they carried the name of Turner on their side. She pulled up alongside a man supervising the process. "Is Mr. Turner here?"

"Just missed him," the man yelled over the loud equipment. "He flew back to the mill. Can I help you?"

"No, thanks," she said. "I'm his daughter, and I stopped to say hi. I'll see him later." The man grinned and gave her a nod. She left the harbor and its smooth shell-covered lot and drove south along the coast on a narrow sandy road. In the distance she saw the little shack sitting off the beach. After a half a mile, she came to the old weathered building. Beyond the shack was a dilapidated wooden dock. Several ill-kept boats were moored to it. She parked next to a few late-model terrain vehicles, apparently belonging to fishermen. After climbing out of her vehicle, she walked through the loose sand toward the building and found it held rusted traps and other tired gear. A fish-cleaning table with a water hose rested against the shack. She turned the handle, taking a sip of cool water, and glanced up at a high pole. Dangling from the pole was a chain and hook used for large fish. A fire pit containing charred ashes was nearby and large, unburned logs circled it for sitting.

A strong wind blew from the ocean as she walked down to the long, rickety dock. The sun was setting on the horizon, and she was glad she brought a light jacket. The night would be cold. At the end of the dock, she sat down on her jacket and waited for Carol and the other girls. The barges left the piers and motored out to open water and their noisy engines engaged, lifting them above the waves. Reaching full throttle, the boats moved at great speed and were quickly out of sight.

Kari reveled in the peaceful setting. The green and yellow seabirds gracefully glided on the wind drafts, and they occasionally squawked for territory before landing on the black beach. Her thoughts drifted to the harpies. To be able to fly must be wonderful. She was so engaged in the birds and tranquility she failed to hear the footsteps on the dock.

"Aren't those birds wonderful?" said a soft woman's voice.

Kari glanced up and saw a young woman, close to her age. "I didn't hear you come down the dock," Kari said, a little surprised.

"I'm sorry I startled you. I'm Lea. May I sit with you?"

"Sure," Kari said. "My name is Kari. Are you here for Carol's cookout?"

Lea nodded and clasped Kari's extended hand.

"I was just thinking that to fly like those birds must be wonderful," Kari commented, looking at the shore.

"You really missed it here," Lea said. "Carol told me of your travels to Earth."

Lea's long brown hair drifted on the wind against the red sky and her large green eyes gazed at Kari.

"You're one of the few people that have said that," Kari said. "That I missed Dora. Everyone thinks I was lucky to go to Earth."

Lea shyly smiled at her.

Kari instantly liked the quiet girl. "So you're a friend of Carol's?"

"I know her, but I'm not sure we're friends," Lea said. "My mother and I make jams and jellies and sell them at Mr. Baker's grocery store."

Kari and Lea heard the slam of a vehicle door. Kari stood and saw Carol and two other girls. They waved at Kari to join them. "I guess we better go say, hello," Kari said. She walked down the dock and Lea followed.

Carol's booming voice rose above the whistling wind and broke the tranquility. "You're early," Carol screeched as Kari approached. "You remember Beth and Cindy from school? And Lea, you showed up. That's a first," Carol said sarcastically.

After Kari said hello to the other girls, Carol took her arm. "Kari, can you help me carry some drinks?" Carol dragged Kari away from the others. "I just want to let you know it was not my idea to invite Lea. My stupid father suggested it at the store. That girl gives me the creeps. She hardly speaks. She and her mother moved here from some hole north of Terrance. I think she's missing a few marbles. Now don't get me wrong, I tried to be her friend and invited her to our activities, but she's never showed up. That's why I'm rather surprised to see her."

"I find her rather charming," Kari said. "Maybe she needs time to get used to strangers." Kari recalled her own isolation on Earth.

"If you enjoy a one-sided conversation, then she's perfect," Carol said.

Kari wondered how a conversation could be anything but one-sided when it included Carol. They unloaded the food and drinks, setting them on a small table. Kari and Lea strolled on the beach gathering firewood, and were happy to be away from the chattering voices. Carol and the other girls arranged the solar lights, and by dark, a blazing fire burned in the large pit.

"Kari, you must tell us about Earth," Carol said as they sat on the logs and watched the fire.

Reluctantly, Kari told them about her experiences in the Earth schools. She didn't reveal the disdain or the depression she endured. They would not have understood. After some time, she changed the subject. "Why do your boyfriend and his friends travel so far to fish and hunt? Isn't the first island over a hundred miles away?"

"That's your dad's fault," Carol said. "Mr. Turner banned hunting on his estate, and Jake has to go to the islands for a harpy."

Kari felt her blood pressure rise and stood. "Your boyfriend is hunting the harpies?" she asked, her repulsion barely contained.

"Of course, silly," Carol said. "Other game animals can be taken here."

Kari grabbed her jacket. "I can't stay here and see this."

"Come on, Kari," Carol mocked. "You've seen dead harpies. Your father holds the record for largest pair of golden wings. I heard he hung them on his porch for years."

"I've never heard that," Kari said angrily.

"Well, everyone in Westend knows about the golden he killed when it went after your mother," Carol said.

"My father does not hunt harpies anymore," Kari said harshly.

"What? Are you still a harpy lover?" Carol taunted. "Thought you grew up and got over that crazy notion."

Lea walked alongside Kari. "Some things are better left unanswered," she whispered.

"Lea, stay out of this," Carol screeched. "It's none of your business."

"It is best if I go," Lea said quietly, walking toward the road.

Kari glared at Carol. "No, I haven't changed, but neither have you. You're still an ignorant bitch." She called to Lea. "Wait, Lea. I'll come with you." Kari ran to the vehicles and approached Lea.

"You should stay here," Lea said, watching Carol come toward them.

"Kari," Carol said, smiling. "I don't know why we're arguing over something so silly. I do want us to be good friends." Carol was obviously sucking up since Kari was the wealthiest girl in Westend. "And Jake rarely gets a harpy. Even if he did, he strips their wings on the islands. Most harpies don't survive the trip. I've only seen one live harpy that they hung on the pole here and dressed out."

Kari gasped. "You watched?"

"It was no big deal. The thing was in shock and never made a sound. It squirmed a little when Jake cut off its wings."

Kari covered her mouth and mumbled, "It was still alive when they took its wings?"

"Yes, Kari. Most hunters prefer to dress them alive. The blood flows out without soiling too many feathers. After the wing is drained and hacked off, the harpy is gutted. But I doubt if Jake got one. Please, stay."

Kari looked around for Lea, but she had disappeared into the darkness. The sound of a motor came from the docks, and she saw the boat lights as it pulled into an empty slot.

"They're here," said Carol, taking Kari's arm "You can lecture Jake on the evils of harpy hunting." She led Kari toward the boat of hunters.

It was like a bad dream, Kari thought, but she had to know the outcome. She was hardly aware of walking alongside Carol toward the bright boat lights. On the dock, a young man jogged to them.

"Baby, you're not going to believe it," he yelled. He reached Carol and picked her up in his arms. "I'm taking you to Hampton for a trip you won't forget."

"What, Jake?" Carol asked.

"I got him. I finally nailed the golden. Been after him for years," Jake said.

Kari couldn't breathe and felt that her heart had been ripped out. She stumbled past Carol and Jake and approached the large boat. A small hovercraft was strapped to the cabin, and a man was securing a line. He smiled as she looked on the deck.

"You want to see the harpy?" he asked.

Kari could only nod, climbing on board. "Is he dead?" she asked.

"Not yet, but we'll string him up soon," he said. "Jake figured you girls would want to see a live golden rather than just its wings. Most Dorians have never seen one. He's tied over here." The man led Kari around some boxes on the deck.

Kari swallowed hard and stared at the yellow feathers partially stained with dried blood. The wings were attached to a lifeless slender frame resting against the boat side. His bound wrists were lashed to a cleat, forcing him to sit up, and his tied ankles were fastened to a wooden beam. The lower half of one wing was twisted and broken from a laser gun blast. The golden's head hung low, his face concealed by his long hair and buried against his arms.

Kari knelt down in a pool of his blood and pushed back the locks, exposing his face. It was Shail. "No," she murmured, tears running down her cheeks. His eyes were shut, and blood trickled from his full lips. She placed her hand against his chest and felt his shallow breath. She spotted another laser blast below his ribs. "This is why you didn't come in my dreams last night," she whispered. "And why you were so scared and said the spell would be broken. My poor Shail." Kari now dwelled in a real nightmare.

"Don't get too close," the man said. "He looks dead, but he can still hurt you." He kicked the harpy's side. The pain jarred the golden awake, and he breathed rapidly.

"Don't," Kari screamed. She put her hand on Shail's face.

His drained eyes stared at her. Turning his head, he nuzzled and softly kissed the palm of her hand.

Carol, Jake, and the other two girls had come on board and two more men emerged from the cabin. They stood around Kari and the harpy.

Jake said, "We found him on an island two hundred miles out. We came across some fledglings, and I winged one. We quickly landed the hover before it could hide. Hank found it under some dried leaves and held it up. Bang, this golden harpy came sailing out of the trees. It was unbelievable. He kicked Hank, sent him crashing into a tree trunk, swooped down, and grabbed the fledgling."

"I think it broke my arm," said Hank, holding his arm in a makeshift sling.

"Well, I got off a shot and hit his wing," said Jake. "He went down, but tried running off. My second blast got his side. We cornered him, but even wounded, he gave us a hell of fight. We got kicked, scratched, and bit by the damn thing. Took all of us to tie him down. Man, I've hunted some harpies, but I ain't ever tangled with one like him. Guess what they say about goldens is true—they're tough little bastards."

Kari half listened, but her mind raced, wondering how she could save Shail.

Jake said to Kari, "Hey, sweetie, keep your hands off him or you'll lose a finger. The sucker bites."

"He'd never hurt me," Kari said.

They watched the harpy nuzzle Kari's caressing hand. "This is Kari Turner," Carol said, smirking. "John Turner's daughter. She likes harpies."

"What are you going to do with him?" Kari asked, fixated on Shail.

"We're gonna string him up and cut off his nuts and wings," said Hank. "I've waited two days to see this baby hang on the pole and wiggle." He adjusted the sling on his arm.

Kari wiped her watery eyes and stood up, facing the people. Hiding her feelings, she glared at Jake. "I'll buy him. How much do you want?" she asked with a controlled tone.

"What are you going to do? Make him a pet?" Jake chuckled. "Even if he survives those wounds, he'll die in a cage. Believe me, I've tried to keep 'em alive for the hell of it."

"What I do with him is my business," Kari said. "Do you want to sell him or not?"

Jake eyed her. "You're like your old man. You Turners think you're better than everyone else." He sneered. "Sure, I'll sell him. I want fifty thousand credits. That's the going price for gold wings in Terrance."

Kari knew she didn't have that kind of money, and even if she could get it, Shail's injuries couldn't wait. She glanced down at the yellow wings. "A pair of wings in perfect shape might be worth fifty," she said, "but one of his is broken, and there's a lot of feather loss." Rather than pleading and crying for Shail's life, she glared at Jake. "But I have an offer that may interest you. Parked by the shack is a brand-new terrain vehicle worth forty. You can have it in exchange for the harpy, but I'll need the use of your old vehicle so I can move him."

Jake scratched his chin and grinned. "Let me go look at it." He stepped from the boat and began to stroll down the dark dock.

"Hurry, Jake," Kari said firmly. "This offer is good only for a live harpy. If he dies before I take ownership, you're stuck with your broken feathers."

"Sure, sweetie," he called and jogged toward the beach shack.

Kari knelt back down to Shail. She took an old knife from a wooden slat and cut the ropes pulling on his wrists and ankles. The harpy feebly collapsed on the deck.

"Hey, he's not yours yet." Hank yelled at her.

Kari ignored Hank and rested the golden's head in her lap. Clasping his hands, she bent over and whispered, "Just hold on, Shail. Don't die on me. I'll get you out of here."

Shail pulled up his legs and curled his long slender frame around her.

Carol and the others watched in bewilderment. Kari stroked his head as the harpy gently licked her hand and nuzzled his nose in her lap.

Beth and Cindy moved closer. "I've never seen a live one," Beth said. "He's beautiful." They heard the sound of running feet on the dock's wooden planks. Jake appeared out of the darkness and hopped on the boat.

Jake glanced down at Kari and the affectionate golden and frowned. "Did you tame that little devil?"

"What's your answer?" Kari said.

"Throw in that new laser gun, and you got a deal," said Jake.

Kari quietly breathed a sigh of relief and removed herself from the harpy's grasp. Shail was too weak to move.

"I can't believe you're selling it to her," Hank complained. "I want to see it hang."

Jake took Hank aside. "Look at it. It's almost dead," Jake said. "Probably die, right after it was hung. And she's right about that mangled wing. I won't get much for the pair, and her vehicle is worth plenty."

"The deal isn't over until the harpy is in a vehicle and still alive," Kari said.

"Sure, Miss Turner," Jake said, and leaned over the comatose harpy. He placed one of his arm under the harpy's neck and the other arm under its legs and wings, scooped up the harpy and cradled it in his arms.

"Want some help?" offered one of the guys.

"Nay, Tom, these scrawny harpies are like birds . . . don't weigh much," Jake said. "Bet this little golden tops out at eighty-five pounds. As long as Miss Turner will open the rear door when we get up there." He stepped off the boat and strolled down the dock carrying the limp body, and Kari walked alongside. They reached Jake's old blue vehicle, and she opened the back. Jake placed the harpy on a worn blanket and put his hand on its chest. "Still alive," he said. "You got yourself a harpy."

5

Kari jumped into the driver seat and pressed the start button. "I'm not sure when I can return your vehicle."

"Take your time," Jake said, leaning in the window. "Didn't your daddy give you that new vehicle?"

Kari nodded and pushed the starter again.

"I was fired from your dad's mill for poaching on his land," Jake said. "Wait'll your old man finds out you traded that expensive vehicle for a busted-up harpy." He laughed. "Tell him it's payback time."

The vehicle engines engaged, and the transport started to hover. Ignoring Jake, Kari threw it in reverse and pushed the old vehicle to its top speed down the coastal road. She sped passed the harbor and reached the highway to Westend. She decided to take Shail to Doc. There was no time for another doctor or vet. She glanced back at the motionless body and wondered if the golden male was alive. "Please don't die, Shail," she cried. Her earlier assertive attitude dissolved into tears, and she wiped them away with her sleeve. Ten long years of waiting and dwelling on the harpy, and now he lay dying. She glanced at her hands, stained with his blood. "This can't be happening. It can't end like this." She sobbed as the dark jungle flew past. The trip to Westend was taking forever.

Kari finally arrived in the little town and zipped down the quiet main street. Seeing the yellow cottage, she took the terrain vehicle over the lawn and parked by the front door. The cottage was dark inside, and the outside lit by a porch light. She leaped from the vehicle and ran to the porch. She rang the bell, beat on the door, and shouted for Doc. An inside light came on, and the door opened. Dressed in his Pajamas, Doc stared at her.

"Hurry, Doc. It's an emergency," she screamed, leading him to the vehicle.

"Okay, okay," he said calmly. "I'd be disappointed if it wasn't."

Kari flung the back door open, and the vehicle light revealed the harpy. Doc peered down at the still creature. He turned and looked at Kari with a frown. "You got me out of bed for a miserable harpy? I ain't no damn vet," he growled, and turned toward the cottage.

Kari grabbed his arm. "Please, Doc," she cried. "He's dying. I don't have any other place to take him." She dropped to her knees and held Doc's hand. "Please, I'm begging you," she moaned. She lowered her head and wept.

"Come now, dear," he said, guiding her to her feet. "It's only a harpy."

"He's not just a harpy to me," she whimpered.

The porch light illuminated her damp face. "Aren't you the Turner girl who was here yesterday?" he asked.

Kari nodded.

He walked over and looked at the harpy. Pushing the bloodstained feathers away, he saw the yellow wings and hair. "I'll be darned. This is a golden. Haven't seen his likes . . ." He paused in midsentence and gazed at the girl, leaning over the harpy. She was gently caressing the young male's face. Her hands trembled, and she whimpered. Doc sighed. "Is this the golden that pulled you out of the lake and used the licing moss?"

Kari nodded again.

"I'm awake now," he grumbled. "Might as well have a look at him. I owe him that much." He lifted the wing and examined the curled up body. "That blast wound is at least two days old. I'm surprised he's alive." He straightened and took Kari by the arms. "I know this harpy saved you, and now you want to save him, but this poor thing has suffered enough. Let me put him out of his misery. I have the drugs. He won't feel a thing. It's the kindest thing we can do," he said gently.

Kari jerked free of the doctor's hold and stepped back. She stared at the old man in horror. "You want to kill him?"

"He's beyond help and suffering. It's cruel to keep him alive."

"No," she said. "He's not some injured animal, not to me. He's been my whole life. I love him. If you kill him, you might as well kill me, too." She kissed the harpy's cheek and wrapped her arms around his neck. She buried her face in his silky blond locks and cried.

Doc watched her for a long moment as she held the frail body. He calmly placed his hand on her shoulder, and she glanced up at him through her wet hair. "I don't know anything about a harpy's insides and haven't done this kind of surgery in years, plus he's very unstable. But I can't turn you and your golden away without trying."

Kari threw her arms around the old doctor. "Thank you, Doc. Thank you," she said between sniffles.

"Don't thank me," he said seriously. "I want you to understand something. He's probably not going to make it, so don't get your hopes up."

"I understand," she said.

"All right, I'll get a stretcher so we can get him inside," he said, and hastily walked into the cottage. He soon returned with the floating bed. Kari and Doc rolled Shail onto it and pushed his limp body into the cottage. Doc flipped on the lights in his small hospital room.

"If word gets out that I'm treating harpies," he said, pushing the harpy on the operating table, "the whole damn town will think I'm nuts." The full extent of the harpy's injuries was revealed under the bright floodlights of the exam room. Cuts and abrasions covered the sleek muscles where the men had beaten him. The ropes that bound his wrists and ankles were so tight Doc had to cut them off, exposing deep gashes. Doc shook his head. Not only did the harpy suffer from two laser blasts, but he had also been severely battered. "Who did this?" he stormed.

"Some guy named Jake."

"Jake O'Connell. I know him. I delivered that boy. He was a rotten kid, and now he's a rotten man. He should be arrested for animal cruelty," Doc grumbled. "It's one thing to hunt wild game, but this kind of torture of harpies goes too far." He placed an oxygen mask over the harpy's face.

"Why did they do this to him?" Kari asked.

"I don't think these guys see harpies as game," Doc said, preparing the harpy and medical equipment for surgery. "It's some kind of twisted

justification. They think the harpies are seductive males that steal and molest women, so the hunters show no mercy. I've heard of some pretty unspeakable things that have been done to harpies. Your boy here could have
gotten worse." He scanned Shail's injuries with a monitor and pushed back
the locks to examine a cut under the harpy's left eye. He smiled at the
stunning creature. "Personally, I think those hunters are just plain jealous.
These harpy males are always good-looking, and they can fly. Makes me
wonder why they'd have to steal women." Doc finished with the scanning.
"Well, he's got a few busted ribs, but they'll heal, and so will that wing.
But this blast to his intestines is the major concern, and his blood pressure
is low. I don't dare operate without a blood transfusion," he said, looking at
Kari. "And you, my dear, are going to provide the blood."

Kari was puzzled, her face frowned with doubt. "I'm no doctor, but don't
blood types have to match? We're not even the same species. Won't my
blood kill him?"

"Without blood, he'll surely die. Most animals don't have blood types,
and he's animal enough. I don't have time to argue about it. Either trust
me or take him elsewhere."

"I have no choice but to trust you," she said. She sat down in a living
room chair, and Doc drew her blood.

"I took quite a bit, so stay put," he ordered, returning to the exam room.
"I'm too old to pick you up if you faint."

Kari waited in the other room and agonized over the blood transfusion.
She stood up and did feel dizzy, but managed to walk to the doorway. "Is
he all right?"

"He's got your blood, and it's compatible. He's doing okay," Doc said,
not even looking up from his patient. The machines buzzed as Doc worked
on the harpy's wound. "I'm surprised these old lasers still work. Haven't
used them in years."

Doc appeared to be enjoying himself and hummed throughout the operation. Kari leaned against the threshold and watched, feeling a little
nauseated and weak.

"I'm cutting out these damaged intestines, but he's got plenty to spare,"
Doc said, glancing up at her. "You look pale. If you're going to vomit, take
it outside."

"I do feel a little sick," she admitted, backing out of the room. "May I use your communicator to call home?"

"On the desk."

Kari looked at it and called, "Do you have a portable com?"

"There's one on the kitchen counter with a location shutoff."

Kari went to the kitchen and called home.

Maria answered. "I was just leaving for the night," she said. "Your father is in his den. Do you want to talk to him?"

"No, just tell him I'm spending the night with Carol."

"Okay, Miss Kari. I will tell him," Maria said.

Kari wandered back to the small hospital room. "I'm feeling better now. Can I help?"

"Not with the surgery, but you can clean up the deep cuts with antiseptic, save me some time," Doc said. "I'll seal them and deal with that broken wing later. I put an antibiotic patch on him. Should fight the infections."

Kari cleaned the injury on Shail's broken wing that hung down from the table and then washed his wrists and ankles. As she removed the dry blood, his wounds were revealed. Rage started smoldering in her when she saw how terribly Shail had suffered. "I should've got my laser gun and killed them for this," she muttered under her breath.

Doc glanced up. "You do care a hell of a lot about this harpy."

"Yes, and I can't even explain it. Since I came back from Earth, I've been fighting these feelings, but the moment I touched him, the battle was lost. Charlie says the harpy has a spell on me."

Doc chuckled. "I don't know about that superstitious Indian and his talk of spells, but I know love is the worst spell. Makes us do crazy things. Well, I'm finished," he said, stretching his tired back. "I sometimes surprise myself."

She looked at him, questioning the outcome.

"I'd say his chances are fifty-fifty. Better than a few hours ago," Doc said. "I got to say this harpy's looks are deceiving. He's got a slight, almost delicate-looking body, but underneath the skin, he's tough and resilient . . . heartier than most humans. Must be the animal blood. Strange these creatures don't hold up in captivity."

"I really must thank you, Doc."

"No thanks until the final results are in. Now let's have a look at that wing," he said, pulling the long wing from the floor and resting it on a small table. "It's a clean break. He's lucky it's not in a million pieces or blown clean off. A good old-fashioned splint will fix it. But it'll be some time before he flies. I don't have the expensive equipment they have in Terrance that can mend a broken bone in a week."

Doc set the wing with a clear plastic splint. "That should hold it, and he'll have a hell of time getting it off." He sealed the open cuts and lacerations with a small laser. "If I'd gotten him sooner, he'd have no scars, but these little scratch marks will give him character, especially the one under his eye. He'll still be a handsome thing." Doc chuckled. "We need to put him in the spare bedroom. Don't have that many visitors, but it wouldn't be wise if they saw a harpy in my cottage."

Kari and Doc moved the harpy on the floating stretcher down the hallway to the spare bedroom. They placed him on a double bed, and Doc sat down in a chair, gazing at his winged patient. "I'm beat," he said. "When you called home, did you tell your father about him?"

"No, Dad would kill him."

"Yes, John doesn't care for harpies, especially gold ones," he said. "When you used the portable com, I figured you didn't want your father to know you were here. What are you going to do with the harpy? He can't stay here. The whole town would find out before long, and you can't take him home. If he survives the night, he's going to need a lot of quiet care. Turned loose too soon, he'd die from those injuries. Plus he can't be caged. They get depressed and suffer from shock. When he starts feeling better, I don't know how you're going to keep him still. Your problems are just beginning, keeping a wounded harpy."

"I don't know what I'll do," she said, realizing that Doc had a strong point. The harpy stood a chance at survival, but her father was Shail's greatest threat.

"Don't worry about it now," Doc said. "If he's alive in the morning, we'll figure it out. Besides Jake, who knows you have him?"

"Three of Jake's hunting buddies, Carol and—"

Doc interrupted. "Carol Baker from the grocery?" he asked with a raised voice. Kari nodded, and Doc continued, "That blabbermouth. By tomorrow the whole town will know about the harpy, including John. You better move your vehicle into the garage, or they'll know you're here. If he survives, you better move him tomorrow night. I can picture your dad storming my door."

Kari rose to move the vehicle, and Doc followed her out of the bedroom. "It's late," he said. "I'm going to bed. The closet has some clean medical gowns. You can use one for sleeping, and there are some blankets and pillows for the couch. Make yourself at home."

"Doc, you act like an old crab, but you really have a heart of gold." She hugged him. "I appreciate all you've done for me and the harpy."

He weakly smiled and ambled off to his bedroom.

She moved the vehicle into the garage, shut the door, and came back into the cottage through the back kitchen door. Grabbing a medical gown, she went to the bathroom to change. She saw in the mirror that dried blood stained her clothes, her face, and hands. After cleaning herself and her clothes, she slipped into the gown, grabbed a blanket for the couch, and decided to check on Shail once more.

A dim bedroom light illuminated his six-foot frame, and Kari saw he breathed easier. Touching his sleeping face, she comprehended he might die in the night. "You shouldn't go alone," she said softly. She turned off the light and climbed on the bed, carefully putting her arm around him. A feeling of contentment consumed her, as though she had always belonged near him. She closed her eyes and snuggled against the golden male.

6

The throbbing pain in Shail's side caused him to gasp, and he detected the scent of men. Startled, he opened his eyes and stared at the ceiling. He struggled to sit up, but lacked the strength, and the slight effort made his suffering worse. He shook his head, trying to clear his mind. He had been taken from the floating structure and put into a large cage. His body shuddered with fear, for he had lost his courage and fight.

Shail smelled fresh air flowing into the musty room and glanced toward an opening. It was night, and the safety of the dark trees lay beyond. Lured by the open window, he gritted his teeth and again tried to rise, but unbearable pain shot through him, making him cringe and sweat. He breathed hard with anxiety, knowing the hunters had far worse plans for him. Though he didn't understand their sounds, he sensed their poisoned minds. Their thoughts had dwelled on hanging him by his wrists and then removing his sex organs and wings. His heart beat faster, dwelling on this fate. Shail grasped the material to drag himself closer to the window and noticed his wrists weren't bound. Perplexed, he glanced around the shadowy room.

On the far side of the bed rested a sleeping female. Her long blond hair hid her face, but when Shail leaned over and sniffed, her scent was unmistakable and unforgettable. Her presence made him relax and breathe easier. He had waited ten long seasons to hold her again, and now she rested beside him, but how? Traumatized by the abuse, his memory was foggy. He shook his head again, trying to remember. She had held him as he waited for death, but he thought it was dream, the same dreams they shared since her return to his land. He nuzzled her cheek, making sure she was real. Shail closed his eyes, trying to recall the last few lights.

On a southern island, Shail had met Aron after his long flight over land.

"You found her?" Shail asked.

"Near the human river city," Aron relayed. "It was wise I was sent to watch over her. She is your match, Shail. Like you, she fearlessly but foolishly faced a pack of grogins alone. This darkness she comes to her father's home."

"Tomorrow I shall go to the lake of our meeting," Shail said. "There, she expects me." Shail and Aron lifted their heads, detecting the distressing sound of a metal bird. "It nears the nests of many fledglings," Shail said, darting into the sky, and Aron raced after him.

They flew rapidly to the island, hoping to lure the hunters away, but they arrived too late. Landing on a large limb, they gazed down at a hunter dangling an injured fledgling by his tiny wing. The human beast prodded the terrified, squirming youngster, and Shail sensed the pathetic silent calls from the baby harpy.

Shail relived the feeling of rage, an uncommon emotion for harpies, but it had been growing in him. Only recently, he had found two of his cherished males cut to pieces and hanging from a tree. As a golden, he was the monarch and protector of the flock. He couldn't stand by and allow an innocent fledgling to suffer the butchery. Preparing to attack, he arched his wings.

Aron sensed his intentions and grabbed his arm, saying, "The fledgling is beyond your help. Be not reckless. Your flock needs you."

Shail broke free of Aron and glared at him. "This one needs me now," he relayed, and sailed off the branch. He dove straight down toward the hunter, catching the man by surprise. With both feet, he kicked the man's back, slamming the brute into a tree. He quickly snatched up the fledgling and flapped hard to escape the laser blasts zipping past. Halfway through the open forest, he felt a terrible sting and smelled his burning feathers. He struggled to maintain his flight, but his wing was limp, and he and the fledgling tumbled to the ground. "Flee and hide," he told the baby. The fledgling scrambled into the dense underbrush, and Shail went in the opposite direction, knowing the men would pursue him. As he leaped into the foliage, he heard and felt a second blast hit his side, forcing him to his knees. He gazed up and saw the hunters running toward him.

Aron swooped down and landed between Shail and the men. He fluttered his feathers and flopped his long brown wings hard on the ground, behaving like a wounded bird. "Look, a blast must have hit that brown!" one man yelled.

"Forget the brown," another man said. "He's trying to draw us off the golden." Shail attempted to run during the distraction but collapsed after a few feet. "I am lost, Aron," he silently relayed to his faithful friend. "Do not come for me. I order you to save yourself." Teary eyed, Aron leaped into the air and disappeared in the trees.

Holding his wounded side and dragging the damaged wing, Shail managed to crawl against a wide tree trunk. He coiled up on the ground and shielded his body with his wings. The men swiftly surrounded him. He viciously hissed, warning them to keep away, but they produced ropes and grabbed for his legs and arms. Once in striking range, he battered them with powerful kicks, striking fists, clawing nails, and a flailing wing. He snapped his teeth at their approaching hands. His aggressive assault forced them back, and their eyes conveyed surprise. The young hunters had never encountered a golden male and were accustomed to hunting the docile browns. Shail quietly seethed as they doctored their wounds and discussed the best way to deal with his defiant nature.

The men chose to beat him into submission. They struck and poked him with long sticks. Shail frantically twisted in the dirt, trying to deflect the blows and hide under his protective wings. Toward dark, his body was weak with blood loss and the abuse, and his spirit was crushed. He panted hard, covered his head, and gave up. He curled up into a tight ball and shut his eyes. Seeing he was finished, the men leaped on him and held him down with their weight. He felt the tight ropes tethering his wrists, ankles, and wings. They grabbed his hair and gagged his mouth so he couldn't bite.

They laughed and prodded him, treating him like a trophy. His bravery slipped away, and he watched them with timid eyes. Their leader stood over him, and Shail performed the act of submission. He tilted his head back, exposing his throat, and hoped the man would slit his throat, giving him a quick, dignified death. The ritual was known to hunter and harpy and was a measure of honor between the species. A wounded harpy that performed this act would no longer hinder his enemy, and the ethical hunter could prove his decency by ending the suffering of the dying creature.

"You're not getting off that easy," said the man whose friends called Jake. His sounds were confusing, but Shail sensed the lack of honor. He knew a slow, horrendous death awaited him. Jake tossed Shail over his brawny shoulder and took him to the metal bird, roughly throwing him inside. The noisy bird rose and flew over several islands before it landed on a floating dwelling. Once there, Shail was tied down, and the hellish journey across the water began. The men unmercifully kicked and tormented Shail, forcing him to thrash wildly against his rope bonds. By the second light the wounds and fatigue had taken their toll. He could only softly hiss and tremble. The men stopped the abuse when they feared he would die before the taking of his wings.

Shail remembered how he had tried to will his own death, but he couldn't focus on it. With darkness came the smell of land, and he knew his death wish would soon be answered. It was then he saw her in a dream. She stroked him and said he should hold on to this life.

Shail gazed at her in the dark room. It had been no dream. She had come for him. He mustered his strength and slid closer, placing his arm around her and covered the two of them with his extended, uninjured wing. She continued to sleep, but unconsciously snuggled against his chest. A peace settled over him, and the panic dissipated. He wouldn't leave the cage without her.

Doc woke at daybreak. After only four hours of sleep, he was exhausted, but his anxiety over the harpy forced him from the comfortable bed. He dressed, wondering if the golden had survived the night. He walked through the familiar cottage and saw the empty couch. The Turner girl had already gone to the harpy. He carefully pushed open the bedroom door.

A soft morning light rested on her and her harpy. They slept with their arms encasing one another, and a large wing lay draped over their slender frames. The male's boyish face rested against the lovely girl's head, and their long flaxen hair mingled. Doc was captivated by the breathtaking pair and watched them for some time. They're beautiful, but doomed, he sadly thought. The golden male was the most prized game animal in the galaxy. Even if he recovers, his life would be short, and the girl had no future with a harpy. The creature would only bring her misery. He questioned whether he had done the right thing by saving him, allowing the forbidden love.

The girl moved, and the harpy instinctively nuzzled her without waking. Even in sleep, they were affectionate. Better they sleep and enjoy some peace, Doc thought. He went to the kitchen and made breakfast.

After a few hours, Doc returned to the bedroom, knowing the male was overdue for an antibiotic patch. He had purposely given the harpy a mild painkiller, hoping the pain would force him to lie still and allow the surgery wound to heal. Walking past the sleeping pair, he noticed the harpy stir and sniff the air. Like all animals, the harpy's scent and hearing were acute. His blue eyes opened, and he looked at Doc. A seething sound came from his parted lips, and he grasped the girl while a protective wing completely covered her. The harpy defiantly glared, and his low seething became a noisy hiss.

"Easy, boy. I'm not going to hurt you or her," Doc said as the male become more rattled.

His feathers quivered with the pain and stress, but despite his injury and weakness, the harpy looked prepared to defend the girl.

"Easy now," Doc said. "I just want to check your wound." He moved his small medical scanner toward the harpy.

The harpy's fist swiftly came out from the feathers and struck the scanner, sending it flying across the room. The harpy bared his teeth and snapped, moving his body over Kari. He angrily tossed his locks, and threatening hisses escaped through his teeth. He crouched into a leaping position as he glared at Doc.

"You're a mean little cuss," Doc grumbled, walking over and picking up his scanner.

Kari woke with the commotion and found herself under the harpy's body. "You're alive."

"He's alive, all right, and full of the devil," Doc growled. "He keeps moving, he'll damage all my surgerical work. Come away from him. I believe he's trying to protect you."

"Doc won't hurt me, Shail," Kari said, unclasping the harpy's arms. When she moved off the bed, the harpy tilted his head, looking perplexed.

"Let's try this again," Doc said, approaching the bed. Instead of standing his ground, the harpy retreated, scurrying across the bed. He defensively coiled up and seethed. "This is impossible," Doc said. "He's too wild to be handled."

Kari went to Shail and stroked the soft hair on the shivering harpy. "He's very scared." She cupped Shail's chin. "Doc saved your life. You must let him treat you." She looked up at Doc. "Do you think he understands me?"

"Obviously not," Doc said and watched the harpy. Like a trapped animal looking for an escape, the harpy nervously seethed as his alert eyes shifted from the man to the screen window. Doc rubbed his beard. "If I force him into corner, he'll fight me out of fear or he'll make a dash for the window and smash the screen. But maybe he'll fall for an old hunting trick. It supposedly can calm a frantic harpy." He left the bedroom.

Kari sat on the edge of the bed and watched Shail. Despite his human features, he behaved like a feral animal. His wide terrified eyes hastily scanned the room while he shook and panted. None of her soothing words and touches would tame him. Every inch of him was tense and displayed an unwillingness to yield.

She took his hand. "Shail, you're going to be all right." He swallowed hard and gazed at her, his watery eyes showing distress.

Doc walked into the bedroom with a large butcher knife. "You want this?" He raised the blade over the harpy.

"What are you doing to him?" Kari screamed.

"Trust me," Doc said.

The golden sniffed the knife and turned toward Kari with a look of profound longing. He glanced back at Doc and shivered, then tilted his head back and closed his eyes. Doc moved in, grabbed the harpy's hair, and held his head back. The harpy shuddered, but didn't resist.

"Pretty good trick," Doc said, putting down the knife. "I always wondered if it really worked."

"What's wrong with him?"

Doc frowned. "For such a harpy lover, you sure don't know much about these creatures. Come around here and hold his hair. He'll think I still got him. Keep his throat exposed, and I'll make his exam quick." Doc placed two patches under the harpy's wings and scanned his wound. Removing the old bandage, he treated the injury with antibiotics and sprayed on a sealant bandage. "Watch what I'm doing. You may have to do this next time."

After a few minutes, Doc had finished. He grabbed the harpy's hair and motioned Kari away. "Good boy," he said, releasing the hair and petting his head. The harpy opened his eyes and stared up in bewilderment. "Can't blame him for being trouble. Those hunters gave him a rough time."

The harpy slid across the bed and pulled in his limbs, covering his body with feathers.

Kari scratched her head. "Why did he let you treat him?"

"He expected me to cut his throat," Doc said. "Hunters say that mortally wounded harpies perform this ritual, toss their head back and go dead still. Some men believe harpies just give up because they're spineless, but your golden is no coward. He was fixing to jump me. Healthy, he'd be a hell of a handful."

The harpy cocked his head at Doc.

"He's a curious little fellow. Can't figure out why I spared him." Doc chuckled and stood. "I'm having another cup of coffee and watching the news. There's a sedative patch on his back, and he'll go down in about ten minutes, but you better stay with him. He was eyeing the window. He's strong enough to break the screen and climb out. It's amazing how fast he recovered." Doc left for the kitchen.

Kari sat on the bed, but the harpy ignored her and watched the door.

"Not all men are bad, Shail." She stroked his head and the harpy relaxed, uncoiling his body.

Shail realized the man wasn't coming back, so he focused on the female. He reached up and caressed the side of her face, running his thumb over her moist lips. She didn't reject his advance, so he leaned closer and kissed her mouth while gently forcing her to recline. Uncertain if he would survive the hunters or his wounds, he had no time for harpy courtship. He crawled on her, assuming the breeding position, and stimulated her with soft kisses and his manipulating hands.

Like their dreams, her affection was mutual. She longed to hold him, to have him. He nipped at her neck and pushed up the gown, exposing her small, nude body. Massaging her breast, he suckled like an infant while his firm erection throbbed between her legs, moistening and penetrating. Every part of him worked to inflame her desire to accept his seed and bear his offspring.

"No, Shail," she moaned. "This is happening too fast."

Shail stopped and lifted his head. To force himself on an unwilling female could cause her rejection of his fledgling. Though her sound conveyed doubt, her thoughts said she was his and wished no other male. He had to be sure. He buried his face in her hair and made his penis lightly pulse up and down, fueling her sexual craving. His partly extended wings fluttered with excitement. Detecting her building climax, he shut out the searing pain from his weak and battered body and mustered his remaining strength. His breath quickened as his teeth clutched her neck, preparing to consummate the mating. She totally accepted him.

Unlike a man who mated for pleasure, he was an animal who procreated to ensure his bloodline and willingly endured any hardship to complete this goal. Neither love nor passion played a role in the bonding. He was driven by despair and fear—fear he might not survive the captivity. As the last golden male and reigning monarch of the harpies, he lacked an heir and was obligated to produce a future ruler and protector of his flock. He had waited ten raining seasons for the chosen female's return, but their time for bonding had run out.

Sensing her welling up and the tremendous rush in her head, he positioned his penis for total invasion and to complete his own climax. He suddenly felt dizzy and frantically shook his head, but the off-balance and numbing feeling wouldn't leave. Frightened and confused, he sniffled at her and laid his head on her breasts, hoping to recover. Moments away from completing the breeding, his own body betrayed him. He closed his drowsy eyes and fell into a deep sleep.

Kari lay beneath the slumbering harpy for some time, knowing the sedative patch had taken effect and knocked him out cold. She gently pushed the lightweight male off her and sat up. The control, the spell he had over her faded, and she uneasily stared at Shail. With one kiss, he had seduced her in less than ten minutes. All of Charlie's and her father's warnings came thundering back. Was this the rape men spoke of? She covered her mouth with her hand. The full gravity of the incident sunk in. If the bonding had been completed, would she have lost her mind or her life?

Kari stared at the silky blond hair strands that drifted over his long eyelashes, his small nose, and full lips. Though a mature male, his alluring looks were childlike. "You didn't rape me. I let you," she said quietly, hoping to be convinced of his innocence, but the haunting question remained, could she resist him?

She wasn't even sure what Shail was. He looked mostly human, but his mind and nature was wild animal. She still loved him, but felt her love was tainted with distrust. Even hurt and frail, he had nearly taken her. What would she do when he recovered? Would he obey her wish not to bond? It came down to a choice. Should she choose her own safety or his?

I can't abandon him, she thought. He can't fly, and he's too weak and injured to last long in the jungle. "I have to stay with him regardless of what my father says." She leaned over and kissed his lips. Her heart fluttered and goose bumps covered her body. The desire to crawl into his arms and cuddle him was overwhelming. Even unconscious, he was a magnet, drawing her to him. She quickly stood and backed away from the bed. "I won't kiss you again."

She went to the bathroom, stripped off the flimsy medical gown, and dressed in her clothes. Maybe Doc had some of her answers. Last night he had laughed off Charlie's notion of a harpy spell.

Doc sat at the kitchen table drinking coffee, and Kari joined him. "Want some?" he offered.

"Yes, please," she said, sitting down. She leaned against the table, wearily placing her hands against her forehead.

"You look upset," Doc said, pouring the coffee into her cup.

"I am," she said. "I'm in love with that harpy, but I hardly know or understand him."

"Don't feel alone," he said. "Nobody knows the harpies. They're Dora's greatest mystery, but I think they're more like us than people are willing to admit. I want to show you something." He opened a drawer and rummaged through it, producing a tattered picture. "My grandfather gave this to me. Said it was taken one hundred and twenty years ago, when Dora was a new colony. The motion is broken, but you can see the images." He handed the photo to her.

Kari looked at three smiling men standing under a large tree. Two harpies hung by their wrists from a branch and waited to be stripped and slaughtered. The picture was obviously a trophy hunt. "It's awful."

"Yes, but look closely at those harpies."

Kari studied the picture. "They don't look like present-day harpies. They have more hair on their bodies and look similar to loca eagles."

"Exactly, and they have tails. Do you know why the first settlers named them harpies?"

"Not really, but I know 'harpy' is a Greek word meaning 'to snatch.' Harpies were noisy flying monsters, usually female, in ancient Greek mythology."

"It's documented that our harpies once chattered," Doc said, "but how did present-day harpies change from their ancestors and became mute, sleek males?"

Kari shrugged.

"The male harpies stole the colony women and mingled the races. Your golden has human blood. That's why the blood transfusion worked last night. I'm betting that something happened to the harpy females—a disease, a genetic defect that caused only male fledglings to be born—whatever it was, it wiped out their females, forcing these shy males to enter settlements and risk death to steal a woman. For over a hundred years we've been searching for a female harpy. Some people think the females are stashed on the islands or in the forbidding mountains, but I don't believe they exist. In my retirement I've been studying the harpies, hoping to prove my theory."

"If harpies are part human, they shouldn't be hunted like wild game."

"It's politics, my dear," Doc said. "Do we pass laws and protect a species that steals our women or let the hunters wipe out this threat? If the people knew the harpies were winged men, would the hunting be sport or murder? By the time it's figured out, the harpies will be gone. More and more hunters come to Dora and invade the islands, the last harpy sanctuary. I bet your harpy is the last golden. As a boy, I'd fish the coast and watch the traveling brown flocks, led by a dominant golden male. Those days are over. Besides your boy, I haven't seen or heard of another golden in twenty years, and that golden was killed by your father."

"The one that tried to steal my mother," Kari said. "I guess the golden harpies are valuable because they're so rare."

"Rare, but they're also more aggressive than browns. Your harpy is living proof. A captured brown dies from fright and shock on the first day, and it won't have the nerve to strike my scanner like your golden. Hunters prize a challenging animal. What surprises me is that idiot Jake managed to bring your golden down."

"Jake said they had wounded a fledgling, and the golden flew down and attacked a guy named Hank and broke his arm."

"What a little spitfire." Doc chuckled. "Wish I could've seen those surprised boys. So, how did you get the harpy from Jake?"

"I traded my new terrain vehicle."

"I said that Jake is an idiot," Doc said. "He based the harpy's price on old taxidermy wings found in the Terrance antique shops, but these days a live golden would bring a fortune. Have you decided where you're going to take him? He'll need quiet rest and antibiotics for ten days, and you're right about John. If your father found a golden with his daughter, he wouldn't think twice about killing it."

She bit her bottom lip. "Dad stopped the harpy hunting on the estate. Maybe it's the safest place."

"John may lift the ban when he learns you got the harpy," Doc said, "and it won't be long, with Carol running her mouth. John and every hunter from here to Terrance will hear about your broken-winged pet. It'll be like a treasure hunt for gold. They'll be looking for your helpless golden that can't fly off."

"I have a place in mind, and I'll leave tonight," she said. "Shail may also tell me of a safe place."

"Tell you?" Doc asked.

"Harpies don't speak or make sound, but I can somehow understand their thoughts. A brown harpy told me that Shail needed me. I didn't figure out his message until I found Shail with the hunters."

Doc raised his eyebrows. "I've never heard of anyone communicating with harpies."

"I was told by a vet at the Hampton Zoo that harpies trust me and use their sixth sense to relate to me. The vet is also studying the harpies and hopes to save them from extinction. The Dora government is funding his research."

"The government!" said Doc. "That sounds fishy. It's our senators who promote the harpy hunting. They recently passed legislation to add a bounty on harpy wings. If the governor signs it, the bounty will raise the price of wings, bringing more hunters to Dora."

"Dr. Watkins seemed sincere and concerned with the harpies' future."

"Maybe he's being deceived," Doc said. "Your father had some nasty dealings with our senators. When John ended the harpy hunting on his estate, he lost several big timber accounts because of those senators. They're against large landowners protecting the harpies, but your dad is a stubborn man. No one tells John what to do." He dug out a pen and paper. "What's the vet's name? I might give him a call."

"His name is Dr. Watkins. He was planning to come to the outback."

"Maybe we can collaborate on the harpies," Doc said. "There's nothing like solving a good mystery." He rose from his seat. "I'm tired from staying up half the night. Think I'll lie down. You might do the same if you have a long night of travel. Does the communicator work in that old vehicle?"

"I don't know," she said.

"Take my portable. You might have trouble," he said, handing the small com to Kari. "On the dining room table, I set out ten antibiotic patches and the medical supplies for the harpy, also some sedative patches, if he doesn't behave." Doc grinned. "Young lady, I believe you're in for a hell of an adventure with the golden male. Keep in touch. You've become part of my research. I've never heard of a woman who could speak with harpies and was willing to go off with one. I'd be interested in how you two make out."

Kari rose from her chair and wrapped her arms around Doc. "Thank you. I promise I'll contact you."

Doc left for his own room, and Kari went back to Shail. She lay down on the bed, but was careful not to touch the dozing harpy. She soon was asleep.

Kari woke to the ringing porch bell. A man's frantic voice shouted for Doc. She scrambled off the bed and cracked the door to listen, fearing for Shail's life. She heard Doc's reassuring voice and the front door closed. Out the window, she saw a hover lift off and several vehicles speed down the street. She left the bedroom and found Doc in the hospital room, tossing equipment in his black bag.

"What's happened?" she asked.

"A swarm," he said. "It hit east of town, and it sounds bad. If there're survivors, they'll be brought here so I can stabilize them for the trip to Terrance. You need to take your harpy and get out while the town people are gone. I have to go," he said, hastily walking to the door. He rushed to his old hovercraft, and in minutes, the hover lifted off and was gone.

Kari grabbed the medical supplies and the portable com and raced to the garage. She threw open the garage door, went in, and placed everything inside the old blue vehicle. Jumping in the driver's seat, she pushed the start button. Amazingly, the engines fired right up. She glided the vehicle over Doc's vegetable garden and set it down by the cottage back door. She didn't have much time, and Shail's life depended on an escape. She ran inside the cottage and brought the floating stretcher alongside the harpy's bed. The sedative must have been strong because Shail slept through the noise. She shook him, and he slowly opened his eyes. "Shail! We must go."

He attempted to sit up, but collapsed, shutting his eyes. She screamed and pulled his arm. He shook his head.

"Climb on here," Kari said, patting the stretcher. He made a feeble attempt, and with her help, he was on the stretcher. She pushed him through the cottage and outside. The warm breeze and fresh air seemed to revive him. He sat up and sniffled toward the trees. She opened the vehicle back door and placed the stretcher alongside. "Get in," she said, patting the inside of the vehicle. Moving him out of the cottage had been easy, but she wanted him to climb inside a confining vehicle, and this attempt had a whole different effect on him.

Shail leaned in the metal traveling monster and smelled Jake's scent and the dried blood left by harpy wings. He created a low hiss that was almost a growl and backed away. The female disapprovingly screeched at him and shoved his shoulder toward the deadly trap. He tossed his hair and bared his teeth at her, conveying his unwillingness to enter. She ignored his concerns and scolded him, grabbing his arm to drag him inside. He balked, bracing his feet against the vehicle door. She tussled with his legs and arms, hoping to overpower his feeble body. Having his fill, he snapped at her hands, and she released her hold. He sensed her distress and frustration, but she asked the unthinkable of a harpy male.

She leaned against the vehicle and stared at him. Even lethargic with drugs and weak from his wounds, he was stronger than her. She couldn't force him where he wished not to go. "Please go in, Shail," she begged. "My father will come here and kill you."

He took her hand, the same hand he had mockingly snapped at, and apologetically nuzzled it.

"I know you wouldn't hurt me." She sighed and petted his head. "I understand that the vehicle looks like a cage, and harpies die when caged, but you must go in so I can take you away from the men."

Shail shook his head, hoping to clear his mind. From the beginning of their reunion, he had been on the debilitating drugs that hindered his instincts and destroyed his telepathy. He glanced into her concerned watery eyes and knew she only wanted what was best for him. He would have to trust her.

"Please, Shail," she said. "We're running out of time."

Shail sniffed the vehicle again and shuddered. He reluctantly but slowly slid off the floating stretcher and climbed into the vehicle. He curled up into a tight defensive ball and swallowed hard, staring at her.

"Good boy, sleep now. All this will be over soon," said Kari, stroking his head. She opened another sedative patch and placed it on his back, fearing he might become rambunctious with the journey. She shut the door and locked it.

Kari leaped into the driver's seat and started the engines. The vehicle moved down the deserted streets, and they reached the old highway. She turned left, heading west toward the coast. Glancing behind her, she saw that Shail had fallen asleep, and she breathed a deep sigh of relief.

They came to the harbor, and Kari veered the vehicle north on a small coastal road. She drove past tiny cottages on the ocean cliffs. Overgrown weeds grew in the yards, and the houses appeared vacant. After ten miles, man's imprint on the environment disappeared, and the road became an ill-kept path. She had reached the true wilderness and her father's estate. With each passing mile, the terrain grew rougher, and the path turned into an animal trail that meandered around massive trees hanging over the ocean cliffs. She maintained her northern trek by following the coastline.

Her grandfather's hunting cabin rested a hundred miles away and was nestled between the rocky beach and the mountain range. Though she had been very young when she last saw it, she still remembered the wondrous and remote place, reachable only by hovercraft. Few humans would find her and the harpy there.

Her father and Charlie wouldn't search for her at the cabin, thinking she was too little to remember it and its location, but she had played a secret game with her dying grandfather. When her grandfather became bedridden, he'd pull out a dilapidated map of the western continent and quiz her about locations. She never hesitated to point out his magical cabin. She'd sit on his bed, and they'd reminisce of fishing and jungle adventures when he was well. "I wish you were alive now, Grandpa," she mumbled. "I know you'd understand and help me save this wounded harpy." The old man had always embraced her rebellious nature and love of the wild.

The vehicle sluggishly traveled over and around large boulders and fallen trees while thick branches scraped its sides. The old engine whined as it struggled to maintain the chassis's balance. Even a new terrain vehicle would have difficulty navigating this course. Kari frequently wiped her sweaty palms on her pants and gripped the wheel, pushing the ancient vehicle forward and hoping it would make it to her destination. She was grateful she had given Shail a second sedative. Awake, he would have added to her worries.

The sun began its descent into the ocean, turning the sky a scarlet red. Another hour and it would be dark. Kari increased the speed. Traveling in daylight on the rugged trail was bad, but at night it would be worse, and the cabin was still hours away.

She wondered how she would find the place after fifteen years. When she glanced around the vehicle, it held nothing of value except the old blanket, Shail's medicine, and the portable com. There had been no time to bring food, water or a weapon for dangerous animals. If they came across a hunter, she couldn't even protect the harpy. Kari realized how ill prepared she was for the trip. She had no extra clothing, other than her thin bloodstained jacket resting on the floorboards. She looked ahead at the towering black mountains that ran parallel to the coast, making the path steeper and more difficult to navigate. She breathed deeply, determined to cross one obstacle at a time.

The sun slipped into the ocean and the landscape became dark and shadowy, forcing Kari to turn on the headlights. The lights could be seen for miles up and down the coast. She nervously scanned the night sky for hovercrafts. By now her father would have learned from Carol and the others that Kari was with a golden harpy. All his warnings had been in vain. It upset her, knowing the worry and trouble she'd create. *Dad has to realize that Shail saved my life, and now I must save his.* She lowered the window and listened for a hover, her father's hover. He'd search for her now. Except for her vehicle engine, all was silent on the starless night.

Kari slowed to a stop and turned on an overhead light to check on Shail. He still slept under his wings. Though drugged and injured, he had surprised her with his strength when he fought entering the vehicle. She saw why it had taken four hunters, two laser blasts, and a severe beating to subdue him. His lofty slender frame resembled an elegant water bird, his girth half the size of a man's. But Shail's elfin look was misleading. Under his luxurious feathers and sleek muscles, he was physically powerful. She'd be at his mercy if he chose to breed. Was he capable of rape? She put her faith in her instincts, knowing he'd never hurt her. She turned off the inside light, focused on the drive, and moved the vehicle over the next ridge.

7

Early in the morning John Turner arrived at the wood mill and entered his makeshift lab, off his office. The new batch of insecticide had arrived on a Terrance hover. He poured the yellow liquid into a spray bottle and removed a palm-size black beetle from the holding tank. For a year and a half he had handled the large insects, hoping to discover the correct poison to kill them. The beetle bit him.

"Damn it," he cursed, jerking his hand and dropping the beetle. It scurried across the floor, opened its wings, and flew against the window screen. He examined the bite and noticed a sizable chunk of flesh missing from his thumb. "This is a first," he grumbled and treated his wound. He walked to the window and examined the beetle. It looked like the rest of the beetles in the tank. Taking a net, he caught it. "Thought you guys only liked trees," he said, putting the beetle in a pail with a see-through lid. He sprayed the beetle with the new insecticide and waited. There was no effect. The beetle ambled around the pail. "Damn government, sending me this crap." He walked out to the mill.

Charlie was instructing another employee when John strolled up to them. "Got an order this morning for ten blocks of the blue," John said. "Have them trim what we have, and I'll radio the crews in the north."

Charlie glanced at the giant bundle of aqua logs. "There is enough for half." Then he looked at John. "What happened to your thumb?"

John grinned, realizing that nothing escaped the old Indian. "You're not going to believe this, but one of the beetles bit me."

Charlie examined the inflamed wound. "That is a bad bite. Lucky they're not poisonous. Do those beetles have food?"

"They eat better than me," John said. "Their tank is full of leaves and wood chips."

"Maybe you hurt it or antagonized it."

"The damn thing was sitting in my hand, and bit me for no reason," John said.

"This is very strange," Charlie said. "Perhaps your hand held the scent of wood, and the beetle became confused."

"Maybe," John said, and turned to leave. "By the way, that new insecticide is worthless. I might as well have used water." He walked back to his office.

Inside, John sprayed a bandage over the wound and went to the lab. The energetic beetle still walked around the pail. John rubbed the back of his neck and sighed. He returned to his office and plopped down in the chair behind the desk. He punched in the com key and the screen rose. As Maria appeared, he asked, "Is Kari home yet?"

"No, Mr. Turner," Maria said, "but she probably still sleeps at her friend's. Young people party until late. Do you wish me to call the Bakers and check on her?"

"No," he said. "She was with a group, and I'm sure she's fine, but call me when she gets home."

"Okay, Mr. Turner."

John pushed the key, and the screen dissolved into the desk. He glanced at a picture of Kari when she was a little girl. When he waved his hand, the motion sensor brought the photo to life. "Hi, Daddy, see my caboo?" she said, holding up her little arm and revealing the clinging small creature with reddish fur. "His name is Harry." She smiled and kissed the animal's head.

John figured he had watched and listened to the picture a million times, and it still made him grin, but Kari was no longer his little girl. She had matured into a stunning woman, similar to her mother. The past haunted him, and he feared his daughter, like her dead mother, might face tragedy due to a harpy. During their last talk, he learned that distance and time had not smothered Kari's devotion for the harpies, in particular the golden male. John questioned his decision to let the golden live, even protecting the creature on his land. If he had known then what he knew now, he would have killed the brazen young harpy and ended this threat to Kari.

"If she loves him . . . ," he said, closing his eyes. "I faced a no-win situation." If he killed the harpy now, he'd end their relationship forever. "Better she hate me, than lose her to a harpy."

John picked up the picture. She's a smart girl, he thought. Maybe I'm worrying needlessly. He wondered how her evening had gone with the young people of Westend. It was a small town, and he was aware that Carol Baker dated Jake, an avid harpy hunter. Perhaps Kari's peers could convince her to stay clear of the harpies. He rose from his desk and went back to the mill. In a few days, he would travel to the northeast part of the estate and check the crews cutting timber.

The cool morning gave way to a hot and muggy afternoon. John, along with Charlie, supervised the cutting and loading of timber. Robotic machines moved the large logs through the lasers, and the rare timbers became neatly stacked piles of fine boards. John wiped the sweat from his brow. "It's strange Kari hasn't checked in with me," he said to Charlie.

"You forget." Charlie grinned. "She is your daughter and has your stubborn nature. As a child, she rarely checked in."

"I suppose," John said. "I'll call the Bakers' store when I get to the house."

Charlie saw one of the men running toward them. "Trouble," he said. "No man runs in this heat."

"A swarm," the man gasped. "A swarm hit east of town. They're saying some people died."

John raced to his hovercraft and Charlie followed. They hopped inside, and the hover lifted off before Charlie had shut the door. They flew past Westend, heading east. Before long, they saw the barren patch of dirt encompassing a space of several city blocks. In the center of black soil were the scattered hovercrafts and terrain vehicles belonging to the town residents.

John landed his hover and leaped out before the engine blades had come to a stop. He hurried toward the small group of people, his thoughts focused on Kari. When he approached, the somber crowd became silent. A woman wept in her husband's arms, as the man consoled her. It was the Bakers, Carol's parents. John swallowed the lump in his throat and walked past them. The red terrain vehicle stood with its doors open. The once new and shiny transport was covered with beetle waste and full of dents, where it had crashed into trees in a futile attempt to escape the swarm. He stumbled toward it, fighting back his tears.

A man caught his arm and stopped him. "Mr. Turner, you don't want to see her like this," he said. The whole town was aware that the special vehicle had been a coming-home gift for his daughter.

John pulled away and kept walking. He looked inside of the gutted vehicle and saw the skeletal remains of three bodies. Two others lay on the ground a few feet away. "No!" John cried, shaking his head.

"I'm so sorry, Mr. Turner," the man said.

"Why didn't they keep the doors shut?" John uttered.

"Best we can tell," the man answered, "the beetles clogged the engine and burrowed through the floorboards. These kids didn't stand a chance."

Charlie walked up to John and put his arm on his shoulder. "Come away, John. Kari would not want you to see her like this."

John broke down and cried. "I can't tell which one is her, Charlie," he sobbed. First his beautiful wife, and now Kari. There was nothing left to make living worthwhile.

Doc landed his hovercraft and climbed out. A man approached him and said, "They're all dead, Doc. There's nothing you can do."

"Who are they?" Doc asked, walking toward the damaged vehicle with the man.

"Carol Baker and her boyfriend, Jake O'Connell, also John Turner's daughter. They were in her new vehicle. There're two others that we're not sure of. We're thinking they may be Jake's buddies, Hank and Tom. The beetles didn't leave much."

Doc saw John with his faithful Indian friend, Charlie, near the vehicle. John's face was buried in his hands and his body shuddered as he wept. Charlie rubbed John's shoulder, attempting to comfort him. Doc stroked his beard and watched them for a moment. He huffed deeply and strolled to them. "John, I need to talk to you."

"Leave me alone, Doc," John stammered. Charlie nodded to Doc and walked away.

"You'll want to hear what I have to say," Doc said. He and John's father had been good friends, and Doc had watched John grow into a powerful man, but now, believing his daughter was dead, he appeared shattered. Doc wasn't eager to tell John the truth: that his daughter was alive and with a golden harpy. John lowered his hands and his bloodshot eyes stared at him.

"She's not dead," Doc said, and John frowned in confusion. "Your daughter is not dead."

John brushed away his tears. "That's her vehicle, Doc, and she was with Carol Baker last night. You can't identify those bodies by looking at the remains."

"Kari wasn't with Carol. She was with me."

"With you? But her vehicle," John sputtered.

Doc wearily rubbed his forehead. "I didn't want to be the one to tell you, but I can't let you believe that Kari is dead."

"What is it?" John screamed. "Is she all right? Is she hurt?"

"Your daughter is fine. She gave Jake her vehicle in exchange for a wounded golden harpy. She brought it to my place last night, and I treated its laser blasts."

"You did what? You let that damn thing live?" John ranted. "Charlie, we're going," he yelled to the Indian. The grieving father quickly turned into an angry man.

"Where do you think you're going?" Doc asked.

John glared at him. "To your place and kill it. Something you should have done last night."

"Go ahead and go, but they're not there."

"Where is she?" John said in a rage.

"Aren't you at least glad that she's not here?"

"Don't play games, old man. That harpy is as deadly as a swarm."

"With your frame of mind, that's true," Doc mocked.

Doc's cutting words stopped John cold. This same rage had killed his wife.

Charlie walked up to them. "Kari's not dead," said John, "but she's with the golden harpy. It was shot, and this crazy old fool treated its wounds."

"I've got better things to do than listen to your insults," Doc said. "Your daughter is alive. Be thankful. The Bakers have truly lost a daughter. I need to identify those bodies and learn what other parents will mourn this day. We've got bigger problems than one little harpy. The beetles have evolved into flesh-eaters, and everyone's in danger." He turned toward the red vehicle.

"Where is she?" John demanded.

"You're one pigheaded man," Doc snarled. "I don't know where she's gone, and even if I did, I sure as hell wouldn't tell you. Take some good advice. Leave them alone. If you interfere, you'll bring disaster." He left John and Charlie as an ominous wind blew across the vacant land.

"Doc is right, John," Charlie said quietly. "Be grateful Kari is alive, even if she is with the harpy. It was foolish thinking that they could be kept apart. There is no more to be done."

"That's bullshit," John growled, and stomped off toward his hover. Charlie lowered his head and followed. They climbed inside the craft, but John didn't start the engine. He placed his head against the wheel and shut his eyes. "I can't let this go, Charlie. That harpy will destroy her life."

"It was unlucky that fate brought them together, but Kari was warned of the risks," Charlie said. "And still, she chose to be with him. You have done everything in your power to protect her, but it's time to let her go."

"Even if I stayed out of it, the harpies, and especially the golden male are doomed. I don't want my daughter jumping in front of a hunter's laser blast to protect him." John glanced at Charlie. "You know she would."

"Yes, she would not hesitate to save him, but if Doc is right about the swarms, we are all doomed."

John held up his bandaged thumb. "Maybe that beetle was trying to tell me something." He pushed the start button, and the hover rose from the ground. "Doc's place may hold some clues as to where she took him." They flew toward Westend, and John flipped on the communicator. "Maria, have you heard from Kari?"

Maria was crying. "No, Mr. Turner, but I was told of her vehicle."

"She's alive, Maria. She wasn't in it, but I can't find her. Call me if you learn anything," he said, flipping the com off. Reaching Doc's yellow cottage, he landed the hover on the street, and went to the porch. John opened the unlocked door and walked into the small hospital room. A bloody plastic wrap still lay on the operating table.

"A lot of blood," Charlie commented "The harpy was badly injured."

"There's also some on the porch. With any luck, the little son-of-a-bitch might die," John said, walking through the cottage to the back door. The stretcher still floated in the backyard.

Charlie examined the flattened grass. "She is in a small terrain vehicle, but not Doc's." He pointed to the vehicle parked under a tree.

"I wonder whose," John said. "I need to get the color and description of it." They returned to the cottage and entered the bedroom off the hallway. Scattered pillows and tangled sheets rested around the unmade double bed. "The harpy lay here," Charlie said, motioning to a small blood smear on the sheet. He picked up a tiny yellow feather.

From the floor, John lifted a medical gown. "This wasn't on the harpy, and from the look of that bed, she also slept in it," he said, dropping the gown. John and Charlie were experienced hunters and knew that certain signs would tell a story about their prey, but the prey had become Kari and the harpy.

"I need to go back to the swarm site," John said. "Someone from the beach party must be there, and they'll know the vehicle she's in."

"You intend to pursue them then?"

"Better I find them than some hunter," John said.

"If you succeed, will you kill her harpy?"

John nodded. "It should have been done years ago while Kari was gone and the golden was young and naïve, but he's injured . . . he'll be easier to find and kill. Kari won't like it, but she'll get over it."

Charlie scoffed. "I don't believe she would nor would she ever forgive you. You will lose her, John. There must be another way."

John leaned against the doorjamb. "Let's first find them. If he hasn't touched her, I might let him live, under the condition that the little stud is neutered and no longer a threat. Hell, if Kari is so fond of that blond, she can keep him like a pet canary. I'll even build the cage." He walked out of the room.

Charlie shook his head. John knew to castrate or cage a wild harpy was a death sentence. They left the cottage and meandered out to the quiet, deserted street and the hovercraft.

A short flight later, they arrived back at the swarm site. The townspeople looked on as Doc supervised the men loading corpses into their vehicles. John walked to Doc as he knelt, examining a skeleton. "Must be Tom Spencer," Doc said. "The red hair is a match." He stood up and cringed, rubbing his back. He looked up at John and grumbled, "What do you want now?"

"I want to know about the vehicle Kari was in," John said. "With or without your help, I'm going to find her."

"Get used to the 'without,'" Doc scowled, facing John. "Can't you get it through your thick skull? Your girl loves that harpy and wants to be with him, and the harpy is equally committed to her. Let them have a little happiness. His yellow wings will be hanging on some hunter's wall soon enough." Doc turned away and began talking to another man.

"No sense arguing with him. He's no help," John said to Charlie.

"Even if you learn of her vehicle, it may be too late for a search," Charlie said. "The light will be gone soon."

John noticed two girls Kari's age in the small crowd. One cried and the other held her. He went to them. "I'm sorry, but I'm trying to find my daughter, Kari."

"I was with Kari at the beach, Mr. Turner," said one of the girls. "I'm Cindy Williams. My father works at your mill. Didn't she come home last night?"

"No," John said. "Do you know the color of the vehicle she was in?"

"Blue. It was Jake's old vehicle," said Cindy. "She swapped her new vehicle for a dying golden harpy, and Jake let her use his transport. The harpy attacked Hank on the islands and broke his arm. Jake, Carol, and the other guys flew Hank to the Terrance Hospital last night. They must've come back this morning and gone joyriding, when the swarm struck. I nearly went with them."

"Did his vehicle have a communicator?"

"It might have, but I doubt if it worked," Cindy said. "Hardly anything worked in that piece of junk."

"Thank you, Cindy. You've been a big help."

"Mr. Turner, once the harpy dies, I'm sure Kari will come home."

"Was it in bad shape?" John asked.

"Oh, yes," Cindy said. "Jake shot the poor thing twice, broke its wing, but even then, it fought the guys. They had to beat the life out it, before they could tie it up. When I saw the harpy, it was almost dead."

"Thanks," John said, and walked to his hover and Charlie. "She's in an old blue vehicle," John said, "and the harpy was bad off with a broken wing. I'm betting she'll look for a place to hole up so it can heal."

"A broken wing takes time to mend, and a grounded harpy is very vulnerable," Charlie commented, climbing into the hover with John.

They flew over the highway late into the night, but eventually gave up and headed for home. "We're shutting down. I want the men pulled from the mill and put in every available hovercraft. We'll start our search again at daybreak," John said, landing at the estate.

8

The tired blue vehicle struggled up the steep cliffs, constantly rattling from ocean breezes. Sporadic strong gusts made the hovering transport sway and rock, making Kari nervous. She clung to the wheel and slowly maneuvered the vehicle around the massive boulders and trees. The dim headlights lit the narrow path, and she strained to see ahead, knowing with one wrong turn, she could plummet one hundred feet below, crashing on the rocky beach. She briefly glanced at the instruments, counting the miles. "Please hold together, old girl," she whispered to the vehicle. The northern journey was taking forever.

She stopped several times to check on Shail, but he continued to sleep. The sedative kept him out, plus he had to be exhausted. The last three days his slight body had been pushed to its limits, needing time to rest and heal. She was thankful he didn't add to her problems.

As the night wore on, the nocturnal animals emerged. Hit by the headlights, countless pairs of illuminating white eyes stared back from the thick brush and trees. Some animals were caught by surprise and dashed across Kari's path to hide in the jungle. To take her mind off her worries, she kept count of the different species. She drove around an immense downed tree and slammed on the brakes. A herd of raydons grazed on shrubs, blocking the passageway. The eight-foot brown lizards were equally startled, rearing on their stocky back legs, growling and snapping at the vehicle. Kari waited patiently for them to relax and move on. Although plant-eaters, raydons had big sharp teeth and would attack if threatened. When the last lizard disappeared into the bushes, she continued her journey.

Kari rubbed her eyes and yawned, trying to recall her last full night of sleep. The pale eastern light crested through the trees, and the black sky turned hazy gray. The shadowy foliage took color as morning ascended on the frontier. She looked at the vehicle gauges. "The cabin has to be close." She then saw the large boulder jetting out from the trees. On its side was a washed-out painted "X," her grandfather's mark that had allowed him to locate the cabin by hovercraft. Veering off the coastal path, she entered the jungle. A short drive revealed a small clearing surrounded by imposing trees. The humble log cabin sat to her left, and she breathed a deep sigh of relief.

She parked the vehicle several yards from the cabin door. The vehicle settled on the ground, but when she killed the engine, it sputtered for a moment before becoming silent. She patted the machine's dash and smiled. "Good girl. You got us here."

Kari stepped out and stretched, removing the weight of worries. They had made the hundred-mile journey and without being seen. Shail stood a chance of recovery and freedom. Walking to the cabin door, she pulled on the handle, but it wouldn't open. She looked down at the tree roots growing in front of the doorjamb. After tugging and digging at the rubble, she opened the door and stepped inside.

A pair of flying dell squirrels leaped across the rafters, noisily chastising the intruder for entering their home, before making their escape through a broken window. Kari glanced at layers of dirt and leaves on the floor, knowing her grandfather and Charlie were the cabin's last human occupants. Comforted by this knowledge, she knew it unlikely that a hunter or her father would discover the harpy here.

She returned to the vehicle and opened the back door. Shail stirred with the smell of fresh air and attempted to open his drowsy eyes.

"You're safe now," she said, stroking his head. She stepped to the front of the vehicle, gathered his medicine, and returned. Like Doc had showed her, she treated his wound and placed a new antibiotic patch on his back. "You must be thirsty." She went back to the cabin, and in the cabinets she found outdated food packets and a water jug. Turning the handles on the ancient faucets, she found no flowing water. She grabbed the empty jug and headed outside.

As a child, Kari remembered a meager mountain stream that was a short walk through the jungle. Pushing the colossal ferns and vines aside, she ambled down the overgrown trail. She reached the crystal-clear stream that tumbled over smooth stones. Farther up from the stream, a sheer cliff created a waterfall surrounded by a mosaic of vivid flowers. She relived her youth when she had cooled off under the falls after hot treks through the woods. The place was still magical. A bounty of wild berries grew between the rocks, and she nibbled on them, before splashing the cool water on her face and filling the jug. Concerned with Shail, she tore herself away from the heavenly spot and walked back to the vehicle.

Shail still dozed, but when she placed the water jug to his lips, he swallowed several times in a groggy state. He opened his eyes and glanced at her, but his eyes widened as he realized where he was. He struggled to rise, but she held him, hoping to control his panic. "Easy, Shail," she said. "Don't be scared."

The sedative drug had worn off and he was fully alert and active. He pushed her aside, scrambling out of the vehicle and falling onto the ground. He made a feeble attempt to stand, but his wound and broken ribs forced him to double over, and he collapsed in the dirt. Staring up at the vehicle, he shuddered and panted, then began to crawl away.

"Stop this now," Kari yelled, pushing him down. "The vehicle won't hurt you." He gazed up at her, and his eyes conveyed uncertainty and fear. "You don't have to go back in it," she said, and petted him.

Shail sensed her frustration as she anxiously ran her hand over his head. Though she loved him, she did not understand a wild harpy. He sniffed the air, and, not detecting the scent of men, he curled up and surrendered to her wishes. Her agitated voice became a low song, and her shaky hands gave way to gentle stroking. She was obviously pleased he was calm.

"Good boy, Shail," Kari said, rising. "Lie still and I'll be back."

She went to the cabin and opened an old trunk that stored bedding. Pulling out a tattered blue quilt, she returned and spread it on the ground alongside him. "I want you to lie on this. It will keep the dirt out of your wounds." He leaned over and smelled the material. His nose wrinkled, and he kicked the quilt away into a heap. "No," she yelled, reopening the quilt and pushed his back and wings toward it.

Shail would've been content in the dirt, rather than on the musty human rag, but he wanted to please her. He poked the cloth before reluctantly climbed onto it, wondering how long he must yield to this female to keep her happy.

Her next test became a toxic-smelling object she retrieved from the human structure. Filling it with tempting water, she placed it to his mouth. He hissed at it, preferring to stay thirsty.

"Shail, it's only a cup." Kari took a sip and offered it to him again. He skittishly sniffed it and carefully sucked up the water in the center, his parched lips never touching the plastic rim.

"You really are wild." She sighed, noticing he didn't drink like a human. "I'm going in the woods to get you some food. Stay here." She grabbed a pail from the cabin and left him.

Once she was gone, Shail labored to rise. He couldn't afford to be helpless. Hoisting himself up, he cringed with the pain, and after a few steps, he was out of breath. Walking any distance was out of the question. He flapped his wings, but saw the lower half of his broken wing was bound between the wing tip and middle joint. He seethed at the plastic cast and tried to pull it off.

"Shail!" Kari screamed, walking from the trees. She dropped the pail of berries and rushed to him. She wrapped her arms around him and gently forced him back down on the quilt. "Don't do this, my beautiful bird. You're safe. There are no hunters here," she cooed. "Lie still. The cast must stay on your wing or you'll never fly again." She sat next to him and rested her back against the vehicle. He placed his head in her lap, and she ran her fingers through his hair. "I guess this is the only way to keep you quiet. I don't want to drug you." After a few minutes, she fell asleep.

———

The chatter of squirrels in overhead branches woke Kari. She was lying on the quilt, and Shail was nowhere in sight. She jolted forward and looked around. Behind the vehicle, she heard his soft sniffle and saw he had crawled off the quilt and was nesting on a cluster of dry leaves. His bright eyes twinkled, displaying contentment, and he held a half-eaten red fruit in his hand. Near him lay a pile of assorted fruits and nuts.

"Where did you get all that food?" she asked, knowing he couldn't have picked it.

He glanced upward, and his answer entered her subconscious. "My harpies," he relayed.

"Your harpies?" she said, and then wondered whether she had really heard him.

He intentionally closed his eyes, confirming a "yes." Recuperating from the abusive trauma and free of the debilitating drugs, he could finally focus on harpy telepathy and communicate with her. He didn't understand her sounds, but sensing her mind, he gained a rough meaning of the words. If she rambled with long sentences and did not concentrate on him, her message to him was lost.

"You're finally talking to me. I figured it was only a matter of time, since you talked to me in our dreams." She grabbed a red fruit and stood. Eating the long juicy food, she stared into the branches that held only squirrels. "I don't see any harpies."

The setting sun told Kari she had slept most of the day and needed to prepare for the coming night. In the cabin she found some dusty solar lights. Cleaning the plates, she set them outside, facing the sun, and hoped they would recharge before dark. Sleeping in a bed would have been nice, but the cabin was filthy, and it was nearly impossible to move a claustrophobic harpy inside. She gathered a few blankets from the chest and dropped them and the quilt near him. He showed his disdain by the toss of his hair. "Too bad if you don't like them. It's going to be cold."

He gave her an indignant glance and reached for the water jug. After filling the cup, he leaned over and sucked up the water.

"Very good, Shail," she said. While she slept, he had overcome his fear of the containers.

As darkness approached, Kari spread the quilt next to him and waited. With no argument, he dutifully climbed onto the cloth. She sat down beside him and flipped on one of the solar lights.

Shail carefully placed his hand close to the light, behaving as if it were hot like fire. Discovering it cool, he prodded the metal and flipped the on-and-off switch. He sniffled at her giggles. "You act like a little boy with a new toy," she said. Though harpies were supposedly animals, she saw that Shail was intelligent and learned quickly. She explained the operation of a solar light, but was unsure he understood.

As night approached, the temperature dropped and a cold ocean breeze swept through the small clearing. Kari grabbed the blankets and covered Shail and herself, but he would have no part of them. He flapped his wing and sent the blankets flying. "I'm cold, even if you're not," she said. He moved closer, putting his arms around her and cloaking her under his soft wing.

Kari's muscles tensed as she resolved to resist any sexual advance. Her mind raced with thoughts of how to discourage him, even considered placing a sedative patch on his back. He was now strong enough to easily overpower her. She waited for his seductive kiss, his fondling hands, but her wait was pointless. He submissively lowered his head and was still, with no inclination that he wished to mate.

After some time, Kari relaxed. He knows, she thought. He senses my doubts and fears. Confirming her perception, she felt the light massage of his extended wing against her shoulder. She stared up through rustling tree branches, listening to the whistling wind, as the gorgeous male held her. She had never experienced such elation. Her life had been a tangled web of searching, longing, misery and confusion, but the web had blown away with the howling night wind. The object of her lifelong quest lay sleeping beside her, and it felt right. Perhaps he had cast a spell over her or used hypnotism; it no longer mattered. Despite the controversy and their differences, he was the only one who completed her, and she would love him all her life.

———

Shail opened his eyes as the pale dawn light filtered through the trees. He leaned over and faintly kissed her cheek. Unclasping her arms, he removed his wing. She shivered, but continued to sleep. Kneeling over her in the shadowy darkness, he glanced at the heap of nasty blankets. He rose, and a sharp pain shot through him. He gripped his side, retrieved a blanket, and placed it over her. She clutched the warming blanket and remained asleep.

Shail went to the food and popped a few nuts into his mouth, but he focused on the sky and trees, sensing the approach of a harpy. In seconds, Aron glided into the clearing and landed alongside him. Respectfully, the tall brown harpy lowered his head to Shail, but a glimpse from his bright green eyes reflected his joy. "I am pleased to see you also," Shail relayed with silent telepathy and wrapped his arms about Aron, nuzzling his neck.

Pulling apart, Aron shuddered. "I so feared . . ."

Shail nodded. "I, too."

Aron glanced down at the sleeping female and then at Shail. "At last, she is yours," Aron relayed. "The wait was long, but worthy. She faced the grogins on the road and now the island hunters. And if not for her, the flocks would mourn your loss. Her journey into the stars made her strong, unlike other females."

"She is strong," Shail agreed, "for she orders the harpy ruler around like a pet."

Aron's eyes twinkled. "I am sorry to hear."

Shail raised his head. "Sorry you are not. It pleases you that I learn obedience." He shook his head. "I can endure this and gladly, but our time apart is the worry. Though strong, she is also strange. Confusion fills her mind, and she is unsure in which world to dwell. And worse, I harmed her trust. Fearing my death, I forced the bonding,"

Aron placed his hand on Shail's shoulder. "Do not worry, little brother. Against all perils, she returned and saved you. Her love is true. Time shall heal her doubts."

"But time, I do not have," relayed Shail. "I was once a hunting tale, a glimpse of yellow feathers in the trees, but now all hunters know I live. They shall seek me and my flock . . . the tide of hunters floods our islands."

Aron lowered his head. "I must add to your worries: The beetles have changed. They devour all living things, trees and animals. A swarm killed the hunters who harmed you."

Shail looked up with surprise. "Those men are dead?"

Aron nodded.

Shail walked over to the vehicle and leaned against it, staring at the ground. "I am glad they are dead, but this beetle news is not good." After a few minutes, he lifted his head. "Gather the western flocks, Aron. All females and fledglings must go the islands. No swarm will fly the distance of water."

"The islands are no refuge. Too many hunters go. Last light I lost two, defending their fledglings."

Shail ruffled his feathers. "Your warning I should have heeded. My reckless attempt to save the one now endangers the many, for I am worthless as a ruler. The wound to my side heals, but my wing, I do not know."

Aron looked at Shail's half-wrapped wing and raised his eyebrow. "The western harpies shall follow me. They know I speak for you. But the river and eastern flocks shall only follow a pair of yellow wings. If you do not mend, all may be lost."

"Secure all on the islands," Shail relayed. "When they are safe from swarms, we deal with the hunters. Take these males that guard me, for I wish none spared in this task. Leave a fledgling to bring food and give warning."

"What of my males protecting these lands?" Aron asked.

"They remain."

"I leave you now, but take rest," said Aron, placing his hand on Shail. "I sense the pain and the burden you carry. You trouble me, brother."

"I shall quickly try to heal, but always, I have troubled you."

Aron breathed deeply and put his arms around Shail. "May this long-awaited female bring you happiness." Aron extended his wings and flew through the trees toward the ocean.

Shail poured a cup of water from the jug and took a few sips, his thoughts focused on the beetles and hunters. The survival of his species depended on him, and he was useless. He wandered to the quilt and sat down, easing his hurting ribs, and watched Kari sleep. He longed to crawl between her arms, so her caressing hands would relieve his anxiety, but he refrained. To build trust, he would stay distant, letting her accept him on her terms. He stretched out and studied every inch of the exquisite but headstrong female. "She is your match," Aron had told him on the island. The truth of it made Shail quiver. After so long, he finally was resting alongside his soul mate.

He was distracted when a small fledgling fluttered down from the trees and shyly approached him. Dropping to his knees and lowering his head, he waited for Shail's response.

"Aron sent you?"

The fledgling nervously nodded.

"There is plenty of food," Shail relayed.

"Bring more with the dawn." The fledgling backed away and fled into the trees.

As the dominant male of all flocks, Shail struck fear in young harpies and could intimidate the adult males with the slight arch of his wings. Though he had never abused his power, it was the way of the harpies. All brown-winged harpies respected the daring goldens who, in turn, sacrificed their lives in defense of the flocks. Shail knew the fledgling was terrified, but also very proud. Aron had chosen him to bring food and watch over their injured monarch.

Shail noticed Kari stir. She was beautiful, perfect. She felt the quilt and sat up. He slid beside her and lowered his head, rubbing it against her leg. She smiled and stroked his head.

"You like being petted," she said. "I'd love to lie here all day and play with you, but I have work, starting with treating your wound." She stood and fetched an antibiotic patch and other medical supplies from the vehicle. Sitting down near Shail, she removed his old bandage and reached for the disinfectant. As the spray bottle came near, he swiftly snatched her wrist. Startled, she dropped the bottle. Leaning over, he sniffed it and jerked away. He seethed at her and the bottle.

"I see your defiant eyes," she said. "Don't give me trouble. I know it stinks, but it will help you heal." She picked up the bottle and slowly brought it near his raised head and arched wings.

Shail created a constant low hiss, conveying his unhappiness, but tolerated her spraying the foul poison and applying an equally reeking and sticky substance on his wound. She also placed some annoying thing on his back.

"There. All done," she said, smiling, "and you lived."

He ruffled his feathers to express irritation. Extending a wing, he lay down on his side, and climbed on top of the feathers that rested on the ground. He curled up into a ball by pulling in his arms and legs, and covered his body with the top wing. Before tucking his face deep in the feathers, he glared at her, conveying he was still irked by the lame treatment. With only his yellow hair and feathers exposed, he had transformed into a large nesting bird.

"I'm sorry you're upset and feel humiliated," she said, standing, "but this stuff has to be done." She grabbed the empty jug and went to the woods for more water.

Kari returned shortly and placed the water jug and cup within his reach. "Here's your water," she said, and walked toward the cabin.

Shail lifted his head and watched her disappear inside the man-made structure. She was gone all morning, and he heard brushing and banging sounds coming from inside. His inquisitiveness got to him, and though annoyed, he missed her. He struggled to his feet and slowly walked to the doorway. Peering in, he saw her hard at work, scrubbing a wooden platform. He tilted his head and watched her.

She frowned when she finally noticed him. "You're supposed to be resting," she said. "Since you're here, you might as well come in and lie down. I found some clean sheets for the bed."

She motioned toward a platform that rose from the floor, similar to the one in the old man's home. Shail, realizing his mistake, turned away from the threshold, hoping to return to the quilt and spacious skies, but she quickly caught his arm and tugged on him to enter. He shook his head and planted his feet, refusing to step inside.

"Is everything going to be a battle?" she asked.

Why could she not empathize with his feelings? Human things made him nervous. For decades, harpies were not only shot with weapons, but also were poisoned, netted, and trapped. Every human object posed a potential danger to a harpy. His skittish behavior was a reflection of his caution, for a naïve harpy was a dead harpy.

She now wanted him within the man dwelling. Its solid walls, covered ceiling, and shut door screamed of no escape. A brown-wing would quickly succumb to despair, shock, and even heart failure if placed in a building because harpies, like all nonhuman animals, lived in the present. A future of possible freedom was impossible to foresee.

Shail's golden bloodline made him tougher than most, but the cabin still terrified him. He hissed at the female, who pulled his arm to enter the potential trap. Should he listen to his natural instincts or please her?

Kari released his arm with his hostile sizzling sound. Like the vehicle, he was too strong to be forced. "Please, Shail. I promise the cabin won't hurt you," she said. He pleaded with his eyes and then sheepishly stuck his head inside, sniffing the air. He carefully stepped over the threshold and looked up at the ceiling. His body shuddered, and he retreated outside. She walked to him and gently took his hand. "Come, Shail. It will be okay."

Shail swallowed hard and let her coax him to the doorway. The scent of men was barely detectable in the cabin, conveying a hunter had not been there for many seasons. He glanced down at the little female holding his hand and recalled how she faced down and outwitted four hunters to save him. She expects more of me, he thought. At that moment, he decided to suppress his fears and animal instincts and enter her human world, though his choice could be fatal. He was, after all, a golden harpy who had survived man's worst. He followed her into the cabin.

She led him to the white platform she called a bed and beckoned him to lie down. He placed one knee on the material, but like a snare net, it collapsed with his weight. He jumped away to avoid being tangled. She giggled at him and plopped on the bed. He tossed his hair and sniffled, relaying dislike of her impertinence. Pushing on the sheets, he realized the bed was only soft like a moss nest. He crawled on it and curled up beside her.

"See? It's not so bad," she said, running her fingers through his hair. "You'll heal faster if your wounds stay clean." She got up and went back to fixing up the cabin.

Shail rested his chin on his arm and watched her remove the dirt and leaves, placing them outside. Humans were the oddest of creatures, he thought. After tearing down the trees, they constructed impenetrable buildings, traveled in confining covered machines, and wore heavy clothing, all with the purpose of keeping nature away. Did they truly believe that dirt, wind, rain, and sun could hurt them? The female had laughed at his fears, but he thought hers were far more absurd, observing her eradicate every spot of dust. It concerned him that they had been raised worlds apart, and he wondered where they would live if they remained together. For now, he'd give in and dwell in her world, hoping to gain her trust.

While cleaning the cabin, Kari talked to Shail, explaining chairs for sitting, tables for eating, beds for sleeping. Although he appeared interested, he didn't respond, so she was unsure if he understood, but her rambling kept him tranquil. She took a break and sat down beside him, ruffling the long locks that hung over his royal-blue eyes. "I can tell you're trying very hard," she said. The more he surrendered to her wishes, the more she felt at ease with him, knowing the sedative patches could be thrown away.

"I'm going outside now to climb on the roof," she said, "so I can fix the solar strips, and the cabin will have water and light."

He tilted his head in confusion.

"I know." She sighed. "Way too much information." She put her hand in front of his face. "Stay here."

He again gave her a quizzical look.

"Don't pull that. I know you understand," she said with a raised eyebrow.

He lowered his head on a pillow.

Grabbing a rusted ax she had discovered in a closet, she left the cabin and crawled up a tree and onto the roof. She removed a fallen tree limb and repaired the broken connections on the solar strips. They would take a full day to recharge. She climbed down and glanced through the cabin door. Shail had his face tucked in his feathers and appeared asleep.

Kari turned and looked at the conspicuous vehicle parked out front. Placing the ax inside, she hopped into the driver's seat and pressed the starter. The engine sputtered for a moment before hovering a few feet off the ground. She drove into the jungle and parked the vehicle near thick blue ferns. Using the ax, she cut branches, cloaking the entire vehicle under foliage.

Wiping her sweaty brow, she flexed her back muscles and returned to the clearing. She looked at the quiet cabin and figured Shail had remained asleep inside. It was late afternoon, and she had accomplished a lot in one day. Longing for a cool drink and bath, she set out for the stream. She could hardly wait to strip off her dirty clothes. The waterfall was heaven, washing away all grime and weariness. Halfheartedly she stepped from the gushing water, but immediately heard the sound of an engine. A hunter, my father, her thoughts raced, and Shail is trapped inside. Frantically she pulled on her clothes, grabbed the ax, and crashed recklessly through the underbrush toward the sound.

As the sound came closer, her adrenaline rose as she prepared to fight any man who harmed her harpy. She bolted around a thick cluster of ferns with the raised ax, but came to a stop. In front of her was the old blue vehicle, hovering in idle, and still covered with shrubs. The driver's door stood open, and she quickly looked around. "Who are you?" she called out, holding the ax. Shail slipped out from behind a tree.

"Jesus, Shail!" She heaved a sigh and lowered her crude weapon. "You scared the hell out of me."

He disregarded her ranting and tiptoed closer to the hovering machine. Bending over, he looked beneath it. He was obviously perplexed that it could rise off the ground with no wings.

"I'm glad you're becoming so brave, but some things you shouldn't play with." She reached through the vehicle door and pushed the off button. The terrain vehicle settled on the ground and was silent. Slamming the door, she watched her inquisitive male scrutinize the machine. He placed his ear near the hood and listened for a heartbeat, then tapped, sniffed, and tasted the metal. He tossed his hair, fluttered his wings, and kicked it, adding another dent to the side.

"Come now, Shail. Let's go back to the cabin. You killed it."

He lifted his bloodstained sash and marked the vehicle with his urine.

Kari shook her head at his animal antics and mumbled, "Killed it and used the poor vehicle as a toilet. At least you're housebroken."

They walked out of the trees toward the cabin. At the door, Shail hesitated and then leaped over the entrance as if something would grab him. He glanced at her with a raised head. She bit her bottom lip and turned away, refraining from laughing at his cute idiosyncrasies. He reclined on the bed, and Kari picked up some fruit, offered him a piece, and sat down beside him. As she nibbled, she felt his hand run across her wet hair and down her back. Her skin became covered with goose bumps and his intoxicating touch was overpowering, but she leaped off the bed, away from him.

"No," she stammered, "I'm not sure we belong together." As soon as she spoke the words, she was sorry. Her father's and Charlie's warnings plagued her mind, and she also wondered if Shail would back off when asked. His recovery had been swift, and if he chose to mate, he now might be capable of outrunning her.

Shail lowered his head on the sheet and stared up at her. "I would never force you," he conveyed into her subconscious. "Fearing death and having no fledgling, I sought a bonding too soon. My fears caused yours. I regret this."

Hearing his soft voice and his explanation, she covered her mouth and her eyes welled up with tears. Understanding his motives, she felt ashamed for distrusting him, especially when he had placed his life in her hands. He was incapable of rape. "I'm not afraid of you, Shail. I am afraid of this commitment."

She ran out of the cabin and took the path to the ocean. On a windy cliff, she gazed out at the water. How could she make Shail understand? Her mother had died in a harpy's arms. If she bonded with him, would her life be over? She didn't trust her father, but Charlie would never lie to her. Her heart belonged to the harpy, but her brain told her to hold back and weigh the risks. The tug of war within was agonizing. When Shail was healed and could fly, would she stay or leave him?

She sat on the ocean cliff until the sun sank into the horizon. Making her way back on the dusky path, she entered the shadowy cabin. On the bed, Shail's vague figure rested, offset by the white sheets. She took a seat on the bed near him. "I'm sorry," she said. "I know you've waited a long time for me, and—"

Shail leaned forward and put two fingers to her mouth, stopping her justification. "There is no need to tell," he relayed. "Sleep now." He reclined, and she curled up in his arms. His wing went over them.

Shail held her into the night until her distress gave way to sleep. Although she thought him childlike, he comprehended her dilemma. She had spent her whole life with the human creatures that hated and feared harpies. The men were responsible for poisoning her mind. She loved him, but she did not know him or his kind.

Shail closed his eyes, tortured by his mistake. Distressed, dying, and drugged, he had attempted a bonding without waiting to recover, so he could sense her mind. Their telepathic dreams had confirmed her desires for him, and he had acted, based on the dreams, but the dreams were wrong. Her fragile mind was confused and full of doubt about harpies, and worse, he added to her fears, confirming the men's lies. She was unsure if she would remain in his harpy world and become his mate or go back to the safe human world she trusted. He wanted to talk to her and tell her all these things, but her telepathy was very weak. She could only receive short messages from him, and he was just beginning to learn the human language of noisy words. Now we lie encased in one another's arms, he thought, but so distant.

9

John and Charlie meandered into the dining room and sat down at the table. Maria quietly served them dinner. For two days they had risen before dawn and searched for the old blue vehicle, returning late at night. "Where could she be?" John said wearily, staring at the uneaten food. "We've covered every main road from Westend to Terrance."

"I'd be surprised if we had found her on the highway. Kari is too smart to stay near a road," Charlie said. "She doesn't fear the jungle and has gone there."

"I should have listened to you from the start," John said. "Tomorrow, we'll hit the closest logging roads. God, I hope she's not in the jungle. She has no food, no weapon, and now there're these deadly beetles. Even the broken-winged harpy can't protect her." He poked his food with a knife. "I should've killed that little sucker years ago. She'd be safe now and with a decent life ahead of her. And I wouldn't be walking the floors at night."

"She is safe, John," Charlie said. "The harpy may be crippled, but he is no common brown. He is a golden and precious to his flocks. They would watch over him and her."

"I know you've spent years sneaking around the woods, watching the creatures, but you don't know that for sure."

Charlie glared. "Okay, don't believe me. After all, I am just a stupid old man."

John took a sip of wine and glanced at the irritated Indian. "Let's hear it," he said, setting his glass on the table.

"I've seen brown harpies protect goldens," Charlie said, leaning back in his chair. "Back when there were many goldens, I stumbled upon a nest of yellow-winged fledglings. In seconds, I was surrounded by browns. They fluttered their wings and threw their bodies at my feet, trying to distract me. The flocks prize their blond harpies, treat them like royalty, and Kari has her own harpy guardian. Outside of Terrance, she wandered into a pride of grogins. Before I could fire a shot, a brown flew down and scared off the grogins."

"Why didn't you tell me about it?" John growled, rising from the table.

"She begged me not to," Charlie said. "A harpy in contact with your daughter would raise your concern and anger. It would widen the wedge between you and her. Kari came back as she left, still fond of harpies. I knew she and the golden male would meet again, but I hoped she'd have the strength to walk away. Unfortunately, she found him injured and dying. He saved her life, John. She was obligated to save his."

John returned to his seat and stared at the plate. "You know her better than me. Once he heals, do you think she'll stay with him?"

"Kari has loved him since she was eleven, and after all this time, the golden is still devoted to her. Doc saw them and said they were happy. Though she has doubts, I don't believe she will leave him. If you kill that harpy . . ." He took a deep breath. "You will destroy her. Give up this search, John."

John picked up the wineglass and gulped the remainder. "These damn nervy goldens. I've lost everyone I love to them."

"Face the truth," Charlie said, and rose from his seat. "You blame the harpies, but it is your anger for them that killed your wife and has driven your daughter into the woods. I'm going to bed." He walked to the door and glanced back. "Kari never would have left if she thought you wouldn't hurt him."

"She's not your daughter," John growled, "and I can't let it go."

"I love her like a granddaughter. And if up to me, I'd leave them alone."

John sat at the table and watched Charlie leave the room. "Damn Indian," he grumbled under his breath. "This is partly his fault. He and Dad dragged Kari through the jungle as soon as she could walk, made her wild as hell." He stood, poured another glass of wine, and wandered in the silent big house. Walking into his den, he set the glass on the desk and slumped in the chair. He glanced at a bottom drawer. It held a rarely seen picture that brought tremendous grief. He took another sip of wine and took it out. Staring at the beautiful woman in the photo, his eyes watered. "I'm so sorry."

At dawn, Charlie walked into the empty kitchen, knowing John wanted an early start. He strolled through the house and found John in the den. The large, forty-year-old man slept slumped over the desk, his hand resting on a picture of his dead wife. "Oh, John," he whispered. "Will you ever find peace?" Charlie put his hand on John's shoulder and gently shook him awake. "John, it's morning."

John stirred and sat up. "Must've drank too much last night. Is Maria here?"

"No. She goes to the funerals of those young people this morning."

"Ah, I forgot," John said, rising from the chair.

"About last night—"

"I don't want to talk about it," John said. "Look, I know I've got anger issues, and I'm used to getting my way. If we find them, I'll try and keep an open mind about the harpy, but I gotta keep looking. Hunters are flocking here, ever since the word got out about that young golden. He's no longer a myth. Plus his broken wing makes him easier to track and kill. Westend's inn is booked, and you know their type. Some are animals. God knows what they might do if they find Kari."

John walked out of the den. "So there's no way I'll end the search and sit here. I can't keep hunters off the estate, so I'm considering a reward for the safe return of my daughter. If someone stumbles across her and the harpy, he'll consider the money and stop and think. It might protect her."

"Or a reward might bring more hunters," Charlie said.

"With or without my reward, they're coming for that golden."

"What are you going to do about the swarms?" Charlie asked as they entered the kitchen.

"Been too worried to think about them, but I guess I'd better," John said, pulling a coffee out of a machine and taking a sip, "I ordered in the timber crews. In essence business is totally shut down. The next step would be to reinforce the mill with metal sheets and stock a supply of food and water there in case of a swarm strike. Why don't you stay here and organize it? I know your heart's not in this search for Kari."

"I'm also worried about her, but I want her happy. She did not tell you how she suffered on Earth."

"It was bad?" John asked.

Charlie nodded.

John rubbed the back of his neck. "Guess she suffered for nothing. She ended up with him. Every time I think of that feathered bastard crawling on my girl . . ." He bit his lip. "I'm going."

John left the house, and Charlie watched his hovercraft disappear over the first hill. "I hope he doesn't find them," he muttered. Climbing in his terrain vehicle, he drove to the mill.

10

The night calls gave way to the chirp of birds, and Shail intuitively stirred. Sniffing the air, he detected the fledgling's scent and glanced over Kari's slumbering body. At the door a growing pile of fruit lay in the threshold. Careful not to wake her, he pulled his bottom wing out. He stood, flinched from his aching ribs, and walked out of the cabin. In the clearing, he ruffled his wings and glanced toward the trail where Kari had retrieved water. Dried blood still stained his feathers and hair, and he felt sticky, stinking of the medication. He walked down the path and came upon the stream. He untied his old sash and climbed under the waterfall. For the first time in a week, he began to feel like his old self. The rib pain was an annoyance, but it no longer hampered his movement.

As the water tumbled over him, he glanced at his wounds and thought of the old man that Kari called Doc. The man's kindness had saved his life and left Shail puzzled. How many men were there who meant him no harm? After his wings and body were clean, he stepped from the waterfall. Vigorously shaking the droplets off, he reclined on a rock and pruned the individual flight feathers. With his fingers and mouth, he forced the protective oils down the quill, making the feather whole. He tied the stained sash around his hips and returned to the clearing.

Shail sniffled, and the excited fledgling sailed down from a branch, awkwardly landing. The eight-season youngster dropped to his knees and waited.

"Find a cave maker and bring me new cloth," Shail relayed. The fledgling scrambled to his feet and was airborne.

Shail peeked in the cabin and saw Kari still slept. He shuddered at the doorway before lightly stepping inside, determined to be rid of his harpy fears. Facing his death at the hands of the hunters had given him more courage, and he recalled his father's words, instilled in him when very young. "A golden is not born, he is made. Every challenge faced and survived makes one stronger." Shail had finally learned the truth of his father's words and looked up at the oppressive cabin ceiling for the last time.

He picked up a piece of fruit and plopped down on the floor near the bed. He chewed and watched her sleep, longing to touch, but refrained. It might cause fright. Patience, he thought. I must learn patience. She will come when ready.

Kari opened her eyes, and Shail handed her breakfast. "Thank you, Shail," she said. Before taking the fruit, she ran her hand through his long, wet hair. "You've been busy this morning. I'm glad you feel better."

They nibbled while their eyes were fixated on one another. After eating a few pieces, she rose and gathered his medication. "It's time for your treatment."

Shail leaped to his feet and hissed. He had washed and finally rid himself of the smell.

"Stop. I know you don't like it, but the medicine is healing you." Conveying aversion, he stood with a raised head, but endured the treatment. "I need to wash this," she said, and pulled on his stained sash.

This was all the domestication Shail could tolerate. He tugged back, shaking his hair, and retreated outside.

"Come back in here! You need to lie down, and I want to wash your sash," she said. He gave her an indignant glance and walked toward the ocean.

"I rule all harpies." He huffed and kicked a flower on the path. "Yet she treats me like a lame human pet."

Kari ran after the lanky harpy with an apparently bruised ego. She began to fathom that Shail's personality was complex. Initially, his body language displayed his devotion and fears, but she now saw his pride, which could be wounded, and a stubbornness matching hers. Her perception of him was changing. He was not a wounded jungle creature requiring her care, but a person with deep feelings and emotions.

Kari found him standing on a cliff and gazing out at the ocean. "I didn't mean to push you around." She rubbed his shoulder. "You can keep your old sash."

Shail lowered his head and nuzzled her neck, but quickly withdrew. He walked down the animal path toward the water, and she trailed along. Near the dunes, he stopped and watched several hand-size insects in search of smaller prey, gliding in and out of the stick weeds. He held up his hand and one of the purple insects lit on his finger. He brought it to Kari's face for a closer look.

She smiled. "It's beautiful."

He moved his finger, and the insect took flight. He turned his head toward his bandaged wing, his concerned eyes questioning.

"Don't worry," she said. "You'll fly again. It just takes time."

They strolled along the seashore hand in hand, taking pleasure in one another's company, bringing an end to the decade of yearning. Kari watched his tiptoed stride with concern.

Shail slightly shook his head at her. "The pain goes. I need not rest," he relayed into her fretful mind.

In late afternoon they returned to the cabin. As Kari approached the door, the fledgling soared down and settled near her feet. Startled, she jumped back. She glanced up at Shail's gleaming eyes. Like an animal, his eyes, not his lips, betrayed his mind-set. "I'm glad you think it's funny," she griped. "He surprised me."

Shail took the new sash from the fledgling's hand and his nod sent the young harpy back to the trees. Untying the old sash, he dropped it, exposing his sex organs that were sheathed under straight blond hair.

"Modesty is obviously not a problem," she said as he placed the clean sash around his hips. "Why bother to wear it?"

Shail held a corner of the sash. "This tells I am no less," he relayed.

"No less than a man?" she asked.

He nodded.

She now understood the meaning of the sash. Unlike humans who used clothing to hide the embarrassment of their nude bodies, the harpies wore a sash to symbolize equality and prove they weren't animals. Without hesitation, he confidently stepped into the cabin.

Toward evening, Kari slipped into a torn sheet fashioned as a dress and washed her dirty clothes in the sink. Shail relaxed on the bed, ate fruit, and watched her. Hanging her clothes over chairs to dry, she joined him as darkness came. He curled his body around her and extended his wing as cover. In the flimsy dress, she snuggled her back up against him and unwittingly stimulated him. He breathed heavy and shuddered. Then moved several inches away from the temptation and pitifully buried his face in a pillow. She glanced over her shoulder, realizing he had become aroused, but controlled his urges. She smiled, respecting him more. He was keeping his promise. There would be no bond unless she consented.

The days began blending together. The pair rose at dawn, ate fruit in the cabin, and went to the stream to bathe. Under the tumbling waterfall, Shail battled his sexual cravings, while she washed nearby in the nude. The gushing water flowed down her long blond hair and dripped from her breasts onto her slender frame. Never had he felt such commitment to one individual. She was his sunrise, the air he breathed, the water that quenched his thirst. She was his future. The torture, not to touch, was unbearable, and he'd retreat from her and the waterfall and sought the consoling trees.

Kari felt equally miserable. She longed to wrap her arms around his neck and kiss the tall, gorgeous male, remembering his slow, seductive kiss, but with one kiss, she could ignite an inextinguishable flame in both of them. Her fears of the unknown had created an invisible wall between her and Shail, and only she could bring the wall down, but his standoffishness and patient approach were wearing her down. Every day she loved him more.

After the waterfall, they set out for a day of exploring. Kari shed her heavy khaki pants and shirt for a short, cool dress made from sheets. Exposed to the sun, her skin became golden tan and her hair lightened, matching his. They drank stream water and returned to the cabin only for sleep. Like two wild creatures of the jungle, they wandered through the wilderness. She had never felt such happiness, following a handsome harpy through the trees. Instead of taming him, she was changing. Her human world slipped farther away with the passing of each day.

Shail's wounds healed, and he no longer needed medication. His only concern was the broken wing. As Kari talked to him, he picked up the English language, and instead of answering her subconscious with a thought, he related using her words. To understand human speech could be valuable knowledge for a ruler.

Kari, too, worked on her telepathy. Giving up her noisy talk, she started communicating with him in silence. A process of learning from one another began.

Shail no longer shied away from human objects, but studied and handled them in the cabin, eager for her explanation of their purpose. Kari, on the other hand, hungered for knowledge of his jungle. Her grandfather and Charlie had taught her the dangers, but it was Shail who showed her its beauty and mysteries. Every day she woke excited to take part in a new adventure. She was amazed that animals, terrified of men, would walk up to Shail. They had no fear of a harpy. At his beckoning, small birds lit on his wings and hand.

One day they traveled deep into the trees, and Kari stopped to rest on a log. With Shail's long stride, he was farther up the path. She heard a low seething sound and crunching leaves. She slowly rose as the head of a giant carnivorous lizard appeared, awakened by her scent. She froze, the blue reptile one leap away, and called silently to Shail.

In seconds, he emerged from the heavy brush and calmly moved to her side. The reptile's long forked tongue flicked toward them. "It's going to attack," she whispered.

"No," he relayed. "Look at her gut. She has just fed and is only curious, but her tongue senses and smells your fear, as I have. You made yourself a target." Shail extended his hand so the lizard could taste him, and then he hissed and leaped toward the reptile.

The startled lizard retreated from the smaller harpy. Fearing it had become prey, it darted into the woods.

Shail turned and held Kari's hands. "You must conquer your fears of the jungle just as I conquer mine of your human world."

She glanced up at him. "Don't become too brave, Shail. Men nearly killed you and would do it again."

"I know the difference between caution and fear," he relayed. "I keep the caution."

Kari nodded and sat back down on the log.

Shail pointed to some orange mushrooms growing on the base of a tree. "These are good. They heal pain, but only a small one should you eat."

She smiled and watched him pick a few mushrooms. He's so intelligent, so honorable and gentle, she thought, realizing she had initially admired him for his flawless looks and wild nature. If only the people knew him as I do. They and my father would not hate the harpies.

Shail stood and faced her. "Your father knows me as do others. It does not stop the hate."

Kari was surprised he had heard her thoughts. "You don't understand. The reason my father hates the harpies, and most of all, you," she said. "A golden harpy tried to take my mother. She died when my father tried to stop the kidnapping."

"I do understand and know his story that stays in your mind. It scares you and keeps us apart, but I shall tell you the harpy side of your mother's death. The golden harpy was my father, and he did not come to take your mother, just as I would never force you. Your mother died when stepping in front of the weapon to protect my father. Turner knows the truth of this, yet he lies, as do all humans. They call harpies dangerous and a threat, but it is the humans who are these things."

Shail turned away and walked up the path, and Kari detected his anger. Was Shail telling the truth? Had her mother died not fearing, but defending a golden harpy? She realized that faced with the same situation, she would shield Shail with her life. Doubts of her father clouded her mind. Why had he lied?

"Shail, wait for me," she called, and hurried to catch up with him.

He stopped and lowered his head. "Forgive me," he relayed. "This anger, I do not know. When it comes, I lack control. I did not wish you to choose between your father and me. Turner saw things through his eyes, and I through my father's. You love us and we you. I learned from other harpies how hard your father looks for you. Do not love him less because of these deaths. I ask only you open your own eyes and judge me. I would rather die than see you harmed."

Kari looked up into his profound eyes and placed her arms about his neck. No longer concerned with the consequences, she kissed him. He embraced her, electrified by the kiss. She ran her hand under his sash and massaged him, and he quickly had an erection.

Shail heaved for breath and quivered, stimulated by her fondling hand. She had caught him off guard, and soon he'd lose all willpower. "No," he relayed, shaking his head, and pushed her away. She stared at him in confusion. "You start something, Kari, that cannot be stopped. What you feel does not bind a pair. It is betrayal toward your father and guilt toward me. Such a bond brings regret. I shall give you my seed when there is only love." He started down the path alone, but stopped and glanced back. "Come, Kari. The darkness is soon."

She stumbled toward him, speechless. Her noble harpy knew her very soul, and he had humbly courted her until she knew his. There were no more doubts. They were made for one another.

Night had fallen when they reached the cabin. The fledgling dived from a limb and settled in front of Shail. The little harpy shuddered and sniffled excitedly. Shail bent down and grabbed his arms to calm him. Kari watched them silently converse, realizing it was serious. The fledgling nodded and darted off toward the ocean.

"What is it?" she asked.

"A hunter in a metal bird was here. I must leave this night. The cabin is no longer safe."

"A hovercraft?" she said. "Did the hunter see the hidden vehicle? Does he know we're here?"

"The answers are unknown, but I must go and not take the risk. For you, the choice comes sooner than wished. Come with me and be my mate. The life I offer can be short and hard, but I promise always to love you or return you to a human life. It is safe and long and may hold a man who shall please you."

"No man could ever please me," she said, putting her arms around him. "I choose you."

"I am glad." He nuzzled her. "I fear my heart could not bear your loss."

They went into the cabin, and Kari turned on a light. Glancing around, she saw nothing that the jungle and Shail couldn't provide.

"Your human clothes," he relayed. "Where we go is cold."

She slipped out of the dress and put on her pants and shirt. She started toward the door and noticed Doc's portable communicator on the table. "This is the only thing I'll bring," she said, picking it up.

Shail looked at the thin silver box. "What is it?"

"It's a com. I can talk to others who are far away."

Shail examined it. "You wish to speak to humans?"

"Not really, but it might be useful," she said. "I can ask the old doctor about your wing and when the splint should come off, or if there's trouble, as a last resort, I could call my father."

"Bring it," Shail relayed. "I distrust it, but I see the value. If I am killed for my wings, it might help you." Kari placed the com in a small cloth sack, and Shail added a few pieces of fruit. "We shall eat as we go. Before the coming of light, we must be far away."

They walked into the dark jungle. "Where are we going?" Kari asked, using her voice.

"North to the high mountains," he relayed and turned, putting his fingers to his lips. "You must lose your sound and relate in silence. It is safer."

Kari nodded and followed him on his trek north. The journey was slow, and took them through dense brush and up steep terrain. Using her hands, she traversed the rocky cliffs. "When do we rest?" she asked as she reached the top, huffing for breath.

"With first light," he answered, negotiating the rugged terrain with little effort.

"Why don't we rest now and continue in the morning? The cabin is far away."

"Not far for a hovercraft."

"You certainly learn human words quickly," she relayed, and pushed on.

When the first rays of dawn filtered through the trees, Shail stopped at a mountain stream. He leaned down and drank, waiting for Kari to catch up.

She ambled up and dropped beside him. "I'm too tired to even drink."

"Take rest. We shall stay here and sleep. With the dark, we start again."

"Won't it be easier and faster if we slept at night and traveled during the day?"

"Maybe easier, but not safer. This is the harpy way." He then went into the trees and collected bundles of the soft moss, layering them under some ferns. "Sleep here. Soon I shall seek food. The fledgling returns to the islands and tells my harpies where I go."

Kari drank some water and crawled into the comfortable nest. Shail stroked her forehead until she fell asleep.

She woke in the afternoon and found Shail gone. She stood and walked to a mountain ledge. In daylight she stared out at the breathtaking scenery of mountains and valleys. The vast ocean was still visible through the peaks and trees, but a span of many miles lay between her and the water. They had traveled a lot of territory in one night.

She stripped off her clothes, waded into the stream, and splashed the refreshing water over her. Lying back down on the soft moss nest, she saw Shail. He walked out of the trees carrying two large fruits. He smashed one open against a stone, picked up the pieces, and handed one to her.

He sighed. "It is harder to get food when you do not fly."

She giggled, thinking his frustration was endearing.

He raised his head and glared. "You find humor that I cannot fly?"

"Stop being so serious, Shail." She grinned. "Of course, I don't think your broken wing is funny, but you're awfully cute when you're perturbed."

"So my unhappiness causes this funny?"

"Come here." She pulled him close. "You're normally very self-assured. I just find you sexy when you're a little vulnerable. I do love you." She leaned forward and kissed him. He attempted to tear himself away, but she clamped her arms around his neck and held on, her nude body against him.

"Kari, this is not the place or time," he said, swallowing.

"We've waited long enough."

Shail stared into her eyes. "You give yourself to me? You wish we bond?"

She nodded.

"Once given, there is no stepping away. A harpy bond is forever. Only death shall end it."

"I understand. I want to be yours." Instinctively, she tilted her head back.

Kneeling over her, Shail clutched her exposed throat and said the words of the bond. "This female life is mine and my life, hers. As long as I breathe, I vow to protect her and our offspring." He released his hold, untied his sash, and lowered himself between her legs. He sucked her nipples and rubbed his sex organ against her until she was wet and craved him. He penetrated her and gently began copulation. He wanted the first mating to be tender with his new bride.

Kari wanted no part of his tame sex and his gentlemanly approach. She had waited too long for the gorgeous male. She wiggled under him and bit his neck, drawing blood to encourage him.

Stimulated by the bite, he lost control, the animal taking over. He lunged against her and pumped rapidly, his wings fluttering with the breeding. Sensing her climax, he released his seed and collapsed on top of her.

The deep fathom of stars cleared from her head and she listened to his panting. She stroked his lean muscles, wringing wet with the nervous sweat of a virgin stud. She pushed the blond hair from his face and kissed him. He nuzzled her and slid off to her side, encasing her in his arms. She knew they were both feeling the same thing, an exhilaration and joy beyond words. The love of her life snuggled securely against her, and if they died tomorrow, there would be no regrets of this bond.

They lay still for some time, until their breathing returned to normal. Kari rose to drink and wash in the stream, and he joined her, but thirst was not on his mind. As she knelt by the stream, he sniffed her, detecting her ripe eggs. Terribly excited, he danced around, tossing his hair, and extending and ruffling his wings.

Kari loved his flashy performance. His genes were truly part bird. Her mate was courting her in harpy fashion, taking the appearance of a spooning crane. She sniffled, copying his animal gestures of wanting and gave him consent to mount her. He dropped to his knees behind her, firmly embedded himself, and stroked rapidly to inseminate her egg. Recently depleted, he struggled with a second release. He lunged and nipped at her neck, and with each thrust, he flapped and beat his wings against the hard ground. After several minutes, he ejaculated.

Shail crawled, out of breath, into the stream and relaxed in the cool water. She joined him, kissing and nuzzling his neck. He was too drained to respond. She left the water and went back to the fruit. Under the ferns, she ate, and he climbed from the water. He ruffled his wet feathers, found a flat stone, curled up in the sun and napped.

Kari chewed on the sweet orange fruit and figured her drained mate was done. She reclined on the moss, but didn't realize that unlike a man, Shail was an animal, capable of breeding every fifteen minutes for days.

He rested briefly and returned to her. His hard erection displayed his intention. She happily obliged him, licking and caressing him. Gone was the fondling and kisses, and it was straight sex. She couldn't seem to get enough of his stunning body. She began to comprehend that as long as she consented, he would perform until he dropped. Thus was the beginning of the mating marathon, common for the newly paired.

Rather than travel, they bonded through the night. Shail paced himself, mounting her every half hour. In between, he caught quick naps to regenerate his seed and stamina. The initial pleasure was gone, and it was hard work, his goal to impregnate her, and produce his offspring.

Kari didn't mind his vigorous effort. She'd dozed through the night, awakened by his gentle nuzzle for permission. Lying on her stomach, she gave him the go-ahead by moving her legs. He penetrated her, thrust briefly, discharged his seed and withdrew before she was fully awake.

The copulation continued the following day and night. Kari understood why Shail had said it was not the time or place for the bond. Despite the threat of a looming hunter, he pressed on with the mating without food and little water. He was a fresh stud and no danger would drive him from a willing female.

By the third morning, he was totally exhausted, and Kari had her fill. With his nuzzle, she told him to go away. Almost with relief he curled up alone in the nest and slept all morning.

Kari dressed and sat by the stream, nibbling on the remaining fruit. Shail woke and stretched before joining her. After drinking, he glanced up at her, and she gave him a strange smile.

His eyes lit up. "A fledgling grows." He leaned over and kissed her.

"How do you know that?" she asked.

"I can sense you, and a harpy knows such things."

"Are you telling me your animal senses are so good, you know when I'm pregnant?"

"Not mine, but yours," he relayed. "A male would not know, but a female harpy would sense when my seed entered your egg."

"Maybe that's true, but I'm no harpy."

Shail's features filled with shock. "But you are."

Kari nervously laughed. "Shail, I'm no more harpy than my father."

Shail pushed down the lump in his throat and gently took her hands. "True, your father is no harpy, but your mother was. I thought you knew."

Kari jerked free and stood. She stared down at her lean, blond husband and noticed they did look similar. She breathed hard, realizing their behavior and nature was the same. Like him, she slept curled up, ate a vegetarian diet, loved the jungle, and hated confinement. She stumbled away and gazed out at the mountains. She now understood why she had suffered from severe depression on Earth and had never been attracted to men. Her whole life she was drawn to the harpies and had undying love for Shail. Everything began to make sense. She recalled Doc's blood transfusion that saved Shail's life. Shail had received her harpy blood. She thought of her ability to communicate with harpies. They understood her, and she them. The truth and realization sank in.

Shail lowered his head and meekly approached her.

"Why didn't anyone tell me, Shail?" she asked.

He put his arms around her. "If your mother had lived, she would have revealed the truth and told you we were marked to bond. I thought your long time among the stars and men caused your doubt of us. I now know all truths were kept from you, creating the confusion."

She wrapped her arms around him. "Oh, God, Shail, I have been so confused. I love you, but didn't understand why." They hugged for some time. Kari pulled back and stared at him, seeking long wanted answers. "So I could have chosen a man, like my mother did?"

"Yes," he said. "Because of the hunting, there are more female harpies than males. Some take honorable men as mates. But a male only bonds with female harpies, and never a woman. Female humans cannot bare our fledg-lings. Our females lack wings and look like women. They have learned to hide among them in the cities. When a male and female harpy chose to bond, it can appear the male is stealing a woman. This confusion among humans has brought much death to our flock. If a male is killed and his fe-male mate is recovered by the humans, she, too, can die of grief. The harpies are again blamed for her death."

"If people knew that the female harpies looked like women and our males were innocent, the hunting would stop."

"No, it would not end," he said. "Many hunters and some humans know the truth, but the death continues. If all knew of our female harpies, they could not hide in safety. They would become slaves or worse. The female harpies are the true guardians and protectors of our race. We males only hope to stay alive long enough to plant our seed and protect the male fledg-lings until they can survive on their own."

Kari sat down on a rock, absorbing all his information. She glanced up at him. "Tell me about my father, Shail. Did he know that his wife was a harpy?"

Shail joined her. "Turner knew her nature, and knew you were promised to me. At your birth, your mother told him. Turner rejected the harpy bond, claiming you would be raised human, and have a man mate. Your mother faced a terrible decision. Stay with Turner whom she loved or leave him and return with her daughter to the jungle, securing the golden blood-line. My father met with your mother, hoping to sway her to leave. They died at that meeting, and the harpy decision of your fate died with them. The harpies grew concerned that you were being raised human and losing all contact with your race. They started coming to you at the lake, so you would know and not fear them. I then came to see my future mate. You know how the encounter ended. Turner sent you to the stars, hoping you would find a man and I, another female. For many seasons I flew the length of this land, searching for you. For me, there could be no other. We are the last, Kari, the last goldens. I love you, but I also was bound to produce a pure golden heir for the flock."

Kari breathed deeply. "Everything makes sense now."

"This knowledge you are harpy. Does it displease you?"

"No. It's made me whole." She smiled. "I know exactly where I belong, and it's next to you."

Shail kissed her and she filled with true contentment.

It was afternoon, Kari was hungry, and Shail was famished. They strolled into the jungle in search of food. Shail scaled the tree trunks and dropped fruit into Kari's arms. They returned to the steam and nest to eat. "I guess we should be moving on," she said.

"When dark comes. To move about in light can bring attention to searching eyes. I have no regrets about bonding here, but we have lost time and distance from the cabin. We must travel quickly."

Kari nodded, confirming the complete role reversal. She initially ruled their relationship and made all the decisions, treating Shail like a child. She watched him nibble on the fruit. He had become so much more; a guardian, a mentor, a husband. His knowledge of the jungle and survival exceeded hers, and with the bond, she gave up her authority, making him the dominant mate who would sacrifice himself to protect her. He broke off a piece of fruit and gently placed it in her mouth. She happily yielded her independence to her noble male.

After eating, they curled up in the nest to sleep and wait for night. A few hours passed, and Shail jerked his head up and nervously sniffed the air. The scent confirmed his worse fears. He leaped to his feet, waking Kari and tiptoed to the cliff ledge. He sniffed at the wind that rose from below. Kari saw the fear in his eyes.

"A danger draws near. We must flee quickly and quietly." Walking to the stream, he beckoned to her. "We stay in the water on the rocks, for it leaves no trail."

She grabbed the small sack and rushed to him. "What is it?"

"The scent of men rides the wind," he said with worry.

She understood. Only hunters could terrify him. They followed the stream upward into the mountain, careful to step on solid stones, leaving no footprints. Shail stopped, stepped from the meandering stream, and walked to a high cliff. He scanned the lush valley as the light faded. The ocean horizon was orange atop green. The wind blew against his youthful, regal face, and he tossed his hair and seethed.

"You see them?" she asked, walking alongside and detecting his aversion.

He pointed to a place halfway up the valley. "There," he said. "They come to our bonding nest. We must travel fast in the dark. They know a fresh harpy nest and that we are close. They will retrieve their hovercraft."

Kari caught her breath from the rapid climb and looked hard into the trees. She finally made out tiny figures moving about in the dense foliage. "Why didn't they use their hover now?"

"Smart hunters know a harpy can see and hear a hover from far away and easily avoid it. These found our trail from the cabin and hoped to surprise us. This is how many harpies are killed. Had the wind not shifted, I would not have smelled them. I would now be their trophy. For you, the fate is unclear. Some hunters release the females, knowing you provide offspring and more game. Others are cruel to our females. Their fate is worse than death." He looked at her. "You are ready now?"

She realized Shail had only stopped to give her a brief break. "Yes. Let's go."

"We leave the water and travel this hard ridge," Shail said. "It shall be easier and faster for you. The round moons come out this night. You shall see well."

Kari followed him on to the ledge, hurrying to keep up with his long stride. They reached a summit and started their descent down the other side. A cold, harsh wind blasted them on the open ledge.

Shail turned and saw Kari's arms wrapped about her. "We leave this and go to the covered trees. It shall be warmer."

She glanced up. She was beginning to sense his mind as he sensed hers, and she felt his concern. "It's warmer, but not faster. I'm okay. Let's stay on this trail."

Shail wrapped his good wing around her. "You fear, but not for yourself. Though I cannot fly, they shall not catch us." They continued on the rocky trail, making good time, and Kari's vision adjusted to the moonlight. At steep inclines, Shail stopped and helped her ascend them. She watched him spring from ledge to ledge with the grace of a bird, and if alone, he could swiftly cover the ground.

He caught her thoughts. "You do not hinder me, but complete my life. Do not worry so, my love. The danger has past. Men fear to travel the night winds into the mountains."

Kari smiled, looking into his shimmering eyes as the strong breeze whipped at his glossy hair.

At dawn the golden pair descended into a small valley. Ahead lay the steepest and most dangerous mountains in the range. The morning light reflected off the giant black peaks that crested above all plant life. They walked on the forest floor beneath the enormous trees, thousands of years old, and Kari felt humbled in the giants' presence. These were the trees her grandfather had protected. The pair came to a pool formed between rocks, and Shail stopped. "We shall rest here," he relayed. "The hard rock left no trace of our coming and the tall tree cover shields us. It would be difficult for a hover to land."

"I'm so proud and amazed with you," she said. "The more you relate with the English words, the more you sound like a human."

He shuddered. "I am unsure if this is good or bad. I shall seek food." He vanished into the trees. Kari knelt by the pond, cupping the water in her hands and taking a drink. She coiled up, exhausted from the bonding and the foot travel, not noticing the fearless colorful birds that hopped from branch to branch over her head. Like Shail, the animals instinctively knew she was a harpy.

Shail returned with two large roots that dripped with a sticky substance. He walked passed Kari, who slept. Using a rock, he broke the brown root open and began eating the pale orange contents running with yellow syrup. Having his fill, he crawled next to her, covering her with a wing, as she continued to doze. He rested quietly, but remained awake. His enemies were a safe distance away, but he couldn't afford to sleep. During the daylight hours, the hunters would search hard for him, especially if they had knowledge of his broken wing. Despite his comforting words to Kari, he remained alert and on edge. The truth of the hunt would only worry and terrify her. This distress he had faced all his life.

After several hours, Shail nuzzled her awake. "We go now and put this valley behind us. We must reach the next mountain ridge. There are few trees and we must cross it under the cover of darkness." She sluggishly got up and dragged her limbs forward. "Eat this root," he relayed. "It shall give you strength."

Kari munched on the sweet orange pulp, licking her sticky fingers and tagging along behind Shail. He swiftly moved through the valley, hoping to reach the mountain base and scale the barren ridges at night. After an hour, Kari did feel a renewed stamina. She effortlessly glided around the trees, following her husband.

They came upon a large herd of zels. The deer-size plant eaters momentarily watched the two harpies, but went back to grazing. Kari nearly bumped into Shail when he froze. He raised his head and tilted it to one side. She saw the zels do the same. Every head was lifted toward the sky, eyes alert, ears rapidly twitching. "Come quickly," he said, and the zels scattered, seeking the tree cover. "A hover comes. We hide among the animals and lie on the ground as they do." Shail leaped through the underbrush, and Kari raced after him. Reaching two does and their fawns, he stopped and slowly extended his hand so they could smell him. He curled up alongside the zels and motioned Kari in.

She lay under Shail's wing and watched the shivering zels, who seemed to seek the male harpy's body for protection. She heard the approaching hovercraft. It moved directly overhead and stopped, obviously detecting the heat from the large herd.

Shail saw the fear in the largest zel's eyes, probably contemplating fleeing with her young. He reached over, making a faint sizzling sound, and gently petted her rust-colored head, encouraging her to stay. If the zels left, he and his mate would be exposed. Through Shail's feathers, Kari glanced up at the stationary hover. Part of the herd unnerved, broke and ran. The hover moved off, following them up the valley.

"These are good hunters," he relayed. "They guess the direction we go."

"Yes, they're good. That was my father's hovercraft."

"It proves his love of you," he said, standing.

"Or hate for you." She rose with the zels, who went back to grazing. "How did you know to hide by the animals to avoid the heat-seeking device?"

"I do not know these words."

"Your body gives off heat, and a heat-seeking device can see you despite the trees. This machine is mounted in all hunting hovers."

"I now understand this false sight," he relayed. "We learned the hover-crafts see all, but animal bodies confuse these hovers. A fledgling cannot out-fly the hovercrafts so they are taught to seek the cover of animals."

"Harpies learn quickly," she said.

"We all learn or die. We shall stay near the animals."

Like a collie herding sheep, Shail coaxed the zel herd in the direction he wished to travel. Reaching the base of the mountain, they left the zels with approach of night. The first half of the mountain was an easy upward walk, but the higher they went, the more difficult the climb. Kari stayed close to Shail, knowing his night vision was like a cat's. He came to a halt and stared off toward the valleys. Kari came alongside, happy to catch her breath. "He still searches for you," he relayed.

Kari sensed the pity in his silent voice. Off in the distance she saw the hover lights investigating the valleys. "Why can't he leave me alone? Doesn't he understand I want to be with you?"

"He is a father." He turned away and traversed a rocky cliff.

Kari sighed, watching the distant lights disappear over a crest before she moved on.

As Shail climbed in the dark, he was regretting his decision to send the fledgling to the safe islands. Had he known Turner chased them, and the man would be so persistent, he would have sent the fledgling for Aron. The harpies would have flown him and his mate out of the man's reach, but Shail believed the hover belonged to a typical hunter, one he could easily outwit. The forests were now absent of harpies because all were needed for the evacuation to the islands. He and his mate were on their own. His only consoling thought was that if caught by Turner, he would die, but Kari would be safe.

Shail glanced over his shoulder and saw the hover light scaling an outly-ing crest. Turner faced the strong mountain winds at night. No hunter would risk this danger. The powerful gusts could slam a craft into the dark mountainsides. He knows harpies and that we travel at night in the open, he thought, realizing the sanctuary of the wind, rock, and darkness was lost against Turner. Shail's eyes frequently shifted to the lights, tracing their movement, and hoping they did not come. With no shelter, he undoubtedly would be picked off by a weapon. Though Shail feared Turner, he respected Kari's father and his courage. He endangers his life for his daughter, but does he know I, too, would die for her?

Shail heard small pebbles falling. He sprang off the crest and landed beside Kari, who scrambled to her feet. "Are you hurt?" he asked, helping her up.

"I tripped. I'm fine."

"You become weak with this pursuit. We stop and rest."

She glanced at the barren stone and small bushes. "We can't stop here. You've seen the lights. My father is stubborn. He'll search all night."

"Yes, he faces great hazards for you," he said, "and you travel these dangerous cliffs for me. Maybe it is best I build a fire and let him find you. I could release you from our bond, and you would be safe in the human world. Our fledgling is uncertain."

Kari sat down on a rock, lowering her head. "I slow your escape. If I returned, Dad would stop the hunt and we'd all be safe. But I don't want to leave you."

Shail reached down and lifted her chin. "I fear for you and you for me, but Kari, with or without you, this is my life. I shall always know the hunt."

Kari stood and hugged him. "Please don't make me go."

Shail held her and stared up at the stars. "Life is a journey and we know not where it leads. We shall travel the journey together and honor our bond. The flight may be short, but loved. Let us leave now."

They traveled upward and as Kari climbed, she dwelled on Shail's words. He was simplistic yet an intellectual. She believed he ruled the harpies because of his courage, but slowly she saw the wisdom in her young mate.

Scaling the pinnacle crest, they descended on the northern side. Again the weather was hostile and cold. Kari had slept for only three hours in two days, and the weariness was taking its toll. Concerned for Shail's welfare, she fought the fatigue and staggered ahead. Stepping on the moist rocks, she slipped and fell to her knees. Shail was beside her in an instant.

"No more," he growled. "You shall rest."

"It's too dangerous here," she shouted over the howling wind. Her body and her mind were exhausted, making the telepathy impossible.

"The danger lies in traveling these cliffs when weak," he relayed. "Stay here. You understand?" he mocked, using words she had once used on him. He leaned over and nuzzled her cheek. "I shall find a safe place for us."

He leaped off the cliff as if his broken wing functioned, bounding from one rocky shelf to another until he was out of sight. Although he was grounded, his speed and grace outmatched any human. Kari sat on a smooth stone, clutching her arms, and waited for Shail. She shook her long hair over her arms, hoping to add warmth, but the relentless wind blew it up and away. She was not only cold and tired, but also hungry. The sticky root was her only food since leaving the bonding nest. She shivered and felt faint. She wanted to go on, but was relieved when Shail stopped. Her muscles ached from the rugged climb and though cold, her skin felt hot.

Within a half hour, he returned. "I found a small cave."

Kari stood up, but swayed with dizziness. Shail caught her and lifted her into his arms. He placed his cheek against hers. "You are not well. I should have sensed this."

"You're not at fault," she said. "It's my father's. He chases us." She wrapped her arms around his neck, and Shail carried her down the mountain. "Didn't our first encounter begin like this?" She weakly smiled.

"Yes, but you were smaller and lighter back then."

Kari could have sworn she saw his slight smile.

Shail held his precious bundle and leaped down the crest with a speed close to flight. He reached the large formation of boulders jetting out from the mountainside. Bending down, he entered the narrow crevice, barely a cave. Meager stream water trickled down the rocks on one side. He laid Kari down on the stone floor. "I shall find bedding," he relayed and swiftly disappeared.

Kari huddled and shivered on the cold stone. She shut her eyes and listened to the whistling night wind blasting the entrance and was grateful to be out of it. She woke to Shail pushing the tangle of moss over and under her. He stroked her forehead, and she detected his anxiety.

"I'll be all right," she whispered.

He shuddered and left the cave. More comfortable, she fell asleep.

She opened her eyes when Shail lifted her head off the bedding. "Eat this," he relayed. "It shall fight the sickness."

She ate a few pieces he placed in her mouth and she recognized the flavor. It came from a bright purple fruit that grew on the forest floor. "This doesn't grow in the mountains. You traveled too far."

"Eat, then rest," he relayed. After she ate her fill, he crawled next to her, wrapping his arms, legs, and wing around her shaky body.

"Did you eat, Shail?" she asked.

"Do not worry about me. Sleep."

She knew he hadn't. On the comfortable moss, with his body warmth and the food, she couldn't stay awake and quickly dozed.

Shail nervously watched her, refraining from sleep and food. If he ate the meager fruit, he'd have to remove his warm wing from her to fetch more. He preferred hunger than have her shiver with cold. Worry of Turner and her illness kept him on guard.

At dawn Shail heard the faint sound of the searching hovercraft. He fretted, wondering if the heat device could see through thick rock. The sound grew louder with the hover's approach. He nervously nuzzled his sleeping female and waited. The hover flew past the cave entrance and descended into the valley. He closed his eyes and loosened his hold on Kari, knowing their heat was unseen. She never stirred.

Although it had been three days and nights since he slept, he was determined to stay alert, listening and smelling the wind for danger. In the afternoon, billowing clouds rolled in, covering the mountain in a dense fog and relieved Shail's anxiety. Turner would be foolish to fly in such weather.

Shail rose briefly and filled his mouth with water from the tiny trickle, but did not swallow. He leaned down, kissing Kari. "Drink," he relayed, releasing the water between her lips. She swallowed, but remained semiconscious.

He stood to gather more, when she called out, "Shail! Don't leave me."

He dropped beside her and caressed her forehead, his eyes welling up with tears. "No, my love, I would never leave you," he relayed. She was delirious with raging fever, her breathing rasping and uneven. She was growing worse. He gave her more water, forced the purple fruit between her lips, and then coiled around her. Never had he felt so helpless, so worried. With the silence of one heartbeat, his whole world could slip away.

The second night in the cave, Shail became frantic, fearing her death. He raced through the trees and gathered sticks and moss. He piled them in front of the cave. With the spark of two stones, he lit the dried moss, and created a small bonfire. He stared out across the dark landscape, hoping Turner would see his fire, but the black and vacant mountains held no hover lights. He lowered his head and went back to Kari. For the first time, he wanted a man to find him and was willing to sacrifice his life to save hers. Wrapping his frame around her, he closed his eyes and waited for the hunter.

In the middle of the night Shail woke. The limits of a living, breathing creature had forced sleep. He nuzzled Kari's neck and felt her warm sweat and cool skin. Her fever had broken, and she slept quietly without a shiver. He glanced out the cave and saw the smoldering ashes. Turner had not come. He shut his eyes again and drifted into deep sleep, allowing his drained body to recover.

In the morning Shail saw that the mountain hid under a dense mist. He stretched and Kari stirred. "I go for more food," he told her.

"But it's daylight, and there are no trees. My father may see you."

"I believe he has gone, and with the mist, I go unseen." He rose and stepped out of the cave. He sniffed the air and quickly kicked the charred wood off the cliff, hiding the evidence of his fire signal. Kari would be furious, knowing what he had done. He listened below to the birds' melody, absent of alarm squawks. With that reassurance, he leaped down the boulders until he reached the cover of trees.

He walked through the forest and came to a fruit-bearing tree with a stout vine. He climbed up and dropped the fruit to the ground. Using his sash as a makeshift bag, he gathered the fruit and headed back up the mountain. He noticed a ground vine with tiny pink flowers and dug to the roots, tossing the sticky food also in the sash.

Shail reached the end of the tree line and skittishly looked, listened and sniffed like wary deer before scampering across the barren ground. He entered the cave and saw Kari drinking water from the small flow between the rocks.

She smiled at his nude body. "I love your seductive dress for grocery shopping."

Shail spilled the food on the cave floor and retied his sash around his hips. "You feel better. The color returns along with your humor." They sat on the moss and ate heartily.

"So, we leave tonight?" Kari asked. "I feel great."

"No, we wait. You were very ill. The cave is safe."

"Since we have the time, maybe we can finish the bonding," she said, leaning over and kissing him, while her hand stroked his penis under the sash. "Expect sex when you enter a cave nude."

Shail immediately was breathless. "Kari," he tried to object, but she shoved him back, massaging him. He gave in and reclined. Taking the male's role, she straddled him and nipped his neck. Once penetrated, she rocked him back and forth until he shivered with excitement. This was an uncommon breeding position for harpies, but Shail didn't complain. His gutsy little mate was also uncommon for a female harpy. She finished with him and slid off, returning to eating the fruit.

"Two nights of sleep and rest . . ." He panted and shook his head. "You recover fast."

Kari took a bite of fruit and raised one eyebrow. He rolled over and slept.

Stuck in the cave, Kari was bored, and she felt good. She let Shail sleep for a few hours, but it was hard to keep her hands off him. He's just so darn pretty, she thought, staring at his long lashes, long muscled frame, and long hair. He had explained to her that male harpies would discharge their seed only when breeding with a female, and she decided to put the claim to a test. She fondled him awake and worked him into a frenzied state, but teased him by pushing him away when he attempted to mount her. He puffed, sweated, squirmed, and fought his urge to eject his sperm. He stared at her, clearly confused.

Agitated, he finally hissed, pushed her on the moss, and had his way with her. He hastily pumped and climaxed. He collapsed on the moss and breathed hard. "Did you enjoy tormenting me?"

"I did." She grinned. "I want to learn everything about you, especially your sex capability."

He nodded and heaved a sigh. "My life, I fear, shall never grow dull with you."

Since Kari had apparently recovered from her bout with illness, she encouraged Shail to bond. Only a male harpy gasping his last breath would refuse a willing partner, and Shail mated with her through the day and night.

The following morning Shail slept with his limbs stretched out across the nest, too wiped out to curl up. Kari tenderly nipped his neck and caressed his exposed body, persuading him to rise. He lifted his head, his gaze dispirited. "Female, you have taken all my strength and made me weak."

"Maybe for a change I like you weak."

He sat up. "I believe you like the effort that causes my weakness."

She smiled. "That sarcasm sounds a little bit like humor."

"I learn many things from you, not all good," he relayed, standing. He walked to the cave opening and stared. "My flock worries for me. It is time we move on."

"Where are we going, anyway?" Kari rose and came alongside him.

He pointed to a huge black mountain in the distance. "There. It is the sacred mountain of our people. When we are safely within, we shall bond until you want me no more."

She flipped her hair back and walked to the stream. "More ironic humor?"

He gave her a puzzled look. "I fail to see."

"The day will never come when I don't want you." She leaned over and sipped the water.

"I do see the humor, since you lack to tire of me. I shall be the weakest of all males and happy to be so."

Shail cautiously stepped from the cave, sniffing the wind and listening, but all appeared calm and secure. He glanced back inside. "Though light has come and the way lacks cover, the shelter of trees is near. Do you feel well for travel?"

"I feel good. Your bonding cured me."

"The purple fruit made you well, not my seed."

"I know. I was just teasing you."

"Untrue words, more humor," he drearily said. "I fear I must grow used to the human fun."

"It won't hurt you." Kari walked over and passionately kissed him while rubbing him hard.

Shail became breathless, sliding his hands over her delicate, curvy body and small full breasts, while her titillating hands coaxed his sex organ to perform and give up the remaining seed. "Kari, we must go." He gently pushed her away and gained composure. "If not needed, I would mount you until this cave overflowed with our fledglings."

"All right," she sighed. She slipped into her clothes and tossed his sash to him, it landing on his head. She grabbed the cloth bag and headed for the cave door. "Let's go. I'll be glad to get to your sacred mountain."

Shail tied the sash and grumbled. "I am glad I have only one mate. A second would kill me."

"Good one, Shail, good one," she said, and they left the cave.

Shail took her hand and they swiftly descended the windswept rock. Arriving under the trees, they slowed their pace. Shail's playful and teasing banter vanished, and he became serious and alert, assuming the role of a hunted animal. Several yards ahead of Kari, he quietly tiptoed through the brush, smelled the air, and constantly shifted his eyes in search of movement and danger. He had never been confined to foot travel, making him more cautious, and since pairing with Kari, he had changed. He was no longer a roaming single male who could afford recklessness, but had become a husband and possible father. Her life depended on his instincts and wit.

His broken wing also lay heavy on his mind. If danger came, he lost the option of grabbing his mate and flying away. Now his only choice was to outrun, hide, or fight the threat.

Breaking the harpy caution of traveling at night, Shail and Kari journeyed throughout the day to make up for lost time. They descended into a valley abundant with food. Shail stopped at a stream and knelt to drink. Kari came lumbering out of the trees and plopped down beside him. He leaned over, putting his nose against her cheek. He immediately sensed her raised temperature and weariness. He jerked back. "Your illness returns. This is my fault. I should have fought my urge to bond. I should have made you rest."

"Take it easy, Shail," she relayed. "I'm just a little tired and hot. I'm not sick."

He bounded to his feet and scanned the tree canopy for the lavender fruit that fought illness. "Remain here and sleep. I shall seek the purple food. When I return, I shall decide if we stay or go." He dashed into the trees and was gone.

Kari did feel warm, and was eager to bathe. She took off her heavy clothes and stepped into the stream, splashing water on her face and body. The cool water revived her, and she was determined to move on regardless of Shail's decision.

Behind her, she heard the snap of twigs and froze, knowing it wasn't Shail. As a wild harpy, he never made careless sounds when moving through the jungle. She glanced around, expecting to stare down a large reptile, but the threat was worse. A brawny middle-aged man stood in the ferns, and grinned, holding his laser rifle. Terrified, she watched him and slowly backed out of the stream, hoping he wouldn't pursue her. He took a step toward her, and she hissed.

"Easy, little doll," he said, slowly raising the weapon to take aim. "Don't make me stun you."

Kari leaped into the brush and ran from the harpy hunter.

"She's comin' your way," she heard him yell. She hasily looked around as two strong arms grabbed her from behind and lifted her off the ground.

"Got her, Nick," the man called as she struggled to be free. "Man, she's a lil' beauty and full of fight."

Nick appeared after running through the stream, and a younger third man emerged from the trees. The third man stared at Kari as she fought the hold of his hunting buddy. "I'll be goddamned, Nick," he said. "She's a blonde."

"Yeah, a scrappy, little golden," Nick said, "and she's typical of the aggressive breed. Look at her hissing and putting up a fight. Hold her still, Harry, so I can test her."

"She's harpy, Nick. Light as a feather," Harry said, lifting her from the ground.

"Let's be sure," Nick said, pulling a small monitor out of his pocket. "She might be that lost Turner girl. Sure as hell don't want that son-of-a-bitch on my ass for fucking his little girl." He put a strand of the female's blond hair in the monitor and grinned. "Harpy DNA. Knew Turner's estate was full of 'em." He put his monitor away and reached between Kari's legs, driving two fingers into her. He pulled them out and examined them.

"Well?" asked the third man.

"Little bitch's got a buck, Josh," said Nick, the older and more experienced of the three. "She's recently been fucked and is loaded with sperm."

"Shit. Think it might be that golden buck with the broke wing?" Harry said as Kari frantically tossed in his arms.

Kari was so scared her harpy instincts took over. She couldn't scream or explain that she was Turner's daughter. The only thing she could do was fight the grip of the crude man and think about Shail, who would soon return.

"Good chance her buck is blond," Nick said. "According to old records, goldens usually pair with other goldens. Be a hell of a hunting day if we bagged two." He glanced around at the trees. "Let's hang her and bait him over there." He motioned to a tree limb. "I'll give her a light stun so she can't warn him. A buck doesn't stray far when he's getting laid." He produced rope from his gear. Josh forced her wrists together, while Harry held her, and Nick tied her wrists tightly together. She squirmed to bite their hands.

"This wiggling bitch has made me horny," Harry said. "Let's throw her down and use her, Nick. It might be hours before the buck shows up."

"I'm for that," said Josh, massaging her breasts.

"Forget it. I ain't losin' a golden male so you young assholes can get off," Nick said. "That male can smell human sperm a mile away off. He might not come, knowing his female's done for." At the tree, they tossed the end of the rope over a limb and hoisted Kari a few feet off the ground.

Using her silent telepathy, Kari called to her mate. "Stay away, Shail! It's a trap! Do not come for me. Please hear me and don't come." Instead of thrashing wildly on the rope, she hung quietly and lowered her head.

"Shit, she's already played out and going into shock," Nick said, walking to Kari and petting her head. "Come on, little doll. Don't give up so soon."

Harry moved behind her. "She's done. She'll be dead in a few hours. That buck ain't risking his life for a corpse." He undid his pants. "I caught her. I'm sticking her while she's warm."

Nick jerked her head up by the hair and looked into her dazed eyes. "Can't believe she went down so fast. All right, but I'm first. You boys, can wait. After we're done, we'll toss her body by the stream. The buck might come back to sniff her, and we'll nail him." He put his gun down and stripped off his gear. He jammed a finger into the limp female harpy, who shuddered and breathed hard. "You like that, doll? Wait till you feel what's comin'."

Josh and Harry also dropped their gear and weapons. They unfastened their pants in anticipation, fondling the female while waiting their turn.

As Nick prepared to invade and thrust against the hanging harpy, her knee rammed his testicles with deadly aim, dropping him to the ground. "Fucking bitch," he cursed, holding himself. Harry and Josh chuckled as Kari came alive and kicked at any male in reach.

"After I beat the crap out of her, you guys are next," he grumbled. He looked at Kari and the men, and his eyes widened with shock. "Fuck!"

From behind, Kari heard a heavy thud, and Josh fell unconscious at her feet. "Get back!" she heard Harry scream and a second thud. He, too, lay nearby with blood flowing down his face. She saw the terror on Nick's face as he scrambled backward toward his gear. She then saw Shail. He held a stout wood branch, one end dripping with blood while he walked, almost casually, toward the remaining large hunter, who was three times his girth. With every step, Shail seethed and shook with rage.

Nick crawled across the ground, stalked by Kari's golden mate. The hunter lunged, wildly grasping for his weapon, and Shail attacked, unmercifully beating the man with the limb until Nick's face was a bloody pulp. Her slender mate stood over the huge, immobile body and hissed, a spray of the man's blood on his chest. He glanced up at her, slightly out of breath, and it took a second to snap out of his assault mode. He dropped the tree limb and rushed to her.

"Are you hurt?" Shail asked, releasing the rope and untying her wrists. He looked up and down for marks on her body. She didn't answer, but stood and shuddered with fright. He wrapped his arms around her. "I am here now. I am here. You are safe." She broke down and cried. Shail swept her up in his arms. He glanced at the three fallen hunters, who still breathed. He shook his head, and walked to the stream, carrying his female. Leaning over, he grabbed the cloth bag and her clothing and walked up the valley, cradling Kari.

Hours slipped by and neither spoke as Shail carried her. Kari shut her eyes and clung to his neck, trying to forget the experience. She had learned what it was like to be a wild harpy. Recalling the man's groping fingers, she shivered, and Shail nuzzled her cheek. He left the valley and started the climb up the next ridge. She knew he had to be weary. "Put me down, Shail. I can walk," she said, but he ignored her, as though punishing himself.

The terrain became very steep, and Kari wiggled in his arms, asking him to release her. "Put me down," she ordered. Only when she slapped his face did he come out of his trance and listen to her. He set her down on a slope and she now saw his large, teary eyes. The hunter encounter had affected him worse than it had her. He dropped to his knees, hugging and resting his head against her legs.

"Forgive me," he relayed. "Forgive me. I failed to protect you." His once soft voice was shaky.

"You didn't fail me. You protected me," she said, kneeling to be eye level with him.

A single tear ran down his cheek. "I curse this harpy life," he relayed and sniffled. "It holds no peace and nearly destroyed what I love."

"Oh, Shail," she said, hugging him. "I wouldn't trade this life with you for anything. I'm all right. I'm a tough golden like you." She held and comforted him as he tried to get it together. After some time, she rose. "Come now, Shail. Let's find this mountain and your flock." He nodded and stood. They continued the journey.

They walked for hours uphill. Shail remained quiet as he forged ahead.

Halfway up the mountain, he stopped. "What happened to you, Kari, I promise it shall never happen again. Soon I shall rid our land of these men."

"Let's put it behind us and not think of it again."

They traveled over the next ridge in the darkness, and the following morning Shail and Kari ascended into another valley. He stopped at one of the numerous streams that ran through the tropical jungle. "We rest here."

Kari sat down and drank while she soaked her feet in the flowing cool water. Shail stood nearby, on guard and still paranoid.

"Come, sit by me," she said, but he stared off in one direction. "What is it?"

"A harpy," he answered. Soon a brown-winged harpy sailed low through the trees and landed in front of them. The male dropped to one knee and bowed his head.

With Shail's slight nod, the male humbly rose. "What say you?" Shail asked.

"Aron worries for you," the harpy relayed. "Learning Turner followed your trail, he sent his flock out to search for you. A distraction ended Turner's hunt, but the number of hunters grows in the trees. They know of your broken yellow wing."

Shail glanced at Kari. "We came upon such hunters. Are all females and young on the islands and safe?"

The harpy nodded.

"Tell Aron to end the search. I am found. In two lights, I reach the mountain, and I wish a gathering of all western males. My mate was attacked, and the war begins."

The harpy backed away, head bowed and took flight.

Kari stood. "War! What war?"

"This is not the concern of a female harpy, so do not ask."

"Anything that concerns you, concerns me, especially if you're going to war against men over me."

"The attack on you destroyed my last tolerance. It is time to take revenge for all our raped females, slaughtered fledglings, and my males, who are hung from trees. I shall talk of this no more. The war involves only the males."

She pulled on his arm. "You're acting like a chauvinistic, obstinate man."

He raised his head and arched his wings. "I know not those words, but I think I am glad!" he barked back. "I am the male and rule this bond. It is the harpy way."

"Screw your harpy way! No one tells me what to do or say."

No longer a minor disagreement, it was an angry fight with his little female. He deflated and lowered his wings. "Please, Kari, understand. My flock is dying, and many hunters now know of our females. The time for meekness and fleeing is over. We must face the enemy."

"You said you'd rid the land of men, but I didn't take you seriously. Shail, the men have weapons. They'll slaughter the harpies."

"They slaughter us now, one by one." He touched her cheek. "You worry I may be lost, but long life is unknown to a golden male. I do not wish my son to share this fate. We talk of this no more." He turned and walked toward the jungle.

Kari chased after him, begging him to tell her about the war, but he refused. He wouldn't divulge the when, where, or how of the coming conflict against man.

They traveled up a high ridge as the last rays of light disappeared into the horizon. The temperature slowly dropped on their northern trek. Shail came to some jagged rocks. "We sleep here," he said, motioning to a slight ledge.

Kari looked at the skimpy plant life and sweeping open rocks. "You want to stay here and sleep at night?"

"Yes, you are tired, and it shall be cold. The harpies watch over us," he relayed. "There is less worry now. The next fall of darkness we enter the sacred mountain."

Kari pulled some fruit out of the sack that they had brought from the valley. They sat on a ledge, eating dinner and watching the orange and red sunset. Afterward, they crawled under the ledge to escape the nippy wind. She rested on his soft extended bottom wing, clutched in his arms as he lay on his side. The partially cast top wing was used for cover.

At dawn they rose and were greeted by a large pile of assorted fruit.

"Your harpies brought the food?" Kari asked, taking a piece as Shail stared across the landscape.

"I knew Aron would send a provider and protector," he answered.

"Who is Aron?"

"You know him," Shail relayed. "He came to you when the grogins came on the road."

"I also met him at the lake near Dad's house. He told me you needed me. I didn't understand until I found you with hunters."

Shail whirled around and faced her. "He sent you?" he growled. "He endangered my future mate and sent her to face four hunters?"

"Shail, don't get your feathers all ruffled," she said. "He didn't send me. He just warned me, and it was luck I found you. And I was in no danger. No one knew I was a harpy, including me. You were so hurt that only a doctor could have saved your life. Maybe Aron knew."

Shail plopped down on the ledge. "Maybe he did, but the island hunters saw your devotion to a male harpy. An experienced hunter might have guessed your nature."

"Well they didn't guess." She sat down on the ledge beside him. "Besides, those Westend boys are scared to death of my father. They wouldn't dare harm a hair on my head. So, tell me about Aron. He's a leader like you?"

"He is a leader of a western flock, but not like I," Shail said. "He rules many. I rule all."

"You two are close? He seemed upset at the lake."

"We are of different blood, but he is like an older brother. I seek his words and wisdom often. When my father was killed, Aron's father took me to the islands and raised me." Shail stood up. "Let us now go."

"I suppose you're in a hurry to see him, so you can talk about your war."

Shail shook his head and started the descent down the ridge.

By midmorning they entered the trees again, but they were hardwoods, holding little food. Even in this last valley, the weather was cold. Kari had wished many times she had brought her bloodstained jacket, but they had fled in a hurry. On the forest floor, they stopped at a crystal-clear pond. Shail knelt and sucked up the icy water between his lips, but Kari still drank like a human, cupping the water with her hands and bringing it to her mouth. Shail lifted his head and sniffed. Shaking the droplets from his locks, he stood and stared toward the jungle.

Kari tried to mimic him and sensed the presence of another harpy. A brown harpy soon landed near Shail and handed him a sash bag full of food. Shail and the harpy stared at one another, but Kari did not hear their silent talk. She realized they had purposely excluded her and must be discussing the war. After the brown left, Shail and Kari continued their journey through the valley. They approached the base of the enormous sacred mountain.

Shail stared up at the steep black crest. "The light goes soon. We can travel in the dark and end this journey or sleep here and now."

Kari gazed up at the looming and ominous mountain, her arms wrapped around herself. She preferred to crawl between Shail's warm wings but wanted to end the quest. "Let's keep going."

They started the upward climb, the light fading behind them. Kari had noticed the cold weather rarely affected Shail, but he wrapped his good wing around himself in an attempt to stay warm.

After a few hours, the same harpy flew down, landing in their path. He bowed and handed Shail a large woven cloth of the sash material. The harpy flew off, and Shail turned, placing the cloth on Kari's shoulders. "This shall help."

Kari instantly felt the warmth. They moved on in the darkness, Kari close behind Shail. His night vision was superior to hers, but she noticed since wandering the jungle with him that her instincts of hearing, sight, and smell had improved.

"You have the same senses as I," he told her, "just unused. In time you shall be like me."

They reached a high ridge, and wind fiercely blew. Shail sniffled toward the plastic cast holding his broken wing. Kari detected his frustration, wishing he could remove the cast and spread the latter half and wingtip to ward off chilliness. Many times she had explained that to remove the cast too soon would forever ground him.

Kari saw all plant life had vanished except for small patches of silver moss growing between the rocks. The sacred mountain of the harpies perplexed her. Why would Shail and the harpies treasure an inhospitable place, void of warmth, trees, and food? She realized its safety from hunters; the hurricane gusts would easily slam a large hovercraft into the jagged mountainside. She thought about their little bonding cave, wishing she were there. What drew her mate to this forbidding peak?

The climb became straight up. Shail could no longer gracefully leap from ledge to ledge using his feet that bent and grasped like hands. Scaling the sheer rock, he used his hands and flapped his wings for balance. Reaching an open ledge, he stopped and pulled her up by her arms. "I did not wish my harpies to think me weak, but it has become too risky for you." He turned and sniffled into the wind. "I call them."

After several minutes, three male harpies appeared out of the darkness. They frantically flapped their wings, fighting the blustery weather to set down. A brown-winged male a few inches taller than Shail approached. Kari recognized the handsome harpy as Aron. Shail and Aron embraced as the other two bowed. She watched Shail and Aron nuzzle and lick one another on the neck. Though in some human cultures, men kissed in greeting, she was surprised by her mate's open display of affection to a male.

Aron pulled his face out of the golden locks and held Shail by the shoulders. "When shall your recklessness end?" Aron ranted. "You sent the cabin fledgling away when he should have brought your flock. You allowed the hunt with the lack of flight, risking your mate and your wings, and faced the peril of this mountain, rather than call for me; all for pride. I understand the golden way to prove courage, but think of your flock. We need you."

"Aron, I am cold and hungry, as is my mate. I am too tired to challenge your disrespectful words." Shail glanced at Kari. "He is displeased."

Kari smiled. Aron did treat Shail like a troublesome kid brother.

Aron walked to Kari and bowed his head. "May I have the honor of carrying you?"

"You saved me from the grogins. It's my honor," she relayed. Aron swept her up into his arms and leaped into the draft. Two harpies took Shail. They flew higher up the mountain and finally landed on a sheer cliff, setting Shail and Kari down. The two males disappeared inside the sliver of a crevice. Aron, Kari, and Shail followed. Kari held Aron and Shail's hands into the pitch-black cave, blindly walking between the males who saw in darkness. After some time, she saw a distant glow, revealing the shadowy walls of the narrow passage. The deeper they traveled, the brighter the light.

Kari was finally led into an enormous space with high ceilings. Small stone pits burned with fire, and surrounding each pit were hundreds of male harpies. When Shail entered, they fell to their knees and lowered their heads. She was in awe of the vast place and numerous harpies. She stared at the walls and ceiling, and became breathless, recognizing the place. Instead of black mountain stone, there were rivets and metal beams. The sacred mountain's giant cave was an ancient spaceship.

11

After several discouraging weeks, John Turner returned home, fearing he had lost Kari forever. His resources were limited, having only three other hovercrafts and two freighters to aid in the search. In the hope of finding the old blue vehicle, he and his crew of men had flown over the nearest logging roads and woods, but the job was enormous. His property consisted of thousands of roads, trails, and paths capable of bearing a small vehicle. Old Doc White had obviously saved the golden's life. Kari would have come home if it died.

John went to Doc's cottage several evenings, pleading with the man to reveal Kari's whereabouts. At first Doc stubbornly refused, convinced that Kari and the harpy loved one another and belonged together, and John should give up the hunt. Doc finally took pity on John, telling him he honestly didn't know where they were.

The longer time passed, the more John's hate grew, regretting not killing the golden male. John's harpy wife had told him after their daughter's birth that Kari was destined to bond with a five-year-old golden fledgling in the north. With his wealth and power, John thought he could change destiny and keep his daughter and the harpy apart. He sent Kari to Earth, figuring she would forget the harpy, and hunters would solve the problem of the arrogant teenage male, but his plans failed. She came back still loving the harpy, and the golden beat the odds, surviving the ten years and remaining faithful to their fledgling bond.

John couldn't understand Kari. She was half human and a smart girl. Couldn't she remove the blinders and see her future? There was no future with a male harpy. The harpies were a doomed species, teetering on extinction, and the golden male was the most hunted of all. When he died, she could be in grave danger; if he survived, what kind of life could they lead? They would have to run and hide constantly in fear, and her fledgling sons would face the same miserable existence. John thought about the sorrow she'd feel if her babies were butchered.

If she married a man, she'd live happily and securely with her daughters among humans. Can't she see all this? he thought, making his way into the house.

Like Doc, Charlie had argued with him about the pursuit and sent John into numerous rages. "Too much time has passed," Charlie had said. "The harpy has recovered from his wounds, and they are a bonded pair. They cannot be separated. If you kill her mate, it will destroy Kari."

"There're drugs that will make her forget him," he had told the meddling old Indian. "She may be angry with me, but at least she'll be alive."

Charlie climbed out of John's hover and trailed him to the house. He had finished the construction of the beetle-proof building at the mill and rejoined John in the hunt.

They walked silently to the house. Maria opened the door, her face worried. Charlie shook his head and walked past her. She put her hand over her mouth, fighting back her daily tears, common tears that flowed when a loved one was lost to the unknown. She went to the kitchen to serve John and Charlie a late dinner.

The communicator buzzed in the den, and John walked in and answered it. An unfamiliar young man appeared on the screen. "Hi. I'm trying to reach Kari Turner."

"She's not here," said John. "I'm her father. Who the devil are you?"

"Hello, Mr. Turner. My name is Ted, and I'm a friend of Kari's. We met on the ship from Earth. I was just calling to see how she's doing. When can I reach her?"

"God only knows. She disappeared with the harpies, and for weeks I've been searching for her. I suppose you won't have any useful information on where she went?"

Ted was silent for a moment. "No, Mr. Turner, I don't know where she is, but we became pretty good friends. She said she planned to find the harpies and help them. She was very committed to the gold one that saved her life."

"Yes, I know all about that damn golden," John said. "She's with him now. Her admiration for that animal is misdirected. He'll ruin her life."

"Mr. Turner, I can tell you're upset, and I don't know you, but I know Kari. When she talked about the harpy, her eyes lit up. She really cared about him. It sounds like she's exactly where she wanted to be. Maybe it's best you give her some space. I'm sure she knows what she's doing."

"You're right, boy," John said. "You damn well don't know me, and you sure as hell don't know what's best for my daughter."

John angrily pushed the disconnect key and walked into the dining room. He poured a glass of wine and took a gulp. Maria was setting a plate down in front of Charlie. "Goddamn it," John said, throwing the full glass against the wall. "Some jerk in Hampton telling me how much my daughter cared about that stinking golden male. Did everyone know about this except me? Then this jerk tells me I should give Kari some space. The runt was lucky he was on the other side of a com."

The communicator buzzed again. "The nerve of that bastard to call me back. This time he's getting a piece of my mind," John said, returning to the den and pushing the answer key. "Listen you," he growled, not waiting for the screen to illuminate.

"Mr. Turner?" said a deep voice. A middle-aged man appeared on the com.

"Yes?" John said, collecting himself.

"My name is George McGill. I saw your reward for your missing daughter on a Web memo. Said she was in a late-model blue terrain vehicle and had a pet golden harpy with a broken wing."

"That's right. You know something?" John asked.

"I didn't see her or the harpy, but I think I know where the vehicle is. Does that entitle me to your reward?" McGill asked.

"If it's hers, you got the reward," John said.

"I saw it two days ago on your estate. My hover had mechanical problems and barely made it to Terrance before it quit. The solar strips won't hold a charge. Darn hover put me out of business, but I figure might as well call and collect on the reward. Get something for my trouble."

"I understand, Mr. McGill," John said, knowing he was talking to a seasoned harpy hunter. "So you were poaching on my property and planned to harvest my daughter's pet? I'll still send you the reward if your information is accurate. I keep my word."

"Yes, I've heard you're tough, but honest. That vehicle is about a hundred miles north of Westend, just off the coast by a small cabin. I spotted the cabin and flew down for a closer look. The vehicle is hid pretty good under bushes, but luckily some glass caught the light, giving it away."

"I know the cabin," John said. "I'm faxing you the ticket for the twenty grand. You can collect the reward from the Terrance bank."

"Thanks, Mr. Turner. Maybe we can do business again," said McGill.

John scribbled on a voucher and jammed it into the fax. "I don't think so, McGill," he said, "and if I ever catch you poaching on my estate, I'll hunt you down like a harpy, and remember I keep my word." He disconnected the communicator and rushed back to the dining room.

Charlie was bent over, helping Maria pick up the broken glass.

"I'm sorry, Maria," John said.

"It's okay, Mr. Turner," she said. "I know you are very worried."

"I have good news," John said. "That was a harpy hunter, and he's found her vehicle. I'm going."

"Let me pack the chicken," Maria said. "You may eat it on the way, and I'll throw in some fruit for Miss Kari." She hurried to the kitchen.

Charlie wearily rubbed his forehead and remained quiet.

While working on the beetle-proof building, Charlie had visited Doc one evening. John was gone, hunting for Kari and the harpy. He figured one old man to another he might learn something from the doctor.

Doc welcomed Charlie, and they sat on the cool dark porch, sipping a glass of scotch.

"At first I was skeptical," Doc had said. "The poor girl was on her knees, crying and begging for my help. I thought she was a fanatic, one of those crazy animal-rights people. I then learned the harpy was the same golden that had saved her as a kid and used the licing moss. I told her I'd try to fix him, but honestly, Charlie, I believed it was a lost cause. A laser blast had seared his intestines, and he was in shock from blood loss, not counting a broken wing and a hell of a beating from those hunters, but the little guy surprised me and pulled through the operation. The following morning, he was full of spit and vinegar, but what impressed me was his devotion to that girl. Despite weakness and pain, he was ready to jump me if I hurt her . . . knocked my medical scanner clean out of my hand. Those two are totally committed to one another."

Doc took a sip from his glass. "You know, Charlie, it's the darnedest thing. That young golden looks identical to the one John killed twenty years ago. I bet he's a son."

"I never saw that harpy," Charlie said. "I was with John's father in the high country, cutting timber when Kari was born. We rushed back, learning of Mrs. Turner's death. John had already buried the thieving golden. I only saw the wings."

"Well, I saw the whole live harpy," Doc said. "Mrs. Turner had given birth in the upstairs bedroom and was holding the baby. John and I were admiring his new daughter when, from the balcony, a big golden male walked into the bedroom. He acted like he belonged there. He looked at the baby for a minute and strolled out, as pretty as you please. John and I were so shocked we couldn't move, but Mrs. Turner was smiling. Two days later, she and the harpy were dead."

Doc glanced at Charlie. "There's a connection between what happened twenty years ago and Kari and her golden today. What young woman wants to be with a harpy? Not only that, Kari claims the harpies speak to her, and she can understand them. I think at birth she was promised to the dead golden's son."

"I believe you're right, Doc," Charlie said. "But how will this end? If John finds them, he'll kill Kari's golden, believing he is protecting his daughter. He doesn't want her to live in the jungle and face hunters. I understand his fears."

"If he kills the harpy, he could be killing his own daughter. When she brought me the dying golden, I wanted to euthanize it. She said I might as well kill her, too. You could see it in her eyes. That girl meant it. She truly loves the creature. If John persists, the tragic event twenty years ago might be repeated."

"Charlie, are you coming?" John said.

"I will come," Charlie answered, following him across the dark lawn to his hover.

They soon were flying over the coastal road. "Who would have guessed she'd remember Dad's cabin?" John said. "She was so little when he took her there."

"Good memories are not easily forgotten."

After an hour, they landed on the beach a good distance from the cabin. They crept up silently, John holding his laser gun, ready to kill.

"It is a mistake to take his life," Charlie whispered on the beach. "Let him flee."

"So he can come back later when he can fly? Not a chance."

Holding a light and his weapon, John rushed the cabin door, but found the place empty. The cabin lights worked and water ran from the faucets. The old place was spotless, with clean sheets on the bed. The medicine in the cabinet and bandages in the trash revealed that Kari had definitely brought the wounded harpy there. A bowl of fresh fruit still sat on the table, conveying their recent departure.

"Bet McGill's hover spooked them," John said. Searching the grounds with solar lights, John discovered the camouflaged blue vehicle. Charlie held up the bloodstained harpy sash lying under scattered leaves. It sent John into a rage.

"If he's touched her, I'll hang him from a tree and cut off his balls," John growled.

He eventually settled down, and they decided to wait until morning for the pursuit. In the dark, a footprint could be missed.

With the first rays of light, they canvassed the area, looking for fresh prints. "The harpy leads. She follows," Charlie said.

John bent down and looked at the prints.

"These are the harpy's," Charlie said, showing John the barefoot print. "Harpies walk like waterbirds, toe to heel and tiptoe much of the time. They do not leave the deep mark of a strolling heavy man. It is sad we hunt such a graceful thing."

"That's your opinion," John said and stood up. Eventually, they discovered that the freshest prints led north. "We'll track them on foot. Sneaking up is the only way to catch a harpy off guard."

They traveled the trail, following the two sets of footprints, one of a small shoe and the other the toes and ball of a bare foot.

Halfway up the mountain crest, Charlie stopped. "We should leave their trail and go around. The wind has shifted, and it rides our back. The male will catch our scent. We can pick up their trail at the top."

"The prints are two days old, and they're far ahead," John said. "I'm not wasting time by going around. You have too high a regard for harpy instincts."

Charlie shrugged. "If you say so," he said. They went on and came to a stream. Footprints were everywhere. "They were here for a long time," John said, "but there're no fruit trees or shelter."

"The answer lies under these ferns." Charlie stared at a harpy nest.

John fell to his knees, swallowed, and gazed at the smashed moss, bundled in a circle. In the moss were numerous tiny feathers, all creamy yellow. Half-eaten fruit lay to one side.

"A male builds such a nest only for his mate and young," Charlie said. "They are a bonded pair, and to kill one, kills both. She is lost, John. Let us go home."

John stood, crossed his arms, and stared at the nest. "I'm not leaving without her. Kari is my daughter, and she's strong. She'll survive his death." He looked around for more signs. After a while, he approached Charlie, whose knowledge of hunting and harpies exceeded his. "What do you think?"

"The few tracks that go also come back," Charlie said. "They were flown away by other harpies or they went north into the stream. Either way, we have nothing to follow."

"We'll go back down for the hover."

Following the northern track, they picked up their footprints by a valley stream, but it was the last sign. Two more days of searching in the hovercraft proved fruitless. Even with a broken wing, the harpy evaded them. Regardless of the dangerous mountain gusts that could throw a hover against the sheer cliffs, John pressed on through the night, relying on the heat sensor. He knew harpies came out of hiding and preferred traveling in the dark.

On the third day John's com buzzed. "The swarms hit again," said one of his mill employees. "It's really bad, Mr. Turner. They took out the whole harbor. Every barge and boat is gone. You lost your whole lumber shipment."

"Anyone killed?" John asked.

"No one local, but ten hunters from Terrance died. They were loading a boat for a trip to the islands."

"All right, I'll be back this afternoon to check the damage," John said, and turned off the com. He sighed and glanced at Charlie. "She really is lost to me?"

Charlie nodded, and John veered the hovercraft to the south.

A gentle breeze blew through the porch as Doc sat in his comfortable chair, sipping the last of the lemonade, his tree barren until next year. He glanced down the empty street of the deserted town. After the swarm attacked the harbor, most folks had fled to Hampton and perhaps beyond, into space. Nobody felt safe anymore, but he had stayed with a few others, determined to ride out the plague. He was too old and stubborn to relocate. No bug would drive him from his lifelong home. He glanced at the boarded up Baker store, missing his daily chat with Mr. Baker on current events. After Carol's death, they had left.

Doc enjoyed Charlie's visit, despite the slight hangover the following morning. Charlie had told him about the metal-reinforced room at the Turner mill, safe from swarms, and invited Doc to come if Westend was threatened. They had mainly talked about John's daughter, Kari, and her golden harpy. Doc grinned, pleased he still had the medical skill to save the harpy's life. He recalled Kari had said a vet at the Hampton Zoo was studying the harpies.

Doc took the last swallow and rose from the porch chair. Inside, he punched in the keys on his desk com. "Hampton Zoo," responded a woman.

"You got some vet or researcher there doing a study on harpies?" Doc asked.

"That would be Dr. Watkins. I'll connect you."

A forty-something-year-old man appeared on the screen. "I'm Dr. Watkins. Can I help you?"

"My name is Doc White. I understand you're researching the harpies?"

"That is correct."

"Who's paying for the study?" Doc asked.

"It's a government fund, but I'm not at liberty to divulge the party's name."

"Is your so-called party interested in saving harpies or finding their breeding grounds, so they can be killed? The Dora senators are avid harpy hunters, and it's been their policy to exterminate the species."

"I assure you, sir, I'm a respected scientist and would never participate in a study that endangers an animal, and I'm aware of the senators' policy. A few came to the zoo and voiced their objections to my work. What is your interest in the matter, Doctor White?"

"I live in the outback, Westend. We have a mutual friend, a Miss Turner."

"Westend," Watkins said. "I do remember her. She was extremely pretty and had an incredible encounter with a golden-winged harpy."

"That's her." Doc chuckled. "Well, she found the golden again, and she's with him now. She thought I could shed some light on your research and help the harpies. I have my own little harpy study going on out here."

"Really?" Watkins said. "I'd appreciate any information on the harpies, and I'd love to hear about her and the golden male."

"You'd have to come out here," Doc said. "I don't trust these coms. Too many ears can listen in."

"To be truthful, I'm growing suspicious myself. Last week someone broke into my office and destroyed my research papers that showed the number of harpies killed yearly versus recorded sightings of the creatures. The math proved that the harpies are in trouble. I was preparing to recommend an immediate ban on harpy hunting."

"That's too bad your work was destroyed," said Doc, massaging his white beard. "Makes you wonder who and why they want the harpies extinct. Maybe out here we can put our heads together and unravel some mysteries. My grandfather settled here when Dora was a new colony. His old chest is up in the attic. Sometimes the past holds present-day answers."

Dr. Watkins pushed the hair back from his forehead. "You could be right. Honestly, my research is stalled here. I think I'll accept your offer. Is there an inn in Westend?"

"There was, but it closed. People are running scared because of the swarms, but you can stay with me. I have an extra room and some outdated equipment, but there is a condition: You'll have to bring a few bottles of scotch."

Watkins chuckled. "I drink scotch myself. I need to wrap up a few lab tests and make arrangements to come out with my equipment. I've wanted to go to the outback ever since I met Miss Turner. She's a very intriguing young lady."

Doc nodded. "More than you can imagine."

12

Shail stood in the sacred mountain, staring down at the throngs of bowing male harpies. "I sense your pleased minds," he relayed, "I survived captivity and return when most needed. Though I suffered, I learned from the human creatures. They are unlike other animals that kill to protect or for food. Humans kill for pleasure, excitement, and greed. I detected evil in the hunters' minds. The time nears when we rid our jungle of the deadly and growing human plague."

He stepped off the ledge and walked through the flocks. "Harpies value all life, but we must change. To not, we lose all we love. We shall mourn many lives, but we must see ahead and see our past, before humans arrived, when our fledglings grew to adulthood and when our females dwelled nightly under our wings. This is the hope that comes with the loss."

Shail reached the center of large expanse and raised his wings. He grasped his downy feathers and ripped out several handfuls, tossing the tiny feathers at his feet. "I force a molt so all shall know the gathering begins. Under the light of the next round moons, and deep within the southern river swamps, we meet and do away with our enemy. Fly swiftly, my brothers; my feathers spreading my words." Each harpy walked before him, and picked up a yellow feather, and proceeded to the crevice. The harpies disappeared to the outside. They would travel the continent telling all harpies of the gathering.

Aron moved alongside Shail. "So the death begins," he conveyed.

Shail glanced up into his bright green eyes. "It begins."

Leaving Aron, Shail walked to Kari and put his arm about her shoulders. He detected her concerns. "Your thoughts are known to me," he relayed. "You worry men have an unyielding nature. If we succeed in reclaiming the land, more humans shall come from the stars and keep coming until we are defeated. You think me unaware, but I understand those things. All shall end well."

Kari watched the departing harpies. "On Earth wild animals once defied man. The bear, lion, rattlesnake, and shark showed courage and stood their ground. Those creatures are extinct. Only domestic animals survived." She turned and hugged him. "Years from now, I don't want some book to record the demise of the harpy species. Humans are not only unyielding, they are vengeful. To kill a few men brings the wrath of many, and they outnumber the stars. There must be another way, Shail."

He kissed her cheek. "There is no other way. Though harpies are gentle, we shall not be tamed, and we prefer the death of the Earth bear. If this is our destiny, let it be so. Come. I shall take you to a place so you may eat and rest."

Kari followed Shail around the fire pits and down a long corridor. "I can't lose you to this war. I've waited so long to be with you," she said as they walked.

"The wait was long. Many lights I flew the land from ocean to ocean searching for you. If not told of your life in the stars and your return when grown, I might have given up the hope of our bond." He stopped in front of a doorway. "This is where we nest."

"Who told you that I'd come back?" Kari asked and walked into the room. A circle of rocks encased a small fire in the center of the room. Smoke escaped through a ceiling vent. A moss nest rested near the fire, and at hand's reach, a pile of various fruits. She sat down on the nest and picked up one of the fruits.

Shail sat down beside her. "The old man with long gray hair said that you dwelled among the stars, but would return when grown and free of your father. He is good at sensing an animal's thoughts, and we sense him."

"You're talking about Charlie. When did that happen?"

"Several seasons past, I came upon this Charlie in the jungle. His respect for harpies is well known. He hunts, but only for food. For his kindness, we repay him by letting him watch us at a distance."

"When Aron chased the grogins away, he knew Charlie was there."

"He knew, but to let a man and a weapon too close is unwise. I lacked fear of Charlie after your mogel attack. When I brought you home, he fired his weapon to the sky to scare, not kill. Longing to know if you lived, I sought him."

Kari stopped eating and huffed. "That liar; that hypocrite. He told me to stay away from you. He said you placed a spell on me, and my life would be over."

"Your safe human life is over, and the spell was on you and me, for I wanted no other mate. His words were true. Like your father, he worries for you and warned you away from me and the harpy life I offer. As you learned, it is dangerous and deadly. Do not be angry with Charlie or your father. They, like I, wish to protect you."

Kari leaned back on the moss and stared at Shail. "How can you be so supportive of Dad when he killed your father and also wants you dead?"

"I understand Turner. He is a good and honorable man. For many seasons he chased hunters off his land and protected my flock. His wife and daughter are harpies, and his devotion is unmatched. He does not hate the harpies, only my father and me, for we threatened the safety of his loved ones. My father wanted your mother to leave him, and you left with me. Those are his motives to kill."

"You're so darn rational and easygoing. Just thinking about Dad harming you makes my blood boil."

Shail touched her arm. "You are cool."

Kari smiled. "I mean I'd be angry if he hurt you."

"You and your father see through different times, and that is what causes conflict. You see the present and our happiness. He sees your dangerous future with a harpy mate. Someday he shall learn that without love there is no worthy future, and you shall know his concerns are driven by love, not hate."

She reached up and pulled him close. "For a supposedly wild and ignorant animal, you're pretty insightful." She snuggled against him and stared up at white moss covering the gray metal walls. "So tell me about this old space freighter we're in. Why do you think it's sacred?"

"Kari, I do not yet know all your words. What is a 'space freighter'?"

"This place is an old space freighter. It's like a giant hovercraft that traveled through the stars. Men built it. Surely you knew."

"No, you are wrong. This is the creator's sacred place, where the harpies began. It has always rested beneath the mountain, long before men came to our jungle."

Kari stood and walked to the moss-covered wall. She tapped it, creating a clang. "Do mountain stones sound like this? I'm telling you, Shail, it's a freighter. How many harpies do you know that have traveled to the stars?"

"You are the only one." He rose and went to a wall, and caressed, sniffed and tasted it. "It is different from other mountain caves, but it was here before men came. The story of this place and our creator is long forgotten, but man's coming is well remembered. They came from the stars and killed the males and stole the females."

"Maybe harpies once had technology and traveled through the stars. This craft is definitely hundreds of years old. It belongs in a museum."

He looked inquisitively at her.

"A museum is a place for old things. Humans cherish their past."

He shook his locks slightly and returned to the nest. "No more talk. It is time for sleep."

Kari joined him under his wing. "Shail, what will happen to men like Charlie and Doc when you go to war? You know they're good and would never harm the harpies."

"Like the women and young, they must flee our land. To stay, they perish. I do not have the means to separate the good from bad. I am sad by what shall come. We harpies take great pride and honor in protecting life, but Kari, we shall all die if we do not fight back."

Kari sighed. "I know Doc, Charlie, and my father won't leave. I could lose you and everyone I love with the war."

He nuzzled the back of her neck. "If it is in my power to save the ones you love, I shall, but I make no promise. The light comes. Sleep."

Kari woke and felt for Shail, but the nest was empty. She sensed another person in the room and sat up. A girl with long dark hair was placing a small log on the fire. She saw Kari and dropped to her knees, bowing.

"Forgive me if I woke you," said the girl, using her human voice.

Slightly startled, Kari cleared her throat. She hadn't spoken in weeks, and except for the crude hunters, she hadn't heard a vocal communication in some time. "You didn't wake me, and please don't bow. I'm not a ruler."

The girl slowly rose. "You are a golden harpy. The brown harpies shall always bow to you. It is our custom."

When the girl lifted her head, Kari saw her large green eyes and lovely features. "Lea . . . You're a . . . ? You're a harpy?"

"I am sister to Aron," said Lea.

"No wonder I liked you."

Lea grinned and then became serious. "I am sorry. On the beach, I fled and failed you and our ruler. Aron sent me to help, but Carol's harsh words drove me away. I hid in the dark bushes and watched. You were so brave, facing those hunters alone, and wise, twisting their minds to give you our golden ruler. No other female harpy has your courage."

"Lea, I didn't know I was a harpy at the time, but I doubt if it would have changed things. If those hunters didn't go for my trade, they'd have faced my laser gun. I'd steal Shail before letting more harm come to him. I was pretty desperate that night."

"Those hunters have paid for their cruelty. They are dead, even Carol."

"Carol's dead? How?"

"A beetle swarm attacked your vehicle and ate them. The swarms have changed and now seek flesh. This concerns Aron and our ruler, and they have sent all outback females and fledglings to the islands. Aron brought me to the sacred mountain to serve you. I hope not to fail you again."

"Poor Carol." Kari leaned back in the moss. "She was obnoxious, but she didn't deserve to die." She glanced at Lea. "Stop fretting, Lea. You didn't fail me."

"May I offer you some food?"

Kari popped a few nuts into her mouth. "That darn mate of mine. Shail certainly knows how to keep his secrets. He never told me about Carol or the swarms. I'm glad you're here. I miss talking, and at times, the telepathy is hard for me. Once in a while I feel like screaming at Shail."

Lea giggled. "You would dare scream at our ruler?" She became solemn and backed away from Kari and the fire. She knelt as Shail entered the room.

"You may go," he relayed, and Lea rushed from the room.

"Why is she so scared of you?" Kari asked.

"She is not scared. It is respect she shows."

"It looks like fear to me."

"I am the dominant male of all flocks." Shail lifted his head. "It is the animal way to show meekness. If not for one leader, male would challenge male and cause chaos, exposing the harpies to more dangers. I keep peace and decide what is favorable for the harpies."

"So you rule because of your blond hair and yellow wings."

He frowned. "Always a golden has ruled."

"Because goldens are supposedly braver?"

"You question my courage? In a challenge, I can defeat any male. All harpies but you know this. Taking a mate raised by humans can be trying." He walked to the nest and plopped down on the moss.

"I make you unhappy?"

"I am happy with you. You are unlike all other females; beautiful, smart, and brave, but so brave you challenge me. This I have not known, but you force my eyes open to truths. You ask why I rule. In truth, I do not know. I do not believe the yellow makes me better than other males." He placed his head on her leg.

Kari stroked his hair, sensing he felt vulnerable. Normally Shail was lofty and confident, but she realized that only with his mate would he divulge his lack of knowledge and uncertainty. He didn't know why he was chosen to rule, why the old spaceship was sacred, or who the creator of his people was. All the answers lay buried in the past. She also detected his worry of the coming conflict. Was he smart enough to outwit the humans? "I'm sorry I challenge you. My father raised me not to back down. If you wish, I'll teach you all I know about humans."

"I do not desire the knowledge, but fear I must learn it. Against men, my mind is crippled like my wing. Soon I must fly, and hope to free our people."

Shail and Kari ate the fruit and he left, saying he would send Aron's sister back to the room.

Shail walked down the torch-lit corridor and found Lea waiting. "Go to her and explain the harpy ways," he relayed. "Though my mate is wise with humans, she does not know her own people." Lea nodded and went back to Kari's room.

Shail tapped the metal walls while walking to meet Aron. The clinking echoed in the hallway. He entered a large room. Aron and several harpies lowered their head as he walked past them and headed for a counter with a sink. Shail turned the faucets, and rusty water trickled out. Like the cabin, the room held human things; chairs, tables, and a sink with faucets. The sacred mountain probably had been a spacecraft freighter.

Aron came alongside. "It is unwise to handle the creator's things."

"Send the others away. We speak alone."

With a nod, Aron dismissed the other males. He turned back to Shail. "What troubles you?"

"For many seasons this place has remained empty and unused by female harpies, who dwell among humans and their objects." Shail glanced up at the ceiling. "My mate came here and saw that this place once traveled among the stars, and these things were made by humans. I have seen such things in the human dwellings."

"She is wrong. This is the creator's sacred mountain. Before men, it lay here."

Shail patted Aron's shoulder. "I said those words to her, but who was the creator? Was he harpy or man? I wonder now if the harpies have failed by not learning from our females. They have knowledge of the human world, and knowledge is a powerful weapon."

"To take the evil knowledge, we would become like humans. We would kill the trees for our homes and the animals for our food. We would no longer be harpies, but winged men. Why do you question the golden rules?"

Shail walked to a table and sat on the edge. "The old rules were made when there were many harpies. Now there are few. It is time to change. I do not believe the knowledge is evil. The evil lies in those who use it. If we had shown men our intelligence, perhaps the hunting would have ended long ago. If not, we might have learned how to drive the humans from our land."

"You are no longer the Shail I knew. The hunters changed you."

"They changed me and taught me of fear and pain. I became like all animals that are caught, hurt, and bewildered by human cruelty, but in surviving, I grew in courage. Rather than fleeing, I chose to destroy them, but the knowledge I question comes from my mate. In her effort to discover herself, she forced me to accept many things, and with wisdom comes better judgment and strength. Though I lived in the human dwelling, I am harpy and still long for a jungle nest and fruit."

"Perhaps it is wise you learn of our enemy, whom we must destroy."

Shail took a long deep breath. "To destroy all would be wise if all were evil, but there are good men among them. One chose to spare my life. Understanding brings conflict to my decisions."

"Shail, we cannot attack the bad without attacking the good. Even now I question your judgment. You protect a known harpy killer and his land. He seeks to kill you. It is a mistake that our males defend him."

Shail slid off the table and arched his wings. "You challenge me and my decisions?" He walked to Aron until he was face to face with him.

Aron submissively lowered his head and backed away. "Never would I seek a male challenge with you. Though older and larger, I learned as a fledgling of your unyielding nature. Because of my love and concern for your safety, I question your choice to protect Turner. Four lights ago he nearly hunted you down, and it is known he wishes to kill you as he killed your father."

Shail lowered his wings and folded them against his back, ending the challenge. "I accept your concerns, but I have reasons for protecting Turner. We may fail, Aron. My mate carries our future ruler, and she shall need the strong arm of her father to survive. If these swarms win the land, Turner shall send my family to the safety of the stars. He risked the dangerous night winds of the mountains to find us and would gladly die to protect Kari and my son. This man has the honor, devotion, and courage of a male harpy who gladly sacrifices his life to lure a hunter away from his family. Turner protected my flock for many seasons, and now I shall protect him."

"There is no doubt the man would protect his daughter, but I question your unborn fledgling. He shall be a golden-winged male. Turner may discard or even destroy him."

"As Turner loved his daughter and wife, he shall also love my son. I watched this man at the lake where he met his mate. After many seasons, he still grieves for her. I sensed his heart, and it is not black, only confused. When he sees his grandson carries the same blood, his confusion shall end. He shall fiercely protect the young golden monarch."

"As you wish, we shall continue to watch over him and his land."

"What of the swarms?" Shail asked.

"They are a blessing and a curse. Now that the beetles kill, they drive the humans swiftly across the river. I know you planned to herd the humans, unharmed, out of our jungle, but daily the swarms grow in numbers with the emerging of new queens. They grow harder for the harpies to control. The attack on human villages draws near."

"Yes, the curse of them worries me. I allowed the beetles to multiply and now the blood of many innocent may rest upon my hands, and I fear for our females and young. The beetles might evolve to fly a great distance over water and attack the islands. While we still have control, we shall direct the swarms to known hunting camps. With the hunters' deaths, the women and children in the villages shall flee east and beyond into the stars. Bring your males back in."

On a dusty table, Shail drew the outback with his finger, pointing out the western hunting camps to the harpy males. Once Shail had finished, he followed Aron and the other harpies outside the crevice.

On the ledge, Shail stood next to Aron as the other harpies took flight. "I shall see you at the river, my brother."

"If you can force yourself away from your new mate," Aron relayed.

"It shall be hard. Kari is unlike any harpy. For ten seasons she lived among humans without harpies and the jungle. Most females would have died, but she came back strong and wise."

"And you survived the hunters when others could not and came back the same as her. As I have said, she is your match, Shail."

Shail shook his long hair. "At times she is more than my match." They nuzzled one another's necks. "Fly safe, Aron." He watched Aron leap from the ledge and trail the other males until they were out of sight. He returned to the crevice and Kari. The war of nature against the deadly humans had begun.

Kari was delighted to see Lea when she came into the room. "Our ruler wishes me to teach you about our people," Lea said.

"I've been driving him crazy with my questions, but he's so cute when he doesn't know the answer and becomes frustrated. He's normally too darn confident. It's good to knock him off his throne once in a while."

Lea covered her mouth to hide her giggles. "You truly have the golden blood to treat him so."

"Do you have a mate, Lea?"

"Yes, my mate stays near Westend and guards your father's home. I miss him. Most female harpies have harpy mates, but some seek good men and the man knows their wife is a harpy. These men protect the identity of their mates, their mate's female relatives, and all offspring. The female harpies depend on this help."

"So this is how all female harpies exist?" Kari asked.

"Most of us live this way, since it is safer. When young, we are taught not to do or say anything that would reveal our true nature."

Kari raised an eyebrow. "I guess I broke the rules when I came back to Dora. I ran my mouth about how much I liked harpies and had the ability to communicate with them."

"Yes." Lea nodded. "You took great risk when defending the harpies. Some humans might have guessed you were a harpy. The outcome can be very bad."

"I learned my lesson the hard way when three hunters caught me in the jungle. They planned to rape me. If Shail hadn't come . . ." Kari shuddered.

Lea put her arm around Kari. "Some hunters have discovered male and female harpies together in the jungle and learned of the female's disguise. To choose a life with your mate among the trees is risky, but separation also is painful."

"So how can you have a relationship when you live apart?"

"By day I live as a woman with my mother on the outskirts of Westend. We pick berries and make jams for the humans, but at night I become a harpy. My mate comes at dark and flies me to our jungle nest. One learns to treasure the night."

"You know, Lea, if the humans knew we were related, they might stop the hunting of the harpies, realizing we're not animals."

Lea's eyes widened. "No, our secret must be kept. We know the outcome of exposing our females. Have you not heard of the first men who landed on Dora?"

"I know the Dorial explorers discovered the planet a hundred and seventy-five years ago. The settlers followed twenty-five years later. It's in the history books."

"Yes, the human history books." Lea sighed. "They do not hold the terrible truth of those explorers, and it was hidden from the settlers. From generation to generation, the harpies have passed along the story. The explorers landed on Dora and discovered the harpy community. The harpies, not fearing humans, welcomed those men. The men saw that our females looked like women and learned the harpies were a gentle race. Desiring the females, men caught, caged, and raped them. Many females died of shock and heart failure from the abuse. The males rushed to their mates' defense and also died in great numbers, killed by human weapons. The men cut off their wings, bragging of their trophies. It was the darkest of all seasons for the harpies, yet the history books glorify those malicious men."

Lea added another log to the fire and continued the story. "Some females survived, and, to the men's surprise, became pregnant. When the featherless winged males were born, they disgusted the men, thinking their offspring were four-armed freaks. The men cut the fledglings' throats and started a ritual that exists today. A wounded male exposes his throat to the hunter and hopes to receive the same death as the past sacrificial fledglings. This courageous and honorable death proves we are the enlightened, the civilized ones over the lowly human beasts."

"What happened to the female fledglings?" Kari asked.

"They were spared because they looked human. After that season, the pregnant female harpies hid their labor pains, feeling the male wings in their stomach. At night they gave birth, and through the cage bars, handed their male fledglings to the surviving free adults. The male harpies reared those fledglings as their own sons. The female fledglings remained with their mothers. These daughters grew, and when the settlers arrived, the females passed as women. A wicked partnership began between the Dorian explorers and the harpies; neither would divulge the true nature of the female harpies, and the deception still exists.

"The male harpies were labeled as thieves when they attempted to reclaim their females. If a bonded harpy pair was found by humans, the male was killed and the female was returned to the human world, but she soon died of despair, unable to live without her mate. The second lie was hatched. The humans, thinking a female harpy was a woman, believed that women lost their minds and died after a male harpy took and raped them."

Kari rose from the nest and paced the room. "I know of the despair we face. On Earth, I was so miserable that I nearly lost my mind. I can't imagine existing without Shail; I love him so much."

Lea grinned. "Yes, like some animals, harpies bond for life, unlike a human marriage."

Kari returned to the nest. "Besides going to war, there has to be another way to stop the harpy hunting. Dora has a lot of good people, and if they knew the truth about the harpies, the killing would end."

"There are some good humans, but to reveal the truth to them would also expose every female harpy and could make them slaves."

"It might be worth the risk," Kari said, "if it changed the hunting laws."

"You don't understand. The Dorian explorers' descendants are the senators who make the laws. They rule the planet and know we carry human blood. To hide the disgrace of their ancestors and keep their power, the senators promote hunting and protect the lies. They long for harpy extinction. If harpies attempt to change things, the senators have sworn to bring in the galactic army and kill all harpies. Our males have chosen the hunt, rather than risk their females."

"The truth is slowly coming out, and not by the harpies. Old Doc and a vet at the Hampton Zoo know harpies carry human blood. Eventually the whole planet will know, and there's nothing the senators can do to stop it."

"Someday men may change their ways toward the harpies, but their way takes a long time. The research and history must be proved; seasons must pass before new and fair senators are elected; and then the hunting laws and harpy status must be changed. Kari, we do not have this kind of time."

"But is war the answer? Shail could stop the war and give the vet's research a chance. Dr. Watkins is trying to place a hunting ban on the harpies until the flocks recover."

"The war cannot be stopped. It is years in the making, and the harpies have given up all hope of man treating us fairly. Better we drive them out of our land. The number of hunters grows, while our male harpy numbers shrink. Our kind is losing the race to survive."

"Thank you, Lea. You have explained many things about the harpies. I understand why Shail has been backed against a wall and must strike out. He's tough, but not a killer. I feel guilty for teasing him, now that I know he must be sick with worry."

"No harpy has ever killed a man, but things are about to change. We all feel this sadness. Is there anything else I can tell you or do for you?"

Kari looked at Lea's harpy robe made from the same material as Shail's sash. "You don't wear store-bought clothes here. I'd like to get out of my human clothes and wear a robe like yours."

Lea smiled and bounded to her feet. "I have an extra one. I'll go get it." She returned quickly with the rope and sheets of the material. Kari slipped into the soft robe, recalling the old picture in her bedroom. Her mother had worn the same type of gown.

They sat down by the fire, and Lea began to fashion the second robe as Kari watched. They had become best friends.

Shail walked through the vacant space freighter toward Kari's room. His mind was troubled. So many things could go wrong. The harpies had kept the swarms in the jungle and away from the towns that held women and children, but the swarms turned deadly and were multiplying at an alarming rate. The humans would soon have to flee to the stars or perish, and his flock would then face the swarms, out-flying the beetles and destroying them. All was timing and must be completed before the second rise of the full moons. To delay meant the swarms would be unstoppable, consuming every living thing on the planet.

He flinched the shoulder holding his broken wing. It, too, must be healed and be ready. The eastern and river flocks would follow only a pair of yellow wings. Without a leader to direct the harpies, the flocks would seek the safety of the cold mountains. The humans would die in vast numbers, and there would be no attack on the beetles. After devouring the jungle, the swarm might evolve to travel over water and reach the islands or penetrate the cold mountains, where eastern females and fledglings hid. All could be lost on a broken wing.

Two seasons before, Shail had come upon two beloved males who were slaughtered and hung from a tree. His decision was made there and then. He halted the harvest of new beetle queens and let the swarms multiply, hoping to drive out mankind. The loca eagles ate the beetles and had taught the harpies to control the beetle population and thus protect the jungle. Because of man and his ignorance, both loca and harpy now faced extinction. Once the harpies were gone, the beetle explosion and disaster was inevitable. Shail allowed nature to take its course early, hoping he could save his race and the jungle. With no weapons or technology, Shail launched his silent war against man and let nature do his bidding.

He reached the corridor and felt the weight of the world rested on his wings. He longed to crawl into Kari's arms and forget who he was, preferring to be a simple young male enjoying his new mate and their coming fledgling.

Nearing the doorway, he heard Kari and Lea talking. He entered the room, and with the slight toss of his locks, Lea bowed and left the room. Kari stood up, and her robe hugged her slender figure while her long hair flowed down her shoulders and back. She took his breath away.

Her deep blue eyes sparkled in the firelight. "Are you all right, Shail?"

"Seeing you, I feel I have reached the summit of a lifelong climb. Never have I known such joy."

She walked to him and gave him a long, slow kiss. "I take it you like the harpy robe?"

"Yes, but more what it holds. Come. We shall walk a little before sleep."

They left the room and walked down the corridor back to the large expanse. A small glow came from the fading fires in the pits. The place was empty of harpies.

"Have they all gone?" Kari asked.

"A few remain. When the moons are round, I join them."

Kari stopped walking and stared at him. "The full moons are in seven days. Your wing might not be healed."

"Kari, I must go whether my wing is ready or not." Shail expected an argument from his feisty mate, but she said nothing about the wing or his leaving.

They walked through the crevice and reached the outside. It was night and the moons had reached their crests. The cold wind blew hard against the cliff, and Shail's mate shivered in her robe. Shail moved behind her, hugging her with his arms and warm wings. The couple gazed at the outline of the black mountain range silhouetted by stars and relished the precious moment in time. He nuzzled and kissed the back of her neck, and she tilted her head back, rubbing her cheek against his and giving him permission to breed. He pulled up the back of her robe, holding her against him, and mounted her.

When Shail had finished, Kari turned and faced him. "I don't want to live without you," she said.

He softly kissed her quivering lips and placed her head against his chest, embracing her. "I shall do my best to return."

The wind whipped at their hair, and they clung to one another with feelings of bliss and sadness mixed. The eastern black sky took color as the sun crept above the jungle. They returned to the nest and curled up to sleep.

Kari woke to an empty room. She went to a small water pool formed from rains that had seeped through the old ship's broken hull. After washing, she ate some fruit and waited for Shail. He came in and dropped on the nest. "I have made a decision on your welfare." He sighed deeply. "You shall not like it."

"What is it, Shail?"

"Since you want to know, I shall tell you all of the war that was kept from our females. The females dwell too close to men, and if my plans became known, the humans might have sought revenge and attacked the harpies. If this happened, all could be lost. You shall understand when I tell." He leaned back and told her about the swarms and his plan to drive the men out of Dora, but it was a risky plan, and all could be lost.

"The swarms killed Carol and the hunters in Westend," she said.

"Yes, Aron brought a swarm down upon them, fearing those men would cause me more harm."

"How did you create the swarms, and how will you destroy them?" she asked.

"I did not create them. These swarms have always been. We learned from the loca eagles to control the swarm numbers by removing the new queens from a mound. We shall destroy the beetles the same way, though it now comes at great risk."

She ran her hand across his body. "So what's this decision you have made for me?"

"I am taking you back to your father."

Kari jerked her hand away and jumped up. "No, Shail. I'm not going. I don't ever want to see him again. I'll stay here while you're gone, or you take me to the islands with the other females. I could be with Lea."

Shail leaped to his feet. "I have decided." He felt the urge to raise his wings at her. "You are going back to your father's home."

"You can't force me, Shail!"

Shail tossed his hair and ruffled his feathers as he paced around the room. He finally stopped and gazed at her. "Kari, I and the flocks might never return here. If this happens, there is no way down from the mountain, and you shall die. The islands might also fall under swarms. My harpies protect your father and land, and I have learned he has made a room that is safe from a swarm attack. If we fail and the land is consumed, he shall send you to the stars. He is the only one I trust to save you and our son."

"I told you I don't want to live without you."

"Stop thinking like this!" he growled, and grasped her shoulders. "Stop thinking like a weak harpy. Draw from your human strength. You must survive my death for the sake of our son. He is the future ruler of our race."

Kari stared blankly. "If all are lost, who will he rule?"

Shail embraced her and nuzzled her neck. "There shall be survivors, and he must be among them."

She hugged him. "This scares me so much."

"I, too, am scared. I hope I have chosen wisely."

"You're right," she said quietly. "Dad would protect me at all cost. I'll go so you won't have to worry about me, but I'm not happy about it."

"I thank you."

The next few days they never left one another's side. Kari taught him about the human objects, and she was amazed how quickly Shail learned. She wasn't sure if he could use the information, but he craved the knowledge of hovercrafts, communicators, and vehicles.

Under a torch, she sat on the floor and drew a laser gun in the dust. "I have to talk. It's mentally too hard for me to explain this, and you know the human language." She pointed to the image of the weapon. "This is the trigger. You pull it back, and the laser fires a blast."

Shail knelt and examined the drawing. "Pull where?"

"Okay, you hold it on the grip. Here. You pull the trigger toward you. It's too bad male harpies can't talk. I could teach you faster, rather than trying to communicate with telepathy."

"What makes you think I cannot?" he said, using the same soft voice that had entered her subconscious, but now it was a gentle whisper.

Kari's mouth fell open. "You can speak. Why didn't you talk sooner?"

Shail returned to using telepathy. "Males choose not to speak. The sound can be dangerous in the jungle. We once spoke like our females, but stopped when men came and hunted us. Our females kept the noisy talk to mingle among humans. Also when we met, I did not know your words as I do now."

"Say something else."

He pulled back, puzzled and relayed, "You like hearing my harsh sound?"

Kari ran her finger over his lips. "Your voice is soft and sensuous. I love it."

"What do you want to hear?" he asked with his low, silky voice.

She leaped up and kissed him. "My God, you're sexy."

"I should speak sooner."

Since it pleased her, Shail continued to speak human words. His sentences were initially broken and foreign sounding, but soon his speech resembled a soft-spoken man. He felt no less of a harpy, using the harmless talk, but he had broken another ancient harpy rule, the male vow of silence.

Kari taught him during the day, and their nights were filled with the passion of the bond. In between, his curious mate was determined to discover the secrets of the old spaceship. They strolled down the corridors, finding what Kari called primitive artifacts. He lacked the interest, but going along made her happy.

"I think this is the helm where they steered the ship," she said and pushed against the crushed doorway. Shail ripped at the dilapidated door, creating a crawl-through opening. With a torch, he entered and she followed. "Yes, this is it. Here's the guidance system." She rushed to a large center chair. "It's the captain's log. I can install the power pack from Doc's com. We'll finally learn who piloted this ship."

Shail was less enthusiastic. His mind too occupied by what he must face in few days. They retrieved the communicator, and for hours Kari worked restoring and cleaning the log while he curled up on the floor and napped.

"I think it's ready," she said, connecting a few wires.

Lying on his side, Shail glanced at her through his locks and feathers. A gravelly and broken man's voice filled the room. Alarmed, Shail jumped to his feet and spread his wings.

"It's okay." She giggled. "Come over here and look at the screen." Shail folded his wings and looked at the square box. After she made a few adjustments, the screen held a yellow-haired man. "It's a human ship. He must be the captain, but look at the date." She read the bottom of the screen. "The ship is over three hundred years old."

"I know not your amounts."

"It means the ship was here long before the Dorian explorers and set-tlers."

"I have said the harpies were here before those men."

On the screen the man talked about the cargo to be picked up on the next planet. Kari pushed the keys. "I'm going to fast-forward it and find out if anyone survived the crash." The screen flashed, and she briefly stopped the movement to check the dates.

"Logged star year twenty-eight hundred, forty-seven," said the middle-aged captain. "After the fire, the head mechanic reported the engines and communication are beyond repair. We're adrift in space with only boosters and missed the worm hole to the Oden system. The closest star is called Duran. We're hoping one of its planets holds oxygen, but we're too far out for the sensors, and the journey will take five years. We're heading for an unexplored section in the galaxy and morale among the fifty surviving men is low. Captain James of *The Princess*, star freighter, out."

Kari pushed in a sequence of numbers, adjusting the log ahead five years.

"We are approaching Duran. The food is low, and I daily break up fights among the men. I'm at a point I don't care if they kill one another. Our sensor did detect oxygen and life on the third planet, so we're heading for it. By the calculations, it'll take another six months. Captain James of *The Princess*, out."

Kari adjusted the log to jump ahead again.

"The planet is very close and the men are excited. Honestly, I'm nervous as the devil, since I've never landed a freighter this size using only the boosters. I pray we survive the crash. The planet has one large continent, and I'm steering for it. I have to say, the planet looks like a little jewel. It's so darn colorful. The food has been gone, so we're all just hanging on. Captain James of *The Princess*, out."

"We made it to the planet surface, crashing into the side of a northwest-ern mountain, barely missing the ocean. When the ship hit, it caused a mountain avalanche, and we're working in shifts, slicing through the rocks to get out. The crash claimed the lives of four good men and injured eight. Food is our main concern. I'll organize a food search party made up of my strongest men. Captain James out."

Shail saw the tall blond man was gaunt, his blue eyes sunken and his voice weary. Starvation was a terrible way to die. Was Captain James the creator, the one the harpies revered? It seemed unrealistic that his flock could have honored such a man.

"Star year twenty-eight-fifty-four. I lost another man today. Joe Mahan was a good young man and succumbed to his crash injuries. The crew cut through the black mountain rocks, and with ropes, five of my best men have descended to the jungle. As captain, I'll be the last to leave my ship and have chosen to stand by my injured men, but I can't wait to explore the planet. Looking out the crevice we made in the mountain, I can hardly catch my breath. The landscape is beautiful. I'm wondering if we have discovered paradise. Captain James out."

"The men returned with loads of food. Scanning the fruit, we found it's edible. They managed to bring back two large flying reptiles. They were greasy, but tasted like pork. The men said the hunting was easy, since the animals have no fear of us. The injured men are making progress, and we are all thankful for our lives. Captain James of *The Princess*, out.

"I've decided to leave the ship for an expedition into the jungle with twenty men. My chief mechanic and I are eager to check the mineral content of the planet. The ship is unsalvageable, since a portion of the mountain rests on it, but we're hoping to repair the com and be rescued. Captain James, out.

"After a week in the jungle, we returned to the ship. I lost one man to giant reptiles. We fired on a herd of the creatures, and when one fell, the lizards attacked. We had to kill half the herd before the rest turned and fled. I may have spoken too soon when I said the planet was paradise. It's similar to Earth during the dinosaur period; giant ferns, trees, and reptiles. I'm making plans to evacuate the ship. It's too much of a climb to come and go. We found a place on the coast with ample food and water, and I'll send half the men to build shelters. My logs will be limited, since it's a heck of a climb up the mountain, but I want to keep a record. In case we're never rescued, there'll be some information on what became of *The Princess* and her crew. Captain James, out."

Kari pressed the hold key. "There're a lot of logs. I'm skipping ahead to the end."

Shail nodded.

"Star date twenty-two-sixty. Today is the sixth anniversary of the crash, and we pretty much have given up hope of a rescue. To date we lost two more men to animals and another to a fall. Without women, we're very lonely, but our cook, Sam Wise, found a root and made spirits. This pleased the men. A young man named Jack Harper made a pet out of a tall flying monkey. One of the Spanish boys named them loco eagles, since the creatures are so crazy they fly right to us. I'm concerned with Harper, and afraid the boy is losing it here. After the loco eagle was shot and wounded, he refused to let the cook have it. Oddly enough, the loco eagle is rather affectionate. I believe it thinks Harper is its mate. There is nothing else to report. Captain James, out.

"This is the seventh anniversary since the crash. It's been a rather strange year. The female loca eagle had a baby a few months ago. Except for a tail and some feathers on her shoulders, the baby looks like a little girl. Now every guy in camp wants his own female loca. It shows how desperate they've become. Captain James, out."

Shail glared at the screen. "Turn it off." He paced the helm and finally stopped. "Is this how we were made, Kari? Men made us?"

Kari bit her bottom lip and didn't answer.

"We are better than humans." He shook his head. "Go on. I must know this truth." Kari hit the key, and the next log entry popped on the screen.

"Star year twenty-eight seventy-two. Tomorrow is my birthday, and I'll be sixty-five years old. Don't know how many more times I can climb the mountain, and . . ." He glanced at the panel. "The power pack is low. Well, I broke down and, like the rest of my crew, took a loca eagle for a wife. My crew made a gift of a rare yellow-winged loca. It may be sick, but she won my heart. I've never been happier with a female. She's affectionate and constantly nuzzles me. We have created a whole new race by procreating with these loving animals. My two sons and four daughters make my life complete. The boys have yellow wings like their mother and can fly, and they taunt my little girls, but they are intelligent and the gentlest of beings. Every morning the village is filled with their chatter. My blond fledglings stand out from the other brown-haired and winged fledglings. My oldest boy rules the roost." Captain James chuckled. "He takes after his old man;

won't back down to anyone or anything. God help me, I love him more than my life. We named them harpies after Jack Harper. He started this all. Captain James, out."

Kari stopped the log and looked at Shail. "We were named after a man, Jack Harper, not the ugly thieving monsters from ancient Greek mythology. There's one more," she said, and an old man appeared on the screen.

"Star year, hell I don't know the date, but I think I'm eighty-five years old. I figure I haven't been to *The Princess* in twenty years. My son flew me up here. Before I died, I wanted to make this final log for the harpies. I'm a grandfather with seventeen beautiful grandchildren, and every generation they grow more handsome. My son rules the others. He was chosen because he's wise and defends his flock with his life, and his compassion is beyond reproach. He's a better leader than I ever was. I brought him to the old spaceship to tell him that this is where the harpies began.

"Besides me and three others, all of the ship's crew is dead. We sit and talk about our offspring and what the future holds for them. If someday other men come to the planet, I'm sure they'll be impressed with the harpies. They have mankind's best qualities; gentleness, honor, and they're smart." James sighed. "Thank God they didn't take after us men. We came here, killed the animals, and cut down the trees, but it was our kids who taught us to respect one another and all life. They're a fine race without a malicious bone in them."

"Father, it grows late, and I fear the mountain wind shall be too cold for you," said a soft male voice beyond the screen.

"I'm almost finished, son," James said.

"Anyway, I'm leaving the log as a record so the harpies know how they were created, and if men find it, they'll know the harpies are their brothers and should be treated with equal respect. I guess that's all. I'm ready, son. I want to be home before my great-grandson is born. Do you think . . . ?" James' voice trailed off, forgetting to shut down the equipment.

Shail placed his hand against the blank screen. "I wish all men were like this one. He was kind and loved us."

Kari pulled the disc out and held it to his face. "Shail, do you know what this means?"

"It means you and I carry the man's blood."

"Yes, but it's solid proof we're related to humans, and better yet, it exonerates the male harpies. We didn't become related to humans because male harpies stole and raped women. The disc tells us we have the human DNA because men mated with the loca eagles. The captain's log could put a stop to the hunting. Harpies are not animals, but another race of mortals. Captain James left the log so humans would respect the harpies."

"It comes too late to be of use. Tomorrow the moons shall be round, and I must fly to the gathering. We shall hold the swarms back so the innocent humans can flee to the stars, but after seven lights, my flock loses this control, and the swarm shall descend on all towns, craving human flesh. Kari, I shall not risk my males to save foolish humans who refuse to go. Once the humans escape, we shall attack the swarm. To destroy a swarm, a male harpy must out-fly and guide it. Some harpies shall die. The swarm amounts must be down before the next rise of the round moons. If we have failed, the land may be lost."

"I understand the deadline, but if I took the log to the humans, and you were convinced that they would stop hunting harpies, couldn't you destroy the swarms before they reached the towns? You intend to destroy the beetles anyway."

Shail paced the room. "I am not sure I could be convinced, and there is no trust. Once the swarms are gone, it is more likely the men shall continue the hunt. The greed for our valuable wings leans toward this choice. Letting the humans live and flee is more than fair when they have killed many in the flocks. You ask a lot of me."

"I do ask a lot, but Shail, you have an advantage. The humans will learn that without harpies, the beetles will take over the planet. Fearing the return of the swarms, the humans would protect the harpies now and in the future. The hunting would end."

"It may be wiser to drive them to the stars and end the threat. Let them seek other lands and inflict their cruelty. We have had our fill."

"There are many good humans here and many of them will die. There aren't enough spaceships to evacuate the planet in time."

"Female, you make my head hurt. Take the captain's words and do what you must. I shall think on this. If I save the humans, I could be killing my flock."

Kari leaped up and kissed him. She dropped to her knees, removing the power pack and placing it back into the portable communicator. "I'm calling Doc. He'll know the right people to look at the disc, and I can ask him about your broken wing." She pushed the com keys. "I have to go outside. The satellite doesn't pick up in here." She crawled through the crushed doorway, and Shail followed.

They reached the cliff as the light faded. Kari started to push a key when Shail caught her wrist. "To now tell that the harpies control the swarms would be unwise," he said and released her.

"I won't tell." Kari hit the keys, and Doc appeared on the small screen. "Hello, Doc. It's Kari Turner, the girl with the golden harpy."

"Kari, I've been thinking about you," Doc said. "How are you and your handsome male?"

"We're fine, but I need to know when his splint can come off," she yelled over the wind.

"So you still got him." Doc chuckled. "Well, let's see." He rubbed his beard. "He's young with strong bones, should've healed quickly, and it's the lower bone on the wing, not that much stress. Bet that high-strung fellow is itching to fly. Probably could come off now, but he better take it easy. The wing would be more stable if he waited a few more weeks. How's he treating you?"

"He's a real gentleman, Doc, in the truest sense of the word. I've never been happier." Kari clasped Shail's hand.

"Say, there's a friend of yours here, Dr. Watkins. We've been working on the harpy study and discussing you and the golden quite a bit."

"Dr. Watkins is there? Can you put him on the com?" she asked.

Watkins appeared on the screen. "Hello, Miss Turner. Did I hear you correctly? You still own the golden harpy?"

Kari pulled Shail toward the screen. "Here he is."

Watkins stared at Shail. "Dr. White told me he was a stunning creature. Can you bring him here so I could get a blood sample for my research?"

Shail hissed at the man's image on the screen.

"That was definitely a no," Kari laughed, "but I'll be picking up my vehicle in the morning and plan to be back in Westend tomorrow night. I'm bringing solid proof that can help the harpies and your research."

"I'll be looking forward to it, and to seeing you again," Watkins said, and they disconnected.

Shail and Kari went back inside the spaceship. "I do not wish that you travel alone in the vehicle," he said. "I can fly you to your father's home."

"It's too risky to come to the estate, and you heard Doc. That's a hundred-mile flight with my weight. It will tax your wing. Besides, I may need the vehicle. You can take me to the cabin. It's a short flight along the ocean." She sensed his worry for her safety. "I'll be all right. The harpies keep the swarms off my father's estate, and if I run into hunters, they'll think I'm a woman. Wild harpies don't travel in vehicles."

Shail sniffled toward a doorway, and one of the few remaining male harpies appeared and bowed to Shail. "Go to the islands and fetch an older and reliable fledgling," he relayed to the male. "At dawn have him meet me at the small human structure to the south. The fledgling shall be responsible for watching over my mate." The male nodded and left for the crevice. "I would prefer an adult," Shail said to Kari, "but all are needed at the gathering. The fledgling shall be the eyes and ears of the harpies. If trouble comes, he can retrieve the males who guard the borders of the estate."

"All right, if it makes you feel better."

They returned to their room, and Kari carefully removed the splint from Shail's wing. He stretched it out and saw the new feathers that had replaced the damaged ones. He fluttered off the floor, testing the wing and felt the weakness from injury and lack of use. His mate was right. With her weight, a long flight to the estate would bring soreness, and he needed strong wings for the days ahead.

Kari and Shail curled up on the moss, knowing this was their last night together. Having missed her period, Kari told him she was definitely pregnant, and it was no longer harpy intuition. The bond that night was for pleasure and the possibility of loss.

Shail caressed her slender body, noticing every detail. The memory would have to sustain him in the grueling weeks ahead. She quivered and wiggled against him, her body stimulating his. He slowly made love to her, wishing the night would last forever.

Their uncertain future together heightened the sex drive. With each consummation, Shail rested briefly, and at his mate's urging, performed all night. At dawn their bodies were soaking wet with sweat. He feverishly copulated to release one last climax. Rapidly pumping, he consummated the final bonding and collapsed beside her. His heart pounding, he gasped for air with limbs so weak he could barely move. He closed his eyes and felt his female stroke his exhausted body. She kissed his cheek and cuddled next to him. He placed his arms around her and drifted to sleep.

13

The sun was sinking into the horizon when John Turner stepped out of the hover and slung his traveling bag over a shoulder. After a tiring flight from Terrance, he headed for the house. Charlie greeted him at the door. "Were you able to speak to any of them?" Charlie asked.

"I talk to a guy named Harry. He was the only hunter left still able to talk. One kid is in a coma, and the other guy . . ." John raised his eyebrows. "The golden beat him so badly he's a vegetable and paralyzed for life. Kari's harpy is getting damn mean. This is his second attack on hunters."

"Maybe the golden has reasons. What did this Harry say?"

John entered the house and dropped the bag by the door. "Not much. Didn't say he saw Kari, but the location confirms we were close on their tail. The attack was several mountain ranges north of the cabin." John walked into the den. "What's the latest on the swarms? There was a major hit above Terrance while I was there. Those people are getting plenty nervous."

Charlie pulled out a map of the outback and laid it on John's desk. "Here and here." He pointed on the map. "There have been numerous swarm strikes on hunting lodges. The hits have been so fast and frequent that the death toll of hunters is unknown. Only yesterday four hunters were killed in their vehicle outside of Westend."

"No towns?" John asked.

"Not yet, and none have hit the estate. The governor has ordered a voluntary evacuation of the outback towns."

John eased into his chair. "Guess we've been lucky. I just hope the swarms stay away from the northern mountain range and Kari. You really think she's safe with the harpies?"

"I've seen the harpies fly. They can easily out-fly the beetles."

"The harbor is gone, and most of my men have left for Hampton. I can't rebuild without help, and there's no sense with these swarms. Tomorrow I plan to head back up to those mountains and hope to pick up her trail."

The communicator buzzed on his desk, and John pushed the key. "Hello, Mr. Turner. This is Mr. Schmitt in satellite communications. I have another correspondence on your property. You will be very interested in this one. The communiqué wasn't long enough to pinpoint the exact location, but there was a golden harpy on the screen, and the girl said her name was Kari Turner."

John quickly leaned forward in his seat. "Patch it through."

"Do you want a two-way hookup or just your daughter's?"

"Two-way," John said and stared anxiously at the divided screen. Kari was speaking to Doc. "Son-of-a-bitch," John growled when he saw the harpy. The short transmission ended.

"So what do you think, Mr. Turner?" Schmitt said, coming back on the screen.

"You'll be well paid for this," John said, and hit the off key.

"I thought it was illegal to listen in," Charlie said.

"It is, but some laws are meant to be bent." John rose from his seat. "We have them now. I can get my daughter back and kill the harpy at the same time."

"I heard Kari say she was happy, and he has not harmed her. She is coming back to Westend tomorrow night. Maybe we should stay here and meet her at Doc's house."

"No, I'm going to end this. If I don't, the son-of-a-bitch will come back to haunt me. This is the best shot at getting him. We'll take Sam and Jerry in a second hover. If we get there tonight and stake it out, we can surround him before he takes off. The wind won't be at our backs this time. Let's go."

The two hovers flew up the coast several miles off shore, and aided by the nearly full moons, the headlights were not needed. John and the other pilot landed their hovers on the beach far south of the cabin. The four men piled out and quietly crept toward the cabin. Once they reached the cabin, they fanned out, hid under jungle bushes, and set up a watch.

As dawn broke, John radioed the other men. "They should be here any minute. No talking. Watch for my signal."

Charlie hid alongside John. "I'm begging you for the last time, John. Please don't kill the harpy. Just let him go."

"This is the last time I want to hear that from you," John grumbled.

All was very still as morning came, and they searched the skies and woods for Kari and the harpy. The men finally spotted them.

Shail held Kari in his arms and landed in front of the familiar cabin. He set her down and stretched one wing.

"Does it hurt?" Kari asked, using harpy telepathy when in the jungle.

"No, it is good," Shail answered, and looked up into the tree branches. "I do not see the fledgling. It is unnatural he be late."

Kari wrapped her arms around Shail's neck and kissed him. "You worry too much. He'll come. We could go in the cabin, and fool around while we wait."

"You are not satisfied?" he asked.

"I'm always satisfied with you." She smiled, and Shail embraced her and buried his face in her long hair and nuzzled her neck.

"She's got him pretty distracted," John whispered. He signaled to the other men to close in.

Hearing the faint sound of a man's voice, Shail jerked his head out of Kari's hair and sniffed the air, but it was too late. With their weapons pointed toward him and Kari, Turner and the men hurried from the bushes and raced across the small clearing toward him.

Seeing Shail's startled expression and his arched wings, Kari whirled around and saw her father and the others. "Fly," she relayed.

"I shall not risk it," Shail relayed. "Their weapons could hit you." He held his mate as the men surrounded them.

"Get away from him, Kari," John ordered.

Kari clutched her mate. "So you can kill him? Never."

"Do what I say!" John yelled.

"If you promise to let him go," Kari said, "I'll come home with you."

"I won't promise that," John said. "He'll take off and be right back to ruin your life."

Tears coursed down Kari's cheeks. "Can't you see he is my life? Charlie, don't let Dad hurt Shail."

"I cannot stop him," Charlie said. "I have asked John many times to let your harpy live."

Kari wiped her wet face on her sleeve and glared at her father. "Is this how it was twenty years ago, Dad, when my mother tried to protect a golden male? You'll have to kill me, too." Her sharp words sliced through the jungle air.

"It was an accident," John stammered.

"And you can also call my death an accident," she retorted.

Shail forced Kari to face him. Like her brave golden mother, Kari was ready to accept the same fate. "It is over, Kari," he silently relayed. "You shall not risk your life for me. Go to your father."

"No!" she said out loud. "Shail, he's going to kill you." Her tears flowed again. She glanced at her father. "Dad, I know I'm a harpy, and he's my husband. Please leave us alone." She broke down and sobbed.

Shail kissed her shaky wet lips. "Know I love you, Kari." He took her by the shoulders and moved her in reach of her father.

Kari braced her feet and screamed at Shail. "What are you doing?"

John grabbed her arm and pulled her away from Shail. Holding his struggling and hysterical daughter, he said to Sam, "You and Jerry take her to my hover." They held Kari's arms and dragged her away.

"Let me go!" she screamed, and fought them. Overpowered, she turned to look at her mate for the last time. "I love you, Shail," she sobbed. "I'll always love only you."

"I can't stay for this," Charlie grumbled. "You're making a mistake, John." He walked away and followed the two men and Kari.

Shail anxiously tossed his hair and watched his mate fight the men's strength. Though she was in no danger, he wrestled his natural instinct to leap to her defense. Unable to watch, he shuddered and stared at the ground. Turner pointed the weapon at his head.

John placed his finger on the gun's trigger, and the harpy looked up at him and then at Kari a distance away. Amazingly, the male spoke with a serene human voice. "I do not wish her to see my death. May we go in the cabin?"

John's jaw dropped, and it took a moment to respond. "She taught you to speak?"

"She taught me many things."

"I bet she did," John said. "Get in there then."

The harpy stepped into the cabin, and John cautiously followed. The male swallowed hard and stared into John's eyes. "I know you are a man of honor and would keep a promise. I ask one before I die."

John studied the lofty, captivating creature and was slightly unnerved by its calm. "You act darn brave for a harpy," John said. "So what's the promise? Have your throat cut?"

"How I die is not important, but what I ask shall give me peace," Shail said and fought the growing moisture in his eyes. "I have guarded your lands and defended your daughter. When I am dead, the protection shall end, and Kari shall flee from you. Do not let her. I ask you keep her safe and protect my unborn son. I shall not resist death if you promise me this."

John backed out of the striking range of the slender harpy. He learned from the surviving mountain hunter the golden male had brought down three men with lightning speed. He stared into the harpy's blue eyes, and they showed no fear of him or his weapon. Kari's airy mate could put up a hell of fight if only wounded. "Why did you attack those three hunters in the mountains?"

Shail tilted his head, puzzled by his question. "They caught my mate and threatened harm. They are lucky I am harpy that does not take life."

John's hate gave way to respect. "Okay, if Kari is pregnant, I promise to watch over your fledgling. No hunter will get it."

Shail made a slight nod and lightly stepped in front of him.

John raised his weapon, gripping the trigger, but the harpy dropped to his knees and arched his head back, exposing his throat. His luxurious yellow feathers cascaded across the cabin floor. John sighed and lowered his weapon. The noble male deserved an honorable harpy death. Withdrawing a large hunting knife from his belt, he held the blade toward the harpy's throat and grabbed a handful of its silky hair. He jerked the male's neck back to ensure a clean cut. The male shut his eyes and quivered slightly. With his knife against its throat, John stared at him for a long moment and noticed the young male resembled his daughter and dead wife. "Goddamn it." He dropped the knife and grabbed his laser gun. Pointing the barrel at the harpy's chest, he fired. Kari's mate crumbled to the floor face down, his wings extended unnaturally over him.

Kari heard the laser gun. She ripped free of the unsuspecting man and raced up the path toward the cabin. Her father stepped out of the cabin and caught her before she entered.

"Shail!" she yelled and wrestled to be free. She caught a glimpse of his body lying on the cabin door. "Shail," she screamed, but he didn't move or answer her calls.

"It's over now, Kari," John said, holding her. "You don't want to go in there."

Kari called Shail's name again and again. She tried to reach him with the telepathy, but got no response. Even wounded, he would have answered. Realizing he was dead, she collapsed into her father's arms.

John picked her up and carried her toward the beach. She softly sobbed, repeating Shail's name and begging him to come. Sam started to pass John, heading for the cabin. "Where in the hell do you think you're going?" John barked.

"Mr. Turner, I figured you didn't want the wings," Sam said. "They're worth a bunch, and it's a shame to let them rot."

Hearing the man's statement, Kari shook in her father's arms. All her hopes, happiness, and love had been reduced to a bundle of lifeless feathers that lay on the cabin floor. She felt the dark gloom and heavy weight of despair that crept into her soul and crushed her will to go on. She didn't fight it.

John growled at the man. "It's my land, my kill, and my wings. Leave them as they lay."

"Sure, Mr. Turner, anything you say."

"Get to the hover and get back to the mill," John ordered.

Sam jogged ahead and was joined by Jerry. They disappeared over a bluff.

As John walked up the path cradling Kari, he was met by Charlie. The old Indian just shook his head and slowly strolled up the beach.

"We'll be home soon, Kari," John said. "Everything will be all right."

She softly whimpered in his arms.

He finally reached his hover, and Charlie was waiting in the passenger seat. The other hover had already left for the estate. He placed Kari on the backseat, and she curled up in a tight ball resembling an incoherent, wounded animal. "She'll be okay," he said to Charlie. Charlie didn't answer.

The hovercraft ride was as quiet as a funeral. No one spoke.

The male harpy's words played over and over in John's head. Was Kari pregnant? He had promised to protect the fledgling, but he now wondered if he could persuade Kari to abort it. Kari's sniffles occasionally were heard over the hover engine, and he glanced back her. She looked so much like her mother. Her limbs were pulled in, and she rested in the traditional curled-up way that harpies slept. For the first time his daughter truly looked like a harpy. He leaned back in the hover seat and exhaled deeply. He'd honor his promise to the golden male and look after his son.

In the afternoon, dark clouds had gathered, signaling the beginning of the rainy season. John landed the hover on the front lawn, close to the house doors. He climbed out, opened the hover back door, and lifted Kari into his arms. Her eyes were shut, and she trembled. Maria met him at the door and followed him upstairs to Kari's bedroom where he laid her on the bed.

Maria stroked her forehead. "It will be okay, Miss Kari. You're home now," she said. Kari didn't respond or cry. She stared at the wall in a trance. Maria glanced at John with concern.

"Go call Doc," he said.

Maria left the room, and John heard Maria and Charlie on the stairs. "Kari's harpy?" Maria asked.

"Dead," Charlie answered, and walked into the bedroom.

John sat on the bed and caressed Kari's head. She shivered and her eyes were fixed. "Come on, baby. Snap out of this," he said, covering her with a blanket.

"I doubt she can," Charlie said and left the room.

John became seriously worried, knowing a female harpy could die from the loss of a mate, especially if she had no offspring, but he didn't figure it could happen to his strong, willful daughter who was half human. He paced the room. Doc's arrival was taking forever.

John looked out the balcony window and saw Doc's old hover set down beside his. Carrying a black medical bag, Doc got out with another man. They walked to the door, and he heard their voices as Maria let them in. Doc, the man, and Maria soon walked into the bedroom. Charlie returned to the doorway and leaned against the threshold.

Doc didn't say a word and went straight to the curled-up girl on the bed. He examined her set, dilated eyes and felt her pulse. "Maria, more blankets," he said. "She's in shock."

The other man quickly dug through the medical bag and handed Doc a syringe and a vial. Doc filled the syringe and administered the drug into Kari's arm. Maria covered Kari with more blankets.

"Is she going to be all right?" John asked.

Doc straightened and glared at John. "I doubt it. You damn fool; you killed her golden male, didn't you?"

"It had to be done," John said.

"You probably have also killed your daughter," Doc said. "Dr. Watkins, let's draw some blood and get the DNA scanner out." Watkins reached in the bag for another syringe and the monitor.

"Why do you need all that?" John asked.

"Because I want to know if I'm working on a human or a harpy. There is a big difference."

"I swore to my wife I'd never tell," John said, glancing at Kari. "She's harpy."

"Oh, my word," Maria said, covering her mouth.

"John, you knew your daughter was a harpy, and she had bonded with the young male, yet you still killed him." Doc huffed. "The female harpies are as fragile as the males when caged. They go into shock and die of despair. They're not strong like humans."

"Kari is part human, and I figured she could survive," John said. "How did you learn about harpies?"

"Dr. Watkins and I have been doing a lot research on harpies and their history. It became apparent that the women who were taken and raped by male harpies were really female harpies. Once their mates were killed, and they were forced back to civilization, the females suffered from shock, heart failure, and death . . . just like the males." Doc leaned over and patted Kari's arm. "I'm surprised the poor thing stayed alive all those years on Earth and didn't commit suicide."

"What are her chances?" John asked.

"Small," Doc said. "If she survives the trauma, she'll never be the same. The girl you once knew is gone. She's embraced her harpy side. With the loss of her mate, she only wants to die. It'll take drugs with around-the-clock surveillance to keep her alive. I warned you that disaster would come if you interfered."

John slumped in a chair. "My father also warned me. He said my life would be a disaster if I married a harpy, and the creature could only bring sorrow." John placed his face in his hands to conceal the tears. He finally wiped his face on his sleeve, cleared his throat, and looked up at Doc. "I really believed Kari would be okay. I didn't want her running around in the woods being chased by hunters."

Doc rubbed John's shoulder. "I'm sure you had the best of intentions."

"The harpy said that Kari is pregnant with his fledgling. Do you think it's true?" John asked.

"The male harpy spoke to you?" Dr. Watkins asked.

"It surprised the heck out of me," John said. "He spoke perfect English. I didn't think males could utter a sound, much less talk. He asked me to protect his son."

Doc reached in his bag and pulled out his scanner, the same scanner that the male harpy had knocked from his hand and sent flying across his room. "I liked that blond male. He had balls. Even badly wounded, he tried to defend your daughter." He ran the scanner over Kari. "Congratulations, John. If she lives, you'll be a grandfather."

"She's pregnant?" John asked.

"The fetus is roughly three weeks old," Doc said.

Kari gasped for breath and her eyes rolled back.

"No, girl, don't do this," Doc said, and scanned her again. "Hurry, Watkins. Her heart is racing and she's shut down. Give me the stimulant."

"What's happening to her?" John yelled.

Watkins handed the stimulant to Doc. "She's creating her own death," Watkins explained. "Depressed harpies have enough concentration to shut down their organs. I've seen it when they're caged."

Doc scanned her. "The stimulant is slowing her heart rate. Let's put an antidepressant patch on her and load her with tranquilizers. She'll be a zombie, but it will keep her alive. Some vets came up with this new drug treatment. It prolongs the life of a caught harpy." Doc stood up and faced John. "I'm sorry. This is all I can do. Your daughter will live a life of tranquilizers and semiconsciousness. I'm not sure how those drugs will affect her fetus. The baby might be mentally impaired."

John walked to the bed and placed his hand on Kari's frail, clammy arm and watched her trembling in a coma. "I didn't do it, baby," he mumbled to Kari.

"Didn't do what?" Doc asked.

"I didn't kill her mate," John said. "I only stunned him. I thought I could bring her home and persuade her to forget him. Guess I was a fool to think so."

John glanced up, and everyone stared at him. "Look, I really didn't kill him. I couldn't. After he spoke, I saw him for what he was: not some wild, raping animal that had seduced my little girl with his flashy good looks, but an intelligent, loyal husband. He was damn brave and had so much dignity. He dropped to his knees and threw back his head." John walked near the balcony. "The only thing he wanted was my promise to protect his family. I put the knife to his throat and knew I'd regret it. I've never known a man with that much heart."

Charlie went to John and patted his shoulder. "I'm glad, John."

Doc looked at Kari. "Well, she certainly thinks he's dead. The stunning would have worn off hours ago, and he'd have come here. The male would never let his mate come so close to death. Are you sure your gun was set to stun or that the stunning didn't give him a heart attack?"

"I'm sure," John said. "I checked him, and he was breathing fine. I made sure all the men had their weapons set for a mild animal stunning." John froze. "Goddamn them!" He whirled around. "Charlie, take my hover to the mill and see if Jerry and Sam came back." Charlie raced out of the room, and the hover engine sounded. John looked out the balcony and watched the hover fly toward the mill. The sun was sinking into the horizon.

In minutes, Charlie returned and leaped out of the hover. He yelled to John on the balcony "They're not there and neither is the hover."

John looked up at the orange and purple dusk sky and felt ill. "God, what have I done?" He walked back into the bedroom. "The two men that were with me, they must've doubled back and got him. They killed him for some lousy feathers. Oh, Jesus, I've made a mess of things."

"Are you sure they killed him?" Watkins asked.

John nodded. "They wanted his wings."

Doc stroked Kari's forehead and sighed. "She was coming back to Westend anyway to give Dr. Watkins some kind of proof that would help her harpies."

John searched Kari's pant pockets and pulled out an old disc. "This must be it," he said, handing the disc to Dr. Watkins.

Watkins examined it. "Do you have the equipment to play it?"

"I think I can rig something up," John said.

"Go ahead; I'll stay with her," Doc said and eased into a chair. "She'll sleep for some time."

Downstairs, John and Watkins worked on the equipment while Charlie watched. Maria went into the kitchen and made sandwiches and coffee. She served them to the three men in the den. "I will take a plate up to Doc," she said.

"Thanks, Maria," John said. "I plan to stay up all night with Kari. You might as well go home and get some rest. I might need a break by tomorrow."

"If you're sure, I'll clean the kitchen and go." Maria headed toward the stairs with Doc's sandwich.

John worked on the recording equipment, making adjustments to play the ancient-looking disc, and was grateful to take his mind off Kari and her dead mate. Doc joined them, reporting that Kari was sleeping peacefully.

John, Charlie, Doc, and Watkins sat down and watched the old log of Captain James and his ill-fated space freighter, *The Princess*. When the last log was over, they were too astonished for words.

Dr. Watkins finally broke the silence. "I need to take the disc to Hampton and put it in the right hands. Do you realize the log might vindicate the harpies and prove they are a race of gentle mortals? It's inconceivable that harpy hunting would continue."

Doc slowly stood up. "So all our research and assumptions are correct, and this is how the harpies came about."

"How could two different species create the harpies?" John asked.

"Dora is a young planet with wayward genetics that generates new species," Watkins said, "and I'm guessing that the loca eagles and humans have the same amount of chromosomes, like sheep and humans. A man and a sheep can create a fetus, but it never survives. The procreation of a man and loca eagle produces the harpy hybrids that can subsist and are not sterile."

"Why don't the females have wings?" John asked, removing the disc and easing back into his chair.

"That's the way genetics works," Watkins said. "For example, take domestic house cats. A black female cat with black parents bred to an orange male cat with orange parents will produce a litter of orange, black, and possibly tortoiseshell kittens, but the male kittens will be black like their mother, and the female kittens are orange or possibly tortoiseshell like the father. The female harpies pick up the genetic trait from their human fathers, and the male harpies get their wings from the mother loca eagle. Now if the harpies had bred with the loca eagles, then all harpies would have wings."

Dr. Watkins sipped his coffee and continued. "Like your wife, the female harpies occasionally pair with men, and that ensures wingless daughters. The female's ability to be a chameleon and hide amide the human population has probably saved the species, but the day might come when female harpies stop taking men and in a few generations the females might have wings."

"I thought my wife married me for my good looks." John smiled.

"Speaking of looks, the harpies' features are equally fascinating," Watkins said. "These hybrids get their flawless faces, small noses, big eyes with long lashes and slender frames from the loca eagles. Human features are more diverse. Harpies are gorgeous and magnificent. It would be a crime if they became extinct."

Doc leaned back in a comfortable chair. "We also did research on our senators who promote hunting and have a vendetta against the harpies," he said. "It's no secret that our senators are the descendants of the Dorial explorers who colonized Dora. We discovered the first recorded kidnapping of a woman by a male harpy. The woman was found, but went into shock and died. She was the daughter of one of the Dorial explorers, and she had to be a female harpy. Putting two and two together, it was our glorified founding fathers who raped the harpies. How else could one have a harpy child? This is not theory, but fact. We found the passenger list of *The Hampton*, the Dorial's ship. There were no women listed on board, yet when the settlers arrived twenty-five years later, the Dorial men had daughters. Where did those daughters come from if not from the harpies? The Dorials created the lies about the male harpies to hide their own crimes. Even back then, it was a felony to molest or harm intelligent life-forms found on new planets. By categorizing the harpies as hazardous animals, there is no crime. Our senators are willing to exterminate the harpies to conceal those facts. If it came out that the harpies were harmless mortals, guilty only of rescuing their females, the scandal would destroy our senators' reputations, and they would be booted out of office, especially if they were aware of their ancestors' history."

"There's another reason the senators want to exterminate the harpies," Watkins added. "If harpy DNA was compared to the Dorial explorers' DNA it would verify the two are related and the explorers were guilty of raping harpies, but it also would establish that the senators carry harpy blood. Imagine their mortification!"

John got up and took out a bottle of wine. "Anyone want some?"

"I could use a glass," Doc said.

John poured two glasses. "All these years I've believed some of those lies. I figured since the male harpies were raised in the jungle without civilization that they were wild ignorant creatures and different from the females who were raised among humans."

"How did you meet your harpy wife?" Watkins asked.

"My father and I were cutting trees on a logging road behind the house," said John. "I came across a lake with trisom trees. She sat under the trees eating the fruit, wearing a white gown. It was like a dream. This beautiful woman with long blond hair stood up and walked to me. She said she was a female harpy and had chosen me to be her mate. I felt like a spell was cast; I was instantly in love and didn't care what she was. My daughter met her mate at the same lake."

John took a gulp of wine. "Goddamn it! I should've figured those two men would take him. I had to yell at Sam for heading back to the cabin for the wings. Considering the price of gold wings, I should've protected her mate." John swallowed more wine and rubbed his jaw. "My mind was on Kari. I learned three hunters had attacked her. But despite the danger, she'd run right back into woods with her golden male once the stunning wore off and he came for her. I just wanted time to talk to Kari, maybe convince her to stay." He shook his head. "Guess no one could've convinced me to leave my wife, either."

Doc stood up. "There's so much darn grief surrounding these poor harpies. Maybe the disc can give them a decent future. It's late, and I'm tired. I'll check Kari and give her another dose of tranquilizers. The last ones should be wearing off." He set his empty glass down and headed for the stairs.

John was finishing his second glass. "I'll be right up, Doc."

Watkins looked at the disc. "Would you mind if I used your equipment and made some copies? It makes me nervous that there is only one."

John put the disc in the player, pushed the record key, and then headed for the stairs.

Doc pushed open the bedroom door and looked in. What he saw caused him to freeze. A brown-winged harpy leaned over the bed, its hand on Kari's forehead. Seeing Doc, the male made a panic hiss and moved toward the balcony.

"Don't go," Doc said calmly. "You might be the only thing that can help her." The harpy stopped in front of the balcony and stared at him. Doc heard John's heavy steps coming up the wooden stairs. "Get back, John," Doc whispered out the door and slowly went into the bedroom. The anxious harpy arched his wings and shook his long brown hair. One fast movement, and it would spook, darting out the balcony. "Easy, little fellow," Doc said. "No one's gonna hurt you."

John crept toward the bedroom door and peeked in as Doc coaxed a skittish brown harpy to stay.

"Can you help her?" Doc asked the harpy. The threatened harpy made a low, seething sound and trembled badly. His gaze displayed indecision, shifting back and forth from Doc to Kari. Watching Doc's every move, the harpy left the balcony and tiptoed back to Kari's bed, where he again placed his hand on her forehead. "Good boy," Doc encouraged him.

Kari slowly opened her eyes and drowsily looked up at the harpy. "Aron?" She weakly put her arms up to embrace him. The harpy bent over and nuzzled her, allowing her to wrap her arms around his neck and bury her face in his coffee-brown hair. "He's dead, Aron," she whimpered. "Shail's dead."

Aron sensed the harpy depression had a firm hold on her. He normally would never enter a human house, but the harpies couldn't afford to lose the precious golden female who carried their future ruler. He had planned to take her, but detected the helping drugs that slowed her heartbeat. "It is unknown if Shail is dead," he relayed.

"My father killed him," she said, using her human voice.

"He did not," Aron relayed. "The fledgling saw all as he hid from the men. After you, Turner, and the men left, the fledgling entered the cabin and tried to wake Shail, but then heard the returning men and fled to the trees. On the beach, the men tied Shail with ropes, but he woke and fought them. They used their weapons, and Shail went limp. They placed him in the metal bird, and it flew away. The fledgling could not follow the fast flight. We cannot find Shail and do not know if he lives."

Aron detected a second odor and whirled around, breaking free of Kari's arms. Turner, a known harpy killer, stood in the doorway. To discourage an attack, Aron hissed, tossed his locks, and extended his wings while backing toward the balcony.

"John, you're scaring the shit out of him," Doc said. "Get out."

John backed to the threshold. "Kari, tell him, I won't harm him."

Kari glanced at Aron, and he stopped moving away. He folded in his wings and stood in the balcony doorway. She wiped away her tears and stared at her father. "You didn't kill Shail."

"No, I only stunned him," John said. "Tell your harpy friend to stay."

"He senses your meaning. He's not a stupid animal," she snapped.

"Does he know where Shail is?" John asked.

"Two of your hired guns put him in a hover," Kari said. "The harpies don't know if he's dead or alive." She slid off the bed and attempted to walk. "Aron, take me out of here." Feeling faint, she started to collapse. Aron bounded toward her, catching her before she hit the floor.

John rushed to help, but Aron held Kari and struck out with his wing, nearly smacking the man's face. John backed away, and Aron bared his teeth, hissed and ruffled his dark feathers like a bantam rooster poised for a cockfight. Sensing Kari's revulsion for her father, he would defend his golden queen and her wishes. Holding her, he buried his fear and stood his ground.

John eyed the slender male. "This is the one that protected you from the grogins?"

"You know about that?" she said, surprised. "Yes, his name is Aron."

"Kari, I'm so sorry about Shail," John said. "I didn't want him hurt or captured. I promise I'll do everything in my power to get him back. You belong with him. If you want to leave, I won't stop you, but Shail asked me to keep you here. He wanted me to protect you and his son."

Aron helped Kari stand, but kept his arms around her. "I know not Turner's sound," Aron relayed to Kari, "but there is truth and sorrow in his mind."

Kari spoke to Aron with telepathy. "My father says that Shail wanted me here, but please, Aron, take me back to the jungle."

Aron bent down and nuzzled the head of the clinging female. "Shail also relayed those wishes to me, saying you shall need your father's strong arms if the harpies fail. It is better you stay until we know Shail's fate. Do not fear. I shall remain until your death wish vanishes like a bad dream."

Kari pulled her face away from Aron's chest and looked at her father. "Shail spoke to you then?"

"Yes. He didn't say much," John said, "but what little he said left me overwhelmed. I've been wrong all these years about male harpies. He was no monster, but a devoted husband who loves you as much as I do." He lowered his head. "Maybe more."

Kari bit her bottom lip and tried to speak, but couldn't. She hugged Aron again and wept.

Aron hugged her and wrapped his wings around her body as he defiantly glared at John, sensing the father's longing to touch his daughter.

"Kari, I know you resent me," John said, "and for good reason, but I hope you decide to stay." He walked toward the door and glanced back at Aron. "Please take good care of her." Doc followed John out and shut the bedroom door.

Aron breathed a sigh of relief, never before having confronted a man. "If Shail lives, the harpies shall find him."

Lightning bolts lit up the jungle and meadows, followed by tropical gusts and sheets of rain. Kari and Aron stared out the balcony, and he felt a renewed spirit and a hope growing in her, knowing Shail might be alive.

John descended the stairs with Doc. "You didn't give her the drugs. Do you think she'll be all right?"

"I think that brown can do her more good than anything in my black bag, and she doesn't know if her mate is dead or alive. That's given her some optimism."

"The odds are slim, but I hope he's alive," John said, and they reached the bottom of the stairs. "So you liked her golden male?"

Doc grinned. "What's not to like? He's nervy, loyal, and has the good looks to make women drool and men jealous. Yeah, I liked him, and I'm darn picky. I also got a kick out of that feisty brown, taking a wing swipe at you. I believe these slinky male harpies have been underrated."

"For a change, we agree," John said. "Let's just pray her golden escapes those men. I'll call the authorities and report that my hover and the harpy were stolen off my property. First thing in the morning I'm heading back to the cabin. Maybe I can pick up some clues."

John and Doc walked into the den. Dr. Watkins approached Doc. "I'd like to borrow your hover," said Watkins. "If I fly to Terrance tonight, I can catch the early commercial flight to Hampton. I'm eager to expose the information on the captain's log, and my research computer is on the hover's backseat. I'll leave the extra disc copies here."

Doc glanced at the rain pelting the windows. "It's storming out there, but you're welcome to it."

"I've flown in bad weather." Watkins left the front door and ran across the lawn through the rain. He hopped in the old hover and it soon lifted off. Its lights disappeared in the drenching dark clouds.

John shut the front door. "Doc, you might as well spend the night in one of the spare bedrooms. Tomorrow I'll take you to the mill, and you can borrow a hover."

"Good," Doc said. "I'm in no hurry to get wet."

Charlie took Doc upstairs to a room, and he then also went to bed.

John strolled into his den and placed a com call to the Terrance police department.

The officer filled out the information on the stolen hover, but stopped when John explained about his daughter's missing pet, a golden male harpy. The officer looked up and mockingly grinned. "Mister, you want me to file a report on a stolen harpy?"

John glared at him. "That's right. Put your sergeant on the com."

The sergeant appeared on the screen. "Mr. Turner, the officer is new and wasn't aware of who you were. We'll put out an all-points bulletin on your hover and the harpy, sir."

John thanked him and disconnected the com call. He filled another glass of wine and sat in the quiet, dark house. He sipped the wine, listening to the rain hitting the windows, and wondered if Kari had stayed or gone back to the jungle and harpies. Taking the last swallow, he headed upstairs.

At her bedroom, John nudged open her door and peered in. A small bathroom light dimly lit the room. Kari lay sleeping, coiled up on her bed, and in front of the open balcony, the brown-winged male rested on the floor. He jerked his head out of the feathers and flung the brown hair away from his alert green eyes. He stared at John and softly seethed a warning to stay out. The half human, half bird with the lean frame of a teenage boy was protecting Kari like a vicious little dog. "You're a good boy," John whispered.

The harpy sniffled and tilted his head.

John shut the door. For the first time he was grateful to have a male harpy in his home.

Early next morning, Maria entered the Turner home through the kitchen. She hurried to the stairs, eager to see if Kari was all right. Opening the bedroom door, she saw Kari sleeping on her bed, and then noticed the tall male harpy standing in the balcony doorway. She screamed, and the gutsy thing arched its wings and hissed at her. She slammed the door and raced down the hall to Mr. Turner's room. "Mr. Turner! Mr. Turner!"

John climbed out of bed and opened his door to the hysterical housekeeper. "What is it?"

"There's a horrible giant harpy in Miss Kari's room!" she shrieked.

"Calm down, Maria. I know he's there. He won't hurt her."

Maria looked up at him. "Is Miss Kari really a harpy?"

"She's half harpy. Now go down stairs and fix breakfast and make sure there's plenty of fruit. I have a feeling we'll need it. Doc also spent the night."

"Okay, Mr. Turner. I hope I don't have to feed the harpy." She shuddered and scurried past Kari's door and went downstairs.

John dressed and went to Kari's room. He knocked lightly on the door.

"Yes?" Kari answered.

John opened the door and saw the male harpy had gone. "I hope Maria didn't scare your friend away."

"No, he's gone to find out if the harpies found Shail. If he's dead, I'll never forgive what you've done." She glared. "You didn't kill him, but it's your fault those men have him. I'm only here to honor Shail's wishes." Every one of her words smoldered with hostility.

John eased into a chair. "I don't expect you to forgive me. If he dies, I won't forgive myself. I stunned him and brought you home, thinking I could convince you to leave him, or maybe I needed time to convince myself. I'm so sorry, Kari. I swear I didn't want him harmed."

Kari rose from the bed, distancing herself from him and gazed out the balcony. "I find that hard to believe. You had every intention of killing him. You changed your mind and let your men do your dirty work so you'd be blameless. You're sorry now because I became sick."

"Kari, that's not true. You should know I'd never let some flunkies do my dirty work. I did plan to kill Shail, but he dropped to his knees, and . . ."

Kari whirled around, facing him. "Shail would never beg for his life."

"He didn't beg. He accepted his death, and Jesus, he was so impressive. He was only concerned about you and his son. He's everything a man, a husband should be. How could I kill him?"

"Perhaps you're telling the truth. He's not afraid to die, but would be worried about his family. At the cabin I told him to fly away, but he stayed, fearing a laser blast might hit me. Strangely, Dad, he respected you. I despised you when you chased us through the mountains, but Shail saw you as a protective parent. I love him so much. If he's dead . . ." She sat down on the bed, putting her face in her hands, hiding tears.

John rose from the chair, sat on the bed alongside her, and took her into his arms. "Oh, baby, I know you don't want my advice, but I know your pain. When your mother died, I had to remind myself every day that I was lucky; lucky I'd had her even for a short time, and you were lucky to find Shail. They left us with an irreplaceable gift that makes life worth living. Your mother gave me you, and soon you'll have a son; a son Shail was willing to die for. If he's dead, don't deny him his last wish. Live for his boy."

Kari sniffled and wiped away a tear. "Shail must've known that something might happen to him. He told me to draw from my human strength and survive for our fledgling, but it's hard. I feel so empty, it hurts, and I can hardly breathe."

John took ahold of her shoulders and forced a grin. "Let's be positive that he's okay. We'll eat breakfast and then fly back to the cabin. Charlie is good at finding clues. I contacted the police last night, and they're looking for those two men and Shail, plus the harpies are searching. If it's the last thing I do, I promise I'll find him and bring him back."

Her father left, and Kari got dressed. Going downstairs, she entered the dining room and found Doc, Charlie, and her father seated at the table. "Hello, Doc," she said quietly, taking a seat beside him.

Doc smiled. "I'm glad you're feeling better."

"Not better, just more in control," she said.

"The antidepressant patch on your arm is helping you keep that control," Doc said. "There's more in your room, and I want you to put one on your arm daily."

"I will as long as there's a chance Shail is alive."

Doc patted her arm. "I'm betting he's still with us. He's like an ornery little cat with nine lives and should've died on my operating table. He's a scrapper and has outmaneuvered hunters for years. I pity those men who got him."

"I learned he did fight with those men, but his defiance may have drawbacks." Kari turned to Charlie. "I had a disc in my pocket, but it must've fallen out. Did you see it in the hover, Charlie?"

John spoke before Charlie responded. "We found it and played it last night. Dr. Watkins was here, and he and the disc are on their way to Hampton. It's an extraordinary captain's log. In the right hands, it could bring an end to harpy hunting."

Kari leaned back in her chair. "I thought so, too, but Shail didn't place much faith in it." She chewed on her bottom lip. "Even when people know we carry human blood, they still hunt harpies. Like you, Dad, you killed Shail's father and wanted to kill him."

"Don't compare me with those lousy harpy hunters who kill for profit," John said. "I'd kill a harpy or a man if they were a threat to you or your mother." He shook his head. "Turns out I'm the biggest threat to my loved ones."

"John, stop beating yourself up," Doc said. "For twenty years you've lived with regret over your wife. Are you gonna waste another twenty if her harpy dies? The fact is you didn't want either one of them dead, but accidents and mistakes happen in life." Doc turned to Kari. "And you, young lady, give your father a break. After all, he's only human."

The dawn broke over the eastern jungle, and rather than glide cautiously through the trees, Aron rapidly flew above the canopy in the dangerous open sky. Shail's life and the future of the harpies rested on Aron's wings. According to the fledgling, the men had shot Shail and bound him with ropes. Aron knew a dead harpy would not need to be tied, and the news gave him hope that Shail was taken alive, but time was against the young golden. Although Shail was resilient and courageous, he wouldn't live long in the hands of hunters.

Two hours into his flight, Aron's haste nearly caused his own demise. Hearing laser weapons, he had little time to evade or hide. The blasts zipped past his head and wings. He had inadvertently flown over a pack of hunters. He dipped and staggered his flight, but one blast tore through his brown feathers, barely missing the bone and muscle.

Fearing more hunters lay ahead, he automatically faked an injury and let his limp body tumble end over end until he crashed through the branches. Halfway through the tree cover, he righted himself, fluttered, and grabbed a tree trunk. Clinging to the bark, he tightly folded in his wings and listened. The hunters excitedly called to one another in their search for the downed harpy. Aron gained a sense of each man's location; their cheerful voices echoed through the dense vegetation. After pinpointing each man, he left the trunk and sailed toward the forest floor, and a few feet off the ground, he navigated around the trees. Several miles later and past the danger, he flew up to the treetops and resumed his high-speed flight. The hunters would spend hours combing the area of his descent, vainly looking for his maimed body.

Aron reached the expansive river and followed its flow south. The river marked the divide between the outback frontier and the more human-populated east. He soared above the banks, close to the protective trees, and eventually reached a vast marshland. He breathed a sigh of relief, knowing the saw grass wetland left little for concealment, and a hunter, boat, or hovercraft could easily be spotted before a weapon strike. The marsh was a safe haven for river flocks.

Before starting the twenty-mile journey across the watery flatland, Aron fluttered and pulled up a few of the purple water plants. Chewing on the yellow fleshy root for stamina, he continued his quest to the southeast. In the distance he saw the island's blue and red trees rising amid boundless purple swamp. Secure and detached from humans, Shail had chosen this central place for the harpy gathering.

Aron reached the island, and flying above the trees, he looked down at a multitude of male harpies. Some were curled up in trees and others milled around on the ground, all waiting for Shail's arrival. Aron recognized some members of his flock and landed among them. Their eyes held a question: Where was Shail?

Aron walked to the center of the gathering and was surrounded by numerous unfamiliar flocks. He sniffled and flapped his wings to get their attention.

"I am Aron, flock leader of the islands and northwestern shores. I come bearing ill news of our golden ruler. He has fallen to hunters, and his fate is unknown." His message sent a silent rumble of concern through the large group. Several males moved toward him, their reigning position obvious as the other harpies submissively lowered their heads, and gave them a wide berth.

"We shall continue to hold the swarms west of the river," Aron relayed, "and defend the outback towns, allowing innocent humans to flee. Only hunters and their dwellings face the beetle attack. These are the golden's wishes. All here must seek our golden ruler and learn his whereabouts. The gathering is over until he is found."

A flock leader moved closer to Aron. "Unless my eyes deceive me, your wings are brown, yet you order us like they were gold. Why should we yield to a young brown that lacks the wing length that proves cunning?"

Aron expected a challenge. He glanced at the other flock leaders and knew they were bidding their turn to bring him down. How many would he have to fight after this one?

This day could mark the beginning of chaos among the flocks if Shail was lost, or left no heir. Brown would fight brown for leadership, causing weakness and divide among the harpies. Decades ago, only the goldens fought one another for flock rule, and the browns acknowledged and submitted to the winner and new ruler. Shail came into power by default, all his golden equals were dead by the time he had reached maturity.

"The golden shared my nest and I know his wishes," Aron relayed. "You shall yield to me or know your blood." Aron looked at the other males. "I challenge all, but my defeat comes only at the silence of my heart."

A contest to the death was unheard of by the passive harpies. Most minor skirmishes were over a female or rule of an individual flock. And rarely were harpies injured, much less killed, but Aron meant business. To save Shail and protect his golden mate and fledgling from swarms, he put his life on the line.

The male hissed and stepped toward Aron, beginning the challenge. Aron obstinately flung his hair, teasing his opponent while he moved out of striking distance. Fighting like birds, the two moved in a circular motion around one another, extending their wings, ruffling feathers, and tossing their locks. The other harpies left the trees and the massed group closed in to watch the combat between Aron and the male. The flock leader flapped his wings, becoming airborne and flew at Aron, hoping to swiftly end the fight with a powerful kick. Aron lifted a few feet off the ground. Using his feet, he struck back, and a lucky kick connected against the male's face. They both landed and paced again.

The large male wiped his bloodied nose with his wrist and seethed at Aron. In a minute they fluttered, exchanging more foot blows. Having no time for a showdown, Aron flew straight into the male's striking feet and hammered his rival with his fists, wings, and feet. Caught off guard by Aron's full-fledged attack, the male fluttered backward. A hard hit to the male's testicles finished the fight. The male dropped to the ground, coughed and curled up in defeat, lowering his eyes to Aron.

Aron landed and glared at the others. He realized he had been reared with an advantage; that advantage was a young golden harpy. As teenagers, he and Shail partook in mock male challenges. Though five seasons younger and smaller, Shail would ignore his pain and blindly fly into Aron's striking feet. He'd relentlessly attack until Aron yielded.

Another flock leader stepped from the crowd. "So you are Aron of the west? I am Seth and rule the eastern shore, and you shall cower to me."

Aron quickly sized up Seth. The eastern flock leader was formidable, and his mere presence would cause panic in most males. His paling brown feathers told his age: late thirties or early forties. His massive frame was taller and heavier than Aron's. Aron remained undaunted, arching his dark wings and standing his ground with his head held high. Seth sniffled, and his posturing and strut were meant to intimidate, but Aron refused to flinch under pressure. Seth didn't bother with the customary circling to analyze and search for a weakness in an adversary. The big male knew he was good. With a flip of his hair, he flew at Aron. Aron ducked and rolled, but was instantly in the air, sending a powerful kick into Seth's stomach. They landed out of range of one another and glared.

"Come, Seth. Come fight me," Aron relayed. "My golden brother taught me well."

Seth lowered his wings, staring at the young leader. "To challenge me, you are either crazy or cocky like a golden. Perhaps our ruler was indeed your nest brother. To lower your head would take a beating close to death, and I choose not to maim and crush such bravery." Seth turned to the harpy crowd. "The challenge is over. We shall heed Aron's wishes for one more light and search for our golden ruler while holding back the swarms." Seth turned to Aron. "If the golden is not found, he is surely dead, for no harpy can survive hunters this long. We shall end the search of him and leave the swarms, allowing the humans to suffer their just destiny. I shall not risk my males' lives for these cruel creatures, when I must return to the east and defend my family."

"Our golden ruler can survive, for he has already done so," relayed Aron.

"I shall return to the gathering the following light and hope he is found. I now defend his golden mate and unborn fledgling." Aron walked to his western flock. They nuzzled him while he stared skyward at a cloud made of two thousand pairs of departing wings. A massive search for the golden ruler had begun.

"We must find Shail," Aron relayed to his males. "If unfound, we shall all perish under the swarms." They took flight, joining the other harpies, and he spread his wings and flew toward the west coast and Kari.

In the late afternoon, dark clouds gathered and thunderstorms rolled in. The stinging rain hit Aron's face. He lowered his head, allowing his long hair to protect his eyes. Although the rainstorm was an annoyance, he felt more secure, because the feeble humans sought shelter from the sky water and rarely hunted. He beat his wings and pressed on, knowing it would be dark when he reached Turner's home.

John, Charlie, Doc, and Kari loaded up in John's hovercraft. They stopped at the mill, and Doc took the extra hover back to Westend. They proceeded with the one-hundred-mile northern journey along the coast. The day was overcast, but when they landed on the beach near the cabin, Charlie was relieved to see dry ground. "It did not rain here. We might discover signs of what happened."

Kari hurried up the path to the small cabin and entered its door. She bent down and touched the unoccupied floor where she had last seen Shail's fallen body. Fighting back the tears, she glanced around the place they had first shared. On the counter sat the plastic cup Shail had initially refused to touch, and alongside it was the solar light, its switch becoming his toy. She stood up and moved to the bed where he wrapped her in his arms and wings at night. Sitting on the sheets, she sniffed the pillows, and his sweet scent still lingered. She noticed her father watching from the doorway. He lowered his head and looked down.

"Come," Charlie said from the outside. "The tracks show where they dragged him to the beach where the hover set down." They followed Charlie to the beach. "Here they dropped in the sand, and look at the deep struggle marks. The harpy fought them, but there is no blood. They must have stunned him again."

Looking at the scenario, John rubbed his chin. "Those boys wanted him alive, but why?"

Kari pulled a small yellow feather out of the sand. "For two days, Carol's boyfriend Jake kept Shail alive and planned to hang and torture him elsewhere."

"These men weren't hunters like Jake and won't bother hanging a harpy," John said. "They were only interested in money. If they wanted his wings, they would have cut them off in the cabin and carried half the load to the hover, plus they ended up fighting with Shail. To put up with that, they definitely wanted him alive."

"I believe you are right, John," Charlie said, examining the deep grooves in the sand. "They'd be angry after such a battle, yet they spared him. They could have easily hidden the wings and come back later, but they now also face charges for the hover theft. The harpy was worth more alive."

"Let's head back," John said. "Perhaps the authorities have located my missing hover." As they loaded up into the hover, it began to rain. The daily afternoon thunderstorms were part of Dora's wet season. The strong gusts rocked the hovercraft, and the blinding showers created a rough ride home. John finally landed the craft in the front yard and relaxed for the first time in his seat while killing the engine. "I hate flying at this time of the year."

They unloaded and made a dash for the house. The storms would continue the rest of the day. John and Kari went to the den, and John placed a call to Terrance.

"No, Mr. Turner," said an officer. "Nothing on your hover, but Terrance is pretty shut down due to the swarms. Most people are leaving for Hampton, and the commercial flights have been booked, and tomorrow is the last run. Don't want to take the chance of setting down during a swarm attack. Those men are probably on their way to Hampton in your hover. I'd advise you to contact the Hampton authorities and check the off-planet flights."

"Taking a small hover cross continent during the wet season is risky, and it doesn't have the range," John said.

"People are growing desperate," the officer said. "They're traveling in small hovers, vehicles, anything that will take them over the river and out of the western outback. This morning twenty-three hunters were killed in a big camp thirty miles south, and it's created a panic. As far as your harpy, most don't live long in captivity, but we could possibly recover his wings."

John glanced up at Kari. "The harpy doesn't fear cages so he'd still be alive. Thank you, Officer. I'd appreciate it if you keep me posted." He hit the disconnect key and the transmission ended.

"I'm going up to my room," Kari said.

"All right, dear. If I learn anything, I'll come and get you."

Kari walked into her room and discovered Maria had locked the balcony doors either to keep rain or male harpies out. Kari unlocked them and pushed them open, then crawled into bed. She lay curled up, grasping the yellow feather, and watched the rain splatter on the floor. Maybe Shail will come in my dreams, she thought, closing her eyes.

She woke to the sound of the balcony doors closing and saw her father.

"No, I want them open. Aron will be back."

John opened the doors again. "I didn't mean to wake you. Go back to sleep, and I'll wake you for dinner."

Her father left, and Kari shut her eyes, feeling the familiar depression she had suffered and fought on Earth, but this time it was close to crippling. Without Shail, she barely had energy to move. She managed to maintain with the help of the antidepressant patches. Shail hadn't come in her dreams, causing her more concern. Was he dead? She reached over and replaced the patch with a new one. "I must stay well. I can't help him like this."

Hours passed, and her father woke her for dinner. She went downstairs but didn't stay. She took some fruit back to her room and saw Aron set down on the balcony. He breathed hard and his wings and body were drenched. Apparently he had traveled a great distance. He shook his hair and ruffled his feathers before stepping into the bedroom. His green eyes held a foreboding gaze. "Shail is not found," he relayed, "and the harpies fear the worst."

She put her arms around his muscular streamlined body. "We can't give up, Aron." She sensed he equally grieved Shail's loss. They settled on the floor, and Kari gave him her fruit dinner. Watching the wailing rain drift across the meadow through the open doorway, Kari curled up in his secure arms under the brown wing. Though not her mate, Aron relieved her tension and anguish.

John looked into Kari's bedroom before going to bed. In the balcony doorway she slept on the floor with the male harpy wrapped around her. His brown wing shielded her from the wind, cold, and mist. The harpy raised his head and glared, but no longer hissed.

"She's not mine anymore, is she?" John said quietly before closing the door. Only her promise to Shail kept her in his house.

The first rays of dawn filtered into the bedroom, and Kari felt Aron nudge her cheek with his nose. She opened her eyes and smiled, seeing he still lay beside her.

"I must go and learn if there is news of Shail," he relayed. "I do not wish you more worry, but if Shail is lost, all life might also be lost. The time approaches where you must consider the safety of the stars. Your father knows the way."

Kari climbed out of his arms and stood up. "What do you mean, Aron?"

"Without a golden ruler, the harpies follow none. The flocks shall divide, each male seeking his family in the mountains or islands while the swarms grow too numerous to destroy. Already Shail's wishes fall under question. The attack on the human towns draws near. By the rise of next round moon, the swarms shall own the land, and you must be in the stars."

Kari sat down on the bed. "I thought that with or without Shail the harpies would eliminate the swarms."

Aron shook his head. "A harpy might destroy one swarm that threatens his family, but a mass attack on all beetles requires the leadership of a golden male. The harpies now struggle to hold the beetles in the jungle, and Shail's desire to save the women and children is but a dream. The beetles are drawn to the smell of wooden towns and human flesh. They soon shall cross the river and attack the cities. Those humans who failed to reach the stars shall be the first to die, then the trees, animals, and us. I must fly to the river. I do not know when I return."

"I'll be all right, Aron. Do what you can."

"Some of my males protect this structure from a swarm attack. Do not leave here. There can be no risk to you and your coming fledgling." He walked out on the balcony and spread his wings. With a leap he was gone, disappearing into the morning fog.

As Kari showered and dressed, she was occupied with Aron's words. She fully understood why Shail wanted her with her father. With the beetles turning deadly, there was a real danger the planet could be devastated. Her father would safely get her off Dora. She went downstairs and heard the communicator buzzing in the den.

John pressed the key as she walked into the room. The police officer was on the screen.

"Mr. Turner, I have information on your stolen hovercraft," he said. "An officer heard about your stolen harpy and said those men might have taken it to an old warehouse on the river, just south of town. It's owned by some men who deal in the wild animal trade. I was in the area helping with this evacuation, and I swung by. Sure enough, your hover was there."

"And my harpy?" John asked.

"Gone, I have to tell you the place was bad. There were two dead harpies with stripped wings, but they had brown hair, and aside from decaying animal corpses and some empty cages, the warehouse was vacant. Looks like they left in a hurry. I did a background check on the warehouse owner, Gus Simpson. He has a long rap sheet and was recently released from prison for serving time for assault. He's been arrested for murder and rape, but was never convicted. The witnesses disappeared. I won't tangle with this guy, Mr. Turner. If your harpy manages to survive his care, the harpy's probably on a star freighter headed for a zoo or hunting range. Anyway, do you want me to move your hover to the airport? Terrance is evacuating. I'm leaving in a few hours."

"It can stay at the warehouse. Thank you, Officer; you've been a big help." John disconnected and looked at Kari. "I wish you hadn't heard that."

Kari put her hand to her mouth. "My poor Shail."

John stood up and held her. "Kari, at least we know he's hasn't been killed for his wings, and those men want him alive. Shail is a golden harpy and very valuable. I'm sure they'd take good care of him. I'll call Hampton shipping right now and see if he's left the planet." John sat down in his chair and punched in the numbers.

"Dora Shipping," said a man.

"My name is John Turner, and I need information on wild animal export. I'm looking for a golden harpy."

The man chuckled. "Yeah, isn't everyone?"

"Let me talk to your supervisor, Mr. Davis," John said.

"Mr. Davis isn't here," the man said, "but I can take care of you, Mr. Turner."

"Fine, as I was saying, a golden harpy was stolen from my estate, and he might be shipped off the planet."

"I'll do a search on the outgoing manifests, but Hampton port is a madhouse. Ships are taking off without logging their cargo. Your animal hasn't been inside the port, since a golden harpy would create a lot of interest, but he might have been loaded outside. If I find your harpy, do you have documented ownership papers, or does the harpy have an imbedded chip or tattoo?"

"No."

"I'm wasting my time if you can't prove ownership. Harpies fall under exotic game and don't carry registration papers like domestics. If I did locate your animal on a ship or in the port, you have no legal right to claim him. I'm sorry."

"You locate him, and I'll make it worth your time, say ten thousand credits. I'll deal with the claim of ownership."

"Mr. Turner, I have your com number, and I'll be keeping an eye out for your harpy."

John nodded and turned off the com.

"If you find Shail, how will you get him back without papers?" Kari asked.

"Buy him. I just wonder what a live golden harpy is worth."

14

Turner's two employees Jerry and Sam walked down the beach toward the hovercraft. "I can't believe Turner is going to let those yellow wings rot," said Sam. "They're worth a heck of a lot of money."

"Yeah, but Mr. Turner doesn't need money," said Jerry, "besides, his daughter would freak if he loaded the wings in the hover. Did you hear her? She's already screwed up, loving a harpy."

"Jerry, you realize a mounted golden pair is worth fifty grand in Terrance? That's a year's salary for the both of us, and we're gonna be out of work soon, with the swarm. After Turner leaves with Charlie and the girl, we could double back through the mountains and grab the wings. No one would know."

Jerry stopped in his tracks. "Are you sure they're worth that kind of money? Turner warned you to leave 'em, and he's one guy you don't want pissed off."

"Before he finds out, we'll be long gone with twenty-five thousand in our pockets, and I've seen the price of old, beat-up yellow wings hanging in the gun shops in Terrance. We'll just cure and stash them near the estate and then take 'em to Terrance this weekend. It's sweet."

Jerry thought for a moment. "It does sound pretty easy. All right; it can't hurt anything, and I sure could use the credits."

They reached the hover and took off, heading east over the mountains. After circling around, they landed on the beach, north of the cabin. They crept up to the cabin, making sure that Mr. Turner had gone south to his home. They neared the cabin, and a fledgling bolted out the door.

Jerry leaped back. "That thing scared the shit out of me," he said, and watched the small harpy disappear into the tree branches.

Sam laughed. "Little jumpy, aren't you?"

They went inside the cabin and gazed at the golden male on the floor. Jerry took out his knife and bent down. "Hold his wing back, and I'll cut the tendons near the shoulder." Jerry reached for the wing. "Hey, this sucker's still breathing."

"Well, cut its throat. I want to be back before we're missed."

Jerry grabbed the harpy's hair and lifted its head. "There's no blood under him." He pushed the harpy over on its back. "Look, Turner didn't blast it. He stunned the thing." Jerry looked up at Sam. "It's no wonder Turner didn't take the wings; he wanted this harpy alive." He placed the knife to the unconscious harpy's jugular vein.

"Wait a minute," Sam said.

"I want to kill it before it wakes up and stares at me with those big blue eyes. These harpies look way too human to suit me."

Sam stood up. "We're not killing this one. We're tying him up and taking him to Terrance. I met a hunter in a bar, and he told me about his warehouse on the river. Said if I managed to bag a live harpy he'd give me triple the price of mounted wings. Alive, this baby is worth a hundred and fifty thousand."

Jerry smiled. "Damn, for that kind of money, I can get out of this stinking jungle and live on a real planet. Let's drag him to the beach and bring the hover around."

They grabbed the harpy under each arm and pulled him out of the cabin. "This thing is tall, but he ain't nearly as heavy as he looks," said Jerry.

"Yeah, he's a lightweight," Sam said as they went up the path to the beach. "You stay with the harpy, and I'll get the hover. There's some rope in the hover's storage."

As Jerry waited for Sam to return, he noticed the harpy stir and attempt to open its eyes. Sam landed the hover close by. "Get the ropes out," Jerry said. "He's starting to come around, and I don't want to stun him again. I heard harpies are prone to heart attacks."

Sam grabbed the ropes out of the back and tied the harpy's wrists behind his back. Jerry started with the ankles when the harpy regained consciousness.

Feeling his restrained arms, Shail lay on his side and shook his head, hoping to rid himself of the drowsy effect. He saw two men, and one had begun to put ropes around his ankles. He kicked the man in the face, sending him tumbling backward. The other man lunged at him, and Shail's foot struck his stomach. The man doubled over with pain and gasped for breath. Shail struggled to his knees, but his half-tied ankles kept him from standing.

"Get up, Jerry," Sam called, holding his stomach. "He's going to get away."

Jerry stood and blood ran down his chin from a split lip and bloodied nose. "All right, let's grab him from behind."

Shail hissed, warning them away, but the men closed in. When they were in striking range, he let loose. His long outstretched wings battered the men, and they fell into the sand. The men clamored to rise and were more hesitant in their approach.

Using his feet, Shail attempted to remove the ankle ropes. He couldn't fly unless he stood up. The men gathered their wits and came at him again. He flapped his wings, striking their bodies and forcing them to scramble out of his reach.

The bleeding, sweaty, and bruised men gasped and stared at him with dread. Shail saw they'd had their fill of abuse. He created an intimidating seething sound while cautiously trying to gain his footing.

"Didn't know harpies could fight like that," Jerry panted.

"You're gonna have to stun him. My laser is in the hover," said Sam. "It's the only way to get our hands on him."

Understanding the human words, Shail wildly flapped his wings, trying to get enough wind under them to take off from the kneeling position.

"Shoot him, Jerry! He's trying to fly," Sam yelled.

Jerry grabbed the weapon from his belt and blew the sand out of it. Shail finally lifted into the air when he heard the blast and felt the sting hit his back. He fell several feet into the sand and lay still.

Hearing the men's voices, Shail woke and found himself in the backseat of a hovercraft. He tried to move, but ropes bound his wrists, ankles, and wings. He realized he had been unconscious for some time, because the sun lay low in the west. He lay quietly on his side, waiting for his head to clear.

"Another hour, and we'll be rich," said Sam while piloting the hover.

"I might go back to Earth," Jerry said. "I've got an aunt and two uncles and a bunch of cousins there I've never met." He glanced at the backseat. "Hey, our boy is awake."

Shail exploded, testing the strength of his bonds. He tossed his body against the seat and frantically wiggled to be free.

"Take it easy, harpy. You'll hurt yourself and mess up your feathers." Jerry reached back to pet his head, but Shail lunged to bite. "Damn, he almost took my fingers off. He's a vicious sucker."

"Stun him if he keeps that up," Sam grumbled. "I don't care if it hurts him. I know he cracked a few of my ribs."

"Well, my nose is broken." Jerry pointed the weapon at Shail. "Settle down, or I'll blast you."

Shail seethed and stared at him, but stopped grappling with the ropes, finding they held him securely.

"I swear, he understood," said Jerry, "or he knows what a laser gun is."

"Well, tell him we won't hurt him if he behaves."

Jerry huffed and chuckled. "He ain't scared. He's glaring like he wants to chew me up and spit me out. If he got loose, we'd be in trouble."

"I still can't believe Mr. Turner changed his mind and let this harpy go. Heck, for weeks that man raged about killing it."

"Who knows what makes that guy tick?" Sam said, veering the hover to the left. "I just know it was lucky for us he stunned it. Once we sell it, I'm off this planet."

The men discussed how they would spend the harpy money, and Shail watched them through his long strands of hair. He felt some contentment, learning that Kari's father had spared him. He sensed that Turner was a good but misguided man. His confusion has ended, and he knows I am not a threat to Kari, Shail thought. He no longer stood between Kari and her father, and their rocky relationship would mend.

Shail sensed that Jerry and Sam had passive natures, and if not for the money, they wished him no harm. He worried about the buyer, for there was only one reason to keep a harpy alive; to hunt and slowly torture a male to death. I shall try to remain brave, but in truth I am afraid.

They reached the river and flew north toward Terrance. "There's the warehouse," Sam said. He landed the hover in the parking lot as the light faded. "You wait with the harpy. I'll find Simpson." Sam opened the hover door and climbed out.

"That warehouse looks dark," said Jerry.

"Yeah, he's probably up the street in that crummy little bar." After checking the quiet warehouse, Sam meandered up the street and disappeared.

A half hour later, Sam and three other men were walking down the dark street toward the hovercraft. "Be careful. He's really mean," Sam said. "He beat the hell out of me and my partner." He opened the back hover door.

"Well, let's see if you boys really caught a golden," said Gus Simpson, looking in the hover.

Shail stared into the face of a giant. The grizzly man smelled of whiskey and perspiration, and his grin exposed missing teeth. As Gus reached for Shail's bound legs to pull him out, Shail kicked the unshaven face with his feet and sent the man flying backward to the hard pavement.

"Are you okay, Mr. Simpson?" Sam said, and attempted to help up the big man. "You gotta be careful with that harpy. I said he was mean."

"Get away from me," Gus growled, and climbed to his feet. He went back to the hover and leered at Shail. "I can't believe the little fucker knocked me down. Lester, Bert, drag him out the other door. I'll keep his feet busy. I'm gonna enjoy taking the fight out of this one."

Gus's two men opened the door and met Shail's snapping teeth. Lester grabbed his hair, controlling his mouth, and Bert jerked him out of the hover and dropped him onto the ground. Shail curled up in a protective ball. His only defenses were his tied feet and his teeth.

"Before you get paid, I need to see his wings," Gus said to Jerry and Sam.

Shail kicked and snapped but was helpless against five pairs of hands.

The men flipped him on his belly, and Gus's large shoe stepped on the back of Shail's neck, smashing his face and throat against the pavement. Held firmly, Shail felt the ropes cut off his wings, and he attempted to flap them, but the men pulled and stretched his limbs.

"Pull tight," said Gus. "The more length, the more he's worth."

Four men unmercifully yanked his wings, nearly ripping them out of their sockets. Shail panted and his eyes watered with pain while Lester measured the wing length with a laser beam.

"Sixteen ten," said Lester.

"Too bad," Gus said. "A few more years, and this buck would've been fully mature, making a fine trophy."

They released his wings, letting them collapse. Shail trembled with throbbing pain and couldn't move or fold his wings against his back.

"Let see if he's sexually mature," Gus said, taking his foot off the harpy's neck and shoving the creature to its side.

Traumatized, Shail could only lay still. Lifting his sash, the man seized his penis and pulled while his other hand squeezed his testicles. Shail hissed and attempted to pull up his legs, but felt his testicles being crushed.

"Hurts, don't it?" Gus smirked. "You're gonna pay for that kick to my face."

Shail hardly could breathe, and only by lying still did the stabbing pain end. He sensed Gus's mind, and what he detected scared him. Twisted, poisoned thoughts dwelled in the man's evil conscience. Never had Shail encountered such a vile and ruthless human. During his brush with the mountain and island hunters, he had sensed their cruelty, but they paled compared to Gus.

"This buck is well hung and old enough to be a stud," Gus said, examining Shail's sex organs. "Nice balls, too. I can't wait to cut them off and watch him squirm."

"You're taking his balls?" Jerry asked, flinching.

"Yeah, wings ain't the only trophy you take off a harpy. Treat the skin and the balls makes nice money pouches. Tourists love 'em, will spend a fortune." He released his hold and stood. "Tie up his wings before he recovers."

As the men folded and bound Shail's wings, he curled up to relieve the smarting ache to his testicles and shuddered, having learned the purpose for harpy castration.

"So you'll give us a hundred and fifty thousand for him?" asked Sam.

"Sure," said Gus and looked at Lester and Bert. "Go fetch a credit voucher and a cage for this little beauty. Also bring back my training stick."

Jerry hooked his laser gun to his belt and stood next to Sam. "No wonder he fought us so hard," he said, staring at the pathetic, trembling harpy.

Gus came alongside of them. "Yeah, he'll pay for beating up you boys. I've heard you're supposed to stretch goldens for a day before they're defeathered, and stab holes in their liver. The feathers turn bright yellow from the damage. It's a prettier mount."

"Jesus, the poor thing," said Jerry and leaned toward Sam. "Maybe someone else wants to buy him."

"Come on, boys. Don't feel sorry for it," Gus said. "Feel sorry for yourselves." He grabbed Jerry's laser gun, ripping it off his belt, and pointed the weapon at Jerry and Sam. He looked down at the weapon and scowled. "You got this set for stun. That won't work." He adjusted the gun to blast.

"Wait a minute, mister," Jerry cried.

Gus fired at the two dumbfounded men, and their bodies dropped near Shail. Shail stared up at the sick grin on Gus while the man kicked the corpses, making sure they were dead. Lester and Bert returned from the warehouse with a long, narrow cage and a three-foot-long rod.

"You should've seen these assholes' faces." Gus chuckled. "They really thought they'd get paid. Throw their bodies in the river. The jungle will take care of the evidence."

Shail had never seen a man kill another one. He coiled up, tucking his face in his feathers.

After dumping the bodies in the river, the two men returned. "Let's get this buck in the warehouse," Gus said. "I'm ready to celebrate with another drink. Wait'll my brother hears what I got." Gus grabbed for the harpy's neck.

Shail instinctively snapped at the man's hand, clipping his wrist before Gus could jerk away. Shail hissed and showed his teeth, threatening to bite anything that came in reach.

Holding his nipped wrist, Gus glared at the harpy. "You little fucker, you've messed with the wrong man. Give me my cattle prod." Bert retrieved the rod off the top of the cage and handed it to Gus.

Shail managed to sit up, and sniffled. He bravely tossed his long hair at Gus, who was massive, four times his weight. Shail knew it was suicide to defy the monster, but he was golden and king of the harpies. He refused to yield despite the consequences. Better to die challenging an enemy than like a curled-up frightened brown.

"Look at this cocky fucker. I'm going to love this." Gus hit Shail's stomach with the rod and released an electric shock.

Shail doubled over as the stinging pain coursed through his body. Before he could recover, the rod jabbed his testicles. Shail wildly flipped in the ropes as he was assaulted again and again. He tried to huddle under his protective wings, but the rod found his flesh, causing him to thrash against the hard pavement. His heart raced and he panted rapidly. He had never experienced such piercing pain.

"Gus, Bill's gonna be pissed," said Lester. "This sucker's getting all banged up on the pavement."

Gus grabbed the blond hair on the trembling harpy and looked into its eyes. "Yeah, he's dazed and had enough. Put him in the cage. He won't bite now."

Shail barely recalled being hoisted into the cage, but heard the metal rattle from his shaking body. He was numb, but felt like a million thorns had stuck him. Managing to swallow, he tasted his own blood from biting his lip. He lay limp, unable to fight or flee, as the men secured him. His wrists and ankles were freed of ropes, but they were replaced with shackles attached to chains impossible to chew through. Each chain was attached to the cage bars, forcing Shail to lie stretched on his side. The binding ropes that damaged his feathers came off, but the cage was so narrow that he couldn't open or flail his wings. He wondered if the searing pain would ever leave.

The men carried him into the large building and set his cage on the floor. Shail detected the reek of animal waste and rotting death. He closed his eyes and listened to the whimpers and cries of distressed creatures.

After several hours, the throbbing had eased, and he stopped trembling and breathed normally. He lifted his head from his chained arms and glanced around the enormous room. The three men sat on bunks off to one side and drank from a bottle. He saw cages filled with terrified animals along the walls. Each creature cowered and hid in a corner. He sniffed the air, and aside from the stink, he detected a harpy. He hastily looked around, locating two lying on a cage floor in a dark corner. He telepathically called to them, but they didn't answer, and he couldn't see if they breathed.

Gus came to his cage and sipped from the bottle. "This buck is strong. He's already recovered," he said to the other men.

Shail softly hissed, knowing full well it was wiser to remain quiet.

Gus chuckled. "You ain't going to believe it, but the damn thing's still hissing at me." Lester and Bert approached the cage and peered down at the harpy.

"They say these goldens are different from the browns," said Lester and looked at Gus under the bright lights. "Gus, the harpy gave you a shiner." He laughed. "The whole side of your face is turning black and blue."

Gus frowned, and Shail sensed anger. Gus grabbed the rod, adjusting the setting to high. He put it through the cage bars and held it close to Shail's exposed ribs. Shail frantically fought the chain's hold and tried flapping his wings while pushing his body away from the rod. The intoxicated men roared, watching him try to escape the rod in the narrow cage.

"Let's find out how much he can take," Gus said and jammed the cattle prod against Shail's ribs. Instead of withdrawing the rod, Gus held it against his skin and watched Shail go berserk.

Shail thrashed for some time until his sweat-covered body seized up, and he went into convulsions, excreting his body fluids. His limp body twitched and his eyes closed with unconsciousness.

In the middle of the night, Shail woke. His body still suffered from burning numbness. He carefully glanced around for the men and saw they slept on bunks. He shook his hair to remove regurgitated food, and shivered in his own urine. Quietly he tried to pull his bloody wrists out the shackles, but it was hopeless. His body was so weak, he doubted he could walk or fly even if he were free of the chains and cage. He longed to curl up, but the restraints would not allow it. Feeling pathetic, filthy, and afraid, he closed his eyes and worried what the dawn would bring. I must not be seduced by the peace of death, he thought. My mate, son, and flock need me. Shail felt his willpower slipping away after the horrendous assault of the rod. His lightweight frame couldn't tolerate much more abuse. Either his heart would stop or his mind would fall into irreversible depression, leaving him comatose. He glanced at the motionless brown harpies and knew the fate they had suffered.

The morning filtered through the cracked warehouse door, and Shail stared at the sleeping men. They stirred in their bunks, and he hid his face in his extended arms.

Lester approached the harpy cage. "How you doing, little buck?" Shail glanced up, but quickly buried his face again. "Hey, Gus, your golden is awake, but he's damn timid. I think you broke him."

Gus sat on the edge of his cot and touched his painful, swollen face. He stood up and walked over to Lester and the cage.

Peeking up at Gus, Shail cowered and forced his wing up and over his head. He trembled and backed his body against the bars.

"See? He's scared of you, Gus," said Lester, and Bert joined them.

"He can handle a few more prods," Gus said, placing the rod against Shail's ribs. Shail grit his teeth and grabbed the chains as excruciating pain entered his body. His frail body twisted sluggishly against the chains. Gus withdrew the rod and stared at the harpy's dull half-closed eyes. Its chest pounded and it hyperventilated.

One more, Shail thought, and I shall die. He heard the approach of a giant hover. After a few minutes, the men also heard it, and it distracted Gus.

Gus walked to the warehouse doors and slid them open. "The freighter's here. Get the cages ready to load." Walking past a large female grogin, Gus hit the animal's ribs with his rod. The grogin let out a cry and slunk to a corner.

Shail wearily watched and tried to catch his breath and slow his heart. Gus was the worst of men, killing his own kind and finding pleasure in torture. Shail had never sensed such heartlessness in any creature, and the sadistic man was his master.

Shail felt his body and mind shutting down. His nerves were raw, and he struggled to maintain control. He heard a woman's voice enter the warehouse. He looked over and saw her standing by the animal cages.

"Damn it, Gus," she said. "These animals are filthy. You want to sell them, and they're half dead. How many days has it been since you fed and watered?"

"That's Bert's job," Gus said.

"Well, he should be fired," she said. "Now what's this crap about a golden harpy? Bill radioed and said you had one."

"He's over here, Mollie. Look what the little son-of-a-bitch did to my face," said Gus. They walked toward the cage. "I had to get him under control with a little shock therapy."

Mollie looked down at the harpy. "You jackass! You shocked this valuable harpy? When are you going to learn harpies are fragile? It's like shocking a bird. It knocks the life right out of them." She put her hand between the bars and petted Shail's head. "Bet you were really beautiful before that moron got to you." She pulled out a small scanner from her pocket and ran it across Shail's body.

"I'm no moron, Mollie," Gus grumbled.

"Really? Well, the harpy is on the verge of a heart attack," she said. "Your brother pays me to keep the animals alive for his hunting range, and you make my job damned impossible with this abuse."

"The little fucker loves to fight."

"He's a golden. He's supposed to be aggressive. Beside the yellow wings, that's what makes him valuable." Mollie shook her head and walked back to the freighter.

In minutes she was back at Shail's cage with drugs to slow his rapid heart rate and treat his depression, pain, and signs of shock. Covering him with a blanket, she inspected the other animal cages, giving orders to a few men who had arrived with the freighter. She crawled into the cage with the two lifeless browns. "And what did these two do that you had to beat them?" she called to Gus.

"We gave 'em the depression drugs, but it didn't work. The boys and I got bored and thought we'd have a little fun. I'll take care of them."

Mollie returned to Shail's cage. "Let's wash you, little prince. I know you handsome boys like to be clean." She left and came back with a bucket and towels

Shail was soothed by the warm water and glanced up at the thin, coarse-looking woman who shampooed the vomit from his hair. Her short, dark curls dangled over her forehead while she sponged the dirt and dried blood from his smudged face and clammy body. She removed his soiled sash and washed it and the cage. With the bath, drugs, and fresh straw under him, Shail felt more comfortable. The middle-aged woman named Mollie had saved his life. She placed her hand against his face, and he licked her to show his appreciation.

"You're a lover, not a fighter. You just don't like to be bullied." She gazed down at him. "God, you're absolutely gorgeous. I'm going to take good care of you."

Shail turned his head and ignored her and the other men loading cages, but watched Gus and Lester. They dragged the brown harpies out of their cages and tied their wrists together with a long rope. Tossing one end over a beam, they hoisted the harpies off the floor. Shail raised his head and looked for Mollie, but she was in the freighter. He turned back toward Gus and shivered, realizing he was about to witness the brutal removal of a harpy's wings.

Grabbing each wing, Gus took a knife and cut the vein in the wing tip. Blood spurted out while Lester applied a tourniquet on the wings near the harpy's back. Gus castrated one male and placed the organs in a plastic bag. The harpy barely moved, but the second male flailed his wings and twisted on the rope.

Gus laughed. "This one still has his mind," he said to Lester.

"You should see a bull calf when you make it a steer," said Lester. "At least these harpies are quiet and don't bellow."

The harpy stopped thrashing, and its body slowly squirmed while it dangled. Shail panted with anxiety, watching the ghastly torture. Under the harpies, a large pool of blood spread across the floor. The men snapped the cartilage in the wing joints and hacked off the feathered limbs, throwing them in a pile. Lester and Gus picked up the wings and loaded them in the freighter, leaving the harpies to die an excruciating death.

Mollie came back to Shail's cage. "Paul, this golden is ready to load," she said to a man.

Shail wrestled in his chains and pleaded with his eyes.

"What's wrong, prince?" she asked, and saw him glance at the dying harpies. "Gus, cut those harpies down and put them out of their misery, or do I have to? It's scaring the heck out of the golden."

"Let it scare him," Gus said. "Now he knows what to look forward to."

Mollie picked up her medical bag and took a step toward the browns.

"I'll do it," Gus said. "Save your euthanizing drug." He cut the ropes, and the harpies collapsed into the red pool. He snatched up each one by his long hair and slit his throat.

Shail stared at the two dead harpies as two men picked up his cage and carried it on the freighter.

Gus was the last one on board. "Let's get out of here," he called to the pilot and slumped into a seat. "This freighter is slow and can't outrun a swarm. It'll take two days before we reach Hampton."

Mollie sat toward the back, next to the golden's cage. She noticed the male's low hiss when hearing Gus's voice. "You're feeling better," she said, looking at the blond harpy. "I don't like Gus, either." The freighter engines cranked up, and the large transport lifted from the pavement.

"I better hook you up to a catheter, so you stay clean," Mollie said to the harpy and produced a tube. She seized his penis and started to insert the tube.

Seeing what she planned to do, Shail came alive and was no longer lethargic or docile. He angrily hissed, wiggled, and attempted to push her away with a wing.

"I can see how Gus got that black eye," she said, and forced the tube into the restrained harpy. "You must be hungry, too."

When she held his head and put the tube toward his mouth, Shail violently tossed his body in the chains and snapped at her hands and the tube.

"Wow, you really are aggressive," she said, and saw he'd be impossible to tube feed unless knocked out. He was so wound up she barely got the tranquilizer in his arm.

In a few minutes the harpy's eyes became drowsy. Mollie placed the blanket on him and softly talked while stroking his neck. Subdued by the drugs and the gentle handling, the feisty golden nuzzled the blanket and drifted to sleep.

Gus walked to the back of the ship. "You treat that animal like a baby."

"He is a baby," Mollie said. "He may not understand me, but a calming voice soothes him, and all harpies like to have their necks massaged. I'm trying to reverse all the damage you did and build some trust."

"Why don't you soothe me? I can show you a good time when we reach Hampton."

Mollie laughed. "I'd have a better time with the harpy." She pulled out the feeding tube and slipped it down the harpy's throat, feeding him pulpy liquid fruit.

Recovered from the abuse, Shail became more defiant with Mollie's drug-and-tube treatment. She sedated him most the time. When he woke, he found his throat sore and hunger gone. As the freighter traveled toward Hampton, he lost all sense of time, not knowing if it was night or day. His only memory was Mollie and her gentle voice and hands. She groomed, washed, and caressed him, apparently knowing a lot about his race. The tube in his sex organs and the chains were uncomfortable, but he truly became upset when seeing or hearing Gus. Tossing in the chains and loudly hissing, he was quickly reassured by Mollie or one of her sleep drugs.

"There, my pretty little prince," Mollie said as the harpy fell asleep.

Gus walked over to Mollie and the unconscious harpy. "What's this 'prince' crap? I think you're getting too attached to this one."

Mollie smiled. "He is a prince: fiery, arrogant, and unyielding. No doubt he was a dominant male among other harpies. I can see the audacity in those blue eyes when he doesn't get his way. And with his chemistry and looks, it's rather hard not to get attached."

Gus sat down in a nearby seat. "Well, your prince will soon be hanging from a post while all that chemistry is cut up. Besides, you've been handling a drugged and chained harpy, but this sucker's mean. Those boys who caught him had the fuck beat out of them. He got loose, your prince would rape you."

"I don't believe it," Mollie said. "Those old stories of harpy rape are fantasy. Every harpy I've handled is sweet and timid. The golden is a rebel, but with patience he'll tame down. He's alert and intelligent, with a strong will to live. I haven't had to give him the antidepressant. I'm hoping a zoo will buy him rather than a hunter. I can't understand why men want to destroy such an elegant creature."

"One of these days, a harpy's gonna get a hold of you when you don't control it. Maybe then you'll appreciate me."

Mollie fluffed her brown curls. "Appreciate you? It'll never happen."

Gus stood and growled, "Mollie, I'd kill most people for talkin' to me like that." He stormed away from the animal cages.

On the second night of the voyage the large freighter reached Hampton and set down outside the spaceport in the expansive landing strip. The men opened the large hover's doors and unloaded the cages while they waited for the vehicle transports.

Shail smelled the cool night air and opened his eyes to the starry sky. The sedatives were wearing off, and he stirred in his bonds. He heard the men's voices while they unpacked. An unfamiliar young man looked down into his cage, and Shail seethed a warning sound.

"This is a golden harpy?" the young man asked Lester.

"Yeah, but keep your hands out of his cage. The son-of-a-bitch bites," said Lester, and walked back into the freighter.

The man looked down at the harpy. "I wonder if you're Kari's gold harpy."

Shail rattled his chains and grabbed the bars, pulling himself close to the top of the cage. He stared at the man with beseeching eyes.

"I think you are her harpy," he said.

"Get away from that animal," yelled Gus, treading heavily toward the smaller man.

Shail made a begging sniffle and shook his chains, but the young man moved away as Gus reached the cage. Shail saw the rod in Gus's hand that he tapped against the top cage bars. Shail quickly released his hold on the bars and froze with fear.

"Go ahead," Gus said, looking down at Shail. "Jerk those chains again, and I'll give you a good reason to jerk."

Shail lowered his head, tucking it into his wing.

"Mollie's right. You do have some brains."

"Don't hurt him, Gus," Mollie said and hurried out of the freighter and rushed to the cage.

Gus continued to tap the rod against the bars. "He's making a racket. You better knock him out, or I'll be happy to do it."

"He's only excited to see the night sky," Mollie said to Gus. "Be quiet, now, prince." She gave Shail another sedative, and he quickly fell asleep for his journey to the hunting range.

15

The day wore on as Kari and her father milled around the house and waited for the important call from the Hampton shipping clerk, but the call never came. As evening approached, they ate a solemn dinner with Charlie.

"Is your harpy guardian coming back tonight?" John asked.

"Aron is searching for Shail," Kari said. "I'm not sure if he'll be back."

The com buzzed in the den, and they jumped out of their seats. John rushed into the room and pressed the key.

A young man appeared on the screen. "Did Kari come back?"

"She's here," John said, and turned to Kari. "This guy called before when you were gone."

Kari sat down behind her father's desk. John and Charlie left the room to finish dinner and give her some privacy. "Hi, Ted."

"Boy, I've missed you." Ted grinned. "How are you?"

"Things aren't going well."

"Your father sure wasn't happy when I talked to him a few weeks ago and you were with the golden harpy. Do you still have the harpy?"

She wearily rubbed her forehead. "No."

"I didn't think so. That's why I'm calling. A little while ago some hunters landed in a freighter outside the spaceport. The hover was loaded with wild animals. I'm working all hours, due to the swarm threat, but I took a break and walked over to see them. One cage had a golden harpy. I didn't think he was yours until I mentioned your name. He yanked on his chains and looked like he was pleading for my help."

"Chains!" she cried. "Oh God, Ted, that is my harpy. That's Shail. We've been searching for him. Where did they take him?"

"I got chased out of there by some big guy, but I asked another man where the harpy was going. He said they were taking him to new hunting range on the outskirts of Hampton, and the harpy would be auctioned off to the highest bidder. He wasn't sure of the auction date, sometime next week."

"Thank you, Ted, thank you. You have no idea how much this means to me. I'll be coming to Hampton as soon as I can."

"Great. I owe you a dinner."

"Listen, Ted. Don't wait for me. Catch the next space flight off the planet. The swarms will move east soon, and Hampton could fall."

"Kari, the swarms are mostly in the outback. Hampton is safe for at least another year."

"No town is safe. Please believe me."

"I have to get back to work. We'll talk about it over dinner. I can't wait to see you," he said and disconnected.

Kari turned off the com and stood. Do all humans think like Ted? The east is safe? She hurried through the house and found her father in the living room. He rose out of a large stuffed chair. "Shail is in Hampton," she said. "He's going to a hunting range there where he'll be auctioned. I need to go to Terrance and catch the next eastern commercial flight."

"Let's see if there's any room on a flight." John briskly walked into the den and placed a call to Terrance.

"All flights are overbooked," said a woman on the screen, "and there are several hundred people on standby."

John thanked her and turned off the com. "Kari, let's think about this. Shail wants you here, and the mill room is reinforced against a swarm strike. Flying in my little hover is dangerous, with the stormy weather, and my hover can't out fly a swarm. I'll risk it, go to Hampton, and buy Shail's freedom. I'd like you to stay here."

Kari's eyes narrowed. "I'm going."

John's face was grim. "Okay, but I had to try. If we fly day and night, it'll take three days to reach Hampton. When is the auction?" he asked.

"Next week. Ted didn't know the date."

"That's good. I'll have time to go to the Hampton bank for a credit voucher. These hunters know what they're doing. An auction will draw some high bidders. Your golden's price could skyrocket."

"How high?" she asked.

"I don't know. If it's just the locals, I can outbid them, but if the auction is on the universal Web, I'll be up against zoos, big hunting ranges, and sports hunters across the galaxy, and to make matter worse, Shail is one of a kind, making him priceless. Caught up in bidding, people tend to over-pay."

Kari put her hands to her face, overwhelmed.

John put his arms around her. "Don't worry," he said. "I promised I'd get Shail back and I will. Go pack, and I'll tell Charlie. I know he'll want to come. The old guy has been in torment and blames himself for not step-ping up and stopping me. He did his damnedest to persuade me to leave you and Shail alone. If you can, be kind to him. This whole mess is totally my fault."

"I'll go pack," she said quietly.

When Kari came downstairs, Charlie was waiting in the foyer, his eyes downcast.

"Can I take your bag?" he asked.

"Yes, Charlie." She handed the small sack to him. "I'm glad you're com-ing with us."

They went outside into the dark lawn, and the rain had let up. John slammed the hood on the hover. "It's fully charged and ready," he said.

"I have to do something before we go." Kari walked across the meadow toward the jungle.

Lit by the outside lights, John and Charlie waited while she approached the edge of the trees.

Kari called telepathically toward the dark jungle, and a male harpy flew down, landed beside her, and bowed his head. "Find Aron," she relayed. "Tell him Shail is in the big eastern city on the coast. Hunters have him. I am going there to try to save him."

"I am Reaf, Lea's mate," the harpy relayed. "She said you were fearless, but our golden ruler and Aron ordered me to stay here and guard you and the structure from swarms, hunters, and all threats. You must remain here."

"How dare you, Reaf?" she said, and flung her long blond hair. "See my yellow hairs? They are as golden as Shail's. A brown does not tell a golden what she can or cannot do. Heed my wishes and find Aron."

Reaf dropped to his knees, his face by her feet. "Forgive me. I shall go with great haste." He jumped up and disappeared into the black sky.

Kari swiftly walked back toward the hovercraft. "Let's go." She hopped into the hover backseat. John and Charlie also climbed in.

John started the engine. "What did you say to the harpy, Kari?" John asked. "He looked like he was scared of you."

"He should be scared. After all, I'm a golden harpy, and worse, your daughter."

The jungle flew rapidly past as Aron flapped his long wings toward the east and the harpy rendezvous. He feared the harpy gathering would be the last, worry consumed him. All his life he had loved and protected his younger adopted brother, Shail, but it was likely that he was dead. The flocks had frantically searched for him with no luck, and his loss also meant the loss of all life. Even the beetles would die of starvation once everything was gone.

Reaching the river savannah and island, he fluttered before landing among the massive clutch of harpies. Seth was the first to brazenly approach him.

"Is he found?" Seth asked.

Aron lowered his head and shook it. "None in my flock have seen him."

"And none here," Seth said. "He is dead, then." Seth moved closer and placed his hands on Aron's shoulders. "I sense your heavy heart. You truly were raised in the same nest with him."

"Yes, I love Shail, but I refuse to grieve his death. He was unlike all harpies and lived with reckless luck. Captivity would not easily destroy him."

"Perhaps he might survive the cage, but not a human weapon. The hunters would be quick to take his precious wings." Seth turned to the other harpies. "We came here, each holding a golden feather to honor our ruler and follow his words, but he has fallen. We mourn the loss of the golden line and pray for the light when his son rules. These are dangerous times, and I return to the east to protect my family and flock. The harpies shall no longer hold back the swarm. The humans made a destructive traveling path from east to west through our jungle, devastating the trees and animals. It is now ironic that the swarms shall follow the same doomed path, killing the humans as they go. The humans spoil what they touch, and now nature takes its rightful revenge." He extended his wings to fly.

"Seth, when the humans are dead, what of the animals and trees?" Aron asked. "Shall you allow them to die next under the swarms? We must keep this gathering, for only with numbers shall we defeat the beetles, and we must strike before the rise of the next round moons. Afterwards, there shall be too many swarms."

"My eastern flock shall destroy the swarms that threaten the northern mountains where our females and fledglings dwell, and the river harpies shall drive the swarms from the north, and you, my young brother, shall defend your islands and our pregnant golden queen. We shall do as we always have done: protect our own land and flocks."

Aron sadly gazed at him. "Then all your males shall die with this suicide, for there are not enough males in your flock, and the swarms shall sweep through the mountains, killing your mates and young."

Seth leaned over and nuzzled Aron's neck. "The gathering is over." He glanced at the crowd of harpies. "Look into the eyes of these proud flock leaders. They would not follow your brown wings nor mine in an attack against the swarms. You know this." He patted Aron's shoulder. "I would be pleased if my sons grew like you. You have great courage. I shall continue to have my flock search for the golden in the east, and hope he is alive and found."

Aron nodded. "It is also my hope that we survive." He dismally watched Seth and the huge gathering take flight. He stood among a few of his males, realizing that Seth was right. The flock leaders would respect and follow only a yellow-winged male.

His males moved closer. "What do you wish of us, Aron?" one asked.

"We follow Shail's wishes as best we can. Pull our males from the swarms. We can no longer hold them and protect the human women and children. Their fate is no longer our concern. We shall line the borders of the Turner Estate and make our stand, destroying any swarm that threatens the land. The battle against humans is over, and we now face a war against nature. Pray we endure."

Aron slowly flew back in the dark toward Kari, dreading telling her of the terrible news and worrying if she would live without Shail, and worse, he would have to persuade her to leave the jungle and live in the stars. His faith that Shail was alive was wavering; his harpies had risked checking all human dwellings. Tears ran down his cheek as he tried to imagine life without his carefree blond brother.

Late at night he reached the Turner Estate border. As he flew over the tree canopy, he saw a shadow racing toward him. He frantically tilted and flapped his wings to avoid a midair collision. "Watch out!" he relayed. The harpy banked and turned back to him.

"I found you!" Reaf panted as they fluttered. "It's Shail! He is alive, Aron! He lives!"

They landed on a large tree limb. "Tell me all."

"Our golden female says Shail is held by hunters in the large eastern city on the coast. She left the Turner Estate and journeys to save him."

"You let her leave?" Aron fumed. "You let her risk her life and the life of our future ruler?" He raised his wing to strike Reaf.

Reaf cowered his head. "Aron, I could not stop her nor could any harpy. I told her to stay, but she does not respect a male's wishes."

Aron lowered his wing and breathed deeply. "I am glad to learn of Shail, but now must worry for both goldens and their unborn. I shall die of stress, fretting over these rash yellow-haired harpies." He ruffled his feathers and considered his next move. "Gather my flock and leave only the small number to guard the land and islands from swarms. Shail must be saved and his mate protected. We meet at the swamp island with the river harpies. Then we all fly east."

Traveling toward Terrance in the dark, Kari sat silently while John flew the hover low over the narrow highway with one of its flood lights aimed below. Forced to land, he knew the only safe place was the road.

Unknown to him and all humans, the safe highway would become a path of destruction and death. Like bread crumbs, the scent of humans

and cut wood buildings would attract massive swarms, and with no harpies to stop them, they would rapidly march east along the highway and
straight into Hampton, as the flock leader Seth had predicted.

"It'll be light in a few hours, and we'll be in Terrance. We'll stop and get
some food," John said.

At dawn they approached the town of Terrance, and John flew the hover
toward the airport.

Kari looked down at colorful, ornate buildings trimmed with white lattice and hand-carved wooden arches and doorways. The town purposely
resembled the graceful Victorian period on Earth. Beyond the town was
the river, several miles wide. She noticed there was no movement; no
people, no traveling vehicles. "It seems deserted."

"Something must have happened. Looks like everyone left in a hurry,"
John said and landed at the vacant airport. Every hovercraft was gone. A
man ran out of the large airport building and frantically waved and yelled
to them. A woman holding a small child followed him as they raced toward John's hovercraft.

"Take us with you!" yelled the man. "Please, for God's sake."

John stepped out of the hover. "What's happened?"

"A swarm! It's coming from the northeast," the man said, out of breath.
"There's not much time."

"Get in," John said. "I can't take you far. My hover won't hold this many
people."

The man climbed in and the woman sat on his lap. Kari reached for the
child. "I'll hold him," she said, and the woman placed the one-year-old in
her lap. The hover lifted off.

"Can you pilot a hover?" John asked the man.

"I've flown small ones," the man answered.

"With any luck, I've got a hovercraft here. We'll be sitting ducks for a
swarm with this load." John veered his hover south along the river. After
several miles, they came to a warehouse district, and John spotted his stolen orange hovercraft with TURNER written on the side. It sat in a large lot
in front of a dilapidated warehouse. He landed alongside it and got out to
inspect the craft. The man followed him and watched John pushed the
start button. The engines fired up.

As her father spoke to the man, Kari gave the baby back to the mother and climbed out. She walked toward the warehouse and could immediately smell death and feces. Walking inside, she choked and gasped. Her eyes watered when she stared at the two dead harpies. Their throat's slashed, their wings and testicles sliced off, they lay in a bloody mound on the floor, no longer resembling their beautiful race. She cringed, thinking of Shail, and that he was held in the filthy place. The floor was covered in blood, rotting food, garbage, and animal waste. A large bloated lizard lay dead in one of the remaining cages. Smaller animal corpses rested against the walls. By the bunks were numerous liquor bottles and rags. The place spoke volumes about what kind of men held her beloved Shail captive. She jumped when Charlie touched her shoulder.

"You shouldn't be in here," Charlie said quietly.

She nodded and trailed him outside. The family was seated in the recovered hovercraft, and John stood by the pilot door.

"Okay, you think you can operate it?"

"Yes, Mr. Turner," the man said.

"Now follow the highway west past Westend. Ten more miles, and you're at my estate and mill. Tell my housekeeper, Maria, I sent you and to put you up. The mill is secure from a swarm attack. You'll be all right there."

Through the open hover window, the man grabbed John's hand "Thank you, Mr. Turner. You saved our lives."

"Just get going," John said and returned to his hover. Kari and Charlie already sat inside. John jumped in and started the engine. Simultaneously, both hovers rose from the ground. One veered west toward the protected mill while the other swung east toward the unknown.

John forced the hover high and glanced north along the river. In the distance, he saw the giant black mass. He steered the hover to the southeast. "If they swarm, we're in trouble," he said nervously. He saw the beetles take to the air. "Sweet Jesus, here they come." The swarm was heading toward their hover, but when it approached Terrance, the swarm settled on the little town; the multicolored buildings turned black.

Kari stared out the window as the hover traveled farther and farther away from the obliteration. "I wonder how many people didn't make it out."

"I think most of them got out," John said. "The man said the large hover flights came early and evacuated the entire town. His vehicle stalled, and he and his wife had to run for it. They didn't see other people on their way to the port."

The rest of the morning, John, Charlie, and Kari traveled in silence, observing the ever-growing barren areas, the trademark symbol of a swarm attack. At noon they set down on the highway near a small bridge. From the stream flowing beneath it, John filled water containers and stretched from the tiresome journey.

"Should have brought some food," he said to Charlie and glanced around. "Where's Kari?"

"She went into the jungle," said Charlie. "She will be okay, John."

A few minutes later Kari returned to the hover carrying two large roots. She broke one open with a rock and handed a piece of the fleshy orange food to Charlie and her father. "Try these."

The men bit into the sweet root. "This is very tasty," Charlie said. "Your mate taught you well."

Kari glowed. "He did, Charlie. Shail could even teach you a few things."

John lowered his head and exhaled uneasily. "We need to get going."

John journeyed east following the highway. In the afternoon dark clouds covered the sky, and he hit light showers of rain. Charlie offered to pilot the craft, giving John a break so he could drive through the coming night storms.

Kari was in the front passenger seat next to Charlie, and John slept on the cramped backseat. She had hardly spoken to Charlie since her return.

"You didn't tell me the whole story when you met Shail a few years ago," she said.

"The whole story?" Charlie asked.

"You spoke to Shail and told him I was in the stars but would return when an adult and free of my father."

Charlie cleared his throat. "I did tell him those things. He flew down on the path and pawed the ground with his foot and had the look of asking in his eyes. He obviously sought you. The golden saved your life and deserved to know where you were, but like your father, I hoped you had forgotten him. I have nothing against the harpies, but they live a short, dangerous life. When your mother died, it nearly destroyed your father. I didn't want the same for you, but now we are racing to Hampton, and I'm worried. If Shail dies, will you, too, be destroyed?"

"I don't know, Charlie, but I am like Dad. We have no regrets, bonding with our harpy mates. Like the old saying goes, it's better to have loved and lost than never to have loved at all."

John had been listening from the backseat. He closed his eyes. She was right, he thought.

Night and the sweeping thunderstorms descended on the continent. Kari lay in the backseat, and the strong winds rocked the hovercraft. Shutting her eyes, she hoped that Shail would come in her dreams, but she considered he might be drugged, preventing dream telepathy, or perhaps he didn't want her to know the terrible cruelty he faced.

She pulled up her legs and held them with her arms, lowering her head, and recalled how he had curled his body around hers, nuzzling and faintly kissing the back of her neck before covering them with his wing. God, she missed him. A tear coursed down her cheek.

John steered the hover through the waves of rain, and Charlie dozed in the passenger seat. In the vast darkness, John spotted an obscure light in the distance. "I'm going to set down ahead," he said, waking Kari and Charlie. Approaching the light, he saw a small inn with two hovercrafts and numerous terrain vehicles parked out front. "We'll take a break, and maybe get something to eat here."

He landed his hover beyond the other transports. Making a dash through the rain, the three entered the inn lobby. A balding man greeted them from behind a counter.

"Good evening, folks. You picked a lousy night for travel."

John approached the counter. "Is your restaurant open?"

"Sure is, and packed, but I have one table left. We serve the finest in native cuisine, but unfortunately our rooms are booked; half the folks here are sleeping in their transports."

"That's okay. We're moving on after dinner."

"You're welcome to stay and use our parking lot for sleep," said the man, leading them through a wide doorway into a cozy dining room. "The forecast predicts rain all night. You can eat a good breakfast and catch an early start in the morning." He stopped at an unoccupied table.

"Thanks; maybe we'll take some biscuits with us," John said, taking a seat along with Kari and Charlie.

Kari glanced around at the thirty or more weary travelers who talked somberly among themselves. The people hadn't come to the inn for pleasure, but were refugees fleeing the western swarms. Each conversation concerned the hardships ahead.

"Maybe we should go back to our home," said a man at the next table to a woman. "The swarm might have missed Terrance."

John leaned toward the man's table. "Don't go back. We saw the swarm hit Terrance this morning. There's nothing left."

The man, almost in a trance, stood up, and the woman buried her face in her napkin. "This man says he saw a swarm destroy Terrance this morning," he announced to the people in the dining room. There was a hush, then sighs. Most of the people apparently were residents of the little town.

An old man feebly walked to John. His eyes were moist. "Are you sure, mister? Are you sure everything is gone?" he asked. His voice trembled.

"I'm sorry," John said.

"I've lost everything," he muttered. "A lifetime of work, my home, my store." He slowly walked back to his table and embraced his elderly wife, and they sobbed.

John leaned toward Kari and Charlie. "This is just the beginning," he said in a low voice. "It's going to get worse." They ate their food in silence and ordered food for the trip ahead. They were soon back in the hover and flying toward Hampton.

Kari gazed out the window at the distant lightning strikes, crackling and briefly revealing green and gray clouds in the evening sky. She listened to their distant rumbling. Normally she'd love the magnificent stormy weather, the kind of weather that made one feel alive, but for her, Dora had lost all its beauty since she lost Shail.

She thought about the brokenhearted people at the inn. None were malicious harpy hunters. They were simple people who struggled to squeeze out a living in the rough outback. If Shail was alive and freed, if he could save these people from the swarms, if a peace was made between the humans and harpies, if, if, if. Her head spun. Her mate held the keys to everything, but was there time to unlock and open the doors?

A clear, scarlet dawn greeted John as he steered his hover east. It was Thursday, and with any luck, they would descend on Hampton Friday night.

Charlie woke with the sunlight. "Want me to take over, John?"

"Maybe in a few hours." He flipped on the com. A woman appeared on the screen. "Could you connect me to a new hunting range in Hampton?"

Kari sat up from the backseat. "You're calling them?"

John nodded as a big man in a suit came on the com. "Simpson's hunting range," the man said.

"I've heard you have a golden harpy at auction next week," John said. "I'd like some information and the date of the auction."

The man gleamed. "I'm Bill Simpson, owner of the range, and you heard right, sir. We do have an exquisite golden male. He'll be auctioned off next Monday night at seven and the public viewing takes place Saturday and Sunday with a general admission charge of ten credits."

"I'm interested in purchasing him. What's his condition?"

"He's in excellent health with the fiery disposition the golden species is known for. His wingspan is just short of seventeen feet, but the feathers are consistent, undamaged, and still the creamy yellow of a younger male. They'll make a beautiful mount. This little stud is guaranteed to give you a challenging hunt in our three-acre range. Can I take your name and add you to our list of bidders?"

"John Turner. I'll be there Saturday morning to register in person."

"Very good, Mr. Turner; I promise the animal won't disappoint you in looks or action. He's the perfect rare trophy for a serious game hunter."

John turned off the com. "It sounds like he's okay."

Kari huffed. "It's degrading the way that man talked about Shail, like he was merchandise."

"To these people he is merchandise, Kari," John said. "We'll see him first thing Saturday morning, but you have to hide your aversion as well as your love for Shail. You can't act like you know him. Too many hunters could guess you're his harpy mate. If there's trouble, I could lose my chance to bid on him. God knows what Shail will do when he sees you. He may go nuts. It's almost better if you didn't go."

"I'll be calm, Dad, and I'll tell Shail he must be the same."

Thursday remained relatively quiet. John slept on the backseat, and Charlie and Kari took turns flying the hover. They noticed more and more vehicles on the highway, traveling toward Hampton. The rain came in the afternoon and continued all night.

John flew the evening shift and worriedly watched the solar charge on his hovercraft. The all-night flying and the daytime overcast skies weren't helping the engines regenerate power, and the little hover wasn't built for the long, nonstop trip. When morning came, he landed by a small store and told Kari and Charlie that the engine needed recharging in the bright sunlight. They ate and hung around for a few hours before moving on.

At night John breathed a sigh of relief, seeing the glow of lights filtering up from the horizon. Hampton was within reach, and the trip across the continent was at an end. They flew over the city and landed outside the giant spaceport among numerous hovercrafts and starships. They climbed out, and John and Charlie unloaded their bags. "I'm going to look for Ted," Kari said, and walked toward a port employee under a small spaceship. "Do you know Ted?" she asked. "He works here."

The man pointed. "He should be two lanes over, working on a green freighter."

Kari walked through the lanes and spotted the freighter. Ted was on his back, fixing the landing skid. "Hi, Ted," she said.

Ted jumped up, hitting his head on a beam.

"Are you okay?"

"Fine, fine," he stammered. "In fact I'm great, just glad to see you." They talked briefly about Kari's journey.

"Are you going to see your harpy tomorrow?" Ted asked.

"Yes," Kari said. John and Charlie joined them and she introduced them. John shook hands with Ted and apologized for his rudeness on their first com communiqué.

Ted shrugged. "That's okay, Mr. Turner. I could tell you were under a lot of stress. Would you mind if I took Kari to see her golden harpy?"

"That's up to her," John said.

"I think I will go with Ted," Kari said. "If there's trouble, it'll appear I'm not with you and Charlie."

"Considering Shail might react to you," John said, "it'd be better if you were seen with a young man."

Ted wrote down his com number and handed it to Kari. "I took off work this weekend. Call me, and I'll pick you up first thing in the morning."

Kari, John, and Charlie left the port and took a shuttle to the same hotel where Kari had stayed on her return from Earth. Kari had an adjoining room with her father, and Charlie's room was across the hall. After cleaning up, they ate in the small dining room off the lobby and then went to their rooms. Tired from the long trip and sleeping in the cramped hover, John and Charlie were eager to stretch out in a real bed, but Kari was excited. Happiness mixed with worry kept her up half the night, for she would finally see Shail.

16

Gus called on his communicator. "Where are the goddamn transports, Bill? We've been at the port for a half an hour, and I'm ready for a drink."

"We'll be there in five minutes," said Bill, "and I brought a bottle. Figure you earned it, with the golden. How's he doing?"

"He's fine. Mollie's pampered the hell out of him. I can't get near it without her throwing a fucking fit."

"That's why I hired her. Working with those vets, she learned how to keep a harpy alive, and we'll need the golden to pay for our investment on this lousy planet. He's sparking a lot of interest despite the beetle scare. We're pulling into the port lot now."

Gus looked at the spaceport gate and saw the headlights of two large truck transports. He turned to the men relaxing against the cages. "The transports are here. Get your lazy asses up." The trucks drove onto the dark landing field and stopped at the freighter.

Gus's large brother Bill stepped out of the first truck. Pushing back his greasy hair, he twirled his mustache and walked toward Gus. "Where is he?"

Gus pointed. "By Mollie, she won't leave his cage." The two Simpson brothers walked over to the thin handler and the cage.

Bill looked in the dark cage at the sleeping golden. "Is he all right?"

"I just gave him a mild sedative and knocked him out," Mollie said. "He'd be in better shape if you kept your brother away from him. Gus nearly gave him a heart attack, shocking him with his cattle prod. It's lucky I showed up when I did."

Gus frowned. "Look at my face, Bill. That winged bastard kicked the crap out of me when I reached for him. I had to teach him some manners."

Bill laughed, looking at Gus's black eye. "The little harpy did that?"

"He caught me off guard," said Gus. "Never had one fight back."

"We cannot afford to lose this one, so control your temper," Bill said, "Let's get him back to the range. I can't see him in this light."

The animals and Shail were loaded in the transports and taken to the range five miles outside Hampton. Shail was put in a separate room, away from the other wild animals.

Bill peered down into the harpy cage while Mollie and Gus stood nearby. He scowled and said, "This harpy could be a problem."

"What's wrong?" Gus said. "He's perfect. I didn't put a mark on him."

Bill reached through the bars, turned the dozing harpy's face, and lifted his wing, examining the sleek, handsome frame. "He's perfect, all right," Bill said, "maybe too damn perfect. Compared to him, men look like onions. He's going to melt the heart of every woman who walks through our doors. Plus, you said he doesn't act like a frightened harpy."

"Hey, he's frightened of me and hides when I get near him," Gus said.

"He's afraid of your rod, not you," Mollie said. "There's a reason this harpy is different, besides having the characteristics of the combative golden line." She reached into the cage and lifted his wing. "See that little scar? It's a laser-blast wound, and someone did surgery on it. New feathers have grown in where the wing was broken by a second blast, and he has old rope scars on his wrists and ankles. The harpy was wounded, captured, and treated. He survived hunters and lost his natural animal fear. That's why he's so aggressive."

"The men you got him from probably treated him," Bill said.

"Not those guys," Gus said. "The harpy knocked the crap out of them. They were scared to touch him."

"If the harpy had recently been caged and treated with drugs and force-feeding, he wouldn't look like this," said Mollie. "His skin would be pale, and he'd lack muscle tone. He probably escaped and has been free for some time."

Gus poked the harpy. "I could fix his pretty looks and have him shaking like a brown, Bill. Just give him to me for one day."

"And how many hunters will pay good money for a banged-up harpy?" Bill grumbled and glanced at Mollie. "How do you feel about killing this harpy?"

Mollie placed her hand on the golden. "It makes me sick that such a rare and beautiful creature is going to be destroyed."

Gus chuckled. "Yeah, Mollie wants a zoo to buy him."

"Don't get your hopes up, Mollie," Bill said. "Zoos don't have that kind of money, but that's what concerns me. I've already advertised that the golden will be on display Saturday and Sunday to the general public. One look at this pretty boy, the women will be outraged, not to mention the goddamn animal rights people. They'll be protesting we're killing the last golden. It'll be bad for business and bad for the bidding hunters. I wish I'd seen the harpy earlier and made the auction invitation-only. Jesus, I even have reporters coming on Friday to write a story and take pictures."

"So what are you going to do, Bill?" Gus asked.

"Hope we get rid of him before the public organizes. Keep him heavily sedated and overfed Wednesday and Thursday. Friday morning we'll pull the feeding tube and take him off the drugs. He'll get his balance back and hold his weight till Monday's auction."

The harpy stirred in the cage. "He's coming out of it," Mollie said.

"Good," Bill said. "I want to see this attitude of his."

Shail opened his eyes and saw Mollie leaning over his cage. He then noticed Gus, and another large man. He made a low seething sound.

"He also has blue eyes instead of green," the new man grumbled. "Goddamn it, he's going to melt hearts and have women blubbering."

"All goldens have blue eyes," Mollie said.

Shail saw the rod in Gus's hand and became quiet, lowering his head in his wing.

"He saw Gus's rod," Mollie said. "I told you he's scared of it."

"Get rid of the damn cattle prod," Bill growled at Gus. "I want to see how he'll act when he's put on display."

To Shail's surprise Gus was obedient and removed the rod. When Gus returned, Shail lifted his head and gazed at the men.

Bill twisted his mustache. "Look at his antagonistic stare. He's not a bit frightened."

Shail looked around the small room for an escape, but there was none. Bill put his hand through his cage bars, and Shail hissed, wrinkled his nose, and showed his teeth. Bill poked Shail's rib, and Shail lunged to bite, but was restrained by chains and unable to sink his teeth into the hand. The man continued to prod him, and each assault built Shail's rage. He shook his hair, twisted in the shackles, and attempted to strike with his folded wing. His hisses became louder.

"He'd love to take off my hand," Bill said. "You keep poking a dog with a stick, he'll eventually turn into one vengeful animal. The same could be done with the harpy. The hunters would pay a fortune for a vicious harpy, and if he's crashing into the cage bars to attack, the public won't think he's so appealing."

"You could break his spirit," Mollie said, "and then he'd be like a dog with his tail tucked between his legs; not a very pretty sight."

"He survived those blast wounds and Gus's rod," Bill said. "He won't break down. Change of plans. We'll take him off the drugs on Thursday. Gus, you'll have all day to torment him, but I don't want him hurt. By Friday he'll be pissed off and wanting to kill every man he sees."

Gus grinned. "I can get him like that."

"Don't do it, Bill," Mollie said. "No amount of torment is going to make him crash into the bars. I guarantee you'll destroy him, and he'll lie in a cage corner suffering from shock. He could die."

Bill walked to the doorway "That's why I pay you to keep the harpy alive. Things won't get out of hand. Gus knows he's valuable. Go ahead and drug him. I'm ready for a drink." Bill and Gus left the room.

"Morons," Mollie grumbled and pulled out a sedative. "Sleep now, my prince, and save your strength. I'm afraid you're going to need it."

Shail detected Mollie's anger and also her sadness and helplessness. She couldn't protect him from Gus and later, a cruel death. For the first time he nuzzled her caressing hand before drifting to sleep.

The following day and night Shail was unconscious, but Thursday morning he woke, feeling bloated from overfeeding. He was still in the same room that was virtually empty except for his cage. His stomach ached, and it hurt to swallow. Squirming in his bonds, he noticed the catheter tube had been removed from his sex organ. He heard the door open and strained to see Mollie, but Gus entered. Shail stared up, and Gus reached through the bars to grab his hair. Shail swiftly reacted and jerked his head to bite him.

"Pretty damn brave when I don't have my rod," Gus said and left the room.

Gus came back carrying the rod and adjusted the setting. Shail breathed hard, gripped the chains, and attempted to cover himself with his wing. Gus touched his stomach with the rod. It stung, but the pain was milder, compared to the warehouse abuse.

"Don't hurt as bad? Now let's get you worked up," he said. He reached through the bars, ripping off Shail's sash, dropping it on the floor. He held his wing back. Jamming the rod between Shail's legs, he released a shock.

Shail went nuts, frantically flailing his body and wings in the narrow cage and thrashing on his chains. Gus hit him several more times, and Shail's yellow feathers were littering the floor.

In his office, Bill heard the racket and the panicked harpy's hisses. He walked into the room. "What the hell are you doing, Gus?"

"Making him mean," Gus said. "If anyone stung my balls, I'd kill them."

"You're not a damn harpy, and you're only terrifying him. Look at his goddamn feathers on the floor," he yelled. "Get rid of that fucking rod."

Gus glared at Bill. "Don't yell at me, Bill. I'm not a kid anymore, and my money paid for this range. You wouldn't even have the harpy, if it weren't for me."

Bill calmed down. "All right, but use some common sense. Those loose feathers are like gold. If he's banged up, has damaged wings, or goes into shock, he won't be worth shit. Think of a way to turn him into a man-killer without hurting him. I have a lot of office work, with the auction." Bill left the room.

Gus looked down at the harpy. "What makes a male harpy angry?" He grinned and walked out of the room.

Shail closed his eyes and wished the hunt would begin. At least he'd be free of his restraints and able to fight back. They want me to hate, he thought. Although it was a common emotion for humans, hate was unnatural and frightening for harpies. The emotion wiped all reason from a gentle mind. Shail had briefly experienced hate when Kari was attacked by the mountain hunters. He lost control and nearly beat the men to death. A golden ruler couldn't afford to hate. Too many relied on his judgment. I must fight the anger and keep the hope of my escape, he thought. Without hope, the depression would come, but slowly his will to live was whittling away.

Gus returned with his warehouse sidekicks, Lester and Bert. Lester held a five-season-old fledgling. Gus opened the top of Shail's cage. "Throw it in there. Let him get friendly with this orphan," he said. Lester placed the fledgling on top of Shail, and Gus slammed the cage door closed. "Let's get a bottle." The men left the room, leaving Shail with the young harpy.

The fledgling sniffled, and Shail raised his wing, offering cover. He crawled over Shail's body, sliding behind his back and under his feathers. Resting his chin on Shail's ribs, the fledgling gazed at the yellow feathers.

"Your pale wings means you are our great ruler," relayed the fledgling. "My father has told me the stories of the brave goldens. Will you protect me?"

Shail massaged the fledgling's head with his wing. "I cannot make such a promise, for I, too, am helpless. How did you come to be here?"

"A metal bird flew faster than I, and with the sting, I fell to the ground. The hunters put me in a cage and waited for my father. He came, and their weapons found him. I watched my dad slowly die. The hunters brought me here. Master, I am very afraid."

"Come closer," Shail said. The fledgling snuggled up under his chin, and Shail licked and nuzzled the little guy until he fell asleep. Shail breathed deeply, realizing Gus's motives. The men would see his rage if they harmed the fledgling.

Hours passed, and Shail heard Gus's voice and the door opened. The fledgling woke and quickly hid under Shail's wing. Gus and the two men peered down into the cage. Shail seethed and hit the bars with his wing.

"What did I tell ya?" Gus chuckled. "He's defending the fledgling. Get the little one out." Gus opened the cage, and Shail tried to beat them back with one wing. Bert grabbed his flapping wing while Lester snatched out the fledgling. Gus closed the cage. "Hold the little sucker still," he said to Lester.

Shail noticed the shocking rod in Gus's hand and heard the fledgling's silent pleas for help. Hoping to distract the men, he recklessly bashed his wings against the bars and wildly twisted on the top chains while his feet kicked the metal cage.

"He sure is mad," Bert said.

"That's the point," Gus said. "Wait till I shock it." As Lester held the fledgling out, Gus touched its stomach with the rod. The little harpy shook, urinated, and then went limp.

Shail stopped thrashing and closed his eyes. The fledgling's silent screams no longer entered his mind.

"Damn, Gus, you killed it," Lester said and examined the lifeless body.

Gus grabbed the tiny body. "I didn't even use a full shock." He dropped it on the floor. "It was only worth five thousand."

"Hey, Gus, you better have a look at the golden," said Bert. "He don't look so good."

Gus leaned over the cage, and the golden harpy pathetically shook his head as if impaired. "Shit. He must've smashed his head against the bars. See if there's any blood."

Bert opened the cage and turned Shail's head, looking for an injury.

Shail came alive, his nails raking the man's face.

Bert jerked away. "Son-of-a-bitch," he screeched, holding his face. Blood ran through his fingers and onto his shirt.

"Let me see," Gus said. Bert lowered his hand, and Gus looked at the claw marks. "He almost got your eye. That'll take some sealin' at a hospital." He turned and stared at Shail, who glared and seethed at the men. "Mollie said the lil' fucker's smart. He faked that head wound to get us close. We'll finish with him tonight after Bill goes home."

The men left, and Shail stared through the bars at the dead fledgling. His only soothing thought was the men dying under the swarms.

Through a small high window, Shail saw the light fade to dark, and the hunting range became quiet, its employees leaving for home. After some time, he heard Gus and the other men's laughter, and he jerked his head up. Gus entered and stared down at him, and Shail smelled his whiskey breath.

"We can't hurt him too much," said Gus, "'cause Bill will be pissed, but he can take a good ridin'." He opened the cage and grabbed Shail's wing, pulling it away from his nude body. "Look at that tight little ass. There'd be a long line at the prison for this virgin."

Bert's face was bandaged. He reached in and fondled the harpy's rear. "He's rather pretty, prettier than my last woman."

"Fuck, he's better looking than any women you've been with," Lester laughed.

Trying to pull his wing down for cover, Shail snapped and hissed at the gawking men who touched his body.

"Before we get him out, we need to tie down his wings and gag him. Don't want to get bit," Gus said. "Bert, get some oil out of the kitchen, and we'll lube him, so he's not tore up. After we're done, he'll be a man-killer."

"Stuck in prison and then the jungle, I'm ready for a good piece of ass," Lester said, and stretched the harpy by the wrist chains so it couldn't scratch. He bound the wings while Gus grabbed the harpy's hair and jammed a rag in its mouth.

Gus took a sip from the whiskey bottle and chuckled. "I can't wait to see Mollie's face when she finds out we fucked her prince." Bert returned from the kitchen with the cooking oil.

"When we unfasten his chains, I'll get the legs, and you two pull each arm," Gus said. "We'll chain him over the top of the cage."

Shail tried to kick and fight when the men hoisted him out of the cage, but he was overpowered and restrained. Lester and Bert pulled each wrist, stretching his arms across the top bars and fastened them down. They did the same with his ankles, spreading his legs and chaining the ankles to the bottom bars. Next his wings were unbound and elongated across the bars and retied, giving them full access to his naked body. Shail lay draped across the bars and totally helpless and exposed. Unable to hiss because of the mouth rag, he breathed hard with stress.

Gus looked at the vulnerable slender frame, sleek with nervous sweat. "Put some loading mats between him and the cage. Don't want bruises when he's bouncing around."

Bert put the mats between the bars and the harpy and poured oil on him. "You want some?" He fondled Shail's sex organs and prodded his rear.

Shail exploded in the chains, sensing their lust and that he was the target. He tossed against the padded cage to avoid their touch.

Gus pushed Bert out of the way and unfastened his pants. "I'm breaking him in," he said, and rubbed against Shail's wiggling body until he had an erection. "That's a good boy. You just keep bouncing around and fighting me."

Shail became hysterical when Gus's penis penetrated him. Horrified, he could barely grasp that another male had mounted him. With all his strength, Shail pulled on the chains, causing his wrists and ankles to bleed, but he couldn't escape Gus's crushing body that covered and pinned him against the cage. His eyes watered with the demoralizing pain from the man's large invading sex organ and the ruthless humping.

"That's it," Gus grunted while holding Shail's squirming hips. "Keep wiggling . . . almost there. Fuck, this little beauty is good, the best," he gasped.

Lester and Bert watched and masturbated, waiting their turn. "Jesus, Gus, hurry up," said Lester. "Save some fight for us."

As soon as Gus ejaculated and withdrew, Lester leaped in his place and attacked Shail. The man rapidly pumped with quick, rigged jabs. "You like that, baby?" he puffed.

Gus sat down by the cage to recoup. "He does," he said and took a slug from the bottle. "The prince has a hard-on he's so worked up. Just like them little boys in prison, rape 'em and they come in their pants."

Gus pulled a small bottle of pills from his pocket. "Let's really fuck with his head and overdose him," he said to Bert. "A few of these and he'll get so horny, he'll be itching for dicks and last longer."

Gus removed the rag from Shail's mouth, and Bert crammed a pill shooter down his throat. Shail tasted the sickening sweet pills and hissed. His head spun with the burning assault and the emasculation of his soul.

Lester finished, and Bert quickly took his turn. Firmly planting himself in Shail, he reached around his waist and clutched Shail's unwanted erection. Shail was in a state of total panic as the man tugged on his penis and stroked him within. The stimulating drugs quickly took affect and he lost control of his sex urges and released his seed, seed only intended for a mate. So delirious, he never noticed when Bert finished, and Gus slapped his rear and remounted him. Gus spurred his body to perform and Shail was quickly aroused again.

Throughout the night Shail ignored his wet, aching muscles, the binding restraints, the stabbing rape, and their warm seed that ran down his legs. He fought the pain and fatigue and continued to toss his body to dislodge each rider and stop the attack. Free of the gag, he gasped for breath and inhaled the rank smell of whiskey and human odor. The revulsion caused him to vomit several times on the mat.

Unknowingly, Shail's struggle encouraged the drunk men. They were determined to outlast the fiesty harpy, and like most rapes, their motivation became one of power.

As the dawn approached, the men won the battle. Shail stopped fighting and lay drained from the relentless all-night assault on his slight frame. But worse than the physical abuse, he lost his strong will to live and fell into the deepest void of depression. All he had been slipped away, leaving him like an empty shell. The men had not only raped his body, but also his soul.

Bert groped and prodded him to act out, but Shail desregarded him and concentrated on stopping his heart while he still had a mind. He was broken, disgraced, and worthless as a flock leader, and with this last defiant act, his worth to men would be reduced to lifeless feathers.

Bert climbed off the limp body. "Hey, Gus, the harpy's finally given up. He ain't moving."

Gus woke and rubbed his eyes. He clamored to his feet and wobbled over to Bert and the harpy. "I'll make him move," he said, and hit Shail's chest with his shock rod.

Shail jumped and began breathing. The high-voltage shock jolted his heart and forced it to beat again. Gus had unknowingly saved Shail's life.

The three men soon passed out on the floor, and Shail was too far gone to focus on a second suicide. His body twitched and his eyes were fixed and dilated. Shock and the disabling depression owned him.

In the morning Mollie was worried about the harpy, and she hurried through the hunting range and entered the room. Seeing the golden, she covered her mouth. He lay fastened to the cage top with his limbs extended and stretched across the bars. Blood and fluid ran down his legs. Gus and the two men were passed out and rested against the wall. She dashed out and raced to Bill's office.

"Come quick," she said to Bill and wiped her tears. "Your goddamn brother . . ." She turned away and headed back to the room.

"What's he done now?" Bill followed her. He walked into the room and stared at the harpy and the three sleeping men. He kicked his brother awake. "What did you do? You damn fool!"

"What?" Gus scrambled to his feet. "The boys and me were just having fun. Hey, you wanted him angry. A good raping would make the stud hate men."

"Just shut up." Bill watched Mollie remove the harpy's shackles and ropes. The creature slid to the floor like an inanimate doll, and Mollie forced open one of his eyes. "Is he going to be okay?" Bill fretted.

"I don't know," Mollie said. "He's in severe shock. His whole body has shut down. If he ever wakes, he'll suffer from harpy depression. Let's put him in the large display cage, and I'll start treating him. It'll take a lot of drugs, and he still might be too far gone. We'll have to wait and see." She retrieved the harpy's sash from the floor, holding it to her face, and watched Bill pick up the lethargic harpy.

"He's as light as a bird," Bill said to Mollie as he carried the harpy to the display cage.

"He's also sensitive like a bird," said Mollie. "If he lives, I'll be surprised."

They came to the high twelve-by-twelve-foot display cage in the large front room, and Bill took two steps up the short ladder and entered the cage. He placed the harpy on the straw bedding and Mollie administered the drugs. "I'll check back in a little while."

After Bill left, Mollie gently tied the sash around the harpy's slender hips and cried. She had never wept for a harpy, but her handsome golden prince was different. Unlike a frightened brown that slunk in a cage, the young male was tenacious and showed intelligence. If he survived, his princely qualities would be gone.

Hours passed, and the harpy did not move. Molly washed him, doctored his raw wrists and ankles, and covered him with blankets. She had some men roll the cage to the outside hunting range and placed it under an extended awning near the door. She hoped the warm, fresh air would revive him, but he was close to death.

Bill checked in throughout the morning. "Mollie, groom his hair and curl him up, so he appears like he's sleeping. The reporter will be here at two."

After a few hours the drugs began to work. The harpy opened his eyes but had a blank stare, and his body trembled contantly.

In the afternoon Bill escorted a man and woman from the press out to the golden's cage. Mollie sat in the straw next to the harpy.

"Right now he's heavily sedated," Bill said to the woman reporter. "Of course, you know wild adult harpies are fragile and don't do well in captivity."

The woman gazed at the harpy. "My God, he's absolutely beautiful. Where did you find him?"

"We can't disclose that information," Bill said. "I'd like you to meet his handler, Mollie. She can answer your questions about his care."

Bill grimaced at Mollie, relaying she shouldn't divulge the events that had left the golden dysfunctional.

"Hello," Mollie said, and stood, shaking hands with the two people between the cage bars.

"What can you tell us about him?" the woman asked.

"He's a rare golden harpy," Mollie said. "From what I read, the yellow-winged harpies once protected the brown-winged flocks, but this is the last one, so it's hard to know what role he played in nature, but he has exhibited more nerve than a brown harpy."

"I've heard the stories about dangerous male harpies that steal and rape women," said the woman. "Is there any truth to them?"

"I can't confirm or deny those old stories," Mollie said, "but personally, I don't believe them. I've handled a fair amount of male harpies, and they're always gentle and shy."

"Mollie is fond of the harpies, especially this one," Bill said, "but I assure you the golden is vicious and capable of rape. It attacked my brother, and more recently, it clawed another handler, and he nearly lost his eye."

"I imagine most wild animals fight back when they're caged," said the woman. She smiled at Mollie. "I can see why you're fond of him. I've never seen an adult harpy, and he's drop-dead gorgeous. Staring into those big blue eyes and long lashes, I'm weak in knees." She giggled and turned toward her photographer. "Fred, get some close up shots of his face."

The photographer took his camera that hung from his neck and began to snap pictures of the harpy.

"Are all harpies so stunning?" the woman reporter asked.

Mollie looked down at the golden. "All harpies have tall, lean frames and almost a pixie face, but this golden is exceptional. I've been calling him Prince."

"He does looks like a fairy prince," said the woman. "He's enchanting, yet so human looking."

Mollie sat down beside the harpy and stroked his neck. The harpy nuzzled her leg and rested his head in her lap.

"Look how friendly he is," said the photographer and took a picture of Mollie petting the affectionate creature.

Bill grew anxious with the smitten female reporter and her understanding photographer. An accommodating story about harpies could be trouble. "My employees can hold him and extend his wings for another picture. Most of your readers want to see the wingspan. He's going to make quite a trophy."

"That's not necessary, Mr. Simpson," the woman said. "Let me be clear: We're not sport writers doing a story on a game animal. This will be a human-interest article. You claim you've captured the last golden harpy and he'll be auctioned off and killed in your hunting range. Such a thing might concern our readers."

"The only concern is there are still dangerous harpies on Dora. Your readers dislike the creatures and are glad to be rid of them. Write a sympathetic harpy story, and some important people will be upset with your rag."

"I believe most people, like me, have never seen a mature harpy, much less have an opinion on the species. I intend to include the old rumors of harpies stealing and molesting women, but the last recorded accusation was decades ago."

"That's because the hunters have done a good job exterminating the animals," said Bill.

The woman looked at the foliage in the hunting range. "Your range is very nice. It could pass for a tropical garden."

"We went to great expense to make it look natural," Bill said. "The animals and hunters have the illusion they're in the jungle."

"A brief illusion," the woman said, and stared at the heavy log walls and screened ceiling. "I imagine a cornered animal learns quickly it can't escape. It doesn't seem very sporting."

"It *is* sporting," Bill said. "Animals are the most dangerous when cornered."

The woman reporter sadly looked at the curled-up harpy. "So he'll be turned loose in your range, hunted down by the highest bidder, and killed as a trophy?"

"That's about it. Anything else?" Bill asked.

"No, it's just mind-boggling that people allow it to happen."

"Pretty game fowl has been hunted for centuries." Bill smirked. "It ain't going to change. And that's all harpies are, mindless, vicious game fowl."

The range door opened, and for the first time the harpy lifted his head out of the feathers. He sniffled, and his eyes widened, watching a man walking toward his cage.

"Bill, you're wanted on the com," Gus called.

Staring at Gus, the harpy breathed rapidly and shuddered, rising to a sitting position. His hands clutched the straw.

"Get his picture," the woman hastily told the photographer. The despondent harpy had come to life and alertly focused on the approaching large man. The photographer quickly snapped photos.

The harpy sprang to his feet and dove into the farthest cage corner. He frantically burrowed beneath the yellow straw and concealed his body. Only his golden hair and wings were exposed and blended with the yellow straw, creating an impressive camouflage. The harpy appeared to have vanished from the cage.

"The harpy is terrified of you," the reporter said to Gus, who stood by the cage.

"I caught him," Gus said. "See what the buck did to my face? It's still bruised."

The woman reporter looked in the cage at the petrified blue eyes peering out between the straw under his quivering feathers. "I'd be more interested in what you did to him."

Bill interrupted. "The interview is over. Mollie, can you escort these people out?" Mollie left the cage and walked with the reporter and photograph out of the range and through the large front room, where the auction would be held.

"That reporter is a bleeding-heart bitch," Bill said to Gus, "and was head over heels for the harpy. She'll crucify us with her story. I knew the golden's looks would be a problem. To make matters worse, she saw the harpy's reaction to you. It's obvious you abused him."

"Look at the bright side, Bill," Gus said, "at least the son-of-a-bitch reacted. Shows his mind still works."

Mollie came back into the range and approached the men.

"What do you think, Mollie?" Bill asked. "The harpy was able to get up and hide."

Mollie gazed at the hidden harpy. "Thankfully I got to him in time and the drugs are taking effect, but he'll probably never recover his courage or will to live. He'll have to remain on the heart stimulant and antidepressants. He only wants to die, now. Congratulations, Gus. You took the only harpy with backbone and turned him into a frightened dove, and Bill, you'd better keep your brother away from him. One more bad experience, and you'll lose this harpy. His mind is so fragile he could easily slip into a coma from stress, and no amount of drugs will bring him back."

"Gus, stay away from the harpy," Bill said. "There's too much at risk."

"Sure, Bill. He's paid for the kick to my face." He turned to Mollie and fiendishly grinned. "Your prince put out just fine and didn't stop struggling till dawn. Just the way I like it."

Mollie shuddered. She regretted her job with the sadistic man. For two weeks she had worked at the newly opened hunting range, but it was two weeks too long. If not for the golden's needs, she would have quit the job this morning. After the auction, she decided. She'd never grow used to the inhumane deaths of harpies.

Mollie remained with the golden all night. Gus left, but it still took two hours for the golden to come out of hiding. She gave him drugs and poured fruit juice between his lips. He didn't resist any of the treatment. "Those jerks really did take all the fight out of you," she said sadly. Lacking any motivation, the harpy placed his face in the feathers and straw.

Saturday morning the harpy's display cage was wheeled into the large front room and roped off by the range employees. Bill came out of his office with the news media machine. "Well, they did it," he said to the men and Mollie. "Damn reporters. They wrote one big pity story for the harpies and mentioned the lack of proof that harpies molest women. In the picture you can't even see his wings. Damn golden looks more like a movie star."

One of the employees approached him. "Mr. Simpson, there's a line of people forming in front of the building. Do you want us to let them in?"

"Not till ten o'clock. I can't believe there're people here already."

Mollie looked at the article. "They're probably sick of reading about the destruction of Terrance and the swarms in the west. The harpy can take their minds off their fears."

Gus walked in. "Bill, there's a ton of people outside wanting to see the harpy. We'll make a killing. What do you want me to do around here?"

Seeing Gus, the harpy dove into the straw again. "You can get out of here," Bill said. "You got the harpy hiding again, and some of those people are the bidders. They'll be disappointed if they only see a few feathers."

"Hell, I'll go to a bar." Gus headed for the back door.

"Make sure you take your two friends," Bill said, "and don't come back until we're closed."

At ten, the security guards opened the doors, and the people filed in after paying ten credits each. Mollie gave the golden a large dose of tranquilizers to control his trembling. A noisy, packed room with hundreds of humans wasn't the best therapy for the sick male.

The people gathered around Shail's cage, but he was so numb from drugs, he laid on the straw and gazed at them. His only concern was Gus and his two men. The devastating assault played over and over in his head. In one night all his emotions of love, joy, pride, and sadness were stripped away, and he functioned on the basic animal impulse of fear. It was the only thing that held him to the present.

Mollie stood outside his cage along with men called security guards. The people quietly milled around and looked at him. Mollie leaned toward one of the guards. "This is more like a funeral than an exotic animal exhibit," she commented.

"Why is he in the cage, Mom?" a little girl asked. "Was he bad?"

"No, honey," the mother answered. "I don't think he was bad." She bit her bottom lip.

A woman and her husband stared at Shail. "Oh, Frank. I can't believe they're going to kill him. He looks like an angel with his long, flowing wings and his beautiful, chiseled face."

"He's not what I expected," said the man. "These jungle creatures are called harpies, yet they certainly don't fit the description, an ugly female monster. He resembles a nice-looking young man."

Shail sensed that the human minds held sorrow because of his coming death.

Kari and Ted pushed through the crowd and reached the front of Shail's cage. She felt relieved when she saw her mate was unharmed. He lay on his side and calmly stared at the people. "Shail, I'm here," she silently relayed. "We'll get you out of here soon. Shail, do you hear me?"

He glanced at her, but didn't respond. He closed his eyes and moved his feathers toward his face.

Kari silently pleaded to him several more times, but her budding instincts detected a darkness clouding his subconscious, a darkness so strong it choked out his love, devotion, and sublime spirit. He was not her Shail.

Something was terribly wrong. She noticed a woman inside the ropes standing by his cage. "Is the harpy all right?" Kari asked.

"He's fine. He's just sedated to keep him calm with the crowd," Mollie answered.

"You're lying," Kari said. "Something horrible has happened to him."

Mollie turned to look at the golden. He rested peacefully with his eyes shut. "I assure you, miss, he's fine."

Kari moved closer to the rope, becoming increasingly upset. "Answer me, Shail!" she demanded in a loud voice.

The whole room went quiet and stared at her, but soon the people focused on the cage. The harpy uncurled his body and sat up. He slid across the straw, gripped the bars, and leaned toward her.

"I am lost to you, Kari," Shail relayed silently. "Leave this place and forget me."

"No, my father is going to buy you and take you out of here," she said with telepathy. "In two lights we'll be together."

"I wish no rescue. I am dead and of no use to my family or flock. Please leave this dangerous place for the sake of our son." He lowered his head and eyes.

"Shail, you're not dead, and I won't leave here without you," Kari relayed.

He would not respond further and curled up in the straw, covering himself with his wings.

"What did they do to you?" Kari said softly and looked at her handsome husband. Jake and the Westend hunters had nearly taken Shail's life, but they hadn't broken his spirit. She sensed terror in his mind, but could not tell the source.

After Kari's outburst, a security guard approached her and Ted. "I think it's best if you left now," he said.

"Come on, Kari," Ted said quietly. "We don't want any trouble. We'll come back tomorrow, and maybe he'll be better."

Kari nodded and glanced at Shail. "I love you," she relayed in silence. "You may have given up, but I haven't."

She exited the building with Ted, and they sat down on the street curb. Ted put his arm around her shoulder, and she placed her face in her arms and fought the tears.

John and Charlie walked up to them. "Is it Shail?" John asked. "Is he all right?"

"No, he's not okay. Something awful has happened to him," Kari said with a sniffle. "He doesn't want to be saved. He doesn't want to come back to me. He just wants to die."

John sat down on the curb. "Not too long ago you also were depressed and wanted to die," John said, "but you're better now. Shail is strong, and once I get him back and he's free, he'll come around, Kari. I'll hire guards, put up fences . . . whatever it takes to turn the estate into a true harpy sanctuary. I'll guarantee that you and Shail will have a long happy life, and you'll raise your sons in peace."

Kari looked up helplessly at her father. For the first time in years, she felt like a little girl again, and her dad was her hero. He would make everything okay. She hugged him and whispered, "Oh, Dad, it would be a dream come true."

John stood up. "Ted, can you take her back to the hotel? I have to go in there and register for the auction."

"Sure, Mr. Turner," Ted said. Kari and Ted walked down the street to Ted's vehicle.

John and Charlie got in line to enter the hunting range. "They have a lot of security guards posted inside and out," Charlie said.

"I know what you're thinking. There're too many to steal him."

. Charlie nodded.

They entered the building and approached the display cage. Shail was curled up, sleeping under his wings. "It must be hard for her to see him caged like this," Charlie said.

"I'll go register." John walked toward an office marked for the auction catalog. He went into the room and found six other men waiting their turn.

"John Turner," said a man.

John recognized the stubby, balding man seated by the door. "Hello, Senator Blackwell," he said. "I'm surprised they're making you wait."

"I guess senators don't get priority when it comes to bidding on the last golden, but why are you here? You banned hunting on your property. I figured you became one of those harpy lovers."

John grinned. "Maybe the ban is on my property so I can do all the hunting."

"That might have been smart," said Blackwell. "Your estate is probably the last on the continent that still has large flocks of harpies. I remember the magnificent golden you brought down twenty-some years ago."

"I still hold the record for that one," John said, "but I've come so I can have a matching pair."

"This golden won't break any records; too young. He needs to be in his thirties, but he certainly is a seductive creature. All the women spectators are crying over him. These magnetic creatures have always posed a threat."

"A threat?" John said. "I guess they could be a threat if you have something to hide."

Senator Blackwell sheepishly grinned. "I meant they're a threat to a weak-minded woman." The senator's name was called, and he nodded to John and disappeared into an office.

John's turn came, and the large man from the earlier com call greeted him with a handshake. The man resembled a wrestler rather than a businessman. "I'm Bill Simpson, the owner. It's nice you came despite the negative publicity."

"Turner, John Turner."

"Are you the same John Turner who has a timber estate on the west coast?" Bill asked.

"One and the same," John said.

"It's well known your place is loaded with harpies. What brings you all this way?"

"I've been after this golden male for some time, and I'm not about to lose him now, but he seems awfully docile compared to the last time I spotted him. Hate to spend a lot of credits if there's no challenge in the hunt."

"He's tranquilized. Once he's off the drugs, he'll be lively and give you a good hunt. Fill in these papers, and Mr. Turner, you don't even have to verify your accounts. I know you're good for the credits. I'll get you a bidding number."

Bill left the room and returned with a number. "Two hundred and seventy-six. I hope it brings you good luck."

"That's a high number. You have that many bidders?"

"Most are off-planet bidders. This auction is drawing attention across the galaxy. Everyone wants a golden-winged trophy. I look forward to seeing you Monday night."

John walked to the door and turned. "I'll be back tomorrow to check on him. No sense in staying till Monday if he takes a slide downhill."

"We're taking good care of him, but if you come back, show a guard your number. You won't have to wait in line or pay another ten credits to get in."

"Thanks," John said and left. He strolled across the large room to join Charlie by the cage.

"How is he?" John asked, coming alongside Charlie.

Charlie sighed. "Kari is right. He is not the same. He acts like an unnerved wild animal that has suffered a bad trauma. He shivers with fright, yet is indifferent to the crowd. His mind is impaired, and I don't believe a drug would cause that."

John stepped near the rope that held back the people. Shail was awake and gazed down at the straw. Periodically his whole body trembled, and he swallowed deeply.

John approached a security guard by the cage. "I'd like a closer look at the animal," he said, and produced his bid number.

"Sure, mister," the guard said and lifted the rope. "Just don't get too close or touch him."

John looked directly into the harpy's eyes. "Look at me, Shail," he said with a low voice. "You know who I am, and I know you. Don't let these men take your courage. You will survive captivity and be with Kari again. With the same honor I vowed to protect your son, I now promise to protect you. Stay strong. I will free you."

The security guard moved in. "Sorry, sir. We can't have you talking to the harpy. It might upset him."

"I'm done inspecting him. He's going to be fine," John said to the man and glanced up at Shail. He bent under the rope and stood next to Charlie.

Shail stared at him with watery, tormented eyes. He tossed his head and long locks back and for a moment gazed at the ceiling. He lay down and covered himself with his wings. The feathers faintly fluttered over his shivering body.

John shook his head. "He's a far cry from when I last saw him," John said to Charlie. "These men really abused him. Even after he's freed, I wonder if he can be saved."

John walked to the exit with Charlie and recalled his previous encounter with Shail. The harpy had dropped to his knees and offered up his life for the promised protection of his family. It was the bravest act John had ever witnessed.

His face snuggled in feathers, Shail dwelled on Turner's words and felt ill. He tried to swallow the ever-present lump in his throat. He wanted to be strong, strong for his flock and family, for the jungle that only a golden harpy could rescue from the swarms, but he wasn't strong enough to save himself. He felt weak, dishonored, and terrified and didn't know how to rid himself of the doomed feeling.

Hearing the cage door open, he automatically trembled before lifting his head to see who entered. Mollie walked through the straw toward him and held a syringe of drugs. She pulled back his wing and injected his arm. He lacked the willpower to rebel.

She sat down beside him and stroked his head. "You did good, prince. All the people are gone. I'll have your cage moved back outside to the warm air and quiet. I'll stay with you all night. Those men won't hurt you again. Soon, my beautiful prince, you'll have the peace you want."

Shail licked her hand and understood about the peace. It was the peace of death she spoke of, and the peace he wanted. The strange woman truly grasped a trapped harpy's desires. He rested his head on her leg and nuzzled her.

Two men rolled his cage back to the outside hunting range. With the threat of dark clouds and rain, it was kept under the awning. Mollie entered his cage with a bowl of cut-up fruit. Although he preferred starvation, he obliged her and ate the small piece she slipped into his mouth.

Rain and darkness came, and Mollie stretched out in the straw. He curled up beside her and placed his face near her ribs. Her warm body and stroking, kind hands consoled him.

"You won't be much of a challenge for the hunter who wins the auction," she said. "You'll probably curl up at the man's feet. Gus totally domesticated you, but hopefully the bidders will see your docile nature, and you'll sell as a pet." She leaned over and kissed his cheek. Listening to the rain, they drifted asleep.

In the middle of the night Shail heard the range doors opening and quickly jerked his head up away from Mollie's side. He smelled the unforgettable odor of whiskey. Seeing Gus and the two men at the door, he scrambled to his feet and dove into the far cage corner and hid under the straw.

His movement woke Mollie, and she sat up. "You're not supposed to be here, Gus," Mollie said when the men walked to the cage. "Bill doesn't want you near the harpy."

"He ain't my boss, and I do what I want," Gus slurred. "Me and the boys missed your little prince and came to see if he missed us, but I see he's got you. How come you like that thing more than me?"

"You're drunk," Mollie said, and stood. "You need to go home and sleep it off." She walked to the cage door and unlocked it. As she pushed to open it, Gus slammed it shut and grinned. "Gus, leave the harpy and me alone."

Gus glanced at the harpy that cowered in the corner. "I'll leave him alone. I ain't gonna risk all that money and ride him again, but how about you, Mollie? Care to give me a rough ride?" He and the men laughed.

"Gus, open the door," Mollie said.

"So you can get the guards?" Gus asked. "Them boys are crammed in an office with this rain, watchin' sports, but I'll open the door so me, Lester, and Bert can come in." Gus stepped up into the cage. "Bill said all those women today were in love with the harpy, but I bet they'd feel different if the harpy raped you." Gus stood in front of Mollie, and the two other men blocked the door.

She moved out of the vulgar man's reach. "The harpy wouldn't rape me. You turned him into a gentle little bird."

"Yeah, we broke him pretty good," Gus said, "but I, on the other hand, enjoy rape."

"Gus, don't do this." Mollie tried to reason with the drunk. "You're about to be rich. You don't want to go back to prison."

Gus laughed. "What makes you think I'd go to prison? That takes a witness, and the only witness is gonna be the silent bird. I like you, Mollie, but this is business. When they find you dead and raped, they'll blame the harpy. Everyone knows harpies rape women. The bleeding-heart public will change their tune, and the hunters will bid higher for a killer." He shoved Mollie against the cage bars. "See, I'm not that drunk." He ripped her shirt and exposed her breasts. Mollie slapped his face, and he slugged her, knocking her into the straw. He savagely tore off her remaining clothing.

Gus handed her shirt to Lester. "Gag her, so the guards can't hear."

Mollie returned to consciousness and struggled to rise, but the men held her down while Gus unzipped his pants. "I'm gonna fuck you to death, bitch."

"What about the harpy?" Lester asked.

Gus glanced at the hiding harpy and chuckled. "He's too scared to move. The little stud might learn somethin'." Gus opened his bottle of stimulant pills and popped one in his mouth. "I'm ready for another all-nighter." He brutally penetrated Mollie while Lester and Bert held each of her arms and fondled her breasts.

Shail trembled under his wings and watched the men ravage his gentle handler. He heard her murmured screams in the gag and saw her struggling legs, but soon she lay still and quietly moaned. The attack was end-less, each man replaced with another.

The hours slipped by, and slowly Shail's fear subsided. Breathing deeply, he pictured himself beneath the men and relived the pain and humiliation. Witnessing Mollie's rape, he saw his own, and rage and hate flooded the empty shell of his mind.

Gus was on Mollie, thrusting and cursing. "Come on, bitch, move," he said. Lester and Bert had left the cage and leaned against the outside cage bars, joking and sipping from the whiskey bottle.

Mollie lay limp, all fight gone, apparently resigned to her fate. Her half-closed eyes opened wide, and she stared beyond Gus. The harpy stood behind the unaware man.

Shail grabbed Gus by the neck and held him in a sleeper hold. The large man choked and attempted to unclasp his hold. By the time Lester and Bert noticed Shail's attack, he had throttled Gus into unconsciousness. The men scrambled into the cage door, and Shail was forced to release the big man, who collapsed on top of Mollie.

Bert pulled a long knife from his belt. "Grab him, Lester, and I'll stick him," Bert said. The two men backed Shail into a cage corner.

Mollie managed to slide out from under Gus's huge, stunned body and crawled to the cage door. The men were busy with Shail when she tumbled out of the cage. Gathering her remaining strength, she limped to the doors and staggered out of the hunting range.

Lester lunged for Shail, but he fluttered and kicked Lester's face with a blow meant to kill. The man hit the bars and fell stunned into the straw. Bert wildly wielded the knife, slashing at Shail, but Shail swiftly snatched the man's wrist and twisted. Bert dropped the knife and fought to break free, his wrist broken. Shail jumped in the air and kicked the man's ribs, knocking him backward. Bert struggled to his knees, holding his injured wrist and cracked ribs. His face displayed shock that Shail, though slender, was so agile and strong.

Shail calmly retrieved the knife out of the straw and walked to Bert. He clutched the kneeling man's hair and jerked his neck back. "Is this how it is done?" Shail asked, using his soft human voice. "Is this how a hunter kills a harpy?"

Bert screamed and tried to fight off the hold, but Shail quickly cut the noisy man's throat and watched Bert gag on his own blood.

Lester came around and feebly climbed to his feet. Realizing he was Shail's next victim, he made a dash for the open cage door. Shail sprung at him and seized his hair, jerking him off his feet. Lester crawled through the straw, away from Shail. He grabbed the bars and pulled himself up. "No, please, no," Lester begged when the harpy approached.

Shail flipped his hair with annoyance. "Receive what you have given," he said. A kick to the man's testicles, and Lester dropped to his knees.

Clutching the human's hair, Shail sliced the second man's throat. Shail hissed at the dying man and felt the satisfaction of revenge.

Shail turned toward his last victim. Gus was awake and had witnessed Lester's death. The big man glanced at Bert's still body lying in the straw toward the back of the cage. Gus rose, eyeing the harpy's blood-soaked hands clasping a knife.

Shail flung his hair and seethed. His hostile glare conveyed payback time. "Those received a quick death," Shail said, "but you, who taught me to hate, shall die slowly for taking my honor."

Gus backed away, appearing startled. He bumped into the cage bars. "You can talk," he muttered.

"Yes," said Shail, "so you learn, before your death, harpies are not animals."

Gus nervously chuckled. "You're pretty fucking confident. It's gonna take more than you and a knife to bring me down."

Shail arched his wings. "I am the more." He tossed the knife into the straw. "I need no weapon to kill a monster."

Gus lunged at Shail, knocking him down and wrestled his three-hundred-sixty-pound body on top of the harpy. Standing six foot six, Gus tried to pin Shail, who was eighty-five pounds and six feet tall, but Shail fought dirty. His teeth immediately sank into Gus's nose, and he kneed the man's crotch. Gus pulled back, and Shail curled his body under the man and let loose with a kick to Gus's face, striking his already black eye. Shail slid out and sprang to his feet.

Gus climbed to his feet, rubbed his eye, and felt for his nose. Drawing back, he stared at his bloody hand. "When I get ahold of you," he growled, "you'll wish you were dead."

"Already I wish for death," Shail said with his soft voice.

They stalked each other. Gus out-shadowed and out-muscled Shail, but the harpy had six limbs and moved with lightning speed. All his life Shail had tangled with large, dangerous animals and knew how to disable them.

Gus hurled himself at Shail, wildly swinging his fists. Shail ducked the punches and flapped his wings, flying to the top of the high twelve-foot cage. Before Gus could turn and look up, Shail drop-landed on the huge man's back. Gus struggled to throw him off, leaping back and slamming him against the bars, but Shail clung to the man, one arm around Gus's neck and the other gripping his jaw. Shail jerked with all his strength, attempting to snap the thick neck, but he was off balance on the frantic man, who was in a fight for his life.

Shail flapped his wings and righted himself. Gus pulled the harpy's arms to unlock the death hold. With several swift thrusts, Shail heard Gus's neck vertebrae pop. Shail fluttered off, and the giant staggered, collapsed, and jerked in the straw. Gus stared up at Shail, who mockingly sniffled at his defeated enemy. With his last kick, Gus sadistically grinned. Shail ruffled his feathers and stepped out of the open cage door.

Mollie stumbled through the building nude and hysterical. She screamed for help. The two security guards heard her and rushed out of the office.

"Gus and his men are killing the harpy," she cried.

The guards looked at one another and called on their radio for backup. Two other guards finally appeared from the outside.

Seeing their uneasiness in confronting Gus, she screamed at them. "You're taking too long!" The four men went to the range, and she followed them as best she could, none of them expecting the gruesome sight that awaited. The display cage door was open, and inside three large men lay on the red-soaked straw. Blood from their slashed throats dripped from the cage and splattered on the floor.

One guard checked the bodies. "They're all dead. Do you see the harpy?" The men nervously peered into the dark forest of the range.

"The harpy was able to kill Gus," said another guard with disbelief. "I don't get paid enough to go after it."

A guard wrapped one of Shail's blankets around Mollie and helped her into a chair. She broke down and cried. The guards stayed close to the entrance and called Bill.

"The harpy has killed your brother and Lester and Bert," said a guard. "It's loose in the hunting range."

"I'll be right there," Bill said wearily. "It can't get out, but stay by the doors."

Seeing Mollie's bruised face, split lip, and welts, a guard asked, "Did the harpy do this to you?"

"No," Mollie said between sniffles. "Gus and those men raped me and were going to kill me. The harpy saved me. Do you understand? He jumped Gus and saved my life. Don't hurt him."

Bill and the police arrived at the range simultaneously. Bill stepped up into the cage and looked at his dead brother. Gus's neck was twisted, his face smeared red, and part of his nose was missing. "Jesus," he muttered.

A police sergeant approached him. "I just talked to your animal handler, Mollie. She claims your brother and these two raped her and planned to murder her."

"She's confused. Gus wouldn't hurt her," Bill said. "You've heard how a woman loses her mind after a harpy molesting. My brother was probably trying to help her when the creature attacked. Let me talk to her."

"She sounds competent," said the sergeant, "but regardless, the harpy is dangerous and has to be destroyed. At first light we'll go in and get him."

"No, he's too valuable," Bill said and stepped out of the cage. He pulled the police sergeant aside. "I can make it worth your while to keep him alive. Say twenty thousand credits? My men can stun him and get him back into his cage. He'll be auctioned off Monday night and destroyed Tuesday."

The sergeant massaged his chin. "Twenty thousand," he said. "I have no problem letting it live till Tuesday as long as it's caged and properly secured, but your handler could complicate your plans. If her claim is true that the men were the rapists, the sperm DNA will confirm it and drag out the investigation. The courts will take ownership of the harpy and delay your auction. In the same situation, if a guard dog attacked men to save its assaulted owner, there wouldn't be any reprisal against the animal. This situation might apply to the harpy. The courts have the power to spare him."

Bill nodded. "I'll take care of it." He walked over to Mollie. "Come dear; there's a robe in my office." Bill helped her up and led her out of the range.

Bill put the robe on Mollie and closed his office door. "It must have been awful."

"It was." Mollie whimpered. "Gus held me down . . . he was going to kill me and blame it on the harpy."

"You're upset and mixed up. The harpy raped you, and poor Gus gave his life to save you."

She stopped crying and looked up. "But that's not what happened."

"It is what happened. If you say different, I might have to finish what Gus started, and don't even consider telling the police. I know people who can make a witness disappear. Do we understand one another?"

Mollie nodded with fear.

"Good girl. I knew you were smart. One of the officers will take you to a hospital. They can finish their report on how the harpy attacked you."

Bill opened the office door and motioned to a police officer posted outside. "Her memory is coming back."

17

Outside the cage Shail glanced back at the dead men and felt rage. The rain had let up and exposed the stars in between moving gray clouds. Spreading his wings, he flew the length of the dark hunting range and looked for an opening in the heavy top screen. He quickly learned he was still a prisoner, and the screen was impossible to break. Longing to be rid of the men's blood on his body, he found a small pond and landed. They shall never soil me again, he thought and rinsed in the cool water.

Shail assumed his hate would wash away like their blood, but he was wrong. His mind dwelled on the cruel molesting, and he smoldered with revenge. The humans hated and slaughtered his race, and now the prejudice had come full circle. The ruler of the harpies longed to kill them.

He was troubled by the powerful hate that consumed him and realized he would willingly sacrifice his flocks to destroy men. His decision to lead wisely was lost. If free, I would have my harpies slay all survivors of the swarms, he thought. Better I die than have the human weapons harm my flock.

When the blood was gone, he curled up on the ground and focused on his heart, hoping to commit suicide with a heart attack, but Mollie's drugs protected his life. He stood up and shook his head, never feeling so confused. The emotion of hate was foreign to a harpy, and like love, he believed it would remain forever. "The men shall kill me with the coming light," he said, resolved to his fate. "The swarms shall cleanse the land, and my son shall reign in a human-free world."

He flew to the highest tree and perched on the blue limb near the screen. He called out silently in hopes of contacting a harpy. If any were near, they would sense his thoughts and come. The moist wind whipped at his locks, sending them off his shoulders while he stared beyond the walls at the horizon. The first rays of dawn crept through dark clouds. His time was fleeting like the tropical breeze.

A half-grown harpy sailed out of the shadowy sky and landed on the screen above Shail's head. The young harpy stared down in awe. "Your wings are yellow. You are the golden ruler we seek," he relayed, and bowed his head.

"I am he," Shail relayed. "Are the swarms near?"

"In five lights they come east, my father says. I shall seek our flock leader, Seth. He shall save you."

"No, I do not wish to be saved," Shail relayed, and reached back, plucking a flight feather from his wing. "The men's weapons would destroy Seth's flock, and I still would be caged." Shail pushed the feather through the screen. "Listen carefully. Take my feather to your Seth, so all know we shared these words. After the beetles attack this city and the humans have fled or died, the flocks must gather and destroy the swarms with one sweeping strike. Do you understand? This must be done before the rise of the next full moons."

"I understand, master," relayed the teenager.

"Also my mate is here. She dwells in the city with two men. She and these men must be found and taken to a place of safety before the swarms come."

"You wish to save men?" asked the teenager.

Shail arched his wings and growled, "You do not question. You follow."

The teen fell on the screen and hid his face in his arms with the threat of the raised yellow wings, the symbol of reprisal.

Shail lowered his wings. "What is your name?"

"Ribot, Master."

Shail reached through the screen and stroked the young male's head. "Ribot, these things I say are very important. All life depends on you to deliver my words. The beetles must be destroyed before they grow too strong, and the two men protect my pregnant mate." He glanced up at the brightening sky. "Go now before the protection of shadows is gone, and you are discovered."

Ribot grasped the three-foot yellow feather and bound into the gray sky.

In the distance Shail heard many voices coming from the doors. "I shall never be hunted again." He breathed deeply and flew toward the men gathered by his cage. He landed just beyond the extended awning. The twenty surprised men raised their weapons.

"Don't shoot him," Bill yelled at his guards, animal handlers, and policemen. "A stun can bring on a heart attack. Maybe we can get him without it."

Shail looked at Bill. He alone longs to avenge his sibling's death, he thought, and dauntlessly approached the large man.

"Be careful, Mr. Simpson. It's set its sights on you," called a guard.

Shail stopped twenty feet from Bill. The silence was broken only by the squawks of distant birds as the men stared in a trance. Shail waited for Bill to grasp the weapon hanging from his belt and fire a deadly blast. Taunting the man, Shail flung his head, sniffled, and paced closer, ruffling his feathers. Five feet away, Shail arched his wings and hissed, signaling a male challenge.

"Get ready," Bill whispered to the men. "I'll try to grab him."

Bill lunged for Shail, who fluttered, struck the man's chest with his feet, and sent the big man flying on his back. Bill hit the ground, and Shail landed close by. He paced around him, hissing to encourage him to rise.

Bill sluggishly got up. The wind knocked out of him, he gasped for breath. Shail was only an arm's length away. Bill again charged, his fists swinging, and Shail flapped his wings, kicking Bill's face and again knocked him down. Much like a thin matador, the harpy hit the angry bull of a man with each pass. Bill couldn't put his hands on Shail nor defeat him in physical combat. Shail sniffled with aversion, tempting him to fight or kill.

"You little son-of-a-bitch," Bill grumbled and stood up, holding his sore face.

The men closed in, circling the two. Determined not to flee, Shail stood his ground and hissed at them to keep their distance. He brazenly strutted around Bill and teasingly flung his hair. Bill made one final attack, and Shail jumped sideward, his foot striking the man's stomach. Bill dropped with a heavy thud and coughed. This clumsy beast is no challenge, Shail thought, growing impatient with the pathetic human. He walked behind Bill and clutched his head and neck, preparing to give him the same death as his brother.

The twenty security guards and policemen leaped on Shail and wrestled him off the big range owner. Shail struggled briefly, kicking two men in the face, and a wing took down a third, but he was outnumbered and pinned on the ground. Lying subdued, he felt metal shackles with chains placed on his wrists and ankles.

A couple of guards hoisted up Bill, and he breathed hard with exertion and pain. "Goddamn harpy is fast, and uses its feet like a professional boxer." He puffed. "I see how it killed my brother." He went to the harpy, and it insolently glared up at him, ignoring the other men who held it down. "Stand him up."

The men lifted Shail to his feet, and he hissed at Bill.

"You nervy little bastard," Bill said. "I'll knock the shit out of you."

Bill struck Shail with a hard blow to the stomach, and his knees buckled. He slumped in the men's arms and coughed. He lifted his head and angrily seethed.

"Get him up again," Bill growled and hit Shail's stomach a second time. Shail breathed heavily and shook his hair. Instead of becoming meek, he felt growing rage. He fought the men's hold, lunged toward Bill, and snapped his teeth. His defiance purposely fueled Bill's temper, hoping to incite the man to kill.

It was working. Bill was losing control. He again raised his fist to clobber the harpy.

A young police officer grabbed Bill's arm. "That's enough," he said. "I'll not stand by and watch you beat him to death."

Bill collected himself. "Yes, I don't want him damaged." He stared into the harpy's incorrigible blue eyes and turned to his men. "Put a shock collar on him and attach his chains to the bar before he's turned loose in the cage. We'll need some control over him."

Shail bit at the men's hands when the leather collar came near, but they clutched his hair, gagged him, and fastened the tight collar laced with metal strips to his neck. They picked him up and carried him to the cage. An animal handler injected him with a heart stimulant that kept him alive. The cage was clean and filled with fresh straw. The chains held him down long enough to allow the men to exit. The cage door closed, and the chains loosened. Shail sat up in the straw and looked around. Bill and the guards went inside to prepare for the crowds.

The young officer who stopped the beating, and another policeman approached the cage and watched him. "Sure wasn't much of a hunt. He flew right to us," said the other officer.

The young officer moved closer. "I've never seen a harpy. Take away his wings, he'd pass as a good-looking teenager."

"I've seen a few," said the other officer. "They're always thin and pretty, but don't be fooled by their looks. The thing killed three men and raped a woman, and he was just toying with the big range owner. If we hadn't pulled it off, Simpson would also be dead. I sure wouldn't mess with it."

"The female handler made conflicting statements with her story. She initially told the guards the men raped her, and the harpy was protecting her. Then changed her mind and said the harpy attacked. You know this is the first recorded case of a harpy killing men. I get the feeling this creature is getting a bad rap."

The other officer shrugged. "It's possible, but animals can't plead self-defense, and he's been labeled a man-killer. They're auctioning him off to hunters Monday night, and he'll be destroyed. Look, I have to get back to the precinct." He walked to the doors.

The young officer gazed at the harpy and sighed. "It's a darn shame. I think you wanted it to be over. Why else would you fly to a bunch of armed men?" He walked from the cage and was the last police officer to leave the hunting range.

Nestled down on the straw, Shail had detected compassion in the young man. From the men's words he learned Mollie had lied and blamed him for the rape. Shail was not unsettled by her betrayal, knowing humans lacked a harpy's honor. He longed for Mollie's presence and soothing hands. She was devoted to him and must have had reasons for her falseness. Normally he would have beaten Gus within an inch of his life to protect Mollie, but he had taken the attack one step further and killed; revenge, the motivation.

His fear was gone, but replaced with hate. Shail understood fear, a common emotion in animals, but hate perplexed him. Only men could create the unnatural feelings in a harpy. Even in a male challenge, the harpies didn't harbor evil feelings toward one another. I prefer fear over the killing lust, he thought. I have truly lost the harpy in me.

Bill and an animal handler walked up to his cage. Shail slightly lifted his head off the straw and seethed, feeling the wrath to lash out. With each exhale, he released a venomous sizzle and glared at the man from the center of the cage.

"If he wasn't worth so much," Bill said to the handler, "I'd knock that hostile look right off his cute little face." He picked up the harpy's stimulant drug. "Inject him with this tomorrow morning. Don't want his heart stopping."

Once Bill lowered his gaze, Shail flew off the straw and crashed against the cage. He managed to seize Bill's neck and slam his head against the bars. Swiftly wrapping one of his wrist chains around the man's throat, he tugged and cut off Bill's air. The handler was so shocked by the sudden attack he froze for a moment.

"His collar," Bill choked as his eyes bulged with the throttling. The handler grabbed a remote near the cage door and pressed keys.

The collar's electrical charge, similar to Gus's rod, hit Shail's neck, and he let go of the chain and doubled over in the straw, pulling and clawing at the painful leather.

Seeing the subdued harpy, the handler released the shock key and freed Bill from the chain. "Are you okay, Mr. Simpson?"

Bill scrambled away from the cage, gasping. A safe distance from the cage, he placed his hands on his bent knees and tried to catch his breath. He finally stood and fingered the slice on his throat.

Shail shook his head and yanked on the hard and fast collar. The pain eased, and he rose. Looking intently at Bill, he lividly hissed and paced the cage, whipping the rattling wrist chains against the bars.

"That's one nasty harpy," said the handler.

"Give me the remote," Bill said and jerked it from the handler's hand.

He stomped to the display cage and showed the harpy the remote. "You want some more shocks?" he growled.

Rather than scaring Shail, Bill's threat had the opposite effect. He flew toward Bill and slammed into the bars. The whole cage shook from the full-force attack. Bill had been out of reach but he still jumped back with fright. Shail flung his hair and arched his wings like a hawk ready to pounce on prey. He sniffled, beckoning the man to come close again.

Bill lowered the remote and massaged his mustache. "Gus finally did something right, even though it killed him. He turned the harpy into man-killer and one nice prize." He glanced at the handler. "Get some men out here. I want his wrist chains looped over the top bars, and secure his ankles to the lower bars. He'll injure himself if he keeps crashing into the bars. When the spectators arrive this morning, they'll see his full body and wings. His days of curled up in straw and being babied are over."

From outside the cage, the range employees tightened Shail's chains, pulling him down and disabling him on the bedding. "Get his damn sash off," Bill ordered. "The hunters can see all this stud's trophies."

Shail twisted in the stretch hold while one man removed his sash and the others strung his chains over the top bars. Finishing, they left the cage and released him. Pulling his wrist chains from outside the cage, they hoisted him up like a puppet on strings, Shail was constrained to the cage center and forced to stand.

An employee came into the range and approached Bill with the media machine. "Look at today's headlines, Mr. Simpson. The harpy article is as big as the swarm story."

"'Harpy Kills Hunting Range Owner and Two Others,'" Bill read out loud. "'Gus Simpson, part owner of Simpson's hunting range, was killed with two other employees when they entered a golden harpy's cage and attempted to rescue its woman handler who was beaten and being sexually molested by the animal.'" Bill stopped reading and laughed. "This is great. The ladies won't be crying for him today."

The guards rolled Shail's cage to the front room and opened the door to the awaiting throngs of people who came to see the murdering harpy.

Kari and Ted had returned to the hotel, and she spent the afternoon telling him about her adventures with the golden harpy and the discovery of the ancient ship. She left out the fact that she was a harpy who was married to Shail, and the harpies controlled the swarms. Ted was supportive and concerned for her captured golden pet.

John and Charlie came back from the hunting range, and John assured Kari that Shail would be fine once he had his freedom. There was nothing else to do, but worry and wait.

Sunday morning Kari woke to a knock on her hotel door. She opened the door, and her father stood in the threshold. "Bad news," he said and handed her the media player.

Kari sat on her bed and read the headlines about Shail and his crazed attack on the men. "This is a lie. He might have killed the men, but he'd never rape a woman."

John sat down next to her. "Regardless of the truth, the article is very negative about harpies. It confirms the old rumors that harpies are dangerous. It'll take time to change public opinion."

Kari frowned. "More time? For a hundred and fifty years the humans have killed harpies over these rumors, and the truth is, humans are the murderers and rapists." She stood up and walked around the room. "It no longer matters what people think. Their time is up." She smiled sarcastically. "It's actually funny. They want to kill Shail, but, ironically, he's the only one that can save them."

"What are you talking about, Kari?"

"The end is almost here, so I guess it doesn't matter if you know. The harpies can destroy the swarms, but unless their ruler gives the order, the flocks won't attack the beetles. My sweet, young husband . . . he's the ruler, Dad. You kept hunters off your land and protected his harpies. To show his gratitude, he's had his harpies defend your estate. That's why there's been no swarm strikes."

John thumbed his chin in thought. "Shail told me he protected my land, but I didn't know what he was talking about until now. Kari, you should've told me this sooner. I might be able to get the Dora government to free him and stop the destruction."

Kari sat down on the bed. "They'd never believe you, and most of the senators are bidders at the auction and want to kill him. They'd never free him. Besides, I'm not sure Shail could be convinced to save the humans now. He killed three men, proving he's lost his harpy compassion to protect life. And why should he save people who have slaughtered his flocks for generations?"

"Kari, you know most people on Dora have never harmed a harpy."

"That's true, but who is the more guilty? The cruel hunter who shoots the harpy or the indifferent public that turns its backs and allows a species to go extinct. I lived on Earth and saw what apathy and greed did to nature. Dora is at the crossroads of becoming another Earth. Look at Shail. He was wild, beautiful, noble; a symbol of nature and they destroyed him. Even if he heals and decides to save the humans, he has no guarantee the hunting would end."

"But he does have a guarantee, Kari," John said. "He controls the swarms, the power of life and death on this planet. Once people know this, he can make any demand he wishes."

"Dad, we can discuss this all day, but right now Shail needs to be saved. Without him, there is no hope. Dora is doomed."

"I certainly have underestimated Shail," said John. "He was smart to create the swarms."

"He didn't create them." Kari frowned. "The loca eagles and then the harpies have always prevented the beetles from multiplying and turning into swarms. Man destroyed this balance in nature by wiping out the loca eagles on the continent and trying to exterminate the harpies. Shail simply let the beetles take their natural course sooner. He hoped the swarms would drive the humans from the planet and save his flock, but he was also saving the jungle and all of Dora from the beetle plague that would come when the harpies were gone. Of course, Shail didn't know the beetles would turn deadly. He was upset about the loss of life."

"Do you know how they do it, Kari, how the harpies can take out a swarm?" John asked.

"No, but I heard it's dangerous. Some harpies will die. Now I want to get ready and go see him."

"I'll meet you in the lobby, and we'll go together," John said. "If Shail hadn't been caught, his plan would have worked. He would have saved his harpies and brought mankind to its knees. That's astonishing, given he's so young and a harpy that was raised in the trees."

Kari ascended the stairs and Charlie, John, and Ted were waiting in the lobby. They left for the hunting range in John's roomier rented vehicle, but when they arrived, they saw a line of people wrapped around the building.

"It'll take time to get in," Ted said when they climbed out of the vehicle.

"Maybe not," John said, and they followed him to the front of the line.

John approached a security guard near the entrance. "Do I have to wait with the rest of the sightseers?" He showed his bid number to the guard.

"No, sir; you and your party can go in, no charge," said the security guard and unfastened a rope, letting them pass.

The large room was packed with people, and Kari and her group made their way toward the center of the room and display cage. Kari finally saw Shail through the shoulders and heads of the crowd. He stood chained and nude. His lowered head rested between his half-raised arms, with his face hidden by long hair.

She bit her bottom lip, seeing her mate humiliated by the noisy, sneering mob. She looked at her father. "You want him to save *them*?" she asked.

John couldn't answer.

Bill Simpson walked through the crowded room, accompanied by security guards, unlocked the display cage, and stepped inside. "Thank you for coming to see our killer harpy," Bill said into a microphone. "Perhaps I can get him to perform." The audience of mostly men cheered.

John leaned toward Charlie. "Simpson doesn't act like someone who just lost a brother."

Flipping his shaggy locks from his face, Shail arched his wings when Bill entered the cage, but he focused on Gus's shock rod in Bill's hand. He clenched his teeth and exhaled, emitted the sizzling growl similar to a cornered king cobra.

"You're not afraid of this stick anymore," Bill said and touched Shail's rib with the rod, releasing a shock.

Shail jumped with pain, but instead of backing away, he flapped his wings and lunged against his restraints toward the man. The crowd roared, entertained by Shail's struggle to break free and attack.

"Hit him again!" yelled a man in the crowd.

Bill nodded to his employees who stood outside the cage. They pulled the chains and hoisted Shail off the floor. He wildly tossed his body and flapped his wings in the vulnerable and frightening hold. He gasped for air because his own body weight crushed his lungs. When extending his wings, he felt slight relief from the suffocating torture. His heart raced and beads of sweat ran down his body as he learned firsthand why harpies were hung before the slaughter. Like drowning, the hanging position depleted his oxygen. Terrified, Shail quickly used up all his strength and resistance. He thrashed on the chains, but soon gave up. Tossing his head back, he panted in the foreboding trance of harpy fatalism.

Bill prodded his ribs, and Shail squirmed on the chains, ready to accept any handling and butchery. "Now, gentlemen, isn't this stud the perfect trophy?" he asked and displayed the harpy's sex organs, normally hidden by straight blond hair. "He's aggressive, nicely hung, and has no feather damage. His wings are the pale yellow of a young male." Bill gave his wing muscle a mild shock, and Shail fluttered and completely fanned out his wings through and beyond the bars. There were murmurs through the crowd.

Bill reached over and patted Shail's sweaty body. "Yes, this little stud's wing length is sixteen-ten, nearly full grown." Bill mumbled to an employee outside the cage, "This golden is the same as a brown; fades fast when it can't breathe."

With Bill's words, Shail snapped out of his stupor. He lifted his head, folded in his wings, and hissed in between gulps for air.

Bill glared at Shail, who purposely tried to suffocate himself. Taking the rod, he stung Shail, forcing him to elongate his wings, but it had an adverse effect.

Shail went berserk and bashed his wings against the bars with enough force to break bone.

John shoved people out of his way to get to the cage. Reaching the ropes that held the crowd back, he climbed over them. Two guards grabbed his arms and held him. "What the hell are you doing, Simpson?" he yelled to the man in the cage. "He's smothering and breaking his wings. Cut him down!"

Bill backed to the cage door and nodded to the men, holding the harpy's chains. "Sorry, gentlemen," Bill said to the crowd. "The show's over."

The men lowered Shail to the cage floor. Gaining his footing, he sprang at Bill, but the chains held him short of reaching the man. He twisted his body, whacking his wing at Bill. The long flight feathers slapped Bill's face, and he clambered out the cage and slammed the door.

The packed room of people clapped and howled. Bill pushed back his hair and straightened his suit before approaching John. "Happy, Mr. Turner?"

John jerked free of the guards' hold and scowled. "No, I'm not happy," he growled. "If you plan on more torture for the harpy, let me know. I won't waste my time bidding on a damaged and broken-down animal."

Bill lifted the rod. "Don't worry, Mr. Turner. It'd take more than a few mild shocks to break that harpy." Bill lowered his collar and exposed his cut and bruised throat. "After the harpy killed my brother last night, he nearly got me with his chains. Whoever wins him will have the hunt of a lifetime. Good day, Mr. Turner."

Simpson left the crammed room, and the guards escorted John back behind the ropes. He stared up at Kari's mate and saw the meek harpy had changed overnight. Shail savagely jerked on his bonds, flung his hair back and forth, and tousled his feathers. Every muscle quivered with tension and was poised to strike. His wide, edgy eyes shifted constantly at the men. He panted, each breath releasing a deadly shushing between his clenched teeth. The once-calm and stately harpy was gone, replaced with a treacherous creature bent on slaying. Even John would be reluctant to face him.

John noticed that Shail's wild, piercing stare began to vanish, and he focused on the one thing in the room that could quiet his rage. He took several deep breaths, lowered his head, and his arched wings drooped. He swallowed and sniffled. John turned and saw that Shail sadly gazed at his little female who had traveled a stormy continent filled with deadly swarms and stood among the hunters to save him. Wiping the sweat and moisture from his eyes with his arm, Shail worriedly looked back up at Kari, and John knew they were speaking to one another with silent harpy talk. After a few minutes, Shail pawed the straw with his foot and placed his head against his bound arms, his flowing hair hiding his face.

Security guards ushered the people out, and John moved through the crowd toward Kari. They left the building together. "What did he say?" John asked her as they walked to the vehicle.

"He's angry with me, and you," Kari said. "He told me yesterday to leave the city, and I have disobeyed him, and he's upset with you for breaking your promise to protect me. He was concerned with the hunters at the range and that the swarms will hit this city soon. If I don't leave, he's threatened to break our bond, saying I should take Ted for a mate. He's seen me with Ted for the last two days. Other than that, nothing has changed. He doesn't want to be saved and only wants to die."

"But why, when he seems strong and confident now?"

"He's filled with hate, and he cannot foresee that it will ever leave. He's scared and feels lost, since he's controlled by an emotion he doesn't understand."

"Once I free him, his hate will fade and he'll be fine," John said.

Kari somberly gazed at her father. "Will he? I've never felt so much rage in him. Right now he's willing to risk his male flock and attack every human on the planet. This is what he fears and why he'd rather die. Shail is a full-blooded harpy and lives in the present like all animals. He can't see his future, and he lacks optimism. That's why caged harpies die with depression. They don't believe things can change for the better."

John put his arms around his worried daughter. "Your boy is brave and intelligent. He overcame his fear of cages and hundreds of men, and he has the willpower to change and overcome his hate. Of course he's staying angry. Those men are tormenting him to keep him that way for the auction."

Kari smiled. "He did overcome his human fear, but I wish you had seen him when I first got him. He was so cute and skittish, jumping with fright every time he entered the cabin, like something would grab him."

"Why does Shail think the swarms are coming to Hampton? He's been caged and drugged for a week. Does he even know he's on the east coast, and the nearest swarm is over a thousand miles away?"

Kari leaned against the vehicle. "I don't doubt him, Dad. When it concerns his jungle, he's never wrong, but I'm not leaving here without him. I don't care what he knows or wants."

John sighed. "Kari, if you're in real danger here, Shail is right to be angry with me. Can I convince you to leave with Charlie for the estate, and I'll stay for the auction?"

"No, I'm as stubborn as you."

Ted and Charlie walked up to them. "The place was so packed. It took us forever to get out," Ted said and grinned at John. "You were great, Mr. Turner. Yelling at the range owner for hurting Kari's pet. You sure showed him."

"Simpson didn't back off because of me," John said. "I just reminded him of his priorities. Does he want to sell a damaged harpy or a healthy one?"

They climbed into the vehicle and drove to the hotel. John checked the news on the swarm progress and discovered the closest swarm strike was still far away, and his timber estate had yet to come under attack. He focused on tomorrow night's auction and grew concerned. If the huge crowds at the range were any indication of the harpy's price, John could be in trouble financially. Killing the men, Shail had elevated himself from a rare game animal to a much-sought-after prized trophy, testing a hunter's skill and courage. Some men would pay an enormous amount for such a challenge. John would know the next morning the extent of his credit line.

The dark clouds rolled in from the ocean, and sheets of rain flooded Hampton's streets, making a dreary afternoon. John chatted with Ted and liked the hardworking and easygoing young man. There was no doubt that Ted idolized his daughter. He hovered over her, seeking to please her every whim, but Kari was absorbed and worried about Shail, making her subdued. Her mood just rolled off Ted. He was happy to be near her and help her through the crisis. She apparently had not revealed that she was a harpy and Shail was not a pet, but her mate. John, Ted, Charlie, and Kari milled around the lobby, talking about the auction.

As evening approached, the rain let up. Kari suggested dinner at some seafood shack on the water where she and Ted had dined. The group decided to walk to the restaurant. A cool breeze swept through the streets, and Kari and Ted walked ahead of John and Charlie.

"It's too bad things couldn't have been different," John said to Charlie and motioned to the couple half a block ahead of them.

Charlie glanced at Kari and Ted. "That boy could never make her happy, John. He's too tame. She's always been wild like the jungle and her golden mate."

"I know, but her life would have been easier if she had chosen Ted. I don't know if she knows it, but that boy is in love with her."

They reached the restaurant and feasted. Afterward they strolled down to the beach. The clouds had disappeared, revealing the stars and twin moons. Gentle waves rolled and broke against the shore.

"It's been twenty years since I've been on the east coast," Charlie said.

Kari stopped walking and stared ahead at the long, dark beach.

"What is it?" John asked her.

"A harpy is out there," Kari said.

Ted strained to see in the dark. "Where? I don't see anything."

Kari walked alone down the beach, and a brown harpy emerged from the shadow and approached her.

"My God, it is a harpy," Ted said and started toward her.

"No, Ted, wait here with us," John said, calling him back.

Ted whirled around and looked at John. "But it might hurt her."

"He won't," John said.

Ted's face showed that he was clearly puzzled, but he stayed with John and Charlie and watched from a distance as Kari and the harpy met. The harpy lowered its head and knelt on one knee in front of her.

"I'm glad you are here, Aron," Kari relayed.

Aron rose. "I, too, am relieved to find you."

"Shail is in a hunting range, and by tomorrow's darkness, we hope to free him."

"I know where he is," Aron said, "and he does not wish freedom, nor does he wish you here. As your guardian, I asked you to remain in the west. You have disobeyed Shail and me and placed yourself and his unborn son in danger. You are a golden female, but still a female. It is the male harpy's place to decide what is best. We give our lives to protect you."

Although polite, Aron was obviously irritated with her, but she had little tolerance for the subservient female roles in the harpy culture. "Shail has told me this crap many times, and I chose to ignore it," she said. "I'm staying here and taking him out regardless of what you or he wants."

Aron shook his head. "You truly are a golden first. Shail's concern is valid. The swarms shall be here soon, sooner than the humans know. In two lights they fall upon this city, and the blackness shall be so vast that no life escapes. I have come to take you, Turner, and the old man away. This is Shail's wish."

"And I wish to remain until he is free."

"I, too, long to free him," relayed Aron. "I willingly would risk my life and my flock and fly into the weapon blasts to take him from the hunters, but he has forbidden a rescue."

"You spoke to him?" Kari asked.

"No, but he spoke to another and gave up a valued flight feather to honor his words. When the humans are gone, the harpies shall unite and destroy the swarms. The jungle, the animals, and the harpies shall be saved as he had hoped. Already, great flocks gather in the north. Also, with his feather, he demanded you be taken to a place of safety. You must not think of Shail's loss, but of our future monarch you hold within."

"How can I not think of him? You talk like he's already dead."

Aron looked down and kicked at the sand. "I also think of him. He is my brother, and if lost, my mourning shall be endless, but he is also my ruler. His surrender to death must come with good reasons."

Kari saw Aron's watery eyes and detected his agony. She put her arms around his waist and hugged him. "Don't worry, Aron. Tomorrow night I'll do as you ask and leave the city with or without Shail, but I took him from hunters once before and must stay and try again."

Aron placed his hands on her shoulders. "I shall pray to the jungle spirits that you succeed and bring our Shail home, but by tomorrow's darkness, you must leave with haste. The harpies cannot lose the golden bloodline. I shall wait for you in the trees beyond the structure that holds Shail."

"I'll bring him home."

Aron spread his wings and flew over the ocean that sparkled with moonlight and disappeared. Kari slowly walked back to the three men.

"Shail was right, Dad," Kari said. "The swarms will hit Hampton in two days. Whether you buy Shail or not, we must leave with the harpies after the auction. I have promised Aron."

"The swarms are a long ways off," Ted said. "The satellite information says it'll be months before the beetles start moving east."

John ignored Ted. "We'll go to the auction in my hover so we can leave in a hurry. There's a small park nearby where I can land."

"You're taking this threat seriously?" asked Ted.

Kari took Ted's hand. "When we spoke on the com last week, I asked you to get on a ship and leave Dora. The harpies know more about nature than any satellite. Hampton will be gone in a matter of days."

"You really believe in these harpies," Ted said.

"We don't lie," Kari said.

"You talk like you're one of them," Ted joked. When she didn't answer, he released her hand and stepped back. "You're one of them?"

"I am," Kari said. "Because of the danger, a female harpy must not reveal her true identity."

Ted stared at her. "I knew you were different from other girls," he mumbled. His eyes widened. "You love him. You're in love with the golden harpy."

"Shail is my husband," Kari said. "I'm sorry, Ted."

Ted took more steps away from her and stared at the water. "You sure fooled me, Kari, but I should've guessed. You and your husband look an awful lot alike. You're both beautiful."

She walked to him and reached for his hand, but he pulled away. "Just leave me alone for a minute."

Kari went back to John and Charlie. "That boy is hurting," John said quietly. "Let me talk to him." He walked up to Ted and stood beside him. "This is my fault, Ted. When you met Kari, she didn't know she was a harpy. Shail had to tell her. She never meant to deceive you."

"Ten years ago they fell in love at the lake when they were just kids," Ted said. "You knew, and that's why you sent her to Earth, to keep them apart."

"Yes," John said. "I had hoped she'd find a good man like you, and she'd stay out of the jungle."

Ted turned and looked at him. "You should've taken the time to know your daughter, Mr. Turner."

Ted walked back to Kari. "I'll do whatever it takes to help you get him back."

Kari embraced him. "Thank you, Ted. After the auction, you can leave with us."

"No," Ted said. "Once you're back with Shail, I'll find a way off the planet."

"All right," Kari said. "I've never understood why I didn't have many human friends. You've been my best friend, Ted, and even though I'm a harpy, I don't want to lose you."

"You won't," Ted said.

Kari, her father, Charlie, and Ted left the beach and strolled through the empty, windswept streets. In the late hour, Kari glanced at dim lights that glowed from inside the building windows. The moist ocean breeze blew fallen leaves up the pavement, and tree limbs swayed as if yearning to follow and escape the impending storm. The atmosphere was haunting. In two days, the storm would come, but not one of great waves, wind, or rain. It would be a downpour of black that would destroy the city.

Sunday night Shail remained chained, and forced to stand in the display cage. The crowds of men had come and gone. So bitter over his brother's death and his own injuries inflicted by Shail, Bill had no pity for him and ordered his men to make him stand all night and suffer without food or water. Bill and most of the employees were gone, and two guards sat in chairs near his cage. Instead of being rolled out to the range and fresh air, the cage remained in the large front room.

The guards quietly talked to one another, and Shail rested his lowered head between his half-raised arms and shifted his weight, one leg at a time.

"How long you think before he collapses, George?" one guard asked.

"I don't know, but it's pretty damn cruel," said George, an older man with salt-and-pepper gray hair. "When I got here this afternoon, the harpy was covered with sweat. He's gotta be thirsty. I'm giving him some water, regardless of Simpson's orders." The robust guard grabbed his plastic water bottle and stood.

"You better stay out away from him," said the guard. "The harpy was sweaty because he'd been flailing his wings at people all day. Mr. Simpson even gave up going in his cage for fear of getting struck. Did you see the man's bruised face and throat? The winged devil nailed him and it's killed three men. It's mean."

"I'll take my chances, Harold," George said and approached the cage door. "I don't believe he's mean. He's just been mistreated. Mollie told me how Gus Simpson and his two pals tortured him. Well, Gus's luck ran out when he hurt the wrong animal. Those boys got what they deserved, and the same goes for Bill Simpson." He unlocked the door, and the harpy lifted his head out of his arms.

Harold stood up to watch. "You're crazy. The harpy is going to knock your teeth out with his wings."

George grinned and removed his false teeth. "Too late." He walked to Shail, holding up the bottle. "Easy, little guy, I'm not going to hurt you. I'm giving you a drink."

Shail arched his wings and hissed at the approaching man. Despite the man's kind words, Shail didn't trust him. He angrily rattled the chains and flung his hair.

George slowly moved closer. "Look. It's only water."

Despite Shail's threats, the old man kept coming, coaxing him to drink from the bottle. Shail tried to swallow, but his throat was dry. He stretched his neck, and the enticing water touched his parched lips. He took a quick, nervous sip before jerking his head back and curiously looking at the old guard. Shail's judgment was clouded by hostility, and he sniffed the wrinkled hand to gain a sense of George.

"See, I'm just trying to help you." George again offered the bottle.

Shail eagerly sucked down the water, but remained leery, unfamiliar with a man's compassion. Even Doc had held a knife at his throat when treating his lazar biast wounds.

"You were thirsty." George smiled and patted Shail's shoulder.

Startled by the touch, Shail leaped back, snapped at the hand and raised his wing to strike, but hesitated.

"You're a jumpy little guy," George said and looked at the wing poised to whack his face. "Guess I can't blame you." Shail lowered his wing and tilted his head.

George left the cage and refilled the bottle. He went back into the cage and gave Shail a second bottle of water. "Good boy," he said and slowly stroked the drinking harpy's head. "See, Harold," he called to the other guard, "he's not mean, just misunderstood." He stepped out of the cage and returned to his chair.

"You got guts, George," said Harold. "I sure won't go in his cage."

George leaned back in his chair. "That harpy reminds me of an old stray cat I found. Damn, she was a bitch. She'd scratched me every time I reached for her, but she had been abused. A little nourishment and kindness goes a long ways with an animal. She learned to trust me and turned into a great pet. I miss that old girl. That's the only thing wrong with the harpy. Those men turned him sour. If he were treated right, he'd be gentle."

"A cat scratch is one thing, but that skinny winged thing can snap your neck like a twig. He took on Gus and those other two men and killed all of them in one sweep, and they were big tough guys. There're not enough credits on Dora to get me in that harpy cage."

In the morning Shail lifted his head when Bill and the rest of the employees returned to the range.

"How was he?" Bill asked Harold and George.

"He's pretty tired from standing for twenty-four hours," George said. "At tonight's auction he might be hanging from those chains. It could hurt his price."

Bill looked up at the harpy that softly seethed at him. "All right, here are keys to his chains. Loosen them, and I'll let him rest this morning." He handed the keys to George and turned to the animal handlers. "This afternoon hose him down and string him back up. I'll get him worked up before the auction."

George walked to the cage sides and slackened the chains, and Shail eased into the straw. All the men left the cage area except George. He reached through the bars to pet Shail's head.

Shail watched the man's hand come close. With the loose chains, I could easily kill him, he thought, but he couldn't bring himself to attack George or even pull away. Shail lowered his head and allowed the older man to stroke his hair.

"You just rest now," George whispered, running his hand through the silky, blond hair. "When I come back this evening, I'll bring you some food."

Perplexed by George's kindness, Shail curled up in the straw and watched the sympathetic man leave the large room. George liked him and wanted to help him much like the young police officer that had stopped Bill from beating him. They were unlike the hundreds of hateful men he had encountered over the last few days. They are like a few grains of sand on a beach, very few men are worth saving, he thought. Soon the beetles shall come and my suffering shall be over. He wearily placed his face in his feathers and closed his eyes. He fell into a deep natural sleep not induced by tranquilizers.

A rap against the cage bars woke Shail in the afternoon. He leaped to his feet, dragging the noisy chains still attached to his wrists and ankles. Bill stood near the cage, but out of arm's reach. "Damn harpy was tired," he said to several men. "String him back up and tie down those wings. Roll the cage out to the range and give it and him give a good cleaning. I want him pretty tonight."

The men pulled Shail's chains from the outside of the cage and hoisted him off the straw. The six men entered the cage, and Shail beat his wings to strike, but they grabbed each wing and folded them into place. His wings tied down, Shail struggled in the chains and gnashed his teeth, but he failed to intimidate them. The men rolled the display cage from the building that had stale air and smelled of toxins and put it in the warm outside range. Shail inhaled the fragrant, humid air that once represented freedom.

The men washed and lathered Shail with soap, and he squirmed in his bonds and snapped at their hands. Holding him by his hair, they combed out the tangles and blew him and his wet wings dry. The experience was painless but degrading. Shail shook, trying to remove the perfumed soap scent. His cage cleaned and filled with fresh straw, the men moved it back inside the building.

Bill came out of his office and walked to the cage. "Doesn't he look handsome?" He faced the men. "Go ahead and unload the chairs and set up the stage at the back of the room. While the harpy's wings are tied, I'll get him worked up for tonight."

Bill unlocked the cage door and grabbed the shocking rod. Shail hissed and clutched his dangling chains, bracing himself for pain. The men left to unload the chairs from a truck vehicle and brought them in the front door.

"Time to fan the flames." Bill grinned and stepped up into the cage. He hit Shail's rib with a shock.

Shail leaped and twisted in his restraints. Each shock built his hate and desire to rip Bill to pieces. Soon his body ran with sweat, and he trembled from the stings to his side.

Bill stood back and Shail flung his wet hair from his face and seethed between panting breaths. "You're almost there," Bill said, "close to raving." He held the rod on Shail's rib.

Shail thrashed on the chains, but soon collapsed and hung. His heart pounded with exertion, and he shut his eyes, tossed his head back, exposing his throat, a clear sign when a harpy gives up.

Bill withdrew the rod. "Guess you've had enough. Don't want a coward."

The harpy regained his footing. He shook the wet hair out of his eyes and zealously stared at Bill. "A coward?" Shail said in a low, stalking voice. "I shall never be afraid of you. Like your brother, I vow to take your life." Bill staggered backward, apparently unnerved by his words.

"You can talk," Bill said with surprise.

"Your brother, too, spoke those words before I killed him."

A chill went through Bill's body while he stared into the smoldering blue eyes. He collected his wits. "You're the one who is gonna die."

"We all die, but within two lights your death shall come. With your last breath, remember me and my promise."

The harpy's serene male voice resembled an eerie song, unhuman with a damning message. Bill moved away from the harpy and his back pushed against the cage door. He called across the room to the men who set up the wooden stage. "Come over here! The harpy can talk."

Shail shook his head and his locks floated across his face, concealing his lips. "They shall not hear, for I speak only to the condemned."

Bill opened the door, and without using the two steps, he leaped out of the cage onto the floor as the men hurried to him. "He can talk! I swear, the harpy can talk." He and the men stared up at the harpy, and it mockingly sniffled at Bill. "Go ahead and talk," Bill said to the harpy. "Tell them how you promise to kill me in two days, how you killed my brother."

The men waited, but the harpy remained silent. They turned their attention to their boss, who hysterically chattered about the talking animal.

Bill saw their glances and knew they thought he was delusional. "I'm not crazy. I'll prove he can talk." Holding the rod, he adjusted the setting to high and opened the cage door. "I'll shock him until he speaks."

George had walked in to start his night shift. "Mr. Simpson, your auction starts in a few hours," he said. "At that high setting, you're sure to stop his heart. It's a waste of a lot of money."

Bill stopped at the cage door and stared at the harpy. "He wanted this," he muttered, "Mollie said he only wants to die. He's trying to egg me on to kill him." He closed the door.

"Do you want him left strung up like that?" George asked. "You can hardly see his wings."

"Yes, roll his cage onto the stage and then free him from the chains, but leave the shock collar on," Bill said. "We'll need some control over him."

He walked toward his office feeling tormented by the harpy that had revealed it wasn't an animal, but an intelligent being bent on revenge.

The men moved the display cage onto the stage, and Shail listened to them discussing how to free him from the shackles and chains without getting hurt. The five animal handlers were nervous, and the six guards were grateful they didn't have the task.

"Okay, we'll pull him down and undo his shackles through the cage bars," said a handler. "If he attacks, he can be shocked with the collar."

"He's damn fast and strong," said another handler. "I was there when he grabbed Mr. Simpson through the bars and nearly choked him to death."

George walked to the handlers. "Give me the keys to the shackles," he said. "I'll do it. I don't want to see him harmed."

"Old man, the harpy will tear you apart," said a handler, "and the collar might not work quickly enough."

George held his hand out. "The keys?" He unlocked the door and entered the cage. "Let's get this crap off you," he said to Shail.

Shail stood quietly and watched George bend down and remove each shackle from his ankles. The man stood up and untied the ropes that held down his folded wings. When the ropes came off, Shail ruffled his feathers.

"Watch out, George!" one guard yelled. "He's getting ready to smack you with a wing."

George frowned at the man and turned back to Shail. "You're doing real good," he said quietly. Taking Shail's hand, he unlocked the wrist shackle and cringed when he saw the deep welts and sores created from fighting the chains. "You poor little guy," he said and unfastened the last shackle. He patted Shail's shoulder like he had done on the previous night.

Shail sniffled and nudged him with his head, showing affection.

"This temporary job stinks," George grumbled and strolled to the cage door. A handler opened the cage, letting him out, but quickly slammed it shut. He walked to the circle of shocked men.

"Unbelievable," said a handler. "The harpy was like a kitten with you."

Shail sat down in the straw and watched the men. A younger man approached the cage and put his hand through the bars. "Here, harpy," he called. Shail docilely gazed at him. "Look, he is tame. He just hates the boss." He grinned at the men.

As soon as the man glanced away, Shail leaped at him and grasped his arm, jerking it backward. The man screamed and struggled to be free, but Shail wrenched his whole body toward the bars. Hoisting the heavy body off the floor, Shail choked him. The man's feet dangled and wildly kicked in the air.

Holding the collar remote, another handler hectically jabbed at the keys.

Shail jumped with the sharp neck pain but refused to release his prey. The panicked men tugged at Shail's arms, hoping to break the death hold.

"Push a higher setting!" one man yelled. "He's immune to the low shocks!" The young man had stopped wiggling, close to death.

A tremendous jolt hit Shail's neck, forcing him to release his grip on the young handler. He convulsed and wildly flipped in the straw from the stabbing pain.

"He's had enough," George barked and jerked the handler's hand off the remote key, ending the shocks.

The young man slumped on the floor, gasping and choking, and several men lifted and carried him a safe distance from the cage.

Looking at the young man's arm, one man said, "His arm is broken and nearly wrenched out of the socket. It's astonishing that slight creature is capable of this."

"Better take the boy to the hospital," George said.

"George, you were damn lucky," said a guard. "The harpy could've jumped and killed you in the cage, and we couldn't have stopped him in time."

Shail sat up and shook his head, the sting wearing off. He glared at the men and arrogantly seethed, conveying no shock would stop him from attacking again.

George walked up to his cage, but kept his distance. "I guess you're not like my stray cat."

Shail curled up and rubbed his neck under the collar. Between his feathers, he observed the distressed men, who now truly feared him. He had done his best to kill an outgoing, young man who had never shown him ill will, yet Shail felt no regret. If the opportunity arose again, he'd kill and briefly quench his desire for revenge. Is the hate what drives evil men? he thought. Is this why Gus performed such cruel acts? Gone was his gentleness, his logical reasoning, his harpy soul that had longed to protect life;

also gone was his love of the jungle, and his loyalty to his flock. These things were no longer important. Hatred consumed him and even nullified his depression. He now lived for the kill.

An hour later George returned to the cage, and Shail sensed the man's distrustfulness. Shail lifted his head from the feathers and made a friendly sniffle.

George scrutinized the harpy's eager, bright eyes, which conveyed he sought companionship. "You're one confused little guy, who's been pushed to his limits. You don't know what's right or wrong anymore."

Shail placed his head on the straw and sniffled again, longing for the man's acceptance.

"Come on, come over here," George said, and put his hand through the bars. Shail obediently slid across the bedding and meekly lowered his head against the bars below the man's hand. George stroked his hair, and Shail closed his eyes, the calming touch oppressing his rage.

George took some berries out of a bag and offered them to Shail. "You're not to blame," he said while the harpy ate out of his hand. "You're putting out what's been given to you. I sure wish I was rich. I'd buy you tonight and set you free."

Shail ate the last berry and nuzzled his nose against the man's rough hand, encouraging the man to stroke him. George patted him before returning to his guard duties. Watching him walk away, Shail lay down, feeling baffled. This man was his enemy who participated in his confinement, yet Shail lacked the hate to hurt him.

In a brief span of time, Shail accepted George for his soothing words and simple acts of kindness, and George knew his kindness had paid off. The dangerous young harpy had spared his life and had become his friend.

18

In her hotel bed, Kari awoke and stared at the ceiling. It was Monday, the day of the auction. The long, wrenching wait that decided Shail's and her fate would be over. With the help of Doc's antidepressant patches, she had remained calm and upbeat, positive her father would win back her mate. She smiled with the thought of being wrapped in Shail's arms tonight.

She refused to consider the alternative; her father could lose the auction, sealing Shail's fate, or that her abused and unstable husband could remain forever changed; his love for life gone. To dwell on those things might restore her depression, disabling her and making her useless. She had to stay strong for Shail and for her son, the future monarch of the harpy flock.

During her time in Hampton, Ted had been a great distraction. Ignorant that she faced life-threatening despair with her mate's loss, he was cheerful and optimistic. He'd be back to work at the spaceport, but he promised to return this evening and be at her side for the auction.

On the other hand, her father and Charlie ambled about, sullen and worried, knowing the tragedy of a bonded harpy pair. Like one body, her life and Shail's were completely connected. Cut in half, they had difficulty surviving without one another.

Kari climbed out of bed and went to the sink. She splashed water on her face, hoping to wash away her growing stress. I will get Shail back, and he'll be fine, she thought. For a fleeting moment, her eyes welled up with tears when she realized he could be lost. She brought more water to her face in an attempt to squelch her doubts. A knock on her door liberated her from the ominous thoughts.

"Hi, Dad," she said, opening the door and clearing her throat. All the water on the planet couldn't wash away the worry on her face.

John saw it. "Kari, I'll get Shail back. This morning I have an appointment with the bank, and I'm taking out a line of credit on everything I own. No one will be able to bid higher for a single harpy hunt. Tonight he'll be with you." He lifted her chin and stared into her teary eyes.

Kari nodded, afraid to speak, knowing she would break down and cry.

"Come down and have breakfast with Charlie and me. You'll feel better. I know you're doing your best to be brave and hide your fears, but believe me, everything will be okay."

She hugged her father. "I know it will be. Thank you, Dad."

"I'll wait for you in the dining room," he said and left her room.

John met Charlie in the downstairs lobby. "How is she?" Charlie asked.

"She's holding up," John said, "but if I lose him at the auction . . ." He shook his head. "She's so damn in love with him. How could I have been so stupid and blind? For her sake, I'd gladly trade my life for his."

"John, you have to stop this guilt. At the cabin, you made the right choice and let her mate live, knowing they loved one another and would be together again. The rest has been bad luck."

"Say what you want, but the fact is he wouldn't be trapped in the hunting range if I hadn't stunned him, making him helpless. I wanted to protect her, and now I might have killed her just like I killed my wife. I'm guilty of all of this."

"You're confusing blame with fate. Shail's fate was to be sought by hunters. That is who he is, and it was your fate to protect your daughter from danger and unhappiness. That is who you are. No one is to blame. We travel the path of life hoping to make good decisions, but the path is full of missteps and hazards that we must overcome, just as you try now."

"Spare me your Indian philosophy crap. Fate, blame, whatever, all I know is I have to win that harpy, and not only for Kari. Shail can stop the swarms before thousands of people are killed."

Charlie scratched the side of his face, pushing back his gray braid. "Do you really think he would save humans? He has killed three and nearly killed a fourth. This is unlike a harpy. They are gentle vegetarians like sheep and do not have the nature to kill, but the golden's mind has been twisted. He is no longer the passive creature that once fled men. The hunted has become the hunter. Although he rules a meek band of harpies, once freed, Shail might turn his flock and the swarms against humans. He could be a nightmare, worse than the swarms."

Kari ascended the stairs and approached them in the lobby. "What are you talking about?" she asked.

"Just wondering where we should celebrate tonight," John lied. "Think Shail will drink some wine?"

Kari smiled. "Maybe he'll try it."

After breakfast, John rose from the table. "I'm going to the bank now, but I'll swing by and pick you up before heading to the spaceport. I want to check my hover and make sure it's fully charged."

"Perhaps we'll see Ted," said Kari.

"He's a nice guy," said John.

"Forget it, Dad."

"Hey, I know who you love." John grinned. "Ted is literally not your type."

John left the hotel and climbed into the rented terrain vehicle, his mind worried about his credit line. Though he was the largest landowner in the western outback, he wondered about the land and timber's value with the swarm threat. In minutes the beetles could devour the trees, making his property worthless for years. The harpies protected the estate, and it remained undamaged, but a bank official would never believe the harpy tale. To make matters worse, Westend Harbor had been demolished, making it impossible to sell and ship his lumber. Parking the vehicle in front of the bank, he'd soon find out his wealth in credits.

As John walked through the bank door, he realized he had never asked for a loan. He and his father had worked hard, and every credit made went toward more land and running the estate, leaving him land rich, but credit poor.

In an office John met with a bank official at his desk. "Have a seat, Mr. Turner." The official smiled. "I've pulled the file on your assets. You have a remarkable spread in the outback. It takes up a good part of the west coast."

"I know what I have," John said. "Let's get straight to business. How much are you willing to loan on it?"

The official raised an eyebrow. "I've estimated the value. With the transport trucks, freighters, four hovers, plus the mill, its laser saws and the outbuildings, home, and the land, we can give you two million."

"Two million!" John said, jumping up from his seat. "That's not even one percent of its value. You're not even considering the timber? It alone is worth billions."

"Two years ago that would be a fair assessment, but not in these times. The swarm attacks have virtually made it and your property worthless. We're basing the two million on your equipment and the fact that you're a good customer with an excellent credit rating." He pointed to a stack of files. "Those are outback land deeds that we were forced to foreclose. Honestly, Mr. Turner, you're lucky. Our policy has become 'no loans in the outback.' With a swarm strike, we've estimated it could take ten years before the trees grow back and can be harvested, and that's a gamble. Who knows if Dora will ever recover from this plague? I'm sorry."

John knew there was no sense in ranting. Business was business. "Give me the two million and add the half I have in my account."

"Are you buying off Dora?" the official asked, drawing up the paperwork.

"If I told you what I was buying, you'd think I'd lost my mind and wouldn't give me any credits," John mumbled.

"What you buy is your business, but I'm sure it's a wise investment." The official handed him the voucher.

After signing off on everything he owned, John stuck the voucher in his pocket and left the bank. Two and a half million, he thought. Would it be enough? It was inconceivable, but possible that the harpy price could go higher. Only an undefeated champion racehorse with a pricey stud fee and a reputation for producing winning colts, would fall into that price range, but a harpy? Shail was a game animal who would be killed in minutes; his only value was a feathered mount hanging from a hunter's wall. Would men pay millions for the thrill and to gloat? Some would, for the right trophy, regardless of the cost.

John pulled up in front of the hotel. Kari and Charlie were waiting by the curb. "How much did they give you?" Kari asked, getting in the vehicle.

John breathed deeply "Two and a half million credits."

"That's plenty." Kari grinned. "I've heard golden wings are worth fifty thousand."

"They start at fifty, and that's for old, moth-eaten mounts," John said. "I don't want to worry you, but this is different, Kari. Most of Shail's price is based on a challenging hunt, not his wings. A hunter will travel, face hardships, and spend a fortune to bring down big game. If they only wanted a trophy, they could purchase it cheap in a shop. Unfortunately your mate killed those men and has become a unique and dangerous game animal. Hunters will want him."

"How high could he go?" she asked.

"I don't know, but this is all I could get for my entire estate. With the beetle scare, the banks aren't lending,"

"You could possibly lose the estate for only two and a half million?" she asked.

"Half million is mine, but I'm not concerned. Shail's harpies are protecting the timber. We'll make it up, but I'd happily lose the estate if I won your mate."

They arrived at the port for incoming and outgoing spaceships. Ted helped John inspect his hovercraft for a long trip. They agreed to pick up the hover at six and fly to the auction. Ted said he would drive, having no intention of leaving Hampton with them. Despite the hurt, Ted behaved like a gentleman. "Be with your harpy husband, Kari," he had said, "and be happy."

Kari stared out the vehicle window at the gathering dark clouds. It began to rain as her father drove up to the hotel so they could pack and check out. Shortly before six o'clock, John, Charlie, and Kari picked up the hover and flew to the hunting range, landing a few blocks away in the small park.

After dashing through the sheets of rain, they entered the building. Kari walked to Shail's cage and found him calmly sitting in the straw. His arms held his bent legs and his head rested on his knees. His long wings draped around his slender frame. When he saw her, he moved to the cage bars.

"Why are you still here?" he relayed.

"You know I'd never leave you," Kari relayed. "Aron waits outside and will take me to a place of safety whether you're with me or not. I have promised him."

"If Aron is here, then the young harpy spread my words with the feather, and the flocks gather."

"Yes, Shail, they're in the north and will destroy the swarms and save the planet."

"Tell Aron I am very pleased," Shail relayed, "and though I wish you elsewhere, I am happy to see you this last time."

"You can tell Aron yourself when we free you."

Shail lowered his head. "I dare not hope for such things, and even freed, I am not the same mate you loved. I am ruled by a blind rage to kill men. My family, flock, and jungle home are less important. My death would better serve those who care for me."

"Your death would only serve the men you hate," Kari relayed. "Your rage will fade and be replaced by peace of mind. You must trust me on this."

The room was filling with men, and Kari took a seat next to John and Charlie in front of the cage.

Ted came in and sat down next to Kari. "How is he?"

"About the same," Kari answered.

"Who is this man who sticks by your side?" Shail silently asked.

Kari silently communicated, "His name is Ted. I met him on the spaceship." She turned to Ted and said, "Shail wants to know who you are."

"I'm just a friend," Ted said.

Shail glared at Ted. "He lies. His eyes betray his longing. He is no friend, but loves and desires you as a mate. It is plain to see."

"You're jealous, Shail," Kari relayed. "Since a harpy can have several mates, I didn't think you had this emotion."

Shail stood and paced the bars, ending the men's chatter in the room. The hunters gazed at the long cream-colored wings that drifted across the straw and his elegant frame; six feet of tense, lean muscle. Agitated, he flung his shoulder-length hair. He stopped in front of Kari. "I know not this word 'jealous,' but if it means I would attack a male who lingers near my female hoping to replace my seed with his, then I am jealous. Females can share a male mate, since the males are fewer, but no male shares his female with another male."

"But you told me to go with Ted the other day. You were breaking our bond," she relayed.

Shail wearily gazed at her. "Why do you torment me, Kari? I would say anything for your safety and to make you leave this place. With my last breath, I shall always want and love you."

"I needed to hear that," Kari relayed. "I was afraid with all that's happened to you . . ." Kari looked down and chewed her bottom lip. "I love you, too." She glanced at Ted. "Ted is no threat, but a good friend who helped me fight off despair. He knows you're my mate."

Ted leaned toward Kari. "He doesn't look happy with me."

"He's a little jealous," Kari said, "and says you're a liar and want to be more than a friend."

"He's very perceptive," Ted said quietly to Kari and gazed up at her handsome winged husband. "I'd be lying to say I only wanted her as friend," he said to Shail, "but from the day we met, she's only wanted you."

"I'm sorry, Ted," said Kari. "I never meant to hurt you."

Bill Simpson entered the room and walked on the stage. "Welcome, gentlemen," he said into the microphone. Seeing Kari in the front row, he added, "And ladies."

Shail turned away from Kari and Ted and moved toward the end of the cage and Bill. He seethed and flipped his hair, and Kari saw loathing in his eyes and detected his rising anger. Shail truly hated the man.

"We're here tonight to auction off the rarest and most spectacular game animal in the galaxy, a golden harpy," Bill said to the audience. "Some of you might not be aware, but three days ago this harpy brutally killed my brother and two other men who had entered its cage to save a female handler. The woman was severely beaten and raped." Bill pulled down his collar, exposing his neck wounds. "Yesterday morning the harpy nearly got me, and this afternoon it attacked an employee and broke his arm. I bring these facts to light so you've been warned and know exactly what kind of animal is up for bid. He is unlike any harpy you have ever seen or hunted, a beauty and a deadly beast in one package. His wings are sixteen feet, ten inches, and are the typical powder-puff yellow of a young golden. With his teeth and the wing length, we're guessing he's is in his mid-twenties and sexually mature. His aggressive nature suggests that he is a stud, possibly having a mate, and hopefully the female has offspring for a future golden hunt."

John clutched Kari's hand, as Shail flew at the bars, hissing. Bill moved close to the cage, and Shail arched his wings. Bill chuckled. "He's definitely vicious, gentlemen, and it doesn't take much to get him to spread his wings for an attack. As you see, his wings are flawless. There's no feather loss. He's fast, smart, extremely handsome, and dangerous; the perfect game animal for a challenging hunt. The winning bidder will enjoy my new hunting range and have backup hunters for protection. There's no risk to you or having all your money fly off if you first miss your target. Since his wings are valuable, we suggest a stun-gun hunt. His feathers and genitals will stay intact, and you and your friends can hunt him several times. We have a pole for hanging, stripping, and gutting him and a barbecue pit for those who enjoy dining on the harpy delicacy. We'll tan the skin, treat the wings, and ship them to any place in the galaxy. All this is included in your auction bid. So without anything further, let's start the auction."

Ted tapped Kari's arm. "This is barbaric. Do they really do those things to harpies?"

"Yes," Kari answered.

The auctioneer took the microphone from Bill. "We'll start the bidding at one hundred thousand credits," he said. "Do I have a first bid?" A man in the back held up his number. "Thank you. Do I have two hundred thousand? Thank you. How about three? Thank you." The numbers rose, and Kari worriedly glanced at her father.

"Do I hear one million?" the auctioneer said.

John nodded, knowing most of Dora's local hunters and the zoos were now out of the auction and only the truly rich remained.

"One million to the man in the front row; thank you, sir," said the auctioneer. "One million one, do I have a bid for one million one? You'll never get another opportunity like this. This magnificent creature is one of a kind. Thank you, sir, one million one; do I have a bid at two, one million two?"

John nodded and turned to see the opposing bidder. The stubby senator flashed his bid card above his balding head. John had spoken with him when he registered on Saturday. Senator Blackwell nodded at John and made a mocking grin. "Goddamn Blackwell," John quietly grumbled. The price was now at one million three, and kept rising as John bid against the senator.

Kari's heart leaped with each bid. She had come to the auction confident her father would win, but as it reached two million, her hopes wavered. At two million two, the senator put his number down.

"Two million two, do I have a bid for three?" the auctioneer asked.

Kari held her breath and looked around the large room. The auctioneer announced it again, and it seemed her father had won.

"Two million three," Bill said. "I have an off-planet bidder on the com."

"The bid is two million three, sir," the auctioneer said to John. "Do you wish to go four?"

John took a deep breath and nodded.

"Two million four; will he go five?" the auctioneer asked.

Bill related the quote to the bidder on the communicator and nodded.

Kari's heart sank and her eyes watered, knowing her father could go no higher. The auctioneer asked John for the next bid, and he shook his head.

"Two million six, anyone?" the auctioneer asked.

"Wait," Bill said. "I have a second bidder online, and he's made an offer of three million."

"Three million. Will your last bidder go three one?" the auctioneer asked.

The crowd watched as Bill communicated the last bid of three million one and Bill said, "No."

"Anyone here willing to go three million one?" the auctioneer asked the crowd. The whole room was silent. "Sold, for three million," the auctioneer said, striking the small mallet on the podium.

Kari couldn't control herself and leaped to her feet. She shouted to the auctioneer and Bill as they shook hands. "You can't sell him. He's not an animal." The room went dead silent, all eyes fixed on her.

John jumped up. "Kari!"

She ignored her father and ducked under the rope and leaped up on the stage. "He's my husband," she sobbed and gripped the bars, looking at Shail.

Shail dropped to his knees and put his arms through the bars. They embraced one another and kissed.

A guard stepped forward to remove Kari, but John turned and faced him. "Leave her alone. Let her have her good-byes," he said, and the guard backed off. The room of stunned hunters stood and watched the two apparent lovers. The once-aggressive harpy tenderly held and nuzzled the crying girl. His distressed eyes had lost all their fire.

"I love you, Shail," Kari muttered between sniffles. "I'll always love you."

Bill waved both hands at his security guards. "Get her away from him before she's hurt," he yelled. Two guards approached Kari.

"I'll take her," John told the men and slipped under the rope and onto the stage. "Kari, we must go now," he said, and gently pulled her from Shail's neck. Holding his daughter in his arms, he looked into Shail's moist eyes. "I'll protect her, Shail."

Shail made a slight nod and placed his head against the bars while John ushered his trembling daughter toward the doors. Kari wept and leaned against John for support as they slowly walked through the crowd. All eyes stared at them.

Senator Blackwell was standing by the exit door. As John and Kari approached, he reached out and petted her head. "Poor little thing, she could die of depression when her mate is killed. I understand why you wanted the stud, John. You'd own the last golden breeding pair. I'll give you a million for the female and take the risk of losing her."

John leered at Blackwell. "Get your stinking hand off of her," he growled, fighting the temptation to sock the senator.

Blackwell backed out of reach, seeing John's temper. "I take it she's not for sale," he said as John and Kari passed through the door. "Well, you'd better keep her on a short leash," he called. "She's an animal and fair game to all."

Kari had announced to the worst harpy hunters in the galaxy that the golden male was her husband. Many like Senator Blackwell knew she was a female harpy. In seconds she had recklessly tossed away her human rights and become a game animal. John hurried her out of the hunting range.

Bill Simpson spoke into the microphone while John and Kari walked outside. "Gentlemen, please. You know how male harpies affect women. The ladies lose their minds and blubber over these pretty males. We plan to stock our range with harpies, and hope you'll all return for an exciting hunt."

Most of the crowd ignored Bill's comments and focused on the male harpy. Once the girl had left, he curled up and covered himself with feathers almost as if he were mourning.

Bill went to his cage and tapped the bars with his rod. "Get up!" he yelled. The harpy paid no heed of him and lay quietly. "He's upset he couldn't rape that girl." He saw the men, his future customers, didn't buy his explanation for the subdued harpy. He whispered toward the harpy, knowing it understood English. "It obvious she's not a woman, but your harpy mate."

Shail lifted his head, incensed.

"I bet she's pregnant," Bill went on. "It would be worth a trip to the Turner Estate to snatch her."

Shail sprang up and crashed against the bars.

Bill had moved out of reach expecting his response. "I can't wait to hang you," he said. "Then I'll get your female. Every time I fuck her, I'll think of you."

With all other men out of earshot, Shail spoke to Bill. "You shall soon be dead and unable to touch her." He lowered himself in the bedding.

The crowd left the room and wandered out into the night. Shail watched them leave and bitterly thought, When they seek me in the range, many shall die.

George came up to his cage. "I wish I could give you back to the girl. She really loves you."

Shail moved closer to the bars, so George could pet him. The other employees were busy folding chairs and hauling them away. Shail stared up at George with indecision while the man stroked his hair. "You are very kind," Shail said softly. "I shall return this kindness with a warning."

George's eyes widened. "Simpson was right. You can speak."

"Hear my words and heed their warning: The swarms soon come to this city and all here shall die. I do not want you among them. Travel this darkness to the northern mountains." Shail plucked a small feather from his wing and handed it to George. "Show this to the harpies and tell them you have my protection. They shall help you."

George took the feather. "You told Bill he would be killed in a few days. Is this what you meant?"

"Yes. Do not linger with the knowledge and warning I give you. The swarms shall come within two lights."

"Thank you." George glanced around at the men. "I wish I could get you out of here."

"Knowing I have saved a worthy man heals my black heart. It is thanks enough."

George nodded and patted his shoulder.

Seeing the old guard pet the harpy, one guard called, "George, are you friends with that creature?"

George removed his hand from the cage. "Yes. Tell Simpson, I quit." He walked toward the front doors.

A well-dressed man stopped George in the doorway. "Excuse me," said the middle-aged man. "Can you tell me where I can find Mr. Simpson?"

George pointed. "He's the big guy with the cattle prod," he grumbled and left the building.

The man walked through the room toward Bill. "Mr. Simpson, I'm the agent representing the highest bidder. You received the faxed credit voucher, but I need to examine the harpy and get his paperwork in order for shipping."

"Shipping?" Bill said. "You mean your client isn't hunting the harpy here?"

"No, sir," the agent said. "My client has his own private range. As soon as I certify that the creature is healthy, he'll be loaded into a truck outside."

"Now wait a minute," Bill said. "This harpy has to be hunted at my range. He's very dangerous, and we know how to handle him."

"Apparently your handling is inadequate. The harpy managed to injure and kill several men, one of whom was your brother. I'm sorry for your loss, but we're perfectly capable of dealing with wild animals. Furthermore, I've read your purchase agreement. There are no clauses that state the harpy must be hunted at your range. Now, if you please, I'm rather anxious to move him. It's a long journey to the other planet."

"Fine," Bill growled. "I'll be happy to get rid of the murdering little bastard."

In his office, Bill transferred the ownership papers into the agent's name and left for the large room. By the display cage, two men stood with a narrow shipping cage with padded bars.

"He's wearing a shock collar," Bill said and pulled a remote out of his pocket as he and the agent neared the harpy cage. "I'll set it to high and knock him down. It's the only way to get near him."

"That's not necessary. One of my men brought in a stun gun. It's less painful and traumatic compared to an electric shock, and I have a heart stimulant in case of an adverse affect. After he's stunned, he'll be kept on tranquilizers. For three million credits, the harpy can't be stressed or injured."

Shail nervously paced, studying his new adversary. He saw the narrow shipping cage and the small gun.

The agent gazed up at the moody harpy that light-footedly pranced back and forth, constantly extending and ruffling its wings to threaten. "So this is a golden harpy," the agent said. "He's exquisite, absolutely stunning." The harpy hissed at him. "He's also flamboyant; definitely not a coward. His new owner will be very pleased." He retrieved a small stun gun and pointed it at the harpy.

Shail froze and sniffled at the weapon. Kari had taught him about guns, and when the man pulled the trigger, Shail plunged into the straw. The stunner hit a bar behind him.

Bill laughed. "Hope his new owner has better aim than you. You're lucky he's caged."

Shail sprang to his feet and angrily seethed.

"He is very fast," said the agent and carefully took aim again.

Shail jumped sideways and the stun hit his feathers. He felt the numb prick through the feather veins. He shook his hair with animosity.

"He's watching when I pull the trigger," said the agent. "He's not only quick, but smart." The agent moved closer to the bars, ensuring his next shot would hit the elusive creature.

The man was close enough, and Shail dove at the bars, grabbing the man's hand and weapon. Shail twisted the wrist to retrieve the weapon, but he suddenly felt the full voltage of the electrical collar that sapped his neck. He let go of the weapon and fell in the straw, tossing and rolling with pain. He frantically pulled on the collar as powerful shocks ravaged his body. He curled up in a tight ball, gasping, and the hurt forced tears to run down his cheeks. This is the end, he thought before falling unconscious.

The agent saw the harpy and turned to Bill. "Stop!" he screamed. "You're killing him."

Bill smiled and released the remote key. "Thought you could handle him?" He smirked.

"Open the cage!" shouted the agent. A guard unlocked it, and the agent scrambled in and knelt by the comatose harpy. "You damn fool!" he raged, examining the precious animal. "You nearly stopped his heart."

"Mister, I saved your life," said Bill. "That harpy had you and the gun. I wasn't taking any chances."

"Let's get him out of this wretched place," said the agent to his two men. Shail was placed in the small cage and loaded into the waiting transport truck. The truck drove down the wet streets and disappeared around a corner.

Kari and John walked toward the small park. Ted and Charlie followed in silence. There was no more to say. When they reached the hover, a dark shadow stepped from a cluster of trees. Kari broke free of her father's sheltering arm and ran to Aron. She hugged him and cried. There was no need to explain that she had failed to free Shail.

Aron held Kari and glanced with distress at the hunting range. She detected Aron's thoughts and frustrations. Shail was so close, but so far. Aron turned away from the range and looked down at her. "You must leave, Kari," he relayed. "Shail's fate is out of your hands." He sniffled toward the trees, and two male harpies emerged from the dark, keeping some space from the men. "Have the metal bird follow these harpies. They shall lead you to sanctuary in the northern mountains."

"We must follow the harpies now," Kari said to her father.

"She'll be safe?" John asked.

Aron made a slight nod.

"Kari, you and Charlie will go in the hover with the harpies," John said. "I'll stay and get Shail out."

"How?" asked Kari.

John shook his head. "If there weren't so many guards, I'd break in and take him, but there might be a better way. The governor, Henry Blake, and I were once friends. I believe I can convince him to release Shail. The high bidder was off-planet, and I doubt he'll hunt or ship Shail until tomorrow. If I can contact Henry tonight, I'll have enough time."

Charlie stepped forward. "John, don't build her hopes. Tell her of this governor."

John sighed. "Like I said, we were once friends, but we parted ways when I banned harpy hunting on the estate ten years ago. Henry called and voiced his disapproval, and our words were heated, but he knows me, Kari, and knows I don't lie. He'll believe me when I tell him that only Shail can stop the swarms and save the human population."

"But the swarms will be here soon, Dad," Kari said. "I couldn't bear to lose Shail and you."

"Have a little faith in your old man," John said. "The swarms won't get me, and I promised to save your mate. Besides I couldn't run off like a coward and leave Shail and all these people behind to face the swarms."

Kari hugged her father. "Please be careful, Dad. I love you and don't blame you anymore for what has happened. I know you chose not to hurt Shail."

John sighed. "I can't forgive myself. You're my whole life, Kari, and I want you to have the same happiness I shared with your mother." He pulled away from her. "Now you must go."

Charlie approached John. "Are you sure you don't want me to stay? I'm old, but still handy with a weapon."

"No, Charlie, just take good care of my baby," John said and shook his hand.

Kari kissed Ted on the cheek and thanked him before she climbed into the hovercraft with Charlie. The rain had stopped, and a cool wind blew through the little park. Steering the hover, Charlie forced it up into the starry sky. The two harpies spread their long wings and leaped into the air. They flew north over the doomed city with the hover on their heels; its headlights flooded their chocolate wings.

John, Ted, and Aron watched the hover lights slowly disappear. John stepped in front of Aron and Ted. "If something happens to Shail and me, I am asking both of you to protect Kari and help her raise her son. My grandson will be both harpy and man, and he should know about both races. You two are the best of role models." John placed his hand on Ted's shoulder. "This man is called Ted," he said to Aron. "He is a good man and will be a friend to the harpies. And Ted, this brown harpy is Aron. He has faithfully guarded Kari. I gave Shail my word that I would look after his son. I'm asking the same promise of you."

Aron looked at Ted, the man who would take Turner's place if he died. Aron lowered his head to Turner in agreement.

"Sure, Mr. Turner," Ted said. "You know I would do anything for Kari and her kid."

"Good, good." John glanced at Ted's late-model terrain vehicle. "Does your com work in that vehicle?"

"It works," Ted answered.

John walked to the vehicle, opened the driver-side door, and sat down in the seat. He flipped on the com. "The governor's mansion," he said to the operator.

A man appeared on the screen. "Governor's residence."

"My name is John Turner. It's imperative I speak with Governor Blake tonight."

"What does it concern?" the man asked.

"I have information the swarms will soon strike Hampton, but there's a way to prevent it. I need the governor's cooperation, and it must be done tonight."

"One moment; I'll see if he's available to take your call," the man said. After a few minutes, the man returned to the screen. "You are the same John Turner who owns the Turner timber estate in the outback?"

"Yes," John answered.

"He has given you an appointment for ten o'clock tomorrow morning."

"That's too late," John said. "There's a golden harpy that can stop the swarms, but his head is on the chopping block. I have to talk to Henry now."

"A harpy?" The man smirked. "I'm sorry, Mr. Turner, your appointment is tomorrow or not at all."

"This is an emergency." John yelled.

"Good night, Mr. Turner." The communication shut down.

Ted was leaning against the outside of the vehicle when John climbed out. "Where is Aron?" John asked.

"He took off," Ted said.

John thought for a moment. "The spaceport is the only metal building in Hampton that the beetles can't devour, but it'll take some securing. If the inside dome is cleared of cargo, ships, and equipment, it is big enough to hold the residents of the city. Let's go."

"You really believe the swarms are coming?"

"Harpies are as honest as the day is long. If they say the swarms are coming, it's fact. There isn't much time."

John and Ted climbed into the vehicle and were soon racing through the dark streets toward the spaceport.

Arriving at the port, they parked and ran inside. Ted hurried to a group of men working the graveyard shift. He explained that Mr. Turner had absolute proof that the swarms were coming to Hampton and might strike by the next day.

"Ted, we have no authority to move those big freighters outside along with all the cargo," said an employee.

"Fine, just stay out of my way," said Ted. "I'll move them. I have a ground pilot license to move ships to the landing strip."

A supervisor walked toward them. "What is this, break time? We're behind schedule as it is."

"Ted says the swarms are coming tomorrow and wants us to move the ships and cargo out and prepare the dome," said a man.

"Is he drunk?" asked the supervisor "Get your ass out of here, Ted. You're not on the clock. Furthermore—"

John cut in on the supervisor's tongue-lashing unleashed on Ted. "May I talk to you alone?"

The man huffed and walked aside with John.

"I have reliable information that the swarms will be here tomorrow or the next day." John pulled a piece of paper from his pants pocket. "This is a bank voucher for two and a half million credits. If I'm wrong, the money is yours for all your trouble, but if I'm right, we're going to save a lot of lives with the work we do here tonight. What's it going to be?"

The supervisor examined the voucher and glanced up, studying John's face. "This is a lot of money. You're either crazy or serious."

"Try dead serious," John said.

"All right, mister," said the supervisor. "We'll prepare the port for an attack, and I'll call in the day shift and other supervisors. We'll move the ships and lumber stacks outside and reinforce the wooden doors and sliders with metal. The air ventilation and water flow will need protecting. This is an all-night job."

"I figured as much," said John. "You won't regret it."

Thirty men frantically worked throughout the night on the port, and as dawn broke, the place was secured. The supervisor rushed out of an office toward John. "Mr. Turner, you were right. The first satellite report just came in, and there're massive swarms a hundred miles west and on a collision course with Hampton. The alarm is going out, and I've notified the authorities that we've secured the spaceport. How did you know?"

"The harpies warned me," John said.

The supervisor frowned at him.

"I know it's hard to believe, but true," said John. "The people of Hampton owe their lives to the winged hosts of Dora."

In droves, the panicked town people arrived at the doomed port. If the swarms stayed on their present course and speed, the satellites estimated their time of arrival in Hampton would be midmorning, but men and equipment were hardly capable of predicting the intentions of an insect. Only a creature, in tune with nature like a harpy, could prophesize the beetles' movement.

John watched the swarm reports on wall monitors, but suddenly the monitors and lights went out. People screamed in the dark, eerie building. "Relax, everyone," said a booming man's voice. "The generators will kick in shortly." In a minute the lights came on, and people quieted down.

Ted came up to John. "The solar generator came on," he said. "That means a swarm must've taken out the windmill power station. That's only twenty-five miles south, on the coast."

"Ted, I need to borrow a hovercraft," John said. "Your vehicle is useless. The roads are jammed. I've been waiting for the governor to show up here, but even if he does, he'll be too late to help Shail. I have to get to the hunting range. Most of the range security guards will be gone, saving their own hides."

"Mr. Turner, it's suicide. There's not enough time to go there and come back."

John reached in his tote bag and pulled out his laser gun. "There's enough time for me to get there. I have to free Shail. He is the ruler of the harpies who can destroy these swarms, but unless he tells them, they won't do it. Shail is the only one who can save these people and this planet. Understand? Now do you have a hover?"

Ted wearily rubbed his forehead and started for a door. "Yeah, I was working on one on the landing strip. The electrical systems are fried for the air conditioner and lights, but the motor is fine."

They left the domed building and jogged across the vast landing strip. "It's three lanes over," Ted said. They reached the hover. "You might need help. I'll go with you."

"No," John said. "I need you to get my daughter off Dora if everything is in ruin. Aron will find you and bring Kari. I want you to get her on a ship." He clasped Ted's shoulder. "Just stay alive for me, boy. I'm depending on you."

Ted nodded and John fired up the small hovercraft and was soon airborne.

John landed the hover in the middle of the street in front of Simpson's hunting range. He leaped from the craft and bolted through the doors, his laser ready to fire. Walking across the room, he stopped and dismally stared at the empty display cage.

"Sorry, Mr. Turner, we're closed," said a voice.

John wheeled around and pointed his weapon at Bill Simpson, who casually entered the room.

"Where's the harpy?" John asked.

"Gone. The new owner took him last night. I imagine he's on a ship heading for his new hunting range, but I'll have others just as vicious now that I know how to turn one."

John aimed the weapon at Bill. "How do you turn a gentle creature into a man-killer?"

"I owe that to my crazed brother, Gus, and his two pals. They tied that proud little stud to the top of a cage and took turns raping him all night. Gus claimed the blond was the best piece of ass he's ever had." Bill grinned. "It's rather ironic that my brother's best lay ended up killing him. Guess the little stud didn't enjoy it."

John lowered his weapon and felt ill. He understood why Shail had killed and lost his will to live.

"Well, you came all this way, Mr. Turner," Bill said. "I don't want you to leave empty handed. There're a few fledglings through that door in the back room. Help yourself; my compliments." The whole building suddenly became dark as a great shadow passed overhead. "The swarms!" Bill yelled and raced to the door.

John started to follow him, but stopped and ran toward the back room. In the room animal cages lined the walls. He hurried past until he found the two tiny fledglings crouched in the straw. They were weanlings and hadn't completely molted their down, making them incapable of flight. He blasted the cage lock and opened the door.

"Come on, little guys," he said. Too frightened, they cowered in the straw and sniffled for compassion. He reached in, took one in his arm and gently stroked its head. The cherub-looking fledgling clung to John's neck, longing for a parent. He thought of Kari's baby. Scared to be alone, the second fledgling crept across the straw into his arms.

Holding the fledglings, John raced from the building. Although mid-morning, it seemed like evening, with black clouds of beetles blotting out the sun. The swarms were flying to the heart of Hampton and had yet to settle. Looking at the street, he saw that Simpson had taken his hover. "Son-of-a-bitch," he growled.

A vehicle parked by the front door apparently belonged to the range owner. John opened the vehicle door, climbed in, and placed the fledglings in the passenger seat. When he fired the engine, the first beetle hit the windshield and then another. He pushed the vehicle to its top speed, and palm-size bugs pelted the transport. After only two miles, the beetles invaded the engines, and the vehicle fell a short distance to the ground, clogged and silent. Catching a glimpse out the window through the mass of beetles, he saw that everything—buildings, street, trees—was blanketed in black. There was no place to run, no escape.

The crunching and buzzing sound was deafening. The two pint-size fledglings curled up in tight balls covered with their meager wings and trembled. John sighed and bundled them in his arms. Their tiny arms wrapped around his neck. "It's okay, little guys," he said. "It'll be over soon."

19

Shail stirred, and his half-opened eyes attempted to focus, but all was hazy. He was familiar with the groggy effect of tranquilizers that forced unwanted sleep. He lay still, waiting for his mind to clear. Smelling the moist air and the fragrance of seasonal flowers, he realized his jungle was near. His body felt comfortable so he ran his hand across the plush, silky material beneath him. He was resting on a human bed; its white sheets matched the vague white walls. He shook his head, hating the lethargic feeling that hindered his senses and strength. Gazing across the large room, he saw numerous potted plants and fancy carved furniture. He realized no chains or shackles clung to his wrists, and the shock collar had been removed from his neck, a clean harpy sash hung off his hips. Hearing a song-bird, he slightly elevated his head above the pillows, but looked past the bird at the open balcony window at gray clouds. No cage bars held him. Only his weak, drugged body kept him from the freedom of open sky.

Struggling to rise, he reeled with dizziness and then saw the drug patch on his arm. The same patch the old doctor had used on him. He ripped it off and lay down, hoping to recover quickly and regain his balance before the hunters came.

Shail heard the sound of an opening door and footsteps. He half closed his eyes and lay still. The man who had taken him out of the hunting range leaned over his bed and ran a monitor across his body. "Poor little fellow; he's still out of it," said the man.

Closer, Shail thought and felt his rage growing. Come closer to me. I might seem weak, but I have enough strength to reach up and rip your throat from your neck. Shail readied himself to pounce on the oblivious man.

"Step away from him, Doctor, before you're hurt," said a woman's voice. "He's not as weak as he appears, and he's waiting for you to get close so he can rip out your throat." The man moved away from the bed.

Shail curiously watched the slender woman glide across the floor in a long white gown. She had spoken the same words that dwelled in his mind. Could she be harpy? Approaching his bed, she bent over him, and her clusters of her long blond locks nearly touched his face.

"Leave us now," she said to the man, "and thank you, Dr. Watkins." Her blue eyes sparkled when gazing into his eyes. "To answer your question," she said softly, and placed her hand near Shail's nose.

Extending his neck, Shail sniffed her hand and detected harpy scent. The female was a golden harpy, but Shail had thought that he and Kari were the last of the golden line. She gently pushed aside his hair from his brow and stroked his head. "I waited twenty seasons to touch my son again, and like your father, you have grown sleek and beautiful."

Shail swallowed hard and stared with disbelief. His mother had died. How could this female claim to be her?

"I am Windy, your mother, Shail, and not dead, but have been in seclusion in this city of Hampton all this time. I come forth now to help you and the harpies. You must be rid of the human hatred that blocks all reason and destroys your instincts. Your mind is so distorted, you would eagerly rip the throat from a good man who is here to save harpies, rather than sense and judge him fairly. Evil men gave you the hate and you embraced it, but this is not the harpy way. Your flock needs the guidance of a wise and rational ruler."

Shail lifted his head and leaned on his elbow. "I do not know how to rid myself of hatred, nor if I should. The hatred is powerful. It gave me the strength to survive all hardships, and I now fear nothing. With no remorse, I shall have my flock hunt and slay all surviving humans, forever freeing the harpies."

"So honor and decency shall be cast to the winds to gratify your revenge?"

Shail lowered his head. "What has our honor brought except death?"

Windy sat down on the bed next to him. "Perhaps the humans deserve to be slain and the harpies forever free, but forever changed; the once-gentle race becoming savages, tormented, angry killers lacking a peaceful soul. Like warring men, we shall be without honor and grace. Is this the legacy you wish to leave your flock? Your decision must be made with a clear mind, not a wounded heart."

"I do not want to leave such a legacy, but I cannot rid myself of the rage. It grows."

"It grows because you feed and protect it," she said. "The revenge supplied purpose and the will to live, saving you from harpy depression, but it is no longer needed. The vengeance smothers your love and happiness, and in the end, it shall destroy you."

Shail curled up and placed his head against her leg. "How can I release the hate?"

"Expose it and the horrors that created it. These memories dwell deep and are sheltered, too painful to face. This agony holds you captive. Expose them to me, my son, and it shall set you free."

Like a small fledgling, Shail trembled and swallowed deeply. "I do not want to remember what was done to me."

Windy stroked his neck. "You must. You are the golden ruler and must do all for your flock. The harpies deserve a wise leader, not just a brave one. Remember, Shail."

Shail closed his eyes and focused on all the things that created his hate. His mother placed her hand on his forehead, telepathy revealing his thoughts to her. He recalled the knot in his stomach when he and Aron stood before two slain harpies that hung from a tree. He had grown up playing with, loving, and cherishing the two males. It was the beginning of his rage and revenge against men, seeing the unspeakable torture the males endured. Soon after, he released the beetles, allowing them to grow into massive swarms to chase the humans out of his jungle.

He remembered his own suffering. Wounded, kicked, and beaten, he barely survived the island hunters. He shivered, reliving his terrible pain and fear. The vengeance was personal now. And then there was the attack on Kari, causing the war against humans to begin. His hate was further fueled when he was sold to Gus. The man's deadly shock rod nearly stopped his heart. Humiliated and abused, he lost his gentle and reasoning nature.

His thoughts drifted to the most dreadful night of his life; the final blow that consumed him. Drowning out everything he loved, he became as evil as his enemies.

Shail lifted his head and stared teary eyed into his mother's eyes. "I cannot."

"Go on, Shail," his mother said. "Relive that night."

Gus and the two men had tied him to the top of his cage. He recalled his desperate struggle against the chains as each man mounted and brutally ravaged his body over and over again. He vividly remembered the details: the smell of whiskey and their bodies, the sound of grunts and slurred words, and the harsh fondling hands, their crushing frames over him, and the rape. Drained of all fight, courage, and pride, he gave up at dawn and attempted the heart-stopping suicide.

When Shail finished revealing the horror to her, Windy wiped the moisture from her eyes. "There is one more thing," she said. "I feel a dark shadow hiding in your subconscious. It so horrifies you that you have tried to erase it from your memory."

"The drug," Shail said softly. The sickeningly sweet pills Gus had forced down his throat, and Shail had soon lost control of his own body. The men laughed and stroked him, and he frantically fornicated to relieve the itchy sex drive. Stimulated by the pill, the rape, and the man's hands, he strained to release his seed again and again, the lust so powerful he became a party to the men's cruelty.

The men had forced him to violate the sacred right that a male reserved for his female. He had endured the ultimate rape. Revulsion, grief, and tremendous shame turned him into a killer.

Filled with gruesome memories, Shail placed his head in his mother's lap, shuddered, and broke down and cried.

"Let it go, Shail," Windy said and stroked him. "Let it flow out of you. The disgrace and mortification you feel proves your honor and decency. You did nothing wrong, but your grievous shame has created a powerful hate."

Shail pulled his limbs in, became a tight ball, and sobbed. His insides ached with physical pain, and his once-silent vocal cords whimpered. Never before had he released such sorrow, the sorrow of a lifetime full of struggle, fears, and hardship.

The early morning passed with his mother caressing and consoling him. He finally managed to raise his head and shake his wet locks from his face. "I feel so weak, so empty," he relayed. "The rage goes, but I am left numb. My life shall never hold joy again."

His mother smiled. "Like all harpies, you dwell in the present, but the joy shall come, and the hollow feeling will be filled. When you fly from here, you shall feel freedom, and soaring over the trees, you shall see their beauty. When you hold your mate in your arms, the love that binds you shall awaken, and when you look upon your fledgling, you shall be healed. You are strong, Shail. No other harpy has endured such long and terrible hardships and survived it. You are a great and cunning ruler who has saved his flock. Do not allow the hate to return and destroy you."

"How do you know me and all of this?" he asked.

"Though many seasons have passed, you are my son, my blood, and I can sense deep into your soul, and I, too, was once nearly destroyed by hate and loss."

"Aron's father, Rue, told me you had died."

On an end table she reached into a bowl and produced a piece of fruit. "Rue and all harpies believed I had perished after the death of your father." She handed the fruit to Shail. "It is a long story."

Shail leaned against the pillows. "I wish to know it," he said and nibbled on the fruit.

"I shall start at the beginning," she said. "When nearly an adult, I was brought by my father to the harpy gathering at the base of the sacred mountain. I was there to find my future mate, and the males had come from across the land to pick a new ruler. The old ruler had broken his wing and could no longer lead the flocks. For three lights, the golden males fought in challenges to prove dominance and their skill in daring harpy games. I am saddened when I think of all those beautiful blond males, gone now, killed by hunters when they were defending their flocks." She reached over and petted Shail's head.

"At the end of the gathering, one golden male stood alone. He had proven his courage, wit, and strength. He became the new ruler and your father. We made our nest in the northern mountains, and I became pregnant with you. It should have been a happy time, but it wasn't. Seeking rare yellow wings, numerous hunters came west. In the following four seasons they nearly exterminated the golden bloodline. Your father was desperate and helpless. He flew night and day, moving brown flocks out of harm's way and to the islands. With the golden males gone, the flock leadership fell to the browns that would never face down a man. It became flee and hide, with every harpy for himself and his family.

"At age of five, you were the last golden male fledgling who had survived. Your father had heard of a golden female in the south. She sought protection with a powerful young man named Turner. They bonded, and she gave birth to a female.

"Fearing the loss of the golden bloodline, your father met with the female and said that her daughter must bond with our son. Only these future golden harpies would have the strength to save the harpies. As you know, Turner rejected the harpy bond and wanted his daughter to marry a man. A conflict ensued over your mate's future. Would Kari be raised human or harpy? Your father wanted the female and her daughter to leave the unyielding man and return to the jungle, but I told him the decision was not his or Turner's. When mature, Kari would choose her mate. I knew the love would grow once she saw you. Your father agreed and went to tell Kari's mother that she could remain with Turner. It was then that Turner accidentally killed his own mate and then mine with his anger.

"When I learned of your father's death, I became consumed with grief, and I lost the will to live. Rue was your father's best friend, and I asked him to take you and raise you with his son, Aron, on the farthest island that was still free of hunters. Rue sensed my depression and knew that even the love of my son could not save me. After you were gone, I went to the jungle to die. I do not recall how many lights I wandered in a trance.

"A harpy hunter found me under some ferns and close to death. He took me to a cabin and attempted to revive me. At first I was frightened, but my fear turned to anger; anger with the humans who had killed my lover and ruined my life. Like you, hatred replaced my depression and saved me. I fought the middle-aged man who was named Henry. I bit and scratched him, but he remained gentle and calm. I watched him and sensed his worry. Henry knew I was harpy and no woman. He stayed by my side and nursed me back to health, promising to free me when I had healed.

"After many lights Henry released me back into the jungle with tears in his eyes. His kindness had not only saved my life, but also cured my hate and despair. I learned that not all humans were evil. Of my own free will I returned to the cabin and Henry. I did not feel the passionate, undying love for him like with your father, but I cared for the man. You were safer with Rue and Aron on the islands, and with Rue's guidance, you would become a good ruler, and I discovered that Henry was a wealthy, powerful senator. By staying with him, perhaps I could help the harpies. He loved me, but always feared I would leave him for another male harpy. After many seasons, the trust grew. He knew I would not leave him, and I told him about you, my son and the last golden male. We set in motion a plan to end the hunting and save the harpies and you. He campaigned and became the governor of Dora, but the senate decides the laws. We hired Dr. Watkins to perform a study on harpies, hoping to prove we are part human and carry human blood. With hard evidence, a law could be passed to end the harpy slaughter."

Shail sat up. "In the sacred mountain, Kari discovered such proof on a disc and planned to give it to a man called Watkins."

"Dr. Watkins has the disc and I have seen it, but there has been no time to expose it." She stood and stared out the balcony. "All of Henry's well-laid plans to save the harpies fell apart. The beetles, once only a threat to the timber, turned deadly. The town of Terrance was destroyed. Henry was under pressure to kill the beetles or evacuate the planet. Then hunters captured you, and Henry feared my depression would return if you were killed. Henry's heart was weak and had plagued him for many seasons. His heart, that gave me so much love, gave out from the stress. I hid his death and had Dr. Watkins bid on you at the auction. I did not want the senators to know that the governor's wife had bought a golden harpy. It might arouse their suspicions."

Free of the tranquilizer, Shail stood and walked to her. "I am sorry for your loss," he said and hugged her. "I must leave now and find Kari before the swarms strike the city. I fear she refused to leave."

"The swarms destroy Hampton as we speak, but Kari is safe and taken to the mountains."

"How do you know?"

"Aron faithfully slept at the foot of your bed all night. After he sent Kari to the mountains, he went against your wishes and decided to rescue you. When Dr. Watkins and two other men took you from the hunting range, he and his flock followed the vehicle here. Not knowing you had been saved, Aron and the harpies descended on the vehicle. I revealed myself and stopped them from harming the men who work for me." She took Shail's hand and led him out on the balcony. "Look upon your flock, Shail. They have gathered here and await their ruler."

Shail gazed upon several thousand male harpies. Seeing him and his golden mother, the harpies lowered their heads and knelt. "Aron is among them?"

"No, he has gone to find Turner and save him from the swarms," she said. "Why, Shail? Why do you protect such a man who killed your father and caused your capture?"

"Turner is not evil, but very protective. My father wanted to take Turner's mate and daughter away. I can understand such anger if it were done to me. And I was a threat, wanting Kari. Fearing for her safety, he sought us, risking his own life. Though misguided, he is a good man. For many seasons he defended me and my harpies from hunters on his lands and tried to right a wrong by taking me from the hunting range. He has courage and honor. If I died, I asked him to protect my son, knowing he would not fail. For these reasons I want him alive."

She placed her hands around his head. "Never again will I question your leadership. You are wise and fair. Despite all your suffering, you still see the truth."

"Am I a good ruler?" Shail said. "I chose to let the beetles flourish, and now innocent humans are dead. I shall never rest easy with such a decision."

"You did not choose their deaths, only to drive them from the land," she said. "The beetles changed things, and the blame lies with the humans. If they had not killed the harpies and loca eagles, the humans would not face the swarms now. With the death of the last harpy, the swarms would have come. Your decision has saved your flock and the jungle."

"Your words are true, but I feel no pride. I shall always be haunted by the faces of the compassionate women and children who gazed upon me at the hunting range. The hate had spared me from this remorse." Shail stretched his wings and stared at his flock. "I must go to my males and give them confidence. The lights ahead shall be hard, and some of those males shall die when we attack the swarms."

Shail hopped up on the balcony railing and extended his wings. The morning rays turned his creamy feathers into a bright gold. He glided down and landed among the brown heads and wings. Shail raised his head and walked through the crowd. Each harpy submissively lowered his head and moved out of his way, giving him a wide berth. He sensed their relief and high esteem for him.

Shail saw Ribot, the teenager who had found him at the range. The young male still held his golden flight feather. "You did good to spread my words, but a time of danger draws near. I do not want you among us when we fly into the swarms."

"But, Master, I can fly very fast—faster than any here," said Ribot.

An adult male seized the teen's shoulder and shoved him to the ground. "Forgive my son," he said and knelt. "He was raised in the east and has never seen a golden. He does not know his place."

Shail leaned down and pulled up Ribot by his arm. "I am aware of his rude nature, but he has done me a great service by saving my mate. I now ask of his services again." He turned to the teenager. "You can deliver my words and claim to fly fast. I shall send you on a great errand. Do you know the way to the mountains where my mate and others hide?"

Ribot's face lit up. "I know it, Master. My mother and sisters are there."

"Go swiftly and tell my mate that I am alive and free. She hopes for this important news. I shall come to her when swarms are gone and the land safe."

Ribot extended his wings, and Shail placed his hand on the wing feathers. "Also tell her I love her."

20

John held the two frightened fledglings and saw the first beetles enter the demolished vehicle by burrowing though a hole in the plastic floorboards. He plugged the hole with his shoe, but ten more holes soon formed. He heard a thump on the roof and then another. The beetles were scrambling off the transport, and light filtered into the darkened cab. Through a window, he saw the flash of brown feathers. A harpy bent down and gazed at him and then beckoned with his hand.

John slowly opened the door. Standing on the roof, Aron and two male harpies stared down at him. John reached back in the vehicle, grabbed the fledglings, and handed them to one of the males, who rapidly flew away with his precious cargo. John tried to climb out, avoiding the ground that was knee-deep in beetles. Aron and the other male grasped John's arms and pulled him up to vehicle roof. Aron took a gluey sap from a large leaf and smeared it on John's shoes and lower pants.

John saw the same green sap on the harpies' feet. "This keeps the beetles off?" he asked.

Aron nodded and gestured toward the sky.

John returned the nod. "I'm ready to get the hell out of here." Aron took ahold of one of John's arms and the large older male grabbed the other. The harpies furiously flapped their wings and lifted John into the air. With the beetles beneath, they traveled north over the blackened buildings. John literally had a bird's-eye view of the destruction. Hampton was under siege, and no section or neighborhood had been spared from the black death. John wondered how long Aron and the other harpy could carry him. Surely they didn't have the wing strength to take him to the mountains.

In the distance John spotted colorful trees and below recognized the northbound road that led to the governor's estate. He saw the white mansion surrounded by the vast park. The building had been spared from the swarms. Flying into view, he understood why. Hundreds of harpies covered the grounds beyond the front doors. As Aron and the harpy descended on the mansion, John glanced back at Hampton. The capital of Dora would soon be gone.

Shail spoke with the flock leaders to coordinate the attack on the beetles. More and more males were arriving after their long flights over the continent. The harpy gathering was steadily growing.

A harpy flew in carrying two small fledglings. He landed near Shail and set the fledglings on the ground. "Seth, my flock leader, and a harpy named Aron soon come," he relayed to Shail. "They bring a man called Turner. We saved him from the swarms as he saved these fledglings."

Shail glanced at the twin male fledglings nestled under another male's wings. The male licked and cuddled them and was obviously their father. "Turner saved them?" Shail asked.

"He took them out of the hunting range," the male relayed.

Shail knew why Turner had gone to the range, and it was not to save fledglings. Unaware that Shail had left, Turner had come to free him. Over the treetops Aron and a harpy appeared holding a man. Their frantically flapping wings showed that they struggled with the big man's weight. They fluttered over the building steps and set Turner down on his feet.

"Thanks, Aron," John said, and Aron nodded before flying away. Walking up the steps, John approached the front door and knocked. A man opened the door, and John recognized him from the previous com call.

"Mr. Turner," the man said with surprise. "You kept your appointment."

John shook his head at the pencil pusher. "Yes, the city is falling down around our ears, but I keep my appointments." He walked inside. "Now where is Henry? There isn't much time."

A beautiful woman in a white gown entered the foyer. "Time for what, John Turner?" she asked.

"Didn't this idiot deliver my message last night?" John growled. "There's a golden harpy who can stop the swarms, but he's been taken on a space-ship. The governor can order the return of that ship."

"Governor Blake can't help you. He died three days ago," she said. "Are you sure you don't want this golden for his wings? You've already killed two golden harpies and nearly three others."

"I don't want his wings," John said, "and I've only killed one harpy. Anyway, who are you?"

"I am Henry's wife, and you are a liar," she said bitterly.

John realized it was a lie. He had killed Shail's father and his wife—both golden harpies—and he'd nearly killed his own daughter and Shail. Who was this fifth golden harpy? He stared into her brilliant blue eyes that seemed to peer into his mind. "How do you know if I've killed two or ten goldens?"

"She is harpy and my mother, Turner," answered a soft male voice.

John wheeled around and saw Shail standing in the doorway with Aron. "Thank God, you're okay." The piece of the puzzle came together and he turned to Shail's mother. "You're the fifth golden and the anonymous high bidder of the auction."

"I am," she answered. "I almost died when you killed my mate, but Henry saved me, and I bought Shail's freedom. I never would allow my son to suffer the same fate as his father."

John lowered his head. "I'm sorry," he said. "Sorry to both you and Shail."

Shail approached John. "Let us not dwell in these past regrets, for I, too, am guilty. Though I chose not to harm, I unleashed the swarms, and they caused all to perish in the city. It is a heavy burden to carry."

"They're not dead, Shail," John said. "The people are hiding in the metal spaceport. There isn't much food, but once the swarms leave, they should be okay."

"With the smell of so much flesh, swarms shall stay until they find a way in. All those humans shall die," Shail said. He turned and gazed out the door at his harpies, faced with the decision to save the humans or let them die.

John watched Kari's streamlined mate wrestle with his uncertainty. He lightly paced across the smooth floor. Abused and raped, Shail had good reason not to save the humans who had slaughtered his harpies for years, and once the humans were saved, harpy hunting could continue. John walked to the handsome golden male. "Shail, I understand why you shouldn't destroy the swarms and save those people. If I were you, I honestly don't know if I would lift a finger to help them, but most of those people are good and would never hurt a harpy."

"If only women, children, and good men dwelled in the port, I would protect them," Shail said, "but the senators who long to kill us are there, and the hunters who want our wings. If I let all die, only I shall suffer the grief of my decision. If I save them, my flock shall suffer. I must first think of my harpies and let the beetles do their work. The hunting ends with the humans' death."

Dr. Watkins entered the room. "There's another way to end the hunting without those people dying," he said and held up the disc containing the old captain's log. "It's solid proof that harpies are a race related to humans, and I have the DNA evidence to back it. The harpies can't be hunted as game animals any longer."

Shail stared at Dr. Watkins. "I am no fool, Watkins. Those senators who make your human laws have known for many seasons that harpies carry human blood but have lied about us, so the hunting would continue. I do not trust them. To save themselves, the senators would lie again, saying the hunting stops, but once saved, they would allow the killing of harpies. There is little honor among humans."

"He makes a good point," John said to Watkins and turned to Shail. "You told me I had honor and asked me to protect your son. Do you trust me?"

"I do," Shail said. "You are a man of your word and a great protector."

"Then let me try to protect those people and your harpies," John said. "There's a way that both can be done. Right now you control the lives of everyone on the planet. That's power, Shail. If used wisely, the power can give you what you want. I could go to the port with your demands, and Dr.

Watkins could bring proof that harpies are gentle mortals, not dangerous animals. This proof exposes the senators and their lies. That's what the senators have always feared. The senate could be bypassed, and the people in the port hold a majority of the planet's population. Those people could vote on the laws and a treaty that ends harpy hunting and grant your flock equal human rights. I think you should also ask for your own land, say the outback and the islands. Your jungle trees and animals would also be protected from men. I'm a businessman, Shail, and I'd look out for your interests, making sure you got a fair shake."

"It sounds fair," Shail said, "but laws and treaties can be changed and broken. I have seen men's greed and watched one man kill two others, breaking your human laws."

John nodded. "There're always a few men who don't respect our laws and could harm your harpies, but if caught, these men would face a cage. When you save the humans, they'll be very grateful to the harpies, and they know you hold the power of the swarms. If betrayed, you can unleash the beetles again."

Shail glanced down at his damaged wrists, cut from resisting the bondages of shackles and chains. "I vowed my son would never suffer as I have," he said quietly. "My hate for humans slowly fades, but it is still there. It lies in wait, waiting to be called back with a vengeance that would slay all humans, but Turner, your words hold wisdom and have given me choices. I must go and think of this decision that frees or destroys my flock and spares or kills the humans." He walked to the open doorway.

Aron approached Shail at the threshold. "I shall go with you," he relayed.

"No, the decision is mine alone," Shail relayed.

Aron wrapped his arms around Shail's neck and nuzzled him. "May your choice be wise."

Watkins stood next to John as Shail spread his wings and flew from the mansion. "He knew all about the senators, our laws, and human nature," said Watkins. "I never dreamed that harpies were equally intelligent to men."

"Equal?" John said, and watched Kari's young husband disappear beyond the treetops. "With a harpy's instincts, they surpass men. The humans have been fortunate all these years that they dealt with passive mortals who chose to run rather than fight, but Shail is not like other harpies. That plucky golden male is fearless, and he's been badly abused, giving him good reason to wipe out humans. If I were him, I wouldn't have the compassion to save those people. I'd tell mankind to go to hell."

Soaring along the border between the city of Hampton and the jungle, Shail glanced to the left of his wing and saw massive swarms quickly consuming the buildings. In the distance he distinguished the large doomed port, heavily cloaked with beetles. Similar to bees drawn to honey, they sought a way through the metal to get at the humans. The highway's inns, stores, and small towns brought many swarms that followed the bread crumbs rapidly east. Shail had planned to slow the beetle's pace and let the humans flee on ships to the stars, but he was captured, and the harpy river gathering fell apart, allowing the swarms to move at will. With no time to escape, the vast majority of the humans were trapped with ocean at their backs.

Shail fluttered and gazed at the destruction. "Can I be harpy again?" he wondered. "Can I forgive and be a protector of life, even human life?" He thought of the women and children that had come to the hunting range and were saddened by his captivity. He dwelled on gentle Mollie and George, the kind old guard, and the young police officer who protected him from Bill. Then there was Doc. He had saved Shail's life, and the wise Indian, Charlie, who understood him and his harpies, and Turner, whose honor and courage matched his own. How many humans like these inhabited the doomed port?

Wrestling with the dilemma, he flew to the soothing jungle. After a few miles, he spotted a winding stream, glided down, and landed on its pebbled bank. He waded until knee deep in the clear, gushing, flow and splashed cool water on his face and body, hoping to rinse off the worry. Dripping wet, he glanced up and beheld the towering trees and their colorful foliage. They were magnificent, and he realized his mother was right. His hollow soul felt the awe of the all-inspiring jungle and its freedom.

A twig snapped under a fern, and Shail jumped and whirled around. He saw two small children who hid and peered out at him.

"Look, Tom," the little girl whispered. "It's the harpy with yellow wings we saw last Saturday. I'm so glad he's out of the cage."

"Quiet, Anna," the boy whispered. "He'll get us. Dad said he's dangerous."

"Well, Mom liked him," said Anna and crept out from under the fern. "Come here, harpy. I have something for you."

Shail left the stream and took a few steps toward her.

"Get back here, Anna," Tom called.

Anna ignored her brother and approached Shail. "Do you like flowers? I have one for you." Her outstretched hand held a tiny flower, wilted and partially crushed.

Shail crouched down to the girl's eye level and took the pink flower. He brought it to his nose and smelled it.

"He likes my flower, Tom." Anna smiled. "He's so pretty. Mom cried when she saw him in the cage."

Shail realized their mother had concealed the truth of his coming death from her virtuous children.

"Dad, Dad, come quick," the boy shouted. "Anna's messing with a harpy."

Shail heard the approach of running footsteps that crunched the vegetation. In the past he would have fled, but he stood up straight and waited. A man appeared, his clothes muddy and his face sweaty. Shail sensed his terror.

"Come here, Anna!" the man said.

"He won't hurt me, Daddy," said Anna. "I gave him my flower."

"Do as I say!" the man ordered. Anna reluctantly obeyed, and he grabbed her up in his arms.

"She speaks true," Shail said softly. "I would not hurt her or your family."

The man staggered back. "I didn't know harpies could talk."

"There is much not known of one another," Shail said, "but perhaps we should learn."

The man placed Anna on the ground, and her brother joined them. "We just moved to Dora, but what I've heard about harpies doesn't seem to be true. You're kind of like us."

Shail glanced at Anna. "Yes, like you, I long to raise my offspring in safety and live in peace."

The man wiped the sweat from his forehead. "I wouldn't call this planet peaceful or safe. We were heading to the port because of the swarms. I took the wrong road, and when the swarms flew overhead, I got cut off, so I drove into the jungle. My vehicle is stuck over there, got wedged between two trees, and we're lost. Now I'm talking to a harpy." He shook his head. "It's been a heck of day."

A woman emerged from the trees.

"Look, Mom," said Anna. "It's the golden harpy."

The man took his wife's hand. "It's okay, honey. The harpy's all right." He asked Shail, "Can you tell us the way back to the city?"

"Your city is gone. The swarms dwell there. Follow this water west, and it shall lead you from danger."

"But we don't have any food," said the man.

Shail pointed to the yellow fruit in a tree. "Those can be eaten. The jungle shall provide."

"Thanks for your help." The man walked to Shail and offered his hand.

Perplexed, Shail stared at the man's hand.

The man grinned. "When we meet a friend, we shake one another's hand."

"You call me friend?" Shail asked, and slowly extended his hand.

The man grasped Shail's hand and shook it. "Sure, why not? I hope I see you again."

"I, too, shall have this hope," Shail said to the man and watched the human family walk upstream, disappearing among the trees. He gazed at the little flower in his hand; the flower could have been an olive branch. Is it only fear and ignorance that separates harpy from human? he wondered. Must so many die because we do not know one another? While I hold the power, I shall make this peace offering. He was also plagued by a previous conversation with Kari. Even if the Dora humans were driven away or killed, many others dwelled in the stars. Once they learned how to destroy the swarms, they would return to his jungle, and he or his son would again face the hunting threat. He spread his wings and flew toward the governor's mansion.

It was midafternoon when Shail sailed over his flock and landed near the mansion doors. Aron spotted Shail and joined him, entering the building together. John and Dr. Watkins jumped up from their chairs and approached the harpies as Windy entered the room. All were anxious about Shail's decision.

Shail deeply sighed. "Though uneasy, I shall give peace a chance," he said to all in the room.

Aron sniffled and walked in a circle around Shail. "You trust the humans after what they have done?" he relayed. "Let the swarms take them and be done with this threat." The brown ruffled his feathers and lightly stepped around the golden.

"We would not be done, Aron," Shail relayed silently. "The threat would grow. After we defeat the swarms, we again would confront the humans who dwell among the stars, and they shall come and blame us for all the death, knowing we rule the swarms. It shall be worse than now. I do not trust humans, but I trust Turner, and his words are wise. While I have power, I must use it."

Aron stopped in front of Shail. "I am committed to you and stand by your decision, but if I ruled, I would let the humans die. Once rid of swarms, we shall not have to wait for the star threat. It shall already be here. The humans we saved shall pick up their weapons and continue the hunt."

"There is a chance of betrayal," Shail relayed, "but I must risk it."

Aron walked away and leaned against the doorjamb, staring out at the flock that relied on Shail.

John went to Shail. "Aron is obviously not happy with your decision."

"I am not happy with it," Shail said. "All my life I have longed to be rid of the humans, but now I compromise and save them. Am I foolish or wise?"

"Wise," John said. "Today marks the beginning of peace between our two races and ends a tyranny that would eventually destroy your flock. Dr. Watkins and I will use one of the governor's hovercrafts and go to the port. I promise it will work, Shail."

Watkins approached them with a folder. "When the people see the disc and blood evidence that proves harpies and humans are close to the same species, they'll end the hunting."

"The same?" Shail whirled around, facing Watkins. "Never speak such lies. Like birds, harpies have gentle natures, and lack human cruelty, but don't mistake our gentleness for weakness. Even a bird turns vicious when defending her chicks. If peace fails, I shall become that mother bird." The fire in his blue eyes conveyed a smoldering rage, ready to ignite if he were provoked or betrayed.

John and Watkins loaded up in the hover, and Aron provided them with the sap that kept off beetles. After John explained the harpy demands, Shail would come to the port as living proof that harpies weren't ignorant animals. Shail had his own agenda. If he detected one hint of treachery in the human leaders' minds, his decision of peace would change.

John flew to the spaceport, and Watkins dropped the sap near the doors where the hover would set down. "I hope these beetles stay put," John said. "If they take flight, we're in trouble."

Hearing the hovercraft, the men inside the port cracked open the doors and peered out. John and Watkins made a dash through the beetles for the doors. The men slid the doors open, allowing the two men inside.

"Who's in charge?" John asked the men.

"The lieutenant governor and a few senators," said a man. "They're in the offices, trying to contact some spaceships."

John pushed through the crowded room and walked toward the offices. A police officer stood by the door. "It's urgent I speak with the lieutenant governor. My name is John Turner."

The officer opened the door and conveyed John's message.

A tall middle-aged man with jet-black hair came to the door. "I'm Sam Waters, the lieutenant governor. I'm in charge until we reach Governor Blake, but we're unsure if he escaped the swarms. What's your urgent information, Mr. Turner?"

"Blake is dead," John said. "You're in charge."

Waters swept back his hair from his forehead. "I feared as much. The governor's heart condition had grown worse, and he had asked me to take over temporarily. Is that your urgent news?"

"No," said John. "I know of a way to destroy the swarms, but it comes at a price."

"We're desperate. The beetles are blanketing the solar panels for the generator and have penetrated the water system. They're burrowing through the wooden door sliders, and the nearest spaceship is weeks away. All these people are going to die. Name your price, Mr. Turner."

"It's not a matter of money," John said. "The harpies can destroy the swarms, and in return, they want laws passed that end harpy hunting and gives them equal human rights. Also, a land treaty must be drawn up that gives them title to the outback and islands."

Waters frowned. "This isn't the time for jokes. Harpies are animals."

Watkins stepped forward. "That's not necessarily true. Actually harpies should be recategorized as another mortal species. They're part human and very intelligent. I'm Dr. Watkins, and I was hired by Governor Blake to research harpies. I have the scientific evidence and an old disc that explains their ancestry and proves harpies are genetically related to men."

Waters looked at John and Watkins. "You two are serious?"

"Very serious," John said.

"Fine," said Waters, "I don't care what they are, if they can kill the swarms. Tell them I agree to their terms."

"No," said John. "This won't be handled with a handshake or your word of promise. The laws must be voted on, passed, and signed and the treaty drawn up, guaranteeing their rights and land. I'm here to make sure everything is legal. The harpies have been on the losing end for too long."

"That will take time, and we don't have that kind of time," said Waters.

"Well, Governor Waters, I suggest you get busy," said John, "because the harpies have plenty of time. They can sit back, watch humans die, and then claim the whole planet for themselves. They made this offer because they have more empathy than we do. Now that the tables have turned, it proves we're the inferior race. Their ruler will be here shortly, and after years of harpy hunting, his patience is worn thin. You'd better have something to offer him, and don't consider manipulation. He's enough animal to sense deceit."

"I need the senate's approval," said Waters.

"Don't bother," said John. "The senators have their reputation and their office to lose if the truth comes out about their promotion of harpy extermination. Those men won't propose or pass a law that helps harpies. I suggest an amendment, and take the vote straight to the people."

"That's highly irregular," said Waters. "I'm sure the senators will pass a law if it means saving human lives." He grabbed a microphone and walked up on the loading dock. Waters brought the room to a hush and then explained the harpies' demands. The room erupted with the crowd's voices and noisy arguments.

Senator Peterson stomped onto the loading dock. "Harpies are winged beasts, and they can't kill the swarm," he shouted to the crowd. "By tomorrow the swarms will be gone."

Waters fired back. "Suppose the swarms don't leave. Dr. Watkins has proof that harpies are intelligent mortals. What can it hurt if we pass some laws to protect them and give up some land? The only thing we have to lose is our lives." Heated debates ensued, and the place fell into chaos. Two hours slipped by with nothing accomplished. Waters was at his wit's end.

John pulled Waters aside. "I told you you'd waste time with the senate, but there's one who can dispel all doubts and convince the people that the harpies are part human and sincere with their offer." John walked to the doors and Waters followed. John slightly opened the door and looked at the brown harpy sitting on the hover. "Bring Shail," he said to the harpy. The harpy flew away, and shortly Shail fluttered and landed near the doors.

"Come in, Shail," John said and opened the door. Shail entered the port with poise and grace. Mystified by the enchanting creature, the people in the enormous room fell silent. They huddled closer to see his sweeping yellow wings that drifted across the floor, held up by his scantily dressed sleek frame. Shail flung his blond locks from his blue eyes that glittered with confidence and superiority. John smiled. Kari's husband was utterly magnificent.

"Shail, this is the new governor, Governor Waters," John said. "He'd like to give you your demands, but the senators are against it, and the people are confused."

"You rule all these?" Shail asked Waters.

Waters was taken aback by the captivating and speaking harpy. "Yes, yes, I'm the governor now. You speak English?"

"Yes, I speak your words," Shail said, "perhaps better than you, since your humans remain confused. It is a simple question you need ask them. Do they wish to live or die?"

Waters regained his composure. "Of course they want to live."

"My harpies also want to live. It is trust we lack. I shall save your humans from the swarms if you save my harpies from hunters." Shail gazed at the crowd. "It is time to end uncertainty and replace it with understanding." He leaped into the air and lit on a large crate ten feet above the packed human assembly. Shail folded in his wings and looked down at the gawking people. "I come here to offer you life," Shail said, forcing his soft voice to be heard. "In return the harpies want peace, equality, and the western jungle. If you do not accept the trade, then greed seals your fate, for the beetles shall stay here. I can and shall destroy the swarms, but it is your decision if it be done before or after your deaths. By next light you must decide." He glided down and landed near the doors.

John and Waters walked to him. Waters smiled. "I do believe you ended their confusion and made things very clear."

"I shall return with the dawn," Shail said. "Do not fail, new ruler. There are many females and young here. I do not wish their deaths, but if there is no protective law, no treaty for my harpies, the innocent blood shall be on your hands as well as mine." He shoved the sliding doors open and stepped outside. In a flash, he was gone.

"My God, he's charismatic," said Waters, "and direct."

John nodded. "Shail looks like an elegant fowl, but just remember, Governor, under those feathers, he's tough as nails and means every word he says. Don't make the mistake of screwing him over."

"Ladies and gentlemen, please don't listen to the harpy," said a voice on a microphone. Senator Blackwell stood on the loading platform and addressed the crowd.

John glared at Blackwell, the same stubby senator who had bid against him at the auction. "How did that asshole get into office?" he said to Waters.

"Money," Waters said, and moved toward the platform.

Blackwell grinned and spoke to the audience. "Sure, the harpy is handsome, but a talking harpy is a freak of nature, and he's the same despicable golden that murdered three men and raped the woman at the hunting range. It's a trick to get us out of the port. He wants the men dead, so his harpies can molest our women. If he really can wipe out the swarms, that means he set this plague upon us. Harpies are evil creatures. We shouldn't trust them. The beetles will leave when there's nothing left to eat. Just give it some time."

John and Waters walked up to the platform, and Waters spoke into the microphone. "Senator Blackwell, I think the people should hear both sides of this issue. I personally don't know anything about harpies, but a port supervisor told me that the harpies warned us about the coming swarms, giving us time to secure the port. If not for their warning, the ventilation systems would be clogged and the wooden doors penetrated. We would all be dead. Next to me is Mr. Turner. He knows quite a bit about harpies and should be allowed to speak before we rule out their demands."

Blackwell grinned at John. "Of course I have no objection to letting John Turner speak. He's a well-known harpy hunter and holds the record for the largest pair of golden wings." Blackwell handed the microphone to John.

John took a deep, nervous breath. "My name is John Turner," he said, "and I did kill a male harpy twenty years ago, but I regret it. I've since discovered the truth about male harpies. First of all, you should know I was married to a harpy, and my daughter is half harpy."

The people's voices rumbled through the giant room.

"It's true," John said. "Female harpies have no wings and appear human. Since Dora was colonized they have secretly walked among us, living in our cities, towns, and farms. Their disguise saved their species, but now their males face extinction because of overhunting. Their last refuge, the western islands, is being plundered, and soon the shy, gentle race will be lost. They are a race of winged humans. You saw and heard their golden ruler. He's as intelligent as any person in this room and surely can't be called a game animal."

John pointed down at the crowd. "Down there is Dr. Watkins. He was hired by our late governor, Henry Blake, to research harpies. He has the scientific proof that harpies carry human DNA, and he has a three-hundred-year-old ship log, discovered in the western mountains. It explains the harpies' ancestry, and everyone in this port should see the disc. The fact is the harpies are our blood brothers, and they have never stolen or raped our women. These lies were started by the Dorial explorers, the ancestors of our senators. You might wonder why Senator Blackwell and the other senators are reluctant to pass a law that protects harpies. Why they have openly promoted harpy hunting. It's a cover-up to protect their reputation and the reputation of their famous Dorial forebears. When the Dorials came to the planet, they captured and molested the female harpies, and the males were slaughtered when they attempted to rescue their mates. The women who were supposedly taken and molested by harpies were really female harpies who were trying to get back to their mates and the jungle. Our senators know this fact and wish to hide it."

"That's a lie!" Blackwell shouted. "I don't know of any such rubbish, and male harpies are the rapists. Your precious golden ruler recently raped that poor woman at the hunting range. I know her, and she's no harpy."

"Senator Blackwell," Mollie called from the crowd.

"Here she is," said Blackwell. "Come up, Mollie. It's important that we hear the truth about the vicious harpy."

Mollie moved through the people and was visibly shaken when she stood on the platform.

John gave her the microphone.

"Last Saturday night I was attacked and raped," she said. Her voice trembled and tears wet her black eyes. "But the harpy didn't do it. Gus Simpson and his two men raped me and tried to kill me. They planned to blame my murder on the golden harpy so the hunters would bid higher at the auction. The harpy pulled Gus off of me and saved my life. Those men had a knife and cornered the harpy. He had no choice but to kill in self-defense. I lied to the police because Gus's brother, Bill Simpson, threatened to kill me if I told the truth, but I must tell the truth now. I've worked with caged harpies, and they're sweet and timid creatures. They deserve some peace." She lowered her head and handed the microphone back to John and left the platform.

Senator Blackwell grabbed the microphone out of John's hand. "Well, one of those timid creatures had the nerve to kill three men. The harpies are seeking revenge. If it's true that harpies can destroy the swarms, why didn't they do it sooner? I'm telling you they caused this plague, and now they want us out of the protected port to kill us. We should wait and see if the swarms leave before giving in to those devils."

John took hold of the microphone and eyed the senator. "I wasn't quite finished," he said.

Blackwell looked up, handed the microphone to John, and backed away.

"Look, everyone, the swarms aren't leaving," John said. "They smell us and will stay at the port until they get in. We don't have the water or food to wait them out or for a ship to arrive. There is a connection between the harpies and the swarms. For decades the harpies have protected their jungle by preventing the beetles from multiplying. The protection was stopped when the harpies were faced with extinction. We allowed hunters to reduce their flocks. We are the plague and broke the chain in nature. Without harpies, the swarms would multiply and obliterate the planet, and there'd be nothing to stop them."

John turned and looked at Blackwell. "What Senator Blackwell suggests doesn't make sense. If the harpies want us dead, why did they warn us about the coming swarms so we could prepare this port? Why would their ruler come here and offer a truce that could save us when he could do nothing and watch us die? If they destroy the swarm to get our women, they would still face our weapons and be slaughtered None of this adds up unless you understand the harpies' motives. They long for peace, and pride themselves in protecting life, even human life that has threatened their existence. Harpies will die when they attack these swarms. What kind of race are we to deny them some rights, and land, when they're willing to forgive and protect us? As their ruler said, if we're that greedy, we have sealed our own fate."

The people broke into noisy chatter. "Give the harpies their demands!" several men yelled.

Waters took the microphone. "As governor, I'm issuing a state-of-emergency bill, and we'll vote on it by a show of hands. I assume I have the senate's approval."

Blackwell shrugged and several senators nodded.

"Raise your hand if you want to pass a law prohibiting harpy hunting, granting the harpies human rights, and endorsing the treaty, giving the

harpies the entire outback, the land west of the city once known as Terrance, and the western islands."

The massive domed room became a sea of raised hands.

"Those opposed?" Waters asked.

Blackwell and the other senators raised their hands, and there were a
few scattered raised hands in the crowd.

"It's almost unanimous. We'll give the harpies their demands," Waters
said, and a roar of cheers rose from the crowd. He turned to John. "Without your compelling speech, we might have lost the vote. You should have
been in politics."

"No thanks." John grinned. "No offense, but I'm too bad at lying to be in
your line of work. Besides, it wasn't me that convinced them. They voted for
Shail."

"I'll draw up the new law and treaty," said Waters. "When I'm done, you
can read it over before I sign it. I just hope your friend, Shail, doesn't
change his mind."

"He won't," said John. "Harpies are very honest and reliable."

Governor Waters motioned to Watkins to come up on the platform.
"This would be a good time to play the disc on the monitors and answer
any questions."

"It's an extraordinary ship log. It shows the creation of a new species,"
said Watkins. "The disc is loaded and ready to play."

Waters announced to the people that the monitors would show the ancient captain's log. All eyes focused on the large screens normally used for
incoming and outgoing ship times and cargo. The story of Captain James,
his crew, and his ill-fated freighter, *The Princess,* played for the Hampton
people. The port was quiet, and women shed tears when the elderly James
expressed his love for his harpy children and grandchildren. When the
disc was over, men shook their heads and grumbled, disgusted that the
harpies had been so misjudged and mistreated. A new admiration rose for
the harpies that were named after Jack Harper, a lonely young crewman
with the compassion to save an animal called a loca eagle.

Governor Waters sighed. "It's unbelievable," he said to John and Watkins. "For a century and a half an entire race has suffered and died because
of a few lying men. The Dorial monument will crumble, and the senators

have no hope of reelection after this scandal. Regardless of the swarm threat, the harpies should have been protected all these years."

John nodded. "Being afraid and uniformed creates a prejudice that's a tough mountain to overcome, and a few rotten men can stop the climb. Your predecessor, Governor Blake, wanted to expose the truth and help the harpies, but his wife was the real hidden agenda. She's a harpy and Shail's mother."

"I'll be darned," said Waters. "I always wondered how Henry managed to get a beautiful young wife. I'd better go into an office and start drawing up the bill and treaty. I have only until morning. I'm eager to get to know Shail."

"You're a fair man," said John. "Once he gets to know you, I think you'll get along fine."

Through the night Waters and his staff worked on the documents. John wandered through the port of people that attempted to sleep in the cramped quarters. Even with the thick metal walls, they heard the dreadful buzz and hum of the beetles. Most of the water was gone, and the crowd worried. After all the atrocities inflicted on his flock, would the golden ruler keep his word and save them?

After his trip to the port, Shail returned to the governor's mansion and his ever-growing male flock. All knew of the single surviving golden who ruled, but many had never seen Shail. The eastern flocks lived nocturnal lives and dwelled just outside of the large city of Hampton. The strategy had saved them, since the hunters were oblivious to their existence. The river harpies also had adjusted their lifestyle. Abandoning the trees, they learned to live and conceal themselves in the open swampland. The hunters believed the eastern harpies were extinct, and the river area held a few scattered flocks. As a result, Aron and Shail's western males took the full heat; the hunters journeyed west for their harpy prey. When Shail looked at the huge gathering, he was surprised by the numbers. He ruled a flock of several thousand.

Shail walked inside the mansion, and his mother embraced him and kissed his cheek. "I am very proud of you," she said.

"You think it wise I choose to save the humans?"

"I know many who are good in the port, and I would mourn their loss if you chose differently, but your decision must be for the welfare of your flock."

"I have considered all the ways, and I believe this is the best path. If the humans agree to a truce, I shall save them. I gave my word."

After eating a curious human food of nut bread, Shail curled up on a soft rug in the main living room. His mother sat on the floor and stroked his back. He relaxed and stared at the leaping flames in the fireplace. The fear of sleeping in a human dwelling had long passed. Little could frighten him now.

He drifted to sleep under his cream wings and sought Kari in the illusionary state. They connected telepathically, and he embraced his mate. Feeling contentment, he slowly was becoming whole again, the scars of abuse fleeting.

The first rays of dawn filtered through the windows and woke Shail. He went outside and watched the mass of harpies stir in and beneath the surrounding trees. Aron approached and handed him some fruit.

"The next few lights shall be hard on all here," Shail said and nibbled. "Have them rest. I soon go to the port and learn if the humans accept our demands. I shall return before mid-light."

With the repellent sap wrapped in a large leaf, Shail spread his wings and flew south to the domed port. He reached the doors, fluttered, and poured the sap in front of the threshold. The beetles scurried away, and he landed and tapped lightly against the doors.

A man peeked out the door. "He's here!" he yelled to the room of people and slid the door open.

Shail stepped inside, and the bedded-down humans clamored to their feet and quietly stared at him. He waited near the door as John and Waters walked toward him.

"They have agreed to the truce and the new laws," Waters said.

Shail looked at John, seeking validation. "It's true, Shail," John said.

"The harpies are protected by law. There's no more hunting. You have the same rights as humans, and the western outback and islands, even my estate, belongs to the harpies."

"Once the swarms are gone, we'll remove the surviving people off your land," said Waters.

"I do not know of this owning of land," Shail said, "but I do not wish for those humans to lose their homes. If they cause no harm to harpies or the jungle, they may stay."

"That's very generous," said Waters. "So you'll destroy the swarms?"

"You accepted the demands and soon shall be free of the beetles," said Shail. "I vowed so."

Waters turned toward the people and announced, "He has agreed to save us!"

The crowd erupted with cheers and claps. Shail jumped at the loud response, unfamiliar that humans could make such noise. He stared, wide-eyed, at them and slowly relaxed, realizing they were expressing approval.

The noise subsided, and Shail turned to Waters. "They have heard the truths of harpies?"

"Yes, we've learned about your race and all the injustice you've suffered," said Waters. "I can only say I'm sorry to you and your harpies. Mr. Turner gave a full disclosure. He is truly responsible for convincing the people."

Shail glanced at John. "I was told if you take your hand in mine it would make us friends." He extended his hand to John.

John grinned and shook Shail's hand. "We're more than friends. You bonded with my daughter, so you're my son-in-law." He took hold of Shail's shoulders. "And like a son, you couldn't make me happier."

"I am pleased you accept me," Shail said. "When you protected my flock on your lands, I longed for your friendship."

John motioned toward Waters. "Shail, I think you'll be good friends with this man. Whether you destroy the swarms or not, Governor Waters made sure the harpies are always protected by our laws. He's an honest, fair-minded man."

Shail nodded to Waters. "So our trust grows," he said and turned to leave.

"Wait, Shail," said Waters. "Don't you want to say anything to these people?"

Shail stared at the thousands of smiling humans. Followed by John and Waters, he walked toward the crowd that cleared a path. Reaching the center of the room, he stopped and gazed up at the ceiling and then at the people. He recalled his trembling and fear of the little cabin and the old doctor, yet now he stood in an enclosed building among fifty thousand humans, some armed, and he felt nothing but calm. He raised his head and forced his soft voice to be heard. "All my life I have waited for this light when human and harpy are at peace. You learned we carry your blood, but the blood makes no difference. It was fear of the unknown that truly divided us. We shall save you from the swarms or die trying. The survival of both our races has brought this truce. May it continue with our offspring."

The crowd's roar was deafening, and Shail flinched, the sound offending his sensitive hearing. He sensed admiration in their minds, and also the reverence of worship, similar to his own flock. He glanced at John, puzzled.

John patted his shoulder. "They're grateful, but can also see your dignity and grace. They love you, Shail."

Despite the enthusiastic response, Shail remained cautious, not easily exploited. Humans were fickle creatures, and only days earlier they had wanted his death. He was free of drugs and hate, and his keen instincts and telepathy had fully returned. He was on alert. He started toward the doors when he detected strong hate aimed at him. He froze and nervously scanned the room. His wings were slightly raised for flight, and he sniffled with agitation.

"What's wrong?" John asked, seeing his menaced demeanor.

"A threat," Shail said quietly.

A man leered at him from behind several people. Shail put the face with the hateful mind and recognized the hunting range owner. Shail detected Bill's smoldering anger.

Bill pulled a laser gun from his pocket, pointed it at Shail, and stepped out beyond the crowd. "This stinking harpy murdered my brother, and you're fools to trust it."

Seeing the weapon, the people fled, creating a large space between Bill and Shail, with only John remaining by his side. The room became quiet as all watched the drama unfold.

"Put down the gun, Simpson," John ordered.

"No way," said Bill. "This golden is going to die." He pulled the trigger, and John leaped in front of Shail, taking a blast to his back. Shail held John as he slipped to the floor. Bill's mouth hung open. He had just shot a man in front of a ton of witnesses.

Shail leaped across John's body and flew at the big man. His shoulder rammed Bill's gut, knocking him down. The hard blow sent the weapon flying out of Bill's hand, and it slid across the floor. Shail rolled to his feet and sprang into the air while Bill staggered to rise and retrieve his weapon. Like a tenacious mockingbird after a cat, Shail dive-bombed the man. Bill vainly swung his fists at the elusive target as his face and back were hammered with the harpy's swift kicks. A tremendous belt to his nose sent Bill crashing to the floor, and he stared up at the fluttering harpy that flew like a revenging bat out of hell, relentless and lethal.

Shail landed close to the sprawled-out man. "Rise," he shouted, and his feathers quivered with rage.

With his shirt sleeve, Bill wiped his blood off his face. He turned this way and that, and then scrambled toward a six-foot iron suturing rod. Grasping it, he stood up and wildly swung at the harpy. Shail leaped backward, the metal nearly slicing open his stomach.

"Go on, you little coward," Bill growled. "Take to the air." He charged, wielding the iron weapon.

Shail dodged the blows, keeping his feet on the ground. "I need not wings nor flight to defeat you."

Bill swung and missed, and Shail lunged at him, grabbing the rod in the center. They clung to the weapon, struggling to out-muscle one another and force the rod down on the other's throat. Shail and his flapping wings began to out-power the man. In desperation, Bill kneed Shail's stomach and flung him to the floor, slamming the rod toward the downed harpy. Shail rolled out of the way and scrambled from the pursuing man and his crashing weapon. It was only a matter of time before Bill connected with a powerful blow.

"Shail, take this!" yelled a voice from the crowd. Ted tossed Shail a second rod. He caught it and deflected a fatal strike. Bouncing to his feet, Shail held his weapon, the battleground now even. He flung his hair, mocking his enemy. They moved in a stalking circle and then Bill rushed him, flailing his weapon. Shail swung back, and the iron rods collided. The clanging of metal echoed through the dome. The two adversaries wielded their weapons, and the fight resembled a sword duel between ancient knights. With each of Bill's attacks, Shail warded off the blows and swung back.

Puffing and sweaty, Bill hysterically swung his rod at the harpy. Instead of striking back, Shail dropped down, spun around, and rose. His rod hit the unsuspecting man's back. The devastating blow sent Bill flying. He landed and lay on the hard surface.

Shail slightly panted, each breath incensed and softly seething. "Get up," he said.

Lying on his belly, breathless, exhausted, and in pain, Bill slowly rose and then lunged for his laser gun several feet away. Grasping his weapon, he pointed it at Shail and clambered to his feet. "Now you're going to die," he said. A hideous grin formed on his lips.

Shail backed away, still holding his rod, and glared at the man. Before the gun fired, Shail threw his rod straight at Bill. Like a spear, it bayoneted Bill in the chest. Bill dropped the laser gun and staggered. He stared with shock at the rod piercing his chest and looked up at Shail. He dropped to his knees as the harpy approached.

"Two lights have passed," Shail said. "Remember my vow."

"You promised to kill me . . ." Bill gasped. He crumbled to the ground and was still.

Shail looked at John. A doctor leaned over him, attempting to treat the wound, and Waters and Ted stood by. Shail rushed over, slid to his knees, and stopped next to John.

"Even if we could get him to the hospital . . ." The doctor bit his lip.

Shail carefully lifted John's head and cradled it in his lap. "Do not go."

John gazed up. Blood trickled from his grin. "Did you get him, Shail?" he asked.

Shail nodded. "He is dead."

"Good, you're a good boy." John gripped Shail's arm and grimaced with pain. "Promise me . . ." He struggled to speak. "Promise me you'll take care of my daughter?"

"I shall," Shail said.

"I love Kari so much," John said. "I'm glad she chose you. I'm sorry I misjudged you," he said weakly. He gasped and his breathing ceased. His hand went limp, releasing the hold on Shail's arm.

Shail breathed hard, fighting back tears, and watched the doctor check John's pulse.

"He's gone," the doctor said.

Shail leaned over John's lifeless body and nuzzled his rough cheek. "You were a great protector," he whispered to Kari's dead father. "You even protected me." He stood up. His arm dripped with Turner's blood, and he glared at the humans, feeling the rise of rage. "Who else seeks my death?" he asked in a strong, threatening voice. "Step forth. Let us now put an end to all hate." No one in the crowd moved or spoke. Shail shook, trying to throw off his anger. "Then honor this man, for he has saved you. He sought peace and paid for the peace with his life." He walked toward the doors, parting the people.

Waters ran after him. "Shail, wait," he called.

The harpy stopped at the doors and fiercely stared at him.

"Are you still going to destroy the swarms?"

"I shall keep my word, but you had better keep yours," Shail said. "Harpies are not killers, but as you have seen, we can be, if we must." He shoved the doors wide open and gazed at the swarms. Stepping out, he was airborne before any beetles could latch on. Shail's golden wings glided over the backdrop of a black and deadly landscape.

21

Charlie flew the hover all night, following the two brown harpies. Every so often, he heard Kari's sniffles for having lost her golden mate at the auction. She finally drifted to sleep, exhausted from worry and grief. Charlie also worried, but for different reasons. His concern was for John, who once committed to a cause was relentless. If the governor failed to help him, John would go to the range and free the harpy himself, no matter the obstacles. Charlie reflected on their conversation on the morning of the auction. John had said for Kari's sake, he'd trade his life for Shail's. His statement wasn't to be taken lightly. John stood behind every word.

The northern journey dragged on through the night, interrupted by brief rain showers. Charlie slowed the hover several times so the harpies could take a break, but they refused, waving him on. Their energy seemed boundless, but at daylight, Charlie grew tired and landed the hover near a stream. The harpies didn't object and waded into the water to drink and wash off their sweat.

Kari woke and joined the two males by the water. Charlie ate beef jerky and watched the three harpies communicate in silence and eat fruit. Kari returned to Charlie and the hover. "Before the light fades, we arrive." After talking to the harpies, her manner of speaking had briefly changed to their broken tongue.

Revived, the two males fluttered into the air and motioned Charlie to follow. They soon reached the mountain foothills, and the weather became cooler. Kari turned on the hover communicator to reach someone in Hampton, but there was no response. Even the emergency police channel was dead. She nervously glanced at Charlie. Apparently the swarms had struck and the city was under siege.

Charlie reached over and patted her arm. "Don't worry, Kari. Shail is safe. They won't let a three-million-credit harpy get consumed, and your father can outsmart bugs. I wouldn't be surprised if John and Shail were together right now."

She breathed deeply, obviously not convinced, and kept switching the com channels, looking for news.

By late afternoon, they were in the high mountain range, and Charlie landed in a small clearing to give the harpies another break. He grew more amazed by their speed and endurance. They could easily out-fly a small hover and had the stamina of migrating birds. The two males leaned against a boulder, lightly panting and shaking their sweat-soaked locks. Charlie approached them with the offer of food, and their eyes widened with caution before hesitantly snatching the fruit from his hands. They uneasily watched him while nibbling the food. The browns weren't as bold as Kari's fierce golden mate.

Charlie grinned and walked away, leaving them to eat in peace and admire them from a distance. Their slim muscular bodies glistened in the afternoon sun. Wet, tan, and high-strung, they resembled a sleek thoroughbred after a hard-won race. Though related to men, the harpies were totally different from their human cousins, and their highly evolved instincts were aware of every smell, sound, and movement. It would be a crime if they were tamed, he thought. Wild animals, like harpies, placed in a zoo became lazy and relaxed, lost their drive and instincts, while the same animal in the wild lived by its wits and skill. He glanced at Kari, and she was like a freed zoo animal. Bonding with Shail, she had embraced her wild harpy nature and cast out civilization. Even if her mate died, she'd never return to the zoo, the comfortable human world.

They resumed the flight, and at dusk the harpies settled on a small plateau and Charlie landed the hover. He and Kari gathered their gear and started a steep climb up a mountain path led by the harpies. They had traveled only a short distance when the harpies stopped. One male took Kari and Charlie's bags and flung them across his shoulder and wing. The other harpy stood in front of Charlie.

Kari smiled. "He thinks you're too old and wants to carry you."

Charlie frowned. "Too old? He can carry me when I'm dead."

The tall male sniffled at the short old Indian and walked away with no translation necessary. They continued the hike up a narrow rocky path, the cold wind blowing at their back. At dark they reached the cave. Kari entered a large expanse and found female harpies and fledglings gathered around fires. Seeing the blond harpy, they dropped to their knees and lowered their heads.

"Please rise," Kari relayed. She sat down by the fire and Charlie joined her, definitely feeling out of place as the only adult male and human. After a while he wandered out of the cave and was grateful to find one of the male harpies guarding the entrance. The harpy nervously backed away from him.

"Easy, boy, I won't hurt you, and I doubt if I could," Charlie said. The male settled down and tilted his head at Charlie's ramblings. Charlie was more comfortable with the mute male than the talking females in the cave. The wind picked up and the temperature dropped. The harpy curled up under a cliff, covering his body with feathers. Charlie said good night and returned to the cave.

Kari smiled. "You found a friend?"

"Yes, one that speaks less than me."

Kari took Charlie to his soft bed of moss, and after the long trip, he was quickly asleep.

Sitting by the fire, Kari stayed up and talked to the female harpies and discovered that two had bonded with men who worked for the governor, but they were reluctant to discuss it or disclose their involvement at the governor's mansion. She wondered who could possibly demand their silence. In harpy culture, only goldens had such control over browns.

Growing tired, Kari bid them good night and went to her moss bed. Mentally worn out with worry, she soon was asleep.

Every night she found herself in the same exhausting dream, walking through the jungle and pushing the blue ferns aside while calling in search of Shail, but she never could find him. She knew now that he had been sold to hunters, so the dream grew worse, because she was more desperate. Lost and all hope gone, she sat down under a white-barked tree in the dream and cried.

"I'm sorry, you cry, Kari," said a soft male voice.

She looked up and tried to focus through the haze of tears. "Shail, is it you?"

"I am here," Shail said, and pushed the foliage aside.

Kari stood and rushed into his arms. "Is it really you or just the dream?" she cried. "Are you really alive?"

"It is I, and no mere wishing dream." He wearily lowered his head and nuzzled his face into her long hair and inhaled her scent. "I have so missed you."

Kari held him and stroked his head. "Are you well? Are you still caught?" she asked in her illusionary state.

"I am free, but still fight my demons of hate, but a golden female helps me heal so I can find you in my dreams." He gently kissed her. "The light comes, and I must go, but I shall seek you again with the darkness." He pulled away from her and disappeared into the jungle.

Opening her eyes, Kari saw the faint light of dawn entering the cave. She got up and made her way through the dark cave and knelt down by Charlie. "Charlie," she whispered and shook the old man from his sleep.

Charlie woke. "What is it? What's wrong?" he asked and sat up.

"Shail is alive and free. He came in my dream. Everything is all right now."

Charlie smiled "I'm glad," he said, "but it was just a dream—" He stopped.

She returned to her nest and reflected on the golden female who was helping her mate heal. Like Shail, she presumed that she and her mate were the last of the golden harpies.

During the day, Kari happily played with the fledglings. The little males practiced their flying skills and fluttered to the high cave ceiling. The small females chased them in the game. She kept herself busy, but like Lea, longed for the dark and the return of her mate. Charlie wrapped himself in a blanket and went outside. He apparently enjoyed the male harpy's company.

As evening approached, the group gathered around the fire and ate fruits brought by male harpies. An adolescent male flew into the cave and landed. Despite the cold weather, he was sweaty and puffed for air. Seeing him, Kari stood and walked to him. She barely noticed the teen, but focused on what he held, a three-foot yellow flight feather. The battered feather had separated quills and gray dirt nearly concealed the pale yellow. She leaned over and smelled it, confirming it was Shail's.

The young harpy stared at Kari. "Our golden ruler sent me. He wishes you to know he is free and shall come when swarms are gone and the land safe."

Kari bit her lip, trying to control her tears of joy. She, too, had distrusted the dream, but now she had proof. Shail was alive and well.

"There is one other message," said the teen. "The master says he loves you."

"Thank you," she relayed. After a long savored moment, she went to Charlie and told him the good news.

Leaving the Hampton port, Shail started his flight back to the mansion, but changed his mind and flew toward the ocean. He didn't want his harpies to sense his sadness. He soared along the ocean cliffs, and the strong winds and updrafts allowed him to glide with little effort. He had never mourned for a man, but Turner was different.

Shail reflected on the day after the rape, the lowest point in his life. He had lost his courage, pride, and the will to live. Turner came to his cage and told him to be strong, that he would survive all that, and then the man had sworn to protect him. Turner made good on his promise.

Closing his eyes, Shail drifted on the cool breeze and dwelled on Turner, the only man worthy of his respect. He wondered if he'd ever meet another, flawed yet good, devoted and brave. Like a male harpy, Turner lived to protect his family and died for his convictions.

Flying back to the mansion, Shail set down amid his large flock. Aron approached, and Shail knew very little escaped his nest brother.

"Your heart is heavy," Aron relayed. "What trouble has come?"

Shail stared down. "Turner is dead. He stepped in front of a weapon and saved my life."

Aron breathed deeply. "You and all harpies have lost a true friend. These past seasons you were right to protect him and his land from the swarms."

"We both loved Kari, and in the end protected one another." Shail glanced toward the harpy gathering. "I must speak to them and tell of the new truce with the humans." He flew to a giant tree stump and landed. He looked up at the sun. "See the light," he said to the enormous flock. "It is different. From this light forward marks a time of peace between human and harpy. I have gone to the humans and said we would save them from the swarm if they would end the hunting and give us the western jungle where we can dwell in freedom and safety. They have agreed."

Sensing their minds, Shail felt disapproval among the flock leaders. Like Aron, they didn't trust the humans or the peace. "I feel your doubts, and that you would rather the swarms rid us of these enemies. True, we would know peace, but it would be short-lived. Once the swarms were gone, more humans would come from the stars, and again we would face the hunters. This truce must come while the humans value the harpies. By saving them, they shall be grateful and see our honor. A friendship we shall reap, the same friendship that binds the bird and zel. The calling bird warns the zel of danger, and the moving zel chases the insects from the brush so the bird feeds. We shall dwell as these, moving through the land helping one another, apart yet together and no longer as predator and prey. I want our fledglings to grow not knowing fear and slaughter so I have taken this chance. Harpies are guardians of the jungle. We cherish all life. We shall save the trees, the animals, and the humans. To do not, we lose honor and become less. We go now into the perilous swarms. Fly swiftly, my brothers."

Shail spread his wings and leaped from the stump. The sky erupted with brown feathers and the huge flock followed him south to the city. Nearing Hampton, the dome stood in the distance, the only building left. Flying along the border between the colorful trees and blackness, Shail noticed a younger male that tried to match his wing stride. "We shall pair," Shail relayed to him, "I the taker, and you the follower. Retrieve the wood." The male tilted his wings and swooped down into the trees, and Shail slowed, allowing him to catch up. His harpy apprentice soon returned with a stick of wood. Other males also gathered pieces of wood before hitting the swarms.

With the male following, Shail flew straight toward the port, knowing the beetles were threatening its doors. The male remained above as Shail glided down and hovered several feet from the ground, searching among the black mass. His giant wings rapidly fluttered and created a current of air that blew the beetles end over end. He finally saw her, lying exposed and no longer protected by her workers. He swooped down and seized the queen that was slightly larger than the average beetle, though a human wouldn't notice the difference.

Holding her so she couldn't bite his hands, Shail waited. The queen made a desperate clicking sound. He watched the frantic workers and drones below who searched for her. They exposed their wings and prepared to fly. He darted upward and joined the young male. The swarm of thousands rose up to save their distressed queen that called to them. The chase was on.

Shail and the male flew twenty feet off the ground at the same speed as the swarm. If he went higher or faster, the beetles couldn't hear their queen, and Shail would lose the beetles in the hot pursuit. He and the young harpy reached the ocean and continued east for several miles. The swarm was so panicked by the clicking queen that it lost its fear of flying over open water.

"Go ahead," Shail said. "I do not want you caught."

The young male sped up, leaving Shail and the trailing swarm. In the distance the male placed his wooden stick on the water and then fled straight up to the sky. Shail reached the stick and quickly doused the queen with water, wetting her wings. and placed her on the wood. He furiously flapped upward and narrowly escaped the angry beetles. The beetles merged on the queen and landed on the watery grave. With their wings wet, they couldn't fly and helplessly floundered on top of the waves, eventually drowning.

The male and Shail headed back in search of another queen. They saw other harpies performing the same daring feat. Each one used speed, balance, and timing to lure the deadly swarms out to sea.

Reaching the port, the male flew on to the jungle for another piece of wood while Shail waited and surveyed the ground. A slight mound of beetles usually held a queen.

In the past the harpies had destroyed all new queens and kept the beetle population under control. By moving a queen, the harpies could move a swarm and this was how Shail had protected the Turner Estate and towns.

The male returned, and Shail flew down and retrieved a second queen. Once she started click, the race was on to the ocean. Wetting her wings and placing the queen on the wood, Shail darted for a secure elevation beyond the swarm's reach. Once again the swarm set down on the water in a mass suicide. The water churned as hungry fish feasted on the floundering bugs.

Across the ocean Shail saw green waves quickly turning black, covered with struggling and dead beetles. Among the floating palm-size corpses, he noticed logs clustered with scrambling beetles. Gliding into range to investigate, Shail's heart sank when he discovered that it was not logs but two dead harpies. For lack of timing or too slow an escape, they had met their demise. He stared at their majestic wings and handsome but lifeless bodies ravaged by the beetles. Shail agonized about leaving them in the water and grasped a wing tip, but two beetles quickly clung to his hand. He shook off the insects before they could bite, and realized he could not retrieve the bodies for a proper mourning. He hovered over them. "Before the light fades, how many others shall meet this fate, a fate I chose by allowing the beetles to overpopulate?"

Reluctantly Shail left the dead harpies and returned to land with the male. They continued the quest of search and destroy. Toward sunset, his flock had made good progress. The dome and the heart of the city, once known as Hampton, was beetle free, but many swarms still existed several miles away. Shail gave the order, stopping the crusade against swarms. His harpies were drained and the light was fading.

Shail landed near the port, and Aron set down beside him. "Take the flock back to the gathering place for rest," Shail said. "I shall soon come."

"You should come now."

"I must first speak with the human ruler and warn him. Not seeing the beetles, he might think it safe and leave the shelter. Humans lack wisdom about nature."

Aron nodded and motioned to the flock. He flew up, veered north, and the harpies followed. Shail walked to the port doors and tapped. A man opened the door and Shail walked inside.

Waters greeted him. "I'm happy you're here, Shail. We saw the swarms are gone, and we're very thankful to you and your harpies."

Wiping his sweaty brow and pushing his damp locks off his face, Shail shook his head. "Do not be fooled by what is unseen. We removed the swarms that threatened the port, but others lie near. If you left the port, you would soon see more beetles."

Waters folded his arms and sighed. "That creates a problem. Our water is gone, and several men were ready to leave for far wells and to repair the circuit breakers. They won't hold a charge and either were damaged or jammed by the beetles."

"Your men shall die to bring the water," Shail said. "Can one do as you say?"

Ted step up. "I can fix the breakers."

Shail glanced at Ted. "He shall do. He is not so large I cannot lift him if I must."

"All right," Waters said.

Ted ran and got the tools and new breakers. He returned quickly and stepped out the doors with Shail. In darkness they walked across the giant landing strip almost vacant of ships. With the coming swarms, most worthy spacecrafts had left. Hampton harbor also sat empty with many humans seeking the ocean for refuge.

"Do you know if Kari is all right?" Ted asked while they moved in the dark.

"She is well," Shail answered and sensed Ted's mind. The man had deep feelings for his mate and wondered how Shail knew about Kari's welfare. She was in the mountains, and harpies didn't use communicators. "I know she is well. We sense one another in our dreams."

"Really? She sure loves you."

"And I her."

Ted distanced himself from Shail, and Shail sensed the man's fear. Ted had recalled Shail's jealousy at the auction, and had seen Shail in action with the deadly hand-to-hand combat with Simpson. Ted swallowed and kept walking.

"You need not fear of me," Shail said quietly. "My mate cares for you and would be displeased if I hurt you. And I am glateful you helped her while I was caged."

"Man, you're spooky," Ted said. "The way you read my mind is freaking me out."

They reached the well, and Shail leaned against a water tank. "I am sorry it . . ." Shail mustered, "freaks you out. I still learn of humans and their unsure ways."

Ted turned on a light and began to fix the damaged connections and replace the circuit breakers. "I guess you know how much Kari means to me." Ted glanced up, but Shail ignored him and peered out into the darkness.

"We must go," Shail said. "There is no more time."

Ted looked in the same direction. "I don't see anything, and I'm almost done. Just another minute," he said, and snapped in the new breaker.

"My sight does not warn me," Shail said. "It is the sound."

Ted tightened the new part. "I don't hear anything, either."

Shail couldn't waste more time with the stupid man. He grabbed Ted under his arms and jerked him to his feet. "Drop the metal things," he ordered, and furiously flapped his wings. Ted released his tools and was lifted into the air. Still lying by the well, the solar light went dark, covered by a huge shadow. Shail frantically flew across the expansive lot with the heavy load twice his weight.

Reaching the port doors, Shail released Ted. The beetles dropped around the man's feet and hit Shail's extended wings. Ted slid open the doors and jumped inside, and Shail flew sideways over the threshold. Ted slammed the doors shut and heard the full force of the swarm smash into the outside doors. Like heavy raindrops on a tin roof, the constant popping told their numbers.

"Jesus, that was close!" Ted exclaimed as Shail fluttered and landed beside him. "Sure glad you have good ears."

Shail tossed his hair back and ruffled his feathers. It had been close. The extra weight had nearly cost Shail and Ted their lives. He wearily leaned against the doors, trapped among the humans. He was exhausted and wished for a cool stream to bathe and a soft nest to sleep. Leaving the port wasn't an option until the swarm settled and stopped its attack.

Waters rushed to the doors. "Are you two okay?"

"Yeah, but they almost got us," Ted said. "Shail heard them and picked me up. He saved my life." Ted good-naturedly put his hand on the harpy's shoulder.

Shail seethed, showing he didn't like to be handled, and Ted jerked his hand away and shrugged. "Do you have the water?" Shail asked.

"Yes, it came on, and then we heard the swarms strike the port," said Waters.

"Until the beetles lie down, I must stay," said Shail. "I cannot fly out without them flying in." He went back to the doors and curled up on the floor.

"Give him some space," Waters told the nearby people. Everyone stared at the harpy and could tell he wasn't happy with confinement.

"He's probably thirsty," said a woman and walked toward the harpy with a newly poured bottle of water. She sat down next to Shail. "Can I give you a drink and thank you for saving my life?"

Shail took the bottle from Mollie. "You also kept me alive." Taking a sip, he sat up, holding his knees and resting his chin on them. His wings floated in front and around him and the feathered tips joined at his feet. He detected Mollie's desire to caress him as she once had when he was caged and helpless. She no longer saw him as an animal, but like a man she deeply loved.

"Can you forgive me?" she asked. "I betrayed you because Bill threatened to kill me."

Shail took her hand, brought it to his face, and nuzzled it. "Then there is nothing to forgive," he said softly. "We share a memory of misery at the range. One I long to forget."

The thumps of beetles on the door ended with the swarm settling, and Shail stood up to leave. He glanced down at her. "You are a good human, Mollie, but do not waste your love on a dream. Find a worthy man who can give you happiness."

There was a sharp rap on the port door, and a man carefully slid open the doors a crack. The beetles were gone, but several harpies stood in their place. Shail stepped outside. "I am well, Aron."

Aron seethed at Shail. "I had a harpy watch over you, and he has told of the reckless attempt to flee a swarm while carrying the weight of a man. You are the one and only golden ruler and should not take such risks. Perhaps you are the last because all other goldens had the same death wish."

Shail was accustomed to Aron's ranting, and how he often treated him like a rash younger brother. "You disrespect me?" Shail glared and his wings arched. "You spy on me and question my decisions? Do you wish to challenge my rule?" Shail's eye brightened, conveying insincerity.

Aron played along for the benefit of the other harpies and submissively lowered his head. "Forgive me, Master. I dare not challenge you. My worry for you causes me to lose my place."

Waters left the port and stepped into the ring of harpies. He nervously saw that the beetles were only ten feet away, held back by the harpies' repellent green sap. "I just wanted to thank you, Shail, for restoring the water and saving us from the swarms. I hope we'll become good friends, and you'll trust me like you trusted Mr. Turner."

"Honor our truce, and the friendship shall come," Shail said and saw a little girl inside the port. "You have water, but what of food?"

Waters raised his eyebrows. "We don't have much, but we will survive until the swarms are gone."

"Your young should not suffer the hunger." Shail placed his hand on Aron's shoulder. "He is called Aron, and he acts bold enough to bring jungle food to your humans. A good shall come when you learn of one another."

Shail knew the other harpies believed Aron was being punished for his lack of respect toward the golden male. All harpies would gladly rather face deadly swarms than go among the cruel humans with an unpredictable nature.

The harpies left the port and returned to the mansion. Shail stayed with them rather than go to his mother in the building. Finding a moss-covered tree limb, he coiled up and reluctantly closed his eyes, knowing he must seek Kari and give her the bad news about her father.

Their minds merged in his dream, and he found Kari waiting in the fantasy jungle. She ran to him and jumped into his arms. "I can hardly wait until I really hold you," she said. Shail kissed her cheek and didn't respond. She pulled back and looked up at him. "I feel sadness in you. What has happened, Shail?"

Shail looked down and shuffled the dirt around with his foot. "Your father has died."

Kari's face showed panic, and in an instant her image vanished before his eyes. The dream had become a nightmare and woke her.

Inside the cave, Kari sat up in the moss nest and could barely catch her breath. She stared blankly at the dark walls and cried.

Charlie went to her nest. "What's wrong, Kari?"

"Dad is dead."

Charlie sat down and held her while his own tears coursed down his wrinkled cheeks, his worst fears coming true.

The dawn broke displaying a golden clear sky, and Shail slowly stirred in the branches. He stretched his wings and felt stiffness in his muscles. He hopped to the ground, knowing the minor irritation would fade.

The harpies moved out of his way, giving the blond ruler plenty of space. He casually strolled through the gathering of meekly lowered heads, and sensed their awe.

Aron walked up to Shail and handed him a fruit. "Your fearless reputation grows. Not only do you boldly confront many humans, but the flock is also aware you killed four men. It is unheard of, and they are scared of you."

Shail took a bite of fruit. "It is good they fear me, for with our new future among humans, I shall ask them to do things normally refused. The dread of me shall build their courage."

"This asking includes taking food to humans?"

"You do not fear me, Aron, but I still ask you to deliver the food. I also ask you to learn their words and muster your voice that has lied dormant in all males."

Aron stared at him with disbelief. "You wish I make sound, human sound? Only females do this, and only to blend. It is not a male's way."

"Am I less harpy since making the sound?" Shail asked.

"You are harpy, but different from the rest of us. You have lost all caution and your passive nature. And this truce with humans . . ." Aron shook his head. "Your wisdom falls in question."

"Only time, not harpies, shall judge me," Shail said, "and you shall soon see the good behind all I ask. The lack of sound has protected the harpy males from hunters, but that is the past. We must change and embrace human friendship, if the truce is to last. Bringing the food and speaking their words builds trust and knowledge. The peace shall endure if they learn to know us and we them."

"You are either very smart or very naïve, my little brother, but I shall do as you say."

"Take each finger the number of all in your hands for the harpies needed to bring the food. Pick young and old for the task. Only the fastest males shall seek the swarms with me. I do not want more harpies falling to the sea."

Aron picked one hundred males from the flock to help him gather and deliver jungle fruit to the port. Aron's smaller band departed for the jungle while Shail and his flock of thousands flew south toward the swarms.

Collecting the fruit, roots, and nuts, Aron and the males placed the food in makeshift bags, made from the same material as a male's sash. The bags soon bulged, and Aron flew to the port, loathing the chore. Setting down by the doors, he saw that Shail and the harpies had removed the swarm that had come in the night. Males holding food bags stood behind Aron when he lightly tapped on the metal openings.

A man slid the doors open and grinned. "Come in, come in." He beckoned with his hand.

Aron peeked inside and saw thousands upon thousands of humans. He had never realized there were so many. He hesitated for a long moment, mustering his courage, and stepped over the threshold. The smiling humans advanced on him, and he lost his nerve. Overwhelmed, he dropped the fruit bag on the floor and jumped outside.

"Everybody move back," rang out a man's voice. "Can't you see the harpies are scared of us?" Waters stuck his head out the door. "It's all right, Aron. They won't hurt you. Just dump the food right here, and thank you."

Through telepathy, Aron sensed Waters meaning, but didn't understand each sound. He stepped back inside, but kept the open door close to his back. "Put the food here," he relayed to the harpies. Just inside the doors, each male gently dumped out his bag of contents and then scrambled out of the giant human cage and escaped to the sky. Shail truly is brave, Aron thought. He came here alone and faced the huge human mass.

Governor Waters stood next to Aron and rambled on with human talk, but Aron was too distracted to concentrate on his words or sense their meaning. He fidgeted with apprehension and suspiciously stared into the crowd at the men. How many of them have hunted and killed my harpies? he wondered. And now I must feed and protect them. He wasn't as forgiving as Shail and had a hard time believing in the bigger picture, a lasting truce.

Aron forced himself to stay, knowing his presence gave courage to the other males. Without him, they wouldn't dare approach the port with food. Glancing at Waters, he tried to learn the man's words, but his mind wouldn't focus on the impossible task. Kari had taught Shail the human language, Aron thought. For Shail it was fun, an easy game that pleased his female.

"Perhaps I can also make the learning fun," relayed a female voice into Aron's mind.

Aron quickly looked around and saw her. Her green eyes sparkled in the dim building light and her flowing brown hair hung down to her petite waist. She moved closer, and he detected harpy scent on her delicate body.

"Why are you among these humans?" Aron asked her.

"I came to the city seeking a human mate. Although I prefer a male harpy, most have females," she relayed. "When the swarms came, I sought shelter in the port."

Aron was no longer aware of Waters or the giant room of people. The gorgeous female captivated him. "For you, the search for a mate should be short."

She blushed. "Shall I teach you the human words?"

"If it pleases you," Aron relayed. "I, too, have no mate, but never sought one. I am a flock leader, and we do not have a long life. I feared my female's death would follow mine, and I could not bear the loss of my fledglings to hunters, so I chose the loneliness of an empty nest rather than face my fears."

"Our ruler has brought peace to the harpies, and your fears shall fade."

"You believe in the golden ruler and the truce?" Aron asked.

"My belief is unimportant, but I've been among these humans, and they believe in the protective laws and treaty. They have grown to love our young blond ruler."

Lowering his guard and using telepathy, Aron scanned the faces in the crowd. The women stared at him and thought he was exquisite and handsome, and the men saw him as a worthy equal, not an animal, but all were grateful and sought his friendship. Shail had been right about everything.

The female harpy walked to Waters. "Governor, my name is Starla, and I'm a harpy. I would gladly translate your words to our males, since they don't understand all their meaning."

"That would be great," said Waters. "Aron, is this okay with you?"

Starla translated the governor's words. Aron swallowed hard and forced his unused vocal cords. "Yes," he said with a whisper, speaking for the first time.

Like the previous day, Shail and the large flock confronted swarms, taking them out to the ocean to die. Numerous individual swarms had converged on Hampton, making it easy to locate them and their queens. At sundown Shail halted the attack. He and the harpies were worn out, not from flying, but from the nerve-wracking timing and agility required to summon the beetles to their death. The city stood swarm-free, but as the black blanket was lifted, the death and destruction was revealed. Many human skeletons sat in demolished vehicles and the twisted building metal. Not all humans had made it safely to the port.

After sending his flock back to the mansion, Shail wandered alone up the streets that once held tall buildings. The powerful civilization was crippled and sat in rubble.

With his hate gone, he felt the sickness of guilt. He could have prevented so many deaths. Although the flocks were few, they still could have stopped the beetle growth two seasons ago, but he chose to release the swarms and drive out the humans. Aron accused him of lacking caution. If he had been careful, he wouldn't have been captured, and he and his harpies could have slowed the swarms and allowed the humans to escape.

He bent over and placed his hand on a small skull. He had killed the child as surely as if he had snapped its neck. Feeling great remorse, he took Anna's tiny pink flower from his sash and smelled its sweet scent. There was no gratification, no joy in this victory. His revenge had left him, and Shail was a harpy again, a protector of all life.

At dusk Shail spread his wings and slowly flew to the domed port. Governor Waters greeted him and explained they were thankful for the food.

Shail nodded. "The swarms have been removed from your city, and you may leave the shelter."

"All the swarms are gone?" Waters asked.

"No, there are still many in the west. It shall take two round moons before we lower the numbers, but we do not seek to destroy all. Like us, the beetles served the land. Some creatures rely on them for food, and when a swarm eats the large trees, light and space comes to the ground. New trees appear, and the zel and other animals feast on their shoots and tender leaves. Without human hunters, my flock shall grow, and it shall be easier to control the beetle numbers, for we also are jungle creatures that play a role in nature. In time, all shall be balanced again." Shail gazed across the wasteland.

"I talked to Mollie, the woman handler at the hunting range. She told me how terribly you were assaulted and tortured by those men. After something like that, why did you bother to save us, Shail?"

Shail turned toward him. "Harpies value all life, but after the range, I was willing to let you die. I had to put aside my bitterness, for I rule and am the guardian of my flock. Different types of jungle animals dwell together because of a need. This need came to the humans and harpies. Your humans are many, and my harpies are few. Even if your humans died, other humans would come from the stars and kill us. Eventually only the ghosts of a forgotten winged race would drift through the trees. We both needed to be saved."

Waters stared at Shail. "You're wise beyond your years, and shame us," he said. "Despite all that man has accomplished, we could learn from you."

"Maybe we can learn from one another, Waters. You have a good heart, and this eases my doubts."

"I'm glad," said Waters. "I haven't been around you or your harpies very long, but it's darned obvious the harpies aren't animals. The hunters had to know this all along. It's unforgivable."

Shail talked with the governor into the dark. He trusted his instincts more than any treaty or law of words. Turner had said that Waters was a good and fair-minded man, and he had been right. Shail began to relax, knowing that peace had finally come.

Returning to his harpy flock, Shail found Aron waiting. "I told Waters that his humans can leave the port. You no longer need to bring the food." Strangely, he detected disappointment in Aron, but Aron didn't explain it.

"I have learned the number of our losses," Aron relayed. "Three to the number of fingers, plus six, far less than we expected." Thirty-six harpies had died in the attack on the swarms.

"It is less than thought, but one is too many," Shail said sadly. "With the dawn we shall search for the scattered swarms in the area, and the distance to water shall be long. If the good weather holds, we shall be finished here. The next darkness we leave and the gathering ends. All flocks shall spread out and travel west killing only the queens as we go."

"I shall tell the other flock leaders," Aron said.

"When you brought the food, did you speak to Waters?"

"I forced my voice and spoke as you asked," Aron said. "Waters is a worthy man, and as you said, the humans were grateful, longing for our friendship. Your choices were right, Shail. I no longer distrust your wisdom. I believe the truce shall last."

Shail patted Aron's shoulder. "This is good. Knowledge is power; remember this, Aron. I seek my mother now and hope to bridge our lost time apart."

Flying to the mansion, he meet Windy, and they talked for several hours. Once the swarms were gone, his mother would travel west with Kari. She bid him good night, and he again coiled up on the rug in the front room and sought his mate in his dreams. They found one another and passionately embraced and nuzzled, but neither spoke. With the coming of dawn, they returned to the realistic world of the awake.

Shail woke and went out among the harpies. "This light we seek the swarms that are half a light's travel from the sea," he said to the gathering from the tree stump. "The swarms beyond shall lose only their queens, and those beetles shall separate, no longer a threat. Today's task shall be the hardest, for the distance is long and treacherous to the water. If your wings cannot endure the flight, you should not come. Be wise, not brave, in choosing, for I value all your lives."

Despite the risk, all males stepped forward, indicating they would go with Shail.

Aron sighed. "Did you truly expect them to heed your warning? They would follow you with broken wings; such is their devotion. They have given you a new name and call you the prince of dawn."

"Why?" Shail asked.

Aron affectionately touched his shoulder. "Your yellow hair and wings are golden like a dawn sky, and as the dawn chases the darkness from the land, your wisdom and courage have removed the shadow of tyranny and death. No other golden ruler has done this. They know you have also enlightened the humans. When bringing the food, the males sensed the human minds and felt their admiration for you. Do not question this honor, Shail. For me, you are like the precious gem that lies in the riverbed, covered with clay. When the men sought to crush you, they crushed only clay and exposed the bright, unbreakable gem. You outshine all of us."

Shail gazed out into the flock and sensed their fear had turned to worship. He felt uncomfortable with the tribute. Days earlier he questioned his rule for the sake of his flock and preferred death. "When small, I was told a golden proverb by my father. He said, 'That which does not destroy one, makes him stronger.' I thought it meant if I survived the hunters I would become braver, but the saying was more. Destroying my fears and ignorance, I gained the strength of good judgment."

Shail extended his wings in the morning light and announced to the flocks, "We finish what we start." He flew toward the pale golden sky. The harpies burst into flight and followed.

Aron caught up and glided alongside Shail. "I shall pair with you on this last attack."

Shail watched the giant flock disperse over the multicolored treetops in search of scattered swarms. "I plan to fly farther than the others."

Aron unhappily huffed, knowing he and Shail would face the greatest risk with the long, fast flight to the ocean. "Then it shall be like old times when we were fledglings. I shall have to watch your back."

They flew over small swarms, leaving them for other harpies, and traveled west for hours. With each mile Aron sniffled and flung his hair.

"We soon stop, Aron, so end your uneasiness," Shail relayed. "Ahead is what we seek."

In the distance Aron spotted the huge black void that marred the jungle, and he hesitated, slowing his flight to soar over them. "Shail, it is too big. The queens have merged like at the city."

Shail's eyes sparkled. "Then it shall take both of us to gather the queens. Tear some of your sash and place them within. We shall start at each end, meet in the center, and carry the swarm to the sea."

"After taking two queens, they shall be upon us," relayed Aron.

"Not if we fly fast, Aron. There are too many beetles to kill just their queens. All of these must be destroyed."

"Again the death wish," Aron growled, looking down at the massive swarm.

"I do not wish to die. I want to hold my mate again and see my son next season."

"I, too, long for these things."

Shail curiously stared at him. "So this is your disappointment for not returning to the humans. You have found a female harpy."

"Yes, in the port. She was like a beautiful flower standing alone in a meadow among dull blades of grass. I asked her to bond, but I spoke too soon, for I shall be killed with your foolishness."

Shail was accustomed to Aron's ranting. "I love you, my brother, and would not do this if I foresaw failure. We are the swiftest of the harpies, and no swarm shall out-fly us. The sooner the swarms are gone, the sooner I return to Kari. It is her I seek, not a thrill or death."

"Let us do this." Aron sighed. "The crazy loca eagle must be strong in a golden's veins, for this is loco."

"When you see the beetles fly, you know I have my first queen." Shail took off, traveling several miles across the monstrous swarm.

Aron flew down closer to the beetles and fluttered over a mound, waiting for Shail. Their attack had to be synchronized.

Shail became a gold dot against the black terrain, and then the swarm lifted into the air. Shail had captured his first queen.

Aron dove down and seized a queen but didn't wait for her clicking or for the swarm to rise. He flew toward the swarm center and snatched another queen, and then a third. The queens were clicking, and he glanced back. Like a rolling ocean wave, a sea of beetles ascended from the ground, but they were confused by numerous calling queens and attacked one another. Taking advantage of the baffled beetles, Aron flew on and grabbed several more queens. The whole swarm suddenly rose, and Aron tilted his wings skyward and flapped out of their reach. Looking down, he saw the boiling black air. He frantically soared above the chaotic beetles and searched for the gold wings. A frightened sweat dripped from his brow as seconds ticked by without seeing Shail. No living thing could survive the madness below. His heart raced as doubt crept in. He knew the beetles would soon locate his clicking bag and fly upward. He'd be trapped between the swarm and the cold, thin-oxygen sky.

He saw a flash of yellow in the thick black cloud. The creamy wings darted toward him. The swarm followed Shail a few feet beyond his heels. Aron swooped down to draw them off Shail, but he faced the beetles that heard his bag.

"We go," Shail relayed and pointed east toward the ocean. In a frenzy they beat their wings, the pursuing swarm only a stone toss away. Clearing the black, they reached the untouched edge of the jungle and fell into a sharp pace slow enough for the beetles to follow, yet fast enough to stay out of their reach.

Shail flung his long hair. "Feel your heart, Aron. Its fast beat tells you that you are alive, and tomorrow is precious."

Aron became infuriated. "This taunt with danger pleases you. The swarms were upon you, and you should be dead."

"The beetles were so alarmed with many noisy queens that they failed to bite. Do not be angry, Aron. Soon we shall be at peace and lazily lie with our mates and surrounded by fledglings. We shall look back on this memory of when we challenged the giant swarm and were young, fast, and fearless."

Aron turned and glanced at the enormous trailing swarm. "I only hope it is a memory."

The sun was low in the afternoon sky when Aron saw the ocean in the distance. "The port is north," he relayed. "We must not get too close."

"The swarms seek their queens, not human flesh. There is no worry."

"We go south," Aron barked. "I am tired of your risky games."

"Shall you ever give me the respect of a golden ruler?" Shail asked.

"Perhaps not since you act like an unruly fledgling with no common sense."

Shail's lips curled into a slight smile. "I sense you are not sincere."

The people of Hampton were outside the domed port and wandered the streets, looking for salvageable items. A dark shadow blotted out the rays of the setting sun, and they looked up. On the horizon they saw the approaching mammoth swarm. Some people screamed in panic and raced back to the port as others crouched and froze with fear.

Governor Waters stood beside Starla when they saw the swarm. "Everyone back to the port," he yelled.

"No, Governor," she said. "I can see two harpies in front of the swarm, and they control its movements."

Waters stopped and stared in amazement. "Just two?"

"Yes, but one has yellow wings. It is our ruler. He takes the swarm to the ocean, where it shall drown."

"Shail certainly has courage."

"Yes. No other harpies would risk moving such a swarm," said Starla.

The immense swarm passed south of Hampton and continued out over the ocean, and the humans breathed a sigh of relief.

"We have no wood for the queens," relayed Aron.

Shail held up the bag. "The material shall float long enough to hold them."

They increased their speed and moved slightly ahead of the beetles to allow their own escape. Fluttering over the water, they opened up the material pouches and let the wet queen float on top of the waves. Before darting to the sky, Aron noticed the number of Shail's queens. He had collected twice his amount. Aron and Shail madly dashed upward and reached a safe height in the atmosphere.

Gazing down, Aron watched the swarm settle on the water. "Gathering so many queens delayed your getaway. Is all a harpy game for you?"

"If a game, I won," Shail relayed. He tilted his wings and flew over the water toward the shore.

Aron followed him. "You are welcome to the victory. I am glad to still live."

At the beach, Shail landed. "Are you as tired as I?" Shail asked and waded into the cool water until knee deep.

"More," Aron said and joined him.

Sweat covered their bodies, and their wing muscles were exhausted. Shail tightly folded in his wings, and like a seabird, he dove into the waves. Aron took a calmer approach. He sat down and splashed water over his head and watched Shail swim back to shore.

Shail joined Aron and reclined in the water. "My mother told me I would heal and feel joy again. This moment I feel life's joys. I lie in this cool water with you, my brother, as we savor our defeat of the large swarm. I have not known this peace since I was a fledgling, and we dwelled on the islands many seasons ago."

"It is obvious your playfulness has returned. I am glad, for you have been long without it, but I and all harpies feel the joy again because of your rule. Though at times I disapprove of your daredevil nature, I know your bold spirit has brought us the peace."

Shail stood. "My life would be incomplete without your disapproval and fuming for caution. I know I am flawed with a reckless nature, but that is why I have you." He shook his locks and walked up to the beach. "Let us return to the port. I wish to meet the female harpy who stole your heart. She must be special, since you never wanted the burden of a family."

Aron went ashore and ruffled his brown feathers. "This is untrue. I have always longed for a family, but feared the loss. With the truce I am ready to fill my nest. Besides, I shall need a son to look after your golden fledgling if he is like his father."

Shail only nodded.

The shoreline grew dark with evening, and Shail and Aron spread their wings and flew north along the coast toward the port. Approaching the dome building, they saw numerous campfires beyond the port doors and encircling the fires was the human population of Hampton. Farther out was the harpy flock. Seeing Governor Waters and Windy stand on the front steps, Shail and Aron landed nearby.

Shail tilted his head at his mother. "Why are the harpies gathered here?"

"I asked them to come," Windy said. "Having this union of peace would strengthen the harpy-human bond, and I told them it would please you."

Shail gazed at his shy harpies who anxiously forced themselves to remain near the outgoing humans. Some people tried to coax the wild harpies closer with the offer of food. A few bold males skittishly approached and snatched food from the human hands. Fluttering back, they nibbled, not because of hunger, but to prove their courage.

"They're a little frightened of us," Waters said to Shail, "but you can't blame them after years of being hunted."

"Most shall overcome their human fear, learning they are protected, but some shall always have doubts and stay hidden in the trees. The next generation of humans and harpies shall be brothers."

A large hovercraft zoomed overhead and sent panic through the flock. Every male became airborne and fled for the trees. Once the craft landed inside the dome port, the harpies returned to the site.

"Ted and the port mechanics worked hard to get the hover up and running," Waters said. "To show their gratitude, they wanted to bring you a gift, Shail."

Shail wondered what gift he could possibly want from the humans.

Ted came through the doors and held it open. He smiled at Shail. "I've got something for you."

Kari walked out the doors and was followed by Charlie.

Shail stood stunned, unable to move for a moment. He swallowed hard as Kari approached. His shock wore off, and he rushed to her, lifted her into his arms, and passionately kissed her. "I have so longed for your touch," he relayed.

"And I yours," Kari said and tightly hugged him, delirious with jubilation. "So many times I thought I had lost you."

Aron edged closer to Starla and placed his arm around her shoulder, and she rested her head against his chest while the golden pair hungrily quenched their craving for one another with kisses and nuzzles. "This was a good gift," relayed Aron.

Waters noisily cleared his throat, and Shail and Kari pulled apart, not the least bit embarrassed for the public display of affection. Waters put a microphone close to his mouth. "Ladies, gentlemen, and our harpy friends, I give you Shail the noble golden ruler of the harpies. His wisdom, courage, and honor have saved us all. He is the true hero of Dora."

The harpies dropped to their knees and bowed their heads, honoring their Prince of Dawn. The humans noticed and followed suit. Rather than wild applause, they went down on their knees with the same quiet tribute.

Kari and Shail were the only ones left standing. Even the governor knelt and lowered his head. Kari stared at the great crowd and then looked up at her mate. "Shail, they love you, all of them."

"All is well now, Kari, as I promised you." He leaned over and kissed her forehead. He turned and focused on the crowd. "Rise," he said softly.

When the humans stood, they showed their admiration as only humans could: a loud roar of voices and clapping hands escalated from the crowd. The spooked harpies took to the air and soared over the human gathering. Shail put his arm around Kari and gazed up at the brown wings and stars.

Kari watched his blue eyes sparkle in the firelight, and she reflected how initially she saw Shail as a wild, beautiful creature of the jungle who was persecuted by man. How he had changed, but perhaps the change was not his. Maybe his undaunted spirit had finally been revealed to all. She only wished her father were here, but then she smiled. Her dad knew. She stood up on her toes and kissed Shail's cheek as her handsome husband quietly gazed out at his people.